WAX & WANE

A Gathering of Witch Tales

For Mary

WAX & WANE

A Gathering of Witch Tales

Edited by
DAVID T. NEAL
and CHRISTINE M. SCOTT

Published by

NOSETOUCH PRESS

CHICAGO *MMXVI*

TABLE OF CONTENTS

A Circle of Nine

K.A. Hardway

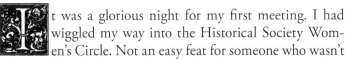t was a glorious night for my first meeting. I had wiggled my way into the Historical Society Women's Circle. Not an easy feat for someone who wasn't born into money. *Those* people are Old Money country-clubbers. Neither my parents, my grandparents, nor any of my family, had ever even set foot in the local country club, let alone been a member.

I had always admired the group from afar, content with not being equal to any of them in my blue jeans and t-shirt. I happened to run into them from time to time while thumbing through the files in the local history department of the public library. I, of course, never engaged any of them in conversation, for fear that they would see the things I had discovered about my ancestors. Old newspaper articles and court documents with titles like: "Drunk in Public," and "Public Drunkenness," were some of the pride-inducing gems I had unearthed. Apparently, my people had exhausted the local newspaper columnists' vocabulary words for people who weren't gracious while intoxicated. In my mind, these things did nothing to lift me up to the standards of the Circle.

One cool fall afternoon, I went to the library to pick up something good to read. Something was in the air that day: I ran into a few members of the Women's Circle as they departed the local history room. One of them, who later introduced herself as Lettie Parsons, gave me an odd look as I passed her at the copier. I assumed it was an inborn aversion to peasants like me. But as I perused the limited paranormal section, I looked up to find her staring at me, a sly smile on her face.

"That book is simply detestable," she said, looking down at the copy of *Idiot's Guide to Tarot* in my hand.

I felt my face flush, realizing that the polish on my toenails was in severe need of a touch-up. Not to mention that I was wearing my worn-out ninety-nine cent Walmart flip-flops.

"Oh? Don't believe in that sort of thing?" I asked, suddenly indignant, poised to tell her to mind her own business.

"I've read it. Out of boredom, of course. But no, I just meant that there are better books on the subject," she answered, searching the spines of the books on the nearby shelf. She made a ticking, disapproving noise with her tongue.

"If you're serious about learning tarot, we have some lovely volumes," she said with a rather pleasant smile, indicating the other members of the historical society. I imagined great weighty, leatherbound books with pages edged in gold foil, and text written in exquisite calligraphy.

Had she really just offered to loan me her books on tarot?

I didn't think that such things were popular amongst the well-to-do, who tend to be the right-wing sort. Those who can afford a seat at "God's table" don't usually clutter it with books on the occult. Ironically, neither would the more liberal atheists. At any rate, I had to admit to myself that perhaps I had been mistaken about the ladies. And perhaps about the rich in general.

The silver in her headful of wild spiral curls set off her violet eyes beautifully, and the dark bifocals perched on the end of her nose drew focus to her kindly smile. I guessed her age to be somewhere in the late fifties to early sixties range, and judged that she was an attractive lady, regardless of her actual age. She radiated a confidence that I admired.

"Forgive me for being forward, but I think you'd fit in nicely with our little group. We've seen you here a lot and have discussed inviting you to join."

I stood, silent as a signpost, allowing myself to feel flattered beyond words.

"I can tell you're one of us," she added with a subtle wink.

One of "us"? Hey, if you say so.

"I am fascinated with local history. I'd love to learn more about it," I somehow finally managed to say.

She took a small notepad and pen from the colorful tote bag on her shoulder and gave me a number to call.

"If you're interested," she explained, walking off to catch up with the group, who waited for her at the exit.

And just like that, there I was, driving through a once-affluent part of the old town, in the chilly autumn twilight, to a local landmark I'd always dreamed of exploring. It was a beautiful white manor house, up on a hilltop overlooking the little town. A wealthy spinster had left it to the historical society in her will, and they rented it out for special occasions. Many weddings, official dinners, and other formal events had been held on the well-manicured grounds. I had never been fortunate enough to be invited to any of those things, and now I was being welcomed into the century-old house by the society that lovingly maintained it.

The paved drive that wound around to the back of the house was narrow and covered in scattered leaves. Against the setting sun, the windows gleamed, reflecting the skyline of the town, the color of rose wine. Venus twinkled down on the autumn patchwork as the colors began fading into dusk. The house was dark inside with the exception of the main parlor where meetings were held, and it glowed from within through that one small window like a one-eyed jack-o'-lantern. As I passed by the front of the house, I could see the shadows of the ladies moving inside.

And now, I get to be one of them.

It was all surreal to me.

My exuberance was neck-and-neck in a race with my diffidence.

I went in through the back door, which I presupposed to

have been the servants' entrance at one time, and heard voices coming from a room at the end of the long hall. I could see the orangey light of a fire dancing on the walls of the room as I passed by the staircase. I walked slowly, giving myself time to take in all the paintings and photos hanging in the hallway. The dark eyes of long-dead people stared down at me, forever frozen in tintypes and oil. A magnificent grandfather clock stood ticking away like a patient watchman near the door of the meeting room.

An elegant dark-haired lady, who introduced herself as Sylvia, welcomed me into the parlor. Though the room was grand, being furnished with many things that looked antique and expensive, the light from the fireplace gave it an air of coziness. I counted seven other women, all standing near a circle of nine chairs in the center of the room. It looked as if someone was either missing or planning on showing up late. They stopped whispering and looked in my direction.

"Ah, you must be young Elizabeth," an attractive woman with long, wavy, reddish-blond hair said, smiling.

Young Elizabeth? I decided to take that as a definite compliment, having just turned thirty. By my estimate, I guessed that I must be a good twenty years younger than the rest of them.

Lettie introduced them all one by one as they began to filing toward the chairs, telling me to sit anywhere I liked.

"Elizabeth, this is Lavinia, to my immediate left, then Sarah, Abigail, Sylvia, Anna, and Chloe."

That makes eight of us. Someone is missing.

I barely heard a word that was spoken, as I was too busy taking in the ambience and décor of the room. The very scent in the air was intoxicating. It was an odd mixture of wood smoke and potent florals. Rather than complementing each other, the fragrances seemed sharply juxtaposed; the lush delicate succulence of flower petals paired peculiarly with the dry, coarse solidity of split wood, acrid and smoldering in the blackened hearth. A random mental image of a young witch being burned alive at a stake, engulfed in flames, sprang into my unsuspecting mind. The thought was so sudden and disconcerting that I gasped aloud. Abigail, who was seated directly beside me, heard me and placed her cool hand on mine. She was wearing an extraordinary ring, with a large black stone on it, which nearly covered two of her fingers. She saw me admiring it and told me that it was obsidian, and that she'd had it specially made.

"For protection," she whispered, leaning in close to me.

That's nice, I remember thinking.

I sat fidgeting with the tail of my new aqua blue polo shirt, regretting the fact that I hadn't tucked it into the khaki pants I'd splurged on for this occasion.

They would have tucked it in, and worn a nice, matching belt.

I was feeling a little like a mud splatter on a stark white designer dress.

The clock in the hallway kept ticking, soothing and lulling my wandering mind against its will. I tried to focus on feeling snug in front of the fire on a nippy night. The light reflected brilliantly off of all the highly polished surfaces in the room, having a very pleasing effect, adding to the atmosphere of opulence. This was way more decadent than sitting at home on my secondhand sofa in pajamas, eating junk food and watching reality TV.

The ninth member decided to finally show up, appearing from the gloomy darkness of an adjacent room. She looked to be closer to my age, with her coppery red hair in a short bob and finger waves. The dark green dress she wore had a sophisticated look of the 1930s, and matched her graceful deportment. It was envy-at-first-sight. She didn't take a seat or speak to anyone, but, rather, lingered in the shadows of the parlor, just beyond the firelight's reach. I could sense that she was smiling at us, though I couldn't see her face properly. I kept watching her, waiting for someone to introduce us. No one seemed to notice her. The air seemed to grow heavy, almost stuffy, and though the fire crackled on, the room had taken on a slight chill. I rubbed my arms to warm away the goosebumps.

Maybe she's a housekeeper, I speculated to myself.

No. Too chic. Who in their right mind would clean a house in such an amazing dress? Besides, you can tell money when you see it. I bet she's the daughter of one of these ladies, home for a visit. Maybe that's why she's keeping herself out of the way.

She walked to the window, and stood looking out at the lights of the town below. A full half hour must have passed since she entered the room, and still no one made an effort to greet her.

Curious. I suppose well-to-do women do have their way of freezing each other out when they've been squabbling over rich gal stuff.

Our mysterious guest decided to take a seat in a sumptuous velvet chair near the window, still with her face mostly hidden in the dimness. Anna, in her grey Chanel suit, noticed that I kept glancing in the stranger's direction.

"Looks like some rain clouds have moved in. Shame," she remarked.

Still no comment about the silent figure at the window. Was she too important to be introduced to me? Was she offended that the others had allowed me to join?

"Yes, and I hate driving in the rain," I answered, tempted to ask who the woman was.

As the last hour of our gathering progressed to a close, the ladies passed around memos and photos of a building. They wanted to start a campaign to save the old place. It looked like a lost cause to me, and I realized that I hadn't looked in the direction of the window for a little while. I also hadn't heard a sound from that area of the room. I carefully turned my head to look over my shoulder, hoping the woman wouldn't catch me gawking at her, but she had gone. I was sure I would have noticed her passing by us on her way out of the room.

Lettie looked at her wrist watch.

"Time for us to clear out, girls," she told the rest of us, and asked Sylvia to help her lock the house up for the night.

I lingered behind with them, hoping that I could tag along for the end-of-the-night rounds. I was thrilled at the prospect of touring the house I'd always marveled at. We walked through the house, checking each room, turning off lights and making sure all windows and doors had been properly secured. Some of the rooms were unfurnished, in the process of being restored, and others had been made into offices. We only briefly checked the second floor. Lettie told me that those doors remained locked at all times. The oppressive darkness seemed to be closing in on us, so we agreed to wrap the "tour" up as soon as possible.

The question of the girl's identity teetered on the tip of my tongue. We walked into the front room, and there, above the marble fireplace mantle, was a large painting of her. There could be no doubt it was her. In her portrait, she wore the dark green dress I'd seen her in. Sylvia saw the look on my blanched face, and explained that it was a portrait of Evelyn Grayson, the damsel who'd donated the house. The painting had been done in the early 1930s, when she had been young and beautiful. Not long before her death.

But it couldn't be her. It wasn't possible.

I was frozen with terror, my mouth hanging open, the warmth gone from my body.

Lettie and Sylvia both rushed close to me with looks of concern on their faces.

"Are you alright, Dear?" they were both asking as they held on to my arms.

"She was in the room with us, sitting by the window for most of the meeting," I said in a small voice that seemed to be coming from someone else. I suddenly felt like a small lost child, bewildered and terrified as the room seemed to spin around me. The tears that came from my eyes surprised me. I was trembling violently, unable to control myself. I feared they would think I was crazy, hysterical, and typical of my kind: the superstitious scullery maid weeping openly in front of the local gentry. I was ashamed of forgetting myself in front of these people, and yet, my fear surpassed my shame at that moment. I had witnessed something shocking, mortifying. Chilling.

The dead walk among us.

What else could they do among us? To us?

The two ladies exchanged a look that strongly resembled excitement, then both of them beamed at me.

"You saw her! You truly are one of us!" Lettie exclaimed.

I was more than puzzled.

What had just happened?

I stood shaking between them, afraid of the dark inside the house, of the dark outside, and of having to drive home alone, in the night, to yet more darkness in my empty little house. Fight or flight took over, and my brain managed to regain control of my body. I ran, thinking only of getting through the dark to the door, and to my car. Sylvia did her best to keep up with me.

Politeness had fled from me as quickly as the reality of what I had just seen set in. I made it out of the house at last. I fumbled nervously with my keys, looking over my shoulder into the nearby trees and shrubs, and clumsily unlocked the car door. I couldn't get in fast enough, and slammed the door shut behind me, locking it with a sweaty hand. Both of the ladies came to the window, apologizing for my horrible experience through the droplets of rain that trickled down the glass. I wished them a good night and sped away, glancing frequently in my rear view mirror. I reached up and turned on the interior light, assuring my worried imagination that nothing waited, watching, in the back seat.

I arrived at my house, not recalling the ride home, and sat gripping my steering wheel, dreading the dash from the car to my front door. I could not remember ever having been so frightened, and shook my house key out of the jumble of others. I would be prepared this time. I would not be caught, unwitting or unnecessarily vulnerable, on the front stoop, in the pouring rain, beneath the exterior light that I had forgotten to leave on.

I made it in unscathed, unharmed by some lurking specter, and ran through the house, purse and keys still in hand, turning on every light. I didn't even allow myself time to hesitate at the doorway to each room. I had just grimaced, prayed aloud, hoping that mentioning the name of Christ would ward off any evil (the way it did in horror movies), and charged ahead. Finally, I made sure all of the curtains were closed and that all of the blinds were firmly drawn down. There would be no opportunity for the Boogeyman to get even the slightest glimpse of me.

At first, I mulled over the details of what I'd seen. In the light of day, and in stimulating company, everything seemed much more benign. However, my solitude had cast a ghoulish pall over things. It sullied the normally cheerful atmosphere in my house with a macabre element. I shivered with each recollection, and decided to work hard at putting the whole thing out of my mind.

"It wasn't real. It wasn't real," was the mantra I spoke aloud to no one.

A flash of the woman in green, sitting in her chair by the window, kept showing itself to me, spasmodically interjecting itself into my mind, and unsettling my settling thoughts. I would reach for the things I typically leaned on in times of stress and uncertainty: TV, food, and alcohol. It wasn't long before I had managed to at least half-convince myself that perhaps I had imagined some of it, or that maybe the firelight had played some sort of trick on my eyes. Or maybe I had unknowingly been the subject of some bizarre initiation. I was determined to rationalize it for the sake of my sanity. Then, a thought sank my heart: Maybe I had been invited as a joke.

"Let's scare the poor girl. Oh, wouldn't that be such fun!" they would all say to each other.

I imagined that there had been a hidden camera somewhere in the room, recording my every movement. Then, in my mind, I could see the ladies gathered around a TV, reliving the whole thing, laughing like a bunch of mean, spoiled, former sorority girls, having tremendous fun. At my expense.

Of course. That had to be it.

Oh well, I could visit a different branch of the public library. Screw those old bitches!

The phone rang. It was Lettie. She was concerned about me, and wanted me to promise to come to the next meeting, which would be conducted over dinner at a swanky restaurant.

Whew.

The Women's Circle was planning a campaign to save an old church. It was a well-known place in our community. I loved that old building. I assured Lettie that I would be there, and hung up feeling extremely silly.

No longer afraid, I changed out of my wet clothes and into my comfiest pajamas, turned the TV on, and settled down on the couch with an unhealthy snack and a cold beer. I was glad the Women's Circle couldn't see the utterly un-classy things I was up to. After several episodes of *Friends* and a couple of cans of Miller, I was feeling much lighter. And drowsy. I finally drifted off on the couch at about 1:00 a.m.

I woke up on the sofa around 9:00 a.m. with a crick in my neck. Hoping to rid myself of the previous day's negativity, I set out on a mission to shop for something spectacular (yet affordable) for my humble abode. There was a wonderful antique shop in town, in a turn of the century brick building on Main Street. I loved wandering through the place. It had a wonderful old house smell, and the creaking of the wood floors was music to my ears.

I stood looking at an oak armoire near the picture window at the front of the store, proud of myself for not quitting the Historical Society in anger and haste. The armoire had unique, beveled glass mirrors on the inside of its doors. I looked away from it to admire the blazing colors of autumn in the trees that lined the street. Even the grey sky couldn't diminish the glory of the fall leaves. In fact, the grey clouds and black tree bark only served to make the bright yellows, reds, and oranges seem even more vivid. When I looked back into the mirrors, I was startled to see Lettie's reflection in them. She laughed and apologized for sneaking up behind me.

"I see you like old things," she remarked.

"I love having antiques around me. It makes me feel connected to the past, like I'm keeping someone alive somehow," I said, the memory of last night returning sharply.

The way Lettie looked into my eyes, I could swear she was reading my mind.

"Interesting," was all she said.

Either I was worrying her a little, or we were on different wavelengths. There was something more behind the single word she'd uttered.

I noticed a golden triquetra pendant on her necklace.

"Oh, how pretty. Where did you find that?" I asked, dodging awkwardness.

"I found it in a lovely shop in Glastonbury. Ever been there?"

"Can't say I have."

"It's magical," she said. More loaded words.

"Are you shopping for anything in particular?" I asked, knowing she probably had everything a girl could dream of, and probably more.

"Not really. Just browsing. I love it in here."

We wandered together through the shop, venturing through both of the upper levels. The rickety stairs had always intimidated me, so I kept one hand against the rough brick wall. The second floor had a large balcony that looked down into the first level. I kept well clear of the railing to keep from getting dizzy. I had always been afraid of heights. Ladders were no-nos. Anything that couldn't be reached by standing on tiptoes was lost to me.

On the third floor, I fell in love with a small round pedestal table. It seemed to call my name. There was a beautiful inlaid star design on its top. It seemed destined to sit in the center of a grand foyer, holding a large vase full of flowers. I preferred not to look at the price tag in front of Lettie, for fear of not being able to afford it. I decided to risk a look anyway. To my surprise, it was ridiculously affordable. The shop owner seemed to be glad to get rid of it, and even loaded it in my car for me.

"I knew you would be drawn to it," Lettie said, standing on the sidewalk as I walked to my car.

"Why is that?" I asked, curious.

The sky had begun to sprinkle again.

"It looks like the perfect table for tarot readings," she answered. I hadn't even thought of that, but I had to agree with Lettie. Except I didn't do readings for other people. I only dabbled in it for fun, and had no intuitive ability with tarot cards. Sure, I had the odd dream that came true, and chance mental images of little significance, but it wasn't anything that I could just switch on or off. Everyone experiences déjà vu, and with a little extra focus, could tap in to their dormant extrasensory abilities. I had a certain attraction to the unexplained, but I certainly wasn't "special" in that regard.

"I'm no good at interpreting tarot cards. Maybe I can use it for a café style arrangement in my kitchen," I said, trying to redirect things.

"You're a natural. I can see it. You're probably just not looking at the cards in the right way," Lettie said. She wasn't going to let this thing go.

"Come up to the house on Friday night. We conduct a séance once a month. Someone always brings a deck of cards," she continued, whispering the last part. "I don't think I need to tell you that it's a well-kept secret, and should remain as such," she added, stern but still smiling.

"A séance? In the house where I encountered my first real ghost?" I asked, incredulous.

Before Lettie had a chance to respond, the rain began to fall in sheets, providing a perfect excuse for a quick departure. I jumped in my car, rolled the window down slightly, and told Lettie goodbye until next time. I had not answered her invitation, but assumed she would understand my reluctance to go back to that house, especially under those circumstances.

She called me later that evening, reminding me that I was now a member of a prestigious organization, and that I should make myself both present and active.

Sigh. Ugh.

I could see that I was going to have to bare my soul to her.

"I feel a little out of place," I tried to explain.

"Nonsense! How so?" she said, sounding genuinely un-aware of our glaring differences, and a little miffed as well.

"Well… I haven't had the same privileged upbringing as the rest of you," I said, hoping that she wouldn't suddenly morph into "Snooty Woman."

I heard her take a deep breath.

"We don't think of you that way, Elizabeth," she said. I could hear her scrambling for a quick save.

"You're *different,*" she finally added.

She explained that I seemed bright, seemed to live with some purpose, had obvious refined taste, and was clearly an open-minded sort. With that, the conversation took a pleasant turn. We talked for a while about everyday things. I was still on the fence about attending the séance, but was less freaked out at the thought. We ended on a positive note, with my promise to seriously consider showing up.

That night, as I sat watching an episode of *Twilight Zone,* something began to formulate in the back of my mind. I start-ed cataloging observances I'd made of the Women's Circle:

Affinity for the occult, spooky old house bestowed upon the group by a spinster, nine chairs, eight ladies, obsidian ring "for protection," triquetra necklace, and séances.

Surely not…

In my eagerness to belong to such an esteemed group, had I innocently overlooked red flags? I would never have pegged the group of women as a secret coven of witches. And as far as my being welcomed into their group, I wasn't as sure as they seemed to be that I would be of any use, if they did turn out to be honest-to-goodness, card-carrying witches. I was, of course, jumping to preposterous conclusions.

The rain pounded against my windows, and the wind had picked up considerably. It whistled in the chimney top. The branches of the tree outside my living room window were moving wildly in the blustery autumn storm, making hair-raising screeching noises against the glass. My new table sat by the front door where I had placed it temporarily. Out of the corner of my eye, the table looked almost like a person, clad in black, standing at the door. It was making me uncomfortable. I carried it into the kitchen and set it by the back door. The living room had gone prematurely dark from the cloud coverage. I turned on the lamp in the corner of the room to dispel the gathering shadows.

Stop it. Get ahold of yourself.

I resolved to stop my imagination from running amok. I decided to drown out the irrational thoughts in my head by watching garbage on TV. The doorknob rattled as thunder rolled, causing me to jump to my feet. My heart was racing.

"It's only the wind. You're safe," I told myself repeatedly.

Still, despite the levity on my TV screen, one nagging question lingered, persisted, refused to be quieted:

Why the ninth chair? Were they leaving it empty for someone?

I must have dozed off, because my suspicions crept into my sleeping brain and manifested as a nightmare.

I was standing inside the hallway of the manor house, alone, with no sound, except that of the ticking grandfather clock. The only light in the house was the moonlight that issued itself through the windows. I walked slowly toward the parlor where I'd seen Evelyn's ghost. I was petrified with fear, but was compelled to put one foot in front of the other by something much stronger than my apprehension.

The women, dressed in dark hooded robes, stood holding hands in a circle. They were chanting something in unison, repeating the phrase over and over in a faint tone. Oddly, I could hear the ticking of the clock over their hushed voices.

Tick, tock, tick, tock...

Two of them stood back, making an opening in the circle. I entered, fearing that if I chose to turn and run, I would be followed. I joined in, noticing the small table in the center of the circle. It was the antique table I'd purchased. There, sitting on the table, was a deck of cards. Beside it, lay a single card, face up. I craned my neck for a closer look and saw that it was a beauti-

fully illustrated tarot card.

The Death card.

A fire spontaneously burst alive in the fireplace, popping and crackling quietly, as if to be polite. The clock in the hallway began to tick louder, as if it had grown, its heavy brass pendulum swinging steadily.

Tick, tock, tick, tock…

Someone, also in a dark robe, her face partially hidden beneath her hood, stepped in front of the empty chair. She uncovered her head, revealing her identity. It was Evelyn Grayson, looking alive and radiant. Her pale skin was luminescent, like blinding white snow in the dead of night.

There seemed to be several clocks ticking now, louder, discordant, competing with the wild hammering of my heart.

Tick-tock, tick-tock, tick-tock…

Evelyn joined hands with the circle, and looked into my soul with her large, arresting green eyes. I was unable to look away from her hypnotic glare. I could not breathe. I feared my heart would stop. I knew then that I would never leave that room as the same person, if I left at all.

TICK. TOCK.

The storm had knocked the power out with a loud snap, startling me awake. The room was eerily black and still.

Had the card been a message?

I suspected that I had been chosen for some unknown purpose. Icy alarm filled my veins. My eyes welled with tears.

And now, I get to be one of them.

She Left Home Under a Cloud of Dragonflies

Lawrence Dagstine

suppose that my mother could have become a full-fledged witch if she had chosen to. But she met my father, who was a rather saintly clergyman, and he canceled out her ambitions. She dwindled from a potential pagan into an English vicar's wife, and ran the parish, as one could in those days—an age of potential dynamism like the late Twenties, when Wicca was fairly new—with a devilish smile and an iron hand disguised by no glove at all. She retained her dominance, her vivid personality, and a small hint of cruelty in her complete lack of sympathy for weakness and incompetence. Back then, paganism was not so much a religion around our parts, but there *were* Wiccan Orders, feminine rituals and midnight observances, burnings and offerings, and there was more than one class of witch.

Personally, I had, I think, a hard upbringing. And so, I believe, must she have had. I remember a photograph of my grandmother, her mother, whom I never met but whose picture terrified me through my childhood: scraped-back hair, piercing eyes, tight wrinkles, and a half-sewn together mouth. She had lived in the wilds of New Zealand and had all the tough virtues of the female pagans of her day; she was a nurse and healer, with whom the friendly Aborigines turned to for what is now known today as shamanism. Still, she would have been classed in an earlier period as a wise woman or even a witch. Minus the sun-bronzed skin, she looked it. My mother, a paler and handsomer version of her, had the same abilities. Merciless to the healthy, disliking all other women as a matter of principle, indifferent to children and animals, she was nevertheless endlessly patient with infants, toddlers, and a splendid nurse to the sick. But there was always that side to her. The one the townsfolk never truly knew about.

We lived in our early years in an ugly coal-mining community in the North of England. Our house was well built, rough and unpaved in some areas, but hideous. The timber made it far too big, and in the winters, between the floor cracks, far too cold.

The vicarage lay at one end of the village, isolated beyond the church in its own large garden, with its peonies and cloud of lilacs. On one side of our grounds ran the main road; on the other three sides were graveyards. Lots of tombstones, lots of crypts. Some dating back two centuries. It was a grim place for a solitary child, but as the daughter of a former witch, my childhood was bleak and comfortless.

It had not always been so. Only when the other brats on our street poked around and made fun. I had my own small golden age to look back on: my brief span of dream days that made the real days of childhood bearable. Until I was eight or nine, I had lived in a village of three hundred souls or thereabouts. Mostly adults. It was an unimportant little parish, and we were very poor, but the place was lovely, and the structure was compact and comfortable, with ivied walls and white roses along the porch. There was even an organ, which the shopkeepers had chipped in for. The back of the parish consisted of farmland and cobblestone, with a small gravel road circling around it. Cars were rare; one usually walked or went by old-fashioned carriage.

Only eight years. But even now, staring out a window in a nursing home, after a lifetime almost ten times as long, some memories are still vivid and exact through the overall staining of times gone by and perhaps *best* forgotten.

The village green, with its grazing goats and stubby ponies, and the white and grey church at its center. Huge trees everywhere, birches and autumn maples, mostly by the cottages, studding the circling meadows and shading the dusty road, where hens strutted and cats lay dozing. But no people. Those golden memories, I suppose significantly, hold no single person. Except *one*. There is no staining of the picture on the day when I first met my mother's oddball cousin Giselle.

She was my godmother, so presumably I had encountered her at my christening, but the first time that I recall talking with her was on a summer's day when I was just a child bored out of my wits.

It was a day like any other day. Which meant that I spent it alone, because my father was out on his parish visits, my mother was too busy to bother with me, and, of course, I was not allowed to play with the village children. Then something happened. Did the sun move? There was a confusion of sound, distorted birdsong from the wood and grasshoppers leaping away from the long, grassy hills.

What I seem to remember is a sudden flash, like a silent bolt of lightning, as if a shape had materialized and scattered the shadows and light. The dreamy color of haze surrounding this figure sharpened. Everything suddenly seemed like an illusion and outlined in the light. The dog daisies, white and yellow and taller than I was at that age, stirred and swayed above my head, as if combed through by a reckless wind. In its wake, the air stilled again, thick with an extraordinary but unusual aroma. The distortion stopped. The birds had stopped singing; some fell dead from their tree branches and nests. The grasshoppers stopped chirping; they began feeding on each other like cannibalistic warriors. I stood there, half-scared and as still as a snail on a stem, and, for the first time knew myself to be a part of what was taking place in the surrounding area.

I looked up, and Cousin Giselle was there.

I swallowed. She could have been much more than forty, but to me, of course, she seemed old and wise, as my parents, who back then were late thirties perhaps, and known for doing what old couples did. She had somewhat of my mother's looks, back when she was a pagan, the proud mouth and nose, the piercing grey eyes, the erect build. But where my mother's hair was auburn with hints of red, Cousin Giselle's was a gloomy black, clouds of it swirled up with tortoiseshell pins. I don't remember what she wore, only that it was dark and voluminous, and it couldn't get any darker.

She sank down beside me on the green, arching her back and bending one knee, seeming to manage it without disturbing the dog daisies. The aroma was still there, but it wasn't perfume. I didn't know what it was. I saw nothing odd about Giselle's sudden appearance. I suppose it was part of that imaginary world of magical appearances and vanishings, timed inevitably as they are for the child's need. Those were the days, especially when all one had to do was believe that conjuring was more than just trickery.

"Do you know who I am, Hannah?" she asked.

"You're Mum's cousin. She has a photograph of you."

"So she has," she laughed. "What were you doing down here?"

Quite apart from the lonely, forbidden adventure outside the neighborhood of the vicarage, I was not supposed to waste time dreaming but, rather, completing my daily household chores. Frightened and fixed by Giselle's straightforward gaze, I said, "Just thinking."

"What about?" Miraculously, she sounded not only unruffled but interested.

"I don't know. Just *things…*"

It was the kind of answer that usually brought a sharp rebuke in that day and age. But Giselle nodded. "Would you like to see something interesting?"

"What?" I inquired.

"Mother Nature," she answered.

"It's already all around us," I said.

"But you're not *binded* to it, Girl. Come, let me help you understand."

Then, a short distance away, Cousin Giselle pointed to where, at the foot of some tall reeds and oaks, the surface of a large puddle bulged—it had looked more like a sinkhole or tiny pond—the water built up from many rainfalls over time and rounded to a circular bubble. She waved her hand at the murky liquid. A brown, grublike creature emerged. Slowly, laboriously, testing the strange element, the ugly creature inched its way up the stem till it clung clear of the water, exposed to the drying sun.

"What is it?"

"It's called a *nymph*. Now watch carefully."

The ugly head went back, as if in pain. I did not see what happened, but all at once there were two bodies there on the stem, the split shell that had been the nymph and, climbing from the empty helmet of the head, another body, newly born—a slimmer, bigger version of the first. It clung there, above the wrinkled discard of its muddy skin, while the sunlight stroked it, drew the crumpled silk of the wings out of its humped shoulders. It slowly pulled them straight, taut and shining, while from somewhere—perhaps from the air itself—color pulsed into the drab body till it glimmered blue as a splinter of sky on a clear day. The wings stretched, feeling the air. The insect's body lifted, straightened. Then into the sun, with a dazzle of light, it was gone.

My mouth was agape. "You blew dust on it, didn't you?"

Giselle laughed. "No, silly. Nature took its course and the sun did all the rest."

"It was a dragonfly, wasn't it?" I found myself whispering.

"It was. *Aeshna caerulea*. Go ahead. Try to pronounce it."

"*Aesh...Aesh-na cae-rule-a.*"

"Again," Giselle smiled. "This time with more tongue."

"*Aeshna caerulea*. But—but you said it was an imp. Was there a dragonfly hidden somewhere inside it?" I asked.

"Yes," Giselle said. "The *nymph*—not 'imp'—lives at the bottom of such deep puddles and ponds in the gloom and dark, and feeds whatever it can get, till one day it finds it can climb out into the light and grow its wings and fly away."

I made a full circle and looked round the village. "Wouldn't it be wonderful if humans could do the same? Wouldn't it be grand if you could use it to leave here?"

Giselle grinned. "Who said they *can't?* Same principle, different result. What you've just watched, however, is a perfectly ordinary miracle."

"You mean nature, don't you? And magic? Tell me, did you
make it happen?"

There came no reply, just a straight face.

"What about all the bluebirds and sparrows falling from the
trees? Or those hordes of grasshoppers going at each other?"

Giselle cleared her throat. "Not that, no. Like your mother
once upon a time, some things I can make happen or need
it to happen, but not that, apt though it was. It was not part
of the binding. Someday, if I'm right, something much like
that miracle will be needed—you're young, so you may call it
magic if you like—and there will be another nymph, another
way, another day." A quick, bright glance. "Do you understand me?"

"I'm not sure. But you just appeared out of nowhere." A
brief pause. "Do you make things happen? Are you really a
witch, then, like my Mum was?"

Giselle narrowed her eyes. "What makes you ask that? Have
they said anything at home?" She shook her head, breaking
down in laughter. She rose and pulled me up after her, and I
felt this strange connection right away. As if our minds and
hearts were one. "Spiritually, I hope, rather than physically.
No—forget I said that. Never mind, Child, we'd better get
you home, hadn't we? And I'm sure your mother is preparing something scrumptious for dinner, made from the finest
herbs. Come."

Cousin Giselle stayed for a few days. Most of them she
spent with me. Some of those afternoons she was very much
like a teacher. Other times, not just a relative but a friend I
could rely on, where the village children taunted me because
of where I came from and refused to let me play with them.
It was halcyon weather, as always in those late faraway sum-
mers, and we were out all day. And during our daylong picnic walks and intellectual conversations on paganism, as I see
now, the *foundation* of my life was laid. When she left, the

light went out of the fields and woods, but what power she had kindled in me remained.

It was the last of the lovely weather. The following spring the bishop purposely moved my father to the big, ugly coal-mining parish, and we settled into the cold discomfort of the house among the graveyards. I had to pass through the tombstones on my walks to school. I was nine, now, and there were no dragonflies and no wildflower meadows. It was boring. I begged for a pet of any kind, even a mouse, but I was allowed nothing. Then, one day, I was given a rabbit by the curate, who bred them. It had floppy ears and I loved it dearly. But within weeks my mother insisted that it be given back; I knew it was my father's sternness coming out of her lips. A few days later, when the curate called, as he did regularly, to talk with my father, he brought my rabbit back, skinned and ready for the pot. I ran upstairs and was sick, and my mother, for once warmly sympathetic and her old self, followed me and mopped up. By the time grief and horror had subsided, the curate, rabbit and all, had gone. I cried for three days, and the incident was never mentioned again. They say that the mind makes its own defenses. Looking back now down the years, I can believe it.

Then one day, without warning, the birdsongs went silent again. Their singing stopped and they fell from their nests just like the previous year. The grasshoppers never returned after the first incident. It was like something was purposely making them die off. I couldn't explain it. Nobody in the village could; a few people cried "plague," but when a veterinarian was called in, the rumors were ruled out. A silent bolt of lightning, and Cousin Giselle paying what she called a farewell visit, before leaving to see family in New Zealand. In those days, before jets and airliners, such a journey took months, and a year was hardly too long to reckon on for a trip that would take the traveler right around the world. There were so many places Giselle wanted to see, and at that age, I must confess, I was slightly envious of her: Paris, Venice, Cairo, Delhi, the Philippines, Peru....She would come back only when she had seen them all or collected a minimum of twenty stamps.

Meanwhile, she had brought a creature for me to keep. A tiny bamboo cage—it looked like it was held together with matchsticks—with a large dragonfly buzzing and zigzagging around inside it, eager and loving. Up until that day, I never knew insects could be loving creatures. A lost nymph she had taken in, and due to certain rites of passage, she would not leave it outdoors to chance or nature's fury.

"It is a *pagan* dragonfly. It needs conversation and companionship. Someone to talk to or watch over."

"What's his name?" I was down on the cold flagstones of the kitchen floor with the tiny cage. It was too good to be true.

"That's for you to provide. He's yours. Why don't you give him a name?"

"I shall call him 'Harry,'" I said into the cage, lying flat with my eyes as close as they could get to the insect's fluttering wings. It had a very long and thin wingspan. "I will put you by my bedside and sing to you or tell you stories every night before I go to sleep. I shall put you in a warm place, and give you your own tabletop and lantern." Giselle smiled and pinched my cheek. "Oh, I almost forgot! What does he eat?"

"Birds or insects much smaller than him I would think. He's a pretty big dragonfly. You remember the nymphs, don't you? You remember my lessons? Ants or termites. Occasionally fruit flies or spiders, but *not* Black Widows."

"Oh no, of course not," I said. "If I saw a Black Widow I'd run!"

"I'm sure you would," Giselle said. "And I'm sure you'll take great care of him."

She did not kiss me when she went. I never saw her kiss anyone, or talk to men for that matter. Not even on past visits with my father or the curate. She walked out of the house under a cloud, and a moment later a horse-driven carriage came along and she climbed aboard.

My father came outside, hands in his trouser pockets.

"That's strange," he said. "I can hear the birds again. It must be a special day. God gave us back the birds." He looked off into the distance. "It must be an extra," he added, looking yonder. "The regular carriage totes eight and left an hour ago. I saw it with my own eyes."

My mother smiled. Then the smile vanished as her eye fell on the caged insect in my hand, and on me holding it tight beside myself.

"A bug. What on earth my cousin was thinking of, saddling my poor child with a bug when there will be nobody here to look after it?"

My father laughed. "She might have given her a frog. Still, better than that wee rabbit."

"I'll look after him. I can easily—"

"You won't be here!"

I gaped at her. One did not question my mother. What she wanted to tell, she told.

She set her mouth till it looked like the one in my grandmother's portrait. "You are to go away to school. Giselle is right. You need companionship,"—she went on, now looking down at the caged insect—"and to be brought out of yourself and made less of a dreamer perhaps. And since she—"

"Ah, don't look so stricken." This was my father talking, gently. "You'll like it. You will, really. And you do need friends. We couldn't afford it ourselves, but Giselle has offered to pay the fees *herself*."

"What?" I was shocked.

"She prefers to be called a *trainer*," my mother said sharply.

My father looked grieved. "Yes. I know. Poor Giselle. But since she is so kindly helping us, we must seize the chance. *Anything* is better for the girl than this mining community."

The school that was chosen for me at age ten was a convent masquerading for a Wiccan Order, of which Cousin Giselle, safely out of reach on the Atlantic, would have surely approved. It was as if my future was purposely set before me; I'd never even had time to thank her for covering my education costs. My mother and father, indeed, made their protests. Leaning out the bedroom window one summer evening with my insect friend, I overheard them talking beside the open window of my father's study just below me.

"My daughter to be brought up by nuns? Absurd!" said my mother. "They may try to turn her out religious."

My father sounded amused. "You gave up a pagan life yourself. So that's hardly something you can expect me to condemn."

She laughed. "I put it badly, but you know what I mean. One hears so much about religious teaching being emphasized at the expense of nature or the sciences, and that's where Giselle's interests will lie. Hannah's got a good brain. She needs good teaching, hard work and competition."

In back of her mind, my mother sensed that this convent was for witches. "Anyway, I should know," she went on. "That's the part of her that was once like *me.*"

Looking back now, after a lifetime, I can see past my own unhappiness to what must have been my mother's. Sacrifices, mostly. Ambitious, beautiful, clever, and with that collective spark of manipulative magic we call *witchcraft,* dormant in her. She must have been worn down, bit by bit, by a life of poverty and loneliness and misunderstanding, then induced by my father's absorption in God and faith and parish affairs. By disappointment, too. But I did not think about all that then.

After a pause she said, in a voice I hardly recognized, "Very well. Bless Giselle's generosity. This so-called convent might be good enough."

And the following school year to the convent I went.

It was a gaunt place, slightly medieval-looking, near the sea cliffs to the east, and my mother hardly need have worried that the good witches would have any undue influence over me. The witches believed in "self-righteousness" and "self-government," which meant that a form leader was selected— the biggest girl in the form, and that all discipline was in her control.

I arrived with a reputation for being "too" smart, fostered by an entrance examination that I passed with ease. I was given a special talisman and put into a class of girls at least three years older than I was. I was soon the youngest head of the class, and no doubt I deserved the jealous dislike that was meted out to me. Then at the end of one term I came home from this secret society of a school to be told that my dragonfly had "gone." That was all. It may be hard for modern children of this century to understand that I did not dare ask how, or when, or even why. Outside of witchcraft, my childhood had conditioned me all over again to unhappiness, to fear, to lack of motivation. I said nothing when at the village on break. I stayed within myself and endured as silently as I could, until, again, help came.

It came in a strange and roundabout way. Foolish and still somewhat innocent as I was, I had confided in females that I believed in magic and practiced it. And it must be admitted, also, that the church-haunted life I once led, with its supposed miracles and its choirs of angels, conspired with fairy tales to make a world of enchantment both real and probable.

Life could not be anything but enriching at the new school. I was still too clever for comfort, yet not clever enough to hide it. However, I was fairly good at conjuring, and my talent for drawing from nature, an acceptable form practiced, was admired. So, though I remember little in the way of my performance, the years went by smoothly enough.

The convent was not only surrounded by sea cliffs and prairies you could run in, but also park and woodland, where we were allowed to wander at will in our free time. Whenever I could escape my schoolmates, I found my way into the woods, where stood tall and thin trees that I thought of as my own. The squirrels and insects whispered to me. They were my friends. And there, one day, it happened: the one memorable encounter of those green and growing years.

A footstep sounded opposite me. Cousin Giselle said cheerfully, "I thought I might find you here. Have you had lunch?"

"Oh, Giselle! No, I haven't."

I don't remember that I ever asked her how she had come, or how she had found me. I suppose I still took her magic for granted. We walked along the banks of the river under some oak trees. Beyond their shadow was a long, sunny curve of meadow where once a bank had been built to keep the river and waves from the Atlantic back in flood time.

"You've gotten so big. How old are you now?" asked Giselle.

"Nearly fifteen. They say I have one more year to go."

"And then? What are you planning to do with yourself, Hannah?"

"What I'd really like is to be a naturalist. But right now it seems more like a dream than reality."

"If that's what you really want, then what's to stop you?" asked Giselle briskly. "You have the talent and wisdom now. You must know it."

"Well, yes, but you see—" I bit my lip and stopped.

She read my thoughts unerringly. "And don't give me any nonsense about not having the chance or the luck. Let me tell you something. The only luck a witch has in this life is the power you're born with. *Natural* talent. The rest is up to you." Her eyes twinkled. "All right. End of sermon. Have a sandwich, and let's talk of something else, shall we?"

"Yes, please." I accepted both offers with relief. The sandwich, a roll bulging with scrambled eggs, was a wonderful change from school meals. "Tell me about the places you've been to. Have you really traveled the world?"

She showed me her stamps.

"Today's a bit like that other time," I said. "You just coming out of nowhere. Almost like a fairy godmother. As a matter of fact, I still think you are. And you did say one thing I've always remembered. When the nymph climbed out of the puddle, became a dragonfly and flew away. Do you remember that?"

"I do indeed. What about it?"

"I asked you if you were a witch, and you said you could make things happen. I obviously believe and know it all now, but what did you mean way back then?"

She was silent. Then she reached into the picnic basket and brought out something about the size of a tennis ball, wrapped in red velvet. Holding it in her palm, she pulled the string and unwrapped it, letting the velvet fall away until the gleaming object lay exposed. A crystal ball. A small reflecting world of green and blue, where the breeze in the boughs threw shadow and shine, and the sun on the water made golden sparks that dazzled the eyes.

"Is—Is that—"

My cousin cut me off. "Whether I can make things happen or not I do not know. But I do sometimes play around with nature and *see* what is going to happen."

"You mean you see things in that crystal?"

"In that, and in other ways. There's a certain technique to it."

I stared, fascinated at the globe in her hand. "Could you look now and see what's going to happen?" I asked her.

A direct look, grave and gentle. "You mean to you, don't you? That's what everyone means when people talk of the future…When caterpillars become butterflies…When tadpoles become frogs…When *nymphs* become dragonflies. It's a very narrow channel, the future."

"I'm sorry. You did ask me what I was going to do when I get out of here, and I wasn't sure—"

"Don't be sorry." She smiled. "I've peered down my own channel already."

I was surprised that anyone already so powerful and advanced in years should have any future worth longing for. She held the ball up to my eyes and read me with ease. She was laughing. "Well? Wouldn't you want to know when it was all going to end?"

"No!" I shouted, suddenly full of fear.

"When you look, you may see what's near at hand, or you may see right to the very end. Would you want to do that?"

The globe in her hand was flickering with light and dark from the flow of the nearby river. I hesitated. "How? Just look, you mean?"

"That's all. Don't be scared. Here, take it." She put the crystal into my cupped palms. "Now empty your mind as best you can, and look."

I saw my own face, small and distorted. The running light of the river and the shadows of the oak trees. The crystal, grey as mist, reflecting my eyes and long hair and the plant life behind me.

I looked up, blinking. The sky was empty. There were no dragonflies, not even *bees*. Only glowing lights and industrial objects. Machines that people carry with them everywhere and other mechanical wonders. Large structures made of metal and glass. And a nursing environment for old people, very up in age.

"Well?" she asked.

I was silent a moment. "Only what you said, the world that's here, like the trees and the river." I looked about me. "Hey, where did they go?"

"In the *crystal*," said Giselle.

"Are you saying they weren't real?"

"Oh, those are real enough." She reached out and took the crystal.

"Then"—I drew a breath—"I disappeared from this plane and *did* see something?"

"It seems so."

"It was like a different world. What does it mean?"

She put the crystal away. "Only that you have told me what I wanted to know. That you are going to live a long life and, for want of a better memory, you'll be thinking about this very day when you're old and grey." And that, in spite of my eager questions, was all she would say. "You said you had looked at your own future. Did you see it?"

"I didn't need to see that in the crystal." We were walking back now. She paused and looked up, but I got the impression that she was looking clear through the branches of the trees to something way beyond. "Time to go."

"Must you?" I said in disappointment.

"A little more traveling here and there, and learning a little more, I hope. A witch *collects* when she travels, and like magic, there's always something new to learn in out-of-the-way places."

"What's it like?" I asked.

"Someday, you will see it for yourself. Lonely as the grave, and every bit as restful." She started walking ahead of me.

To me, at that age, rest was not something I wanted, and the grave was so far off in that crystal as to be almost unimaginable. But there was one essential for any worldly heaven. Cousin Giselle knew it all too well. She gave me a sidelong glance. Then she bid me farewell and left the woods under a cloud of dragonflies.

It's Always Summer
in Daphne's Garden

Lori G. Petroff

he large black bird swooped down through thick
trees, avoiding branches expertly. His wingspan
cast a giant shadow on a small woman in her garden, busy at the task of weeding. At midmorning, with the
sun overhead, there was no way to hide the approach. He flew
over the vine-covered gazebo in the centre of the garden. His
talons gripped the white picket fence that surrounded both
her largish garden and her smallish cottage within it.

"Good Morning." She called to the bird, not looking out
from under her wide-brimmed hat.

He fidgeted on the fence to try to get her attention. She
continued on with her work, keeping her eyes on her hands.

"Old Crone! Old Crone!" He cracked at her.

She smiled at the bird's call from the garden fence but kept
her face hidden from him, under her hat. She didn't look up
from her task, on her knees in the dirt.

"You're perfectly awful. Did you make a special trip to remind me?" She called to him.

"Kra! Old Crone!" The bird bobbed its black head up and
down then hopped down into the dirt, taking two skipping
jumps towards her.

She sat back on her feet, with a small shovel in her hand and
her long skirts swishing in the soil. The huge bird had black
feathers so shiny they sometimes looked white in the sun. His
eyes were alert and focused on her.

"I'm not above throwing veggies." She giggled, raising her eyebrows at him playfully, and shaking the shovel at him. He twisted his head to the side and his quick "Kra-kra-kra" sounded vaguely like laughter. He danced around the garden edge.

"Stay out of the beds, you melon head!" she said, tossing a little stone in the bird's direction, but wide of his dancing body and her precious vegetables.

He opened his wings and with a few flaps of his large wingspan, was back up in the air. Dirt shifted and leaves danced.

She gave a high-pitched sneeze, and then she watched him swing through the trees and away. With him went her smile.

"Happy Birthday to me." The witch sighed, and continued with the weeding.

Late afternoons were made for baths. The bright sun shone into the cottage windows, brightening whitewashed walls.

Daphne sat in the big tub, hot water up to her chin, and sighed. It was a sigh of relief for her aching muscles and bones. She noted that change in the last little while. She felt exhaustion. A morning in the garden felt a little more like work lately. Still another sigh to relax the creaky knee that could predict weather on the outside of her protected property, while sore muscles loosened from squatting in the garden.

And once more she sighed, because that damned bird got her thinking. Another year had passed. Well, it passed everywhere else in the world. Not here, though. It shouldn't count as passing in here. Her magical, witchy homestead was protected from time. Or it should have been. But the feeling of exhaustion and aching body made her feel old. And also made her feel she should check on her spell at the perimeters of the garden, around the white fence.

The witch washed her face, splashing hot bath water up with her hands. Her face still felt firm and square to her. She washed her long hair, stringy, thick and wet. Still as evenly brown as when she was a child. She scrubbed her body from the shoulders down, admiring the freckles on her smooth skin, the soft curves of her short stature, the muscles in her legs, her funny round toes. She watched her long and dainty fingers, and smiled as she remembered her mother so long ago advising her that "You can always tell a woman's age by the wrinkles on her hands." The memory of it brought still another sigh, quickly replaced by the splashing of the rinse.

She patted herself dry in front of the long mirror. Her skin was red and flushed from the bath that still steamed behind her. She examined her face up close, the tiny laugh lines almost imperceptible. A little half-turn to admire the curve of her belly, before stepping away, satisfied.

"Not bad for an old girl" she said to her reflection, grabbed the bunch of clothing on a chair, and left the room in her towel.

Her reflection lingered a minute longer before leaving its room, too.

The bird had sat quietly on a naked tree branch, just outside of the perimeter of the cottage's safe gardens.

He grew antsy in the darkening night, perched in the shadowy trees. An autumn breeze ran through his feathers. He watched for movement in the house. He could only make out the flicker of the fires glow through the cottage's milky windows.

His legs tingled with the cold air. His claws started to itch. He sneezed a few times from deep within, through his black beak. Nearly time.

The crow swooped over the garden, and the change of temperature was perceptible. It both stung intensely and was comfortingly welcome.

It was always summer in Daphne's garden.

His claws hit the ground, scaring the night critters and they scattered out of the garden and into their hiding places. The bird half-loped, half-shuffled into the gazebo to hide himself.

In the dark, in the secrecy of the gazebo, a violent transformation began. As it had happened every night for years, the crow scratched along the floor. He convulsed, flipping and squawking. The pain was as if he were birthing himself every night, breaking out of his own skin. His feathers flexed and then his skin contracted, pushing him out through his own screams. Shifting shape, a man painfully burst out of his crow form.

He emerged from the shelter, naked and sweating, pale from the exertion. The man stumbled across the well-worn, well-swept dirt path around the gazebo. He stuffed his head into the compost pile, and vomited all the things his crow brain thought was a good idea to ingest, and everything his man body knew it could not.

Catching his breath and wiping his mouth, he looked up to the sky. When he was sure he was done retching, he shuffled naked back across the yard. As it always was, a cloak hung on the hook next to the cottage door. He slid into the cloak in the dark, covering his damp body. The light still flickered behind his eyes and he was dizzy from the transformation.

Daphne sat in front of the fireplace, embroidery in her hand. She really wasn't working on it at the moment. She was sitting patiently, hearing his painful noises from the gazebo. From her soft chair, she closed her eyes and reinforced the magic protective energy around her yard, and the healing energy that she immersed her gazebo in. There was nothing more she could do for him. The floor was swept, and swept again.

The waiting was the hardest part.

The man leaned in and pushed open the back door.

He propped his tall frame hard on the door way, and there she was. Her hair woven down her back, he could smell the cleanliness of the little cottage. Everything was tidy here but him.

She put her needlework down. She turned to smile at him, as if this were the most casual of entrances. She pulled her long black dress out from around her ankles so she could get up. Daphne came across the room, wrapping her black knitted shawl around her shoulders, and took the muscular man gently by the elbow. Guiding him into the cottage, she closed the door behind him. She knew his senses would still be burning from the effort of the change. Although he had insisted numerous times that she shouldn't and needn't be so doting, Daphne knew he still needed assistance in this moment, after the shape-shifting.

His eyes still felt glued over, and his mouth was pasty.

He slurred, "You perpetuate a stereotype dressed like that, Pumpkin."

She let out a lilting cackle. She wiped his sweaty face with her hands.

"The tub is ready for you, Kered." She said, guiding him to the bathroom. "Your mug of tea is on the chair beside the tub. Get in there and wash up, so you can get out and have some dinner with me. Besides, you smell funny. What on earth were you digging through today?"

He looked at her and raised an eyebrow, but had no energy for a snappy comeback.

"Never mind. I don't want to know." She giggled, pushing him gently into the bathroom, one hand on the door knob.

Kered let her guide him into the room that smelled of the herbs she put in the hot water. Both in the large tub and in his mug. All, of course, from her blessed garden. He took a deep breath to fill his lungs, and slowly began to feel himself again.

His night-self, anyway.

"Well, are you going to bathe me, too?" He said playfully, still through sticky lips and thick tongue.

She only laughed and closed the bathroom door, before he could throw his cloak off and flash her.

Now that he was here, and settled in, she could relax. Daphne put her feet back up and continued on the embroidery spell she had been working on. She listened to him splashing in the tub, and as he relaxed, she would listen to him softly sing.

She loved this part.

When he opened the door, there was almost an audible "whoosh," as the humidity escaped the confines of the small bathing room. He saw her in her soft chair, her little feet back up on the tiny ornamental ottoman footstool, just peeking out from under the too-long dress.

He loved this part.

His hands were rough on her head as he ruffled her hair from behind. "Hallo, Love!" he said. Kered was tall when they stood side-by-side with her. When she sat, he absolutely towered over her. She craned her neck up to meet his eyes. The bright blue of them contrasted his weathered skin.

"Don't you 'hallo, Love' me!" She said in a stern voice, though a grin peeked out of the corner of her mouth. She smoothed out the top of her head, and pointed from his body, to the empty stuffed chair beside her as if to say, "Sit!"

He sat his cloaked body down and reclined in as best as he could. He made his tall body fit into the smallish chair. The tea steamed hot on the table between them.

Sarcastically, she said, "Thanks again for the lovely birthday reminder today." She held her needle above her embroidery, but looked directly into his eyes in mock anger.

He chuckled. Gracefully, he lifted the painted tea pot with his large hands, to pour them both fresh tea.

"Ah, it never gets old....Just like you!" He said, raising the sugar bowl. "One lump or two?"

"Oh, I'll give you lumps!" she said, tossing her work down, and waggling her fingers at him as if to cast a spell, but a giggle escaped her. It always silently amazed her how his movements were like a dance. His large hands were sturdy and muscular. Once, she had tried to read his palm but was distracted by the lines and rounded hills on them. Hands so strong should be a little clumsy, she always thought.

He cringed at her wiggling finger movements, but knew she would never really hex him. He plopped two sugar squares into her tea.

"Umm, another one, please," Daphne asked. He looked at her with wide and rolling eyes. "It's a big cup!" She said to him, laughing. She loved how he softened her into feeling like a young witch.

They both settled in comfortably, alternately wiggling toes at the fire, and sipping hot tea. They watched the fire dance.

"So, what adventures did you get up to today, Kered? Tell me all of it." She said.

"Well." He sighed "I did quite a bit before I came here to wish you a happy birthday. How old are you again?"

"Never you mind. Get on with your day!"

"I picked through some lovely garbage on the east-end. Lots of nice treats in there."

She made a face to mime vomiting.

"Oh, and then I went shopping." He said with a rather pleased expression.

Her eyebrows raised at that, and she looked over and up into his mischievous face. "Oh, really. Kered, the enormous crow, went wobbling through the malls today? And, what exactly *is* the exchange rate on day old crow-picked bottle caps and old nails now, anyway?" She laughed long and deeply at her own wit, holding her belly and wiping away tears.

"Again, Woman, that crazy cackle is such a stereotype." But he laughed along with her. He secretly loved her laugh. He had never known anyone to laugh as easily as she did. When she finally calmed from her laughing fit, he said "You go all girlish when you laugh out of control like that. As if you weren't a witch who's....How old are you again?"

"Bah!" she yelled at him, and straightened up. "Ok, ok, you went shopping. Tell me what you got. And how you got it."

"Well..." He trailed off, while fumbling with something on his baby finger. "I can't tell you where I got it." He smiled into her eyes. "But, I got you this!" He held his long arm out to her, reaching over the tea pot, fist closed.

"Show me!" she said

"Nope, you gotta unwrap it." He held his fist tightly closed.

Dropping her embroidery to a basket under the tea table, she took his hand and tried to pry it open. Her mock wrestling left them in fits of giggles. She couldn't open his strong large fist. She ended up out of breath, and sitting on the ottoman in front of his chair.

"Look, melon head, I'm not going to tell you how old I am, but what I AM going to tell you is that I'm too old to wrestle you. Give an old lady a break. Let me see!" She pretended to pout.

He moved closer to her, put his closed palm at her face level, and opened it.

Softly, he said "Happy Birthday, Daphne."

On his weathered palm sat a silver ring. An ornate ivy setting held a tear-shaped stone. The stone was red, and polished so it was rounded and smooth. The flickering fire light bounced off it and made the silver shine.

"It's…It's really pretty, Kered," she stammered. He held his hand out farther, and she took it from his hand, and smiled a crooked smile.

"Yeah, you know how crows are with shiny things. Bottle caps and such." He sat back in his chair.

"Kered…" Her voice trailed off and her eyes started to look pleading, and the playful energy in the room melted into something warmer. Kered fidgeted.

"It's a friendship-type ring, Daph. A little token." He trailed off this time. He took her hand, and folded her little fingers over the ring, into her palm.

She took the ring out of her palm, looked at it again, and then slipped it onto her fingers until she found one it would fit. It finally settled on the index finger of her right hand.

"It's jasper," she said, after inspecting it closer. Then she spoke to him softly, "You are so sweet, when you really put your mind to it."

They both felt the room energy change. The firelight got a little softer. The room smelled a little sweeter.

Kered broke the silence, his voice a little louder. "Yeah, I am pretty sweet. And, besides, like I said, there was some pretty good garbage picking to be had over on the east-end today. And gosh darn it, you're worth it."

She laughed and mock-slapped him.

"Jerk." Jumping up, she moved to the kitchen workbench that doubled as the table. "Let's have some dinner. I think the potatoes are done."

The two of them ate dinner, drank tea, and talked the night away excitedly as little children, making each other laugh until their stomachs hurt, as they did every night. Eventually, Daphne and Kered ended up back in the comfy chairs, until they both silently fell asleep in front of the fireplace.

At the first light of dawn, just as the sun peeked over the horizon, the cramps would wake Kered up. They started strong and powerful in his stomach. It was curious to him that even after so long, there was no getting used to this pain.

He looked over at her. She was sleeping on her side in the stuffed chair, with arms and legs pulled up as close to her body as possible to keep her fingers and toes warm. She was still wearing the gift he had brought her.

Breathing deep, Kered rubbed his own eyes, and held his stomach. He slipped into her room, pulled the neatly tucked bed apart to get the quilt from where she only slept when he didn't appear in her doorway at night. And he was here nearly every night.

A step out of her room, and the cramps were spreading from his stomach into his chest and hips. Quietly through the pain, he tucked her under the quilt, managing to not stir her.

Kered barely made it out into the garden before the transformation began again. The change back to crow form from man, was only a little less extreme for him, he had noted through the years. He wasn't sure if it was from spending all night on this protected property, if she slipped something healing into dinner, or if it was just because he was waking from the deepest sleep he would have during his day and night. But there were no more man-thoughts after that.

The cloak lay strewn across the garden walk. The big black crow waddled his way out from under it.

As he burst into the air, his large wings made dirt shift, and leaves dance.

The First Witch

Diana Corbitt

oodwife Alstead…? Are you down there?"

The words, softly spoken, seemed to float down from above. Hands and feet bound by shackles, Alice struggled to rise.

"Who calls?" she whispered. She pulled away from the stone wall where she'd been resting and gazed up at the narrow window above her.

To Alice's surprise, it was Constance Trask, a young girl from the village. Kneeling, Constance peered down at her from between the bars, her normally smooth brow now creased with worry.

"Dear Goody. It must be awful down there all alone, and your husband so recently passed."

Having been treated with contempt every moment since her arrest, it did not surprise Alice when she burst into tears at the first sound of a friendly voice.

"Yes, Dear, it is quite terrible." she sniffed. "And you're right. I do miss my Jonathan."

Constance flashed a cautious look to her right, then pressed her forehead to the bars. "They say you're a witch. But I don't believe them. Hold on. I've brought you some bread."

She reached into a small cotton sack.

"Oh, you dear girl." Immediately, Alice's mouth began to water, having been fed nothing but corn mush since she was cast into the courthouse basement three days earlier. Manacles clanking, she raised her hands, ready to receive the prize, but before Constance could make good her promise something caught her eye.

"S-someone is coming!" she stammered, eyes bright and fearful. "I have to go."

Young and spry, soon, all that was left of Constance was the sound of her receding footsteps.

That afternoon, Goodwife Alice Alstead blinked in amazement as the sheriff, a redheaded man with a great hooked nose, all but dragged her down the center aisle of the courtroom past half the population of Haverhill Township. She had to be dreaming. It was the only explanation, since to think otherwise meant the entire village had gone mad. How could she be accused of witchcraft when she was no witch?

With a hard shove, the sheriff pushed her into the chair provided for the accused, then took two steps back, wiping his hands on his breeches as if he feared contamination.

From his perch behind a high wooden bench, Magistrate Pratt, a clean-shaven man but for a small-yet-lengthy patch of chin whiskers which he stroked frequently, began to speak. "Goodwife Alstead, you are accused of familiarity with the Devil. How do you plead?"

She grimaced as she pushed herself to her feet, more from the rheumatism in her swollen knees than from the shackles grating at her ankles and wrists. Older than most, Alice had reached sixty and two the previous spring.

"I am innocent," she said. "Who accuses me, and what do they say I have done?"

She scanned the courtroom, its two dozen benches packed with well-known faces, all damp with perspiration on such a humid summer day. Most glowered at Alice with the narrowed gaze of burning contempt, but a few looked away as if mere eye contact would damn them to Hell.

"Bring forth the first witness," said the magistrate. As with the rest of the assemblage, the skin between Pratt's bristling black eyebrows had also gathered together, and he scowled at Alice with open disdain as the sheriff, led by his prominent nose, stepped to the front of the courtroom and faced the crowd.

"Gideon Belington!" he bellowed. "Step forward!"

The farmer? She listened as Farmer Belington recalled how, two weeks earlier, Alice had dosed his ailing cow, Bessie, an odorous concoction. At first, the beast's health improved. But three days later, Bessie died, clearly Alice's responsibility since she had gone away dissatisfied with how she'd been compensated.

The farmer's testimony was followed by that of old Samuel Milton's young wife, Theodora. She accused Alice of casting a spell on her husband, her senior by twenty years. He'd nearly died, having spent several days confined to his bed with terrible contractions of the bowels.

As each petitioner spoke, Alice strongly denied their accusations, and on both occasions the sheriff silenced her with a clout to the head. Weeping and frightened, she huddled in her chair and clutched her aching skull, reflecting on her accusers' testimonies.

That one. Bah! It's she who should be sitting here, not me. And Belington's cow was twenty years old if it was a day. He's lucky it lived as long as it did.

Magistrate Pratt ran a hand down the length of his beard and instructed the sheriff to call forth the third and final witness.

Hoping they hadn't saved the worst for last, Alice had no idea who her next accuser might be. She studied each of her neighbors' faces one by one.

"Constance Trask," called the sheriff in a most deep and resonant voice. "Step forward and be heard."

That child? Why she just visited me in my cell this very morn, the only one brave enough to do so! Why call her? She doesn't believe I'm a witch.

As Constance stepped into the waist-high booth built for such a purpose, Alice tried to sort things out in her mind.

Perhaps Constance's words had been misconstrued. Alice had never angered the girl, except—

"'Twas nearly a fortnight ago," Constance began, using an ugly sneering tone Alice had never heard before. "My sister Abby and I were taking an afternoon stroll when we spied Goodwife Alstead scurrying across road in the direction of her home with something bundled in her apron. When she noticed us she slowed and hailed us in a friendly voice, calling us to her. Once we drew near, she gave us a sly wink and revealed the dozen red apples she was carrying. 'Have one,' she offered. But we refused."

Again, the magistrate stroked his substantial length of beard. "And for what cause did you refuse the apples?"

"Why, because they were red, of course." The girl's shoulders rose and fell as if all the world should recognize the significance. "They were obviously from Goodman Simpson's orchard, since his are the only trees of such variety in these parts, and it is well known throughout the community that his wife had quarreled with Goodwife Alstead in the village square that very morn." Her gaze flickered in Alice's direction. "Since the two women were on bad terms, the apples had to be stolen."

Upon hearing the girl speak with such confidence, the room filled with a hive-like drone as the townspeople voiced their agreement. There was no doubt. Alice had stolen the apples. It wasn't until Magistrate Pratt banged his gavel a half dozen times that the discourse was grudgingly ended.

"Tell us," ordered Pratt. "How did Goodwife Alstead respond to your refusal?"

Constance gazed at his narrow face, her great blue eyes now moist with tears.

"With great displeasure. Once it was clear that we would not be a party to her thievery she cursed us each in turn."

Although she knew the sheriff would strike her, Alice could hold her tongue no longer. "Slander!" she shouted, shackles jangling as she rose to her feet. "All lies! I picked no fruit! 'Twas she! I caught them at it when—"

"Silence!" Standing his full height, the magistrate stood and reached across his high wooden bench, the sleeve of his black robes flapping as he swung a long bony finger in the sheriff's direction. "You shall quiet that woman now, Sir!"

Fueled by indignation, the spectators rose as one.

"Witch!" screeched an anonymous voice from the back of the room. The shout was followed by several others, causing the magistrate's already ruddy complexion to redden to the verge of apoplexy.

"Quiet, all of you!" he shouted, and, as if pounding a nail, slammed his mallet-like gavel repeatedly.

The sheriff cuffed Alice across the face, and she fell back into the chair with a groan. Either in consideration of the irate magistrate's health or more likely his wrath, the mob grudgingly settled back into their seats, everyone perspiring profusely from their exertions as well as the sweltering heat.

Once the assemblage had quieted and the magistrate's brow had been suitably mopped, he again addressed the witness.

"And what words did Goodwife Alstead speak to curse you and your sister?"

The girl's chest heaved, and she dropped her gaze to the floor.

"I dare not repeat the words, lest God smite me for such blasphemy."

"My apologies." Pratt bit his lip thoughtfully. "Pray, did you or your sister feel the effects of the curse immediately?"

"No, not immediately. Later...that night."

He leaned forward, his fingers twirling the tip of his beard. "Tell us."

Constance clenched her hands beneath her chin.

"As soon as we were abed, Abby began to cry out in pain. "Father! Mother!" she wailed. "Help me! Goodwife Alstead is upon me! She chokes me! She kneels on my belly! She will break my bowels!" She covered her face with her hands and wept.

"If you can, pray tell the court what became of your sister."

The girl looked up, tears flowing down her cheeks in great rivers.

"She died screaming two days later."

"That poor child," Alice murmured under her breath.

Being that Haverhill was such a small town, the demise of young Abigail was well known to all, including Alice. But it wasn't until that moment that the details of the girl's suffering were made public. Now, it was not only anger surging through the masses, but shock and melancholy.

"And what of yourself?" the magistrate asked. "Were you not also afflicted?"

"Yes, but not as harshly as Abby." She rubbed her arms. "I felt fingers pricking my skin. Invisible fingers, searing hot, as if the Devil himself were pinching me."

The audience shifted impatiently on their benches as Constance drew in a long breath and exhaled deeply. "Then…" She wiped her eyes with her apron. "…suddenly, I felt a great sting on my left cheek, as if I'd been slapped across the face!"

"Let it be noted," said Magistrate Trask, "that the girl still bears the remnants of a hand-shaped bruise on her face. Stand, girl, so those assembled here may bear witness."

Trembling, Constance did as she was bid and drew herself up, the greenish-yellow tint easily visible.

"Reverend Trask," said the magistrate. "Please, step forward."

All heads turned as the reverend, a robust man, made his way through the crowd. Glossy-haired and rosy-cheeked, he was surprisingly hale and hearty, considering the misery he'd suffered during the last year, for his wife and three sons had also been taken from him. Trask stood beside his only remaining child, their fingers locked in solidarity.

Magistrate Pratt cleared his throat.

"Once again, Reverend, I offer my deepest condolences for the recent loss of your daughter, but as a man of the cloth you understand that when the Devil is afoot, he must be rooted out immediately."

Reverend Trask nodded.

"I am well aware."

"Then tell me, sir. Do you abide by such as young Constance has made public?"

"Yes."

"And were you in attendance when all of this occurred?"

"I was." Trask's chin trembled. "And I thank the Lord that my dear wife was not. It was bad enough seeing poor Abigail writhing in pain, but then Constance suddenly arched her back and screamed, 'Goodwife Alstead is pricking my back! Stop her, Father! Stop her!'" The man lowered his gaze to the floor. "I was sending the servant girl for a basin of fresh water when I heard the blow. It was terribly loud. Constance lay on the floor in a heap, the red imprint of a hand on her cheek." He narrowed his gaze on the congregation. "Goodwife Alstead's hand. The Devil's hand."

"Nooooo!" wailed Alice, now fully aware she was not dreaming. "I cursed them not! I am no witch, but a pious, God-fearing woman!"

"God-fearing?" cried the reverend. The people's jeers seemed to fuel his purpose, drawing him taller, straighter. He pointed an accusing finger at Alice, and even though he was several feet away, she cringed as if she herself had been struck. "How many times have you attended church services in the past month? Tell us, how many?"

"I-I'm not certain," she whispered. "I've been so busy…taking care of the farm, my husband." She turned to her audience. "Everyone knows Jonathan was ill and unable to tend the animals. What should I have done, let them starve?"

Trask shook his head. "You should have trusted in the Lord."

Even though she knew it would help her cause naught, Alice chuckled, her lip curled back defiantly. "Oh, I tried. But God sent no angels to pick our corn nor plow our fields. Prayers do not feed cows, Master Trask. That requires human hands. Hands calloused from hard work. But you know not of that. Yours are soft. It's your tongue that works for you!"

There was an immense drawing in of breath, followed by a rumble of scornful chatter.

BANG! BANG! BANG! The sound of Magistrate Pratt's gavel thundered through the courtroom, quieting everyone but Alice.

"No one helped us as Jonathan lay dying. Not one of your fine, pious parishioners, and you know why! They were afraid! Frightened that whatever malady had struck him down might take them, too!" She raised her chin at her audience. "Look at you all, weepy-eyed over the death of that girl. How sad, her young life cut short. But what about my Jonathan? Was his death of less value because he was old? I am sixty and two years old. Am I no longer of value?"

"I'll wager she cast a spell on him too!" hollered Goodwife Simpson, owner of the infamous apple tree.

"She's a witch!" shouted the blacksmith, Goodman Brown.

Again, the word—witch—burst from the crowd, but this time the magistrate did nothing to stop it. Instead, he sat back studying the crowd as their chant echoed through the room.

"Witch! Witch! Witch!" All stood, man and woman, young and old, stomping their feet in time with their angry mantra.

To Alice's surprise, it was Reverend Trask who silenced the horde. As if standing in the pulpit, he raised both arms above his head, turned to the mob, and shouted, "Silence! Let the magistrate pronounce his judgment!"

Alice slouched in the chair, one arm hanging limply in her lap, the other bent at the elbow, her wrinkled cheek resting on her hand. She had no doubt what Pratt's judgment would be. But, strangely, she did not mind. Let them hang her. What life was this, among self-righteous hypocrites who paraded themselves as Christians?

With all eyes upon him, Magistrate Pratt rallied from his stupor and sat up straight. He wiped the sweat from his forehead, adjusted his black skullcap, and cleared his throat.

"Alice Alstead, it is the judgment of this court that thou hast consorted with the Devil and by his evil assistance, brought ill upon the property and health of others. Thou art sentenced to death three days hence."

Cheers rang out through the chamber, followed much hand clapping and back slapping. Young Constance collapsed under the stress, held aloft only by her father's arms. Goodwife

Alstead remained as she was, her only reaction being an almost imperceptible shake of the head.

Three days later, Alice, still bound hand and foot, was lead from her basement cell escorted by four guards, all fully armored, befitting the occasion. She stepped into the alleyway behind the courthouse and smiled as the familiar scents of mud and horse dung entered her nostrils.

"A fine day for a hanging," she murmured to no one in particular.

In the shade of a building a few feet away, one of the miller's boys sat in a small cart drawn by a sagging grey mare. Built from roughhewn branches, the cart appeared new and hastily made. Had it been constructed solely for this occasion? Perhaps no one wished their property sullied by the witch.

Upon a signal from one of the guards, the horse lumbered forward, stopping beside the sheriff and a three step mounting block.

The sheriff rubbed his hands together and grinned, his cheeks already glistening from the early morning heat. "Good morrow, Madame. Ready for your final journey?" He threw open a little door on the side of the cart, his curly red mane hanging lank upon his shoulders.

"As ready...as I will ever be," Alice told him. Winded from her recent climb up the basement steps, she looked for assistance in entering the cart. It did not surprise her when Reverend Trask appeared beside her, he being God's only representative for several miles. With the Bible clasped in his right hand, he offered her his left, and, with his assistance, she clambered into the cart and stood, hands gripping the waist-high railing. The surprise came when the reverend joined her there.

"I don't recall them finding you guilty of anything," she said, hoping to sound brave.

"I can assure you, Madame, I was not." Trask presented the Bible to Alice. "There is still time to clear your soul. Lay your hand upon this holy book. Confess your sorcery, that the Lord might forgive your evil doings."

"Thank you, Reverend." She took the book and pressed it to her chest. "I've had a particular prayer in mind ever since the trial. Would you like to hear it?"

Trask smiled. "Of course." With hands clasped in front of him, the minister closed his eyes and bowed his head.

But instead of following suit or raising her eyes to the heavens, which had begun to darken with clouds, she narrowed them on Trask. "I have many regrets," she began, "but my greatest lament is that I did not proclaim your Constance and Abigail thieves the moment I caught them stealing those apples."

Trask staggered back against the rail, mouth agape.

"I forgive little Abigail." Alice snarled. "For she was but a child and only doing as her sister bid her. But Constance!" She all but spat the words. "May she burn in Hell for her lies!"

In his haste to exit the cart, Trask stumbled, and if it were not for the sheriff and his guards, he might have landed face-first in the mud. But once both his feet touched ground, he quickly recovered.

"The only one going to Hell on this day is you, Witch!" barked the red-faced minister.

The sheriff grinned and addressed the young cart driver, "It appears there will be no salvation for Goodwife Alstead today, Steven. Off with you, then."

With a lurch, the cart proceeded slowly down the alley with the sheriff trailing and a guard on either side. A small procession, but when they turned onto the cobblestoned street, everything changed. It appeared that everyone in the village had turned out for the hanging, and they lined the street leading to the town square, jeering and laughing as she passed.

"Let the Devil take you!" shouted the barrel maker.

The village baker, a circular man who Alice remembered as kind, jovial man, burst from the crowd, still clad in his flour-dusted apron. He jogged alongside the cart. "Die, Witch!" he hollered, one fat fist raised and shaking.

She gripped the rail with both hands, struggling to keep her feet, and as the cart jounced along the cobbles, a small pumpkin struck her shoulder. Rotten, it was much too soft to do any real damage, but the implication was clear. The people she once considered friends all wished her dead. If that was how they felt, then to Hell with all of them. With the reverend's Bible still clutched in her hand, she fell to her knees as more pumpkins rained down on her, along with several eggs and a few moldy squash.

It wasn't until several minutes later that the cart pulled to a stop and the assault stopped. Always a proud woman, she dragged herself to her feet and, chin raised, peered in the direction of the village green, the most likely setting for a scaffold.

What she saw there made her breath catch.

Instead of the gallows she expected, a great mound of lumber had been gathered, from the center of which protruded a freshly-cut pine, its branches hewn down to the bark.

"You seem perplexed," said the grinning sheriff. "Is something amiss?"

"The…the gallows," Alice rasped, suddenly unable to catch her breath. "Where are the gallows?"

"There will be no gallows for you, Witch. Yours will be a more drawn-out death, and, from what I'm told, exceptionally more painful."

With no husband, friend, or family to speak of, Alice had resigned herself to being hanged. There was nothing left for her in Haverhill. Dead, her suffering would be ended, and although hanging was a dishonorable death, it would be quick if done correctly.

But this…

Having grown up in England, she'd been present for several executions, most for theft, a few for murder. Only once had she witnessed a burning. Accused of sorcery, the man's shrieks still echoed in her mind more than fifty years later. To her knowledge, no one had ever been accused of witchcraft in the New World, and for certain, never burned as one.

"'Tis a jest." she croaked the words with little confidence.

Instinctively, the crowd parted, leaving her a wide berth to pass. But by then, Alice had gone limp and in no condition to walk. Seeing this, the sheriff ordered one of the guards to climb up into the cart. He removed the shackles and lowered her muck-splattered body down to his partner. With the expression of men obliged to bear a decaying carcass, they draped her lifeless arms across their shoulders.

"I am no witch," she muttered, inspiring peals of laughter from those close enough to hear.

Someone shouted an insult, but all Alice heard was an unintelligible buzz, for it was as if all the blood in her body were coursing through her skull, drowning out all but the loudest of sounds.

It wasn't until the men carrying her began to climb the mountain of firewood that her mind grasped the full extent of what was happening. At that moment her entire body stiffened, and a shriek burst out of her, sharp as a razor's edge. Arms and legs thrashing, she drained her lungs and drew in a second breath, but before she could scream again, one of the guards punched her in the stomach.

"Shut your filthy hole!" he bellowed. When the audience roared their approval, he turned and waved, a proud grin stretched across his face.

Stunned, Alice gasped for breath, gaping at the massive crowd as the two men bound her trembling body with chains, this time encircling her waist and shoulders. When Jonathan was dying and she needed help with the farm, no one had come to their aid, but for this all had turned out but the aged and infirmed.

There stood Magistrate Pratt and his wife. Beside them, the richest man in town, Master Simons, along with his three sons and four daughters. But in no way did her audience consist of only men of property and wealth. Folk of every age, gender and walk of life had turned out, many more than the tiny population of Haverhill. It was obvious that in the three days since her sentence was pronounced, word had spread to neighboring villages, for there were many of faces she did not recognize.

A raised platform had been erected, and Alice watched, dumbstruck, as the mayor, a large fleshy man with shoulder-length hair the color of winter snow, climbed the four steps up to it. Old Mayor Bedford was followed by Magistrate Pratt, having traded his faded skullcap for one of freshly-dyed wool, black as onyx, befitting the occasion. The mayor raised both arms, and the throng grew silent, anxiously watching as the magistrate passed him the document he was about to read. Facing the crowd, Old Bedford unrolled the paper scroll and drew in a deep breath.

"It has been made public that, with the aid of Satan's hand, Alice Alstead has acted things in preternatural ways. She has been found guilty of entertaining familiarity with Lucifer, the grand enemy of God and mankind." He paused to cast a gaze of pious disdain upon Alice before drawing in another lungful of air. "In adherence with the words of our Lord and Savior, specifically, Exodus 22:18 'Thou shalt not suffer a witch to live,' it is the sentence of the court and the established law of this commonwealth that she must burn."

Finished with his speech, the mayor gave a solemn nod to the sheriff, who had been standing nearby, literally bouncing on his toes with anticipation. He snatched a torch from a deputy, its flame the same color as his hair, and all but ran the few yards to Alice's mound, a childlike grin beneath his red moustaches.

"Wait!" shouted Alice, her heart nearly splitting from fright. "I have yet to be afforded the opportunity to speak! Pray, allow me my last words."

"Why?" replied the mayor. "To fill our ears with Satan's lies?"

The sheriff lowered the flame, but before he could touch it to the dry branches at his feet, Reverend Trask pushed through the crowd, stilling the sheriff's hand.

"Let her speak."

The two men on the platform looked at the reverend as if he had grown a third eye.

"It is only right," Trask continued, "and her words will harm no virtuous man."

Shoulders slumped, the sheriff grumbled as his superiors drew together, foreheads all but touching. After a few moments they'd made their decision, and Mayor Bedford raised his hands to silence the complaining onlookers.

"As all convicted citizens of this commonwealth have the God-given right to speak their last words, let it not be said that Haverhill would deny—even a witch—that opportunity." His eyes narrowed on Alice. "Speak, woman…but mind thy tongue."

Alice could not believe her ears. Finally, she was being allowed to speak, but what would she say? Terrified, her mind seemed empty as if, unlike Alice, her thoughts had seen their chance and fled.

Studying the peoples' faces, she found there neither sympathy nor sadness. If anything, it was impatience. She saw it in the shifting of feet, the release of a deeply drawn breath. Their eyes shifted anxiously from her to the darkening sky and back. Were they concerned that an ill-timed shower might ruin their afternoon plans?

Alice had always been a religious woman, but her partiality to praising her Lord from the privacy of her own home had made her unpopular in the village. She closed her eyes and begged God to help her find the words. After a few moments, they came.

"I have never intentionally harmed another soul, either by my own hand, or with the help of Satan. What I *am* guilty of is keeping to myself, of not conforming to the public expectation that I attend church services twice each week. That makes me different, but it does not make me a witch."

She located the man who had accused her of poisoning his prized cow and fixed her gaze upon him. "Gideon Belington! You, more than most, know that I am innocent. When your cow fell ill and none could find the cause you called on me to help. 'Please,' you said. 'Help me save my Bessie.' And I went. In the middle of the night, I went." Her eyes narrowed into slits. "I did my best for that ancient beast...and this is the thanks I get. Am I to burn because I expected more than a dozen eggs in payment?"

Belington's face churned with conflict, fear, anger, shame, all battling for position. For a moment, Alice thought he might change his tune. But it was anger that won out.

"You killed my Bessie!" he shouted, "You're a witch, and you deserve what you get!"

She chuckled and shook her head. "I expected as much from a man like you. And what of Theodosia Milton? Where is she? Cringing beneath her bed, I'll wager."

"Not so," said a reedy voice.

To Alice's surprise, Samuel Milton stepped through the crowd, his much younger wife, Theodora, bringing up the rear, her eyes downcast. When they reached the foot of the pyre, Samuel raised his bony chin. "We would never miss your demise, foul sorceress." His feathery whiskers waggled as he spoke.

"You're lucky you're not dead," Alice told the old man. "I cast no spell on you. But I cannot speak for your little child-wife. She came to me with questions not long before you fell ill. 'Where grow the venomous herbs, and how do they appear?' she asked me."

"Heed her not!" Theodora clutched her ancient husband's arm. "She's a witch! It is their nature to lie!"

Old Samuel cleared his throat and regarded his wife with doubtful eyes.

"You are right to worry," Alice continued, "I sent her away empty-handed. Your aching belly was due to someone else's effort, and it appears that task is yet to be finished."

Young Theodora attempted to comfort her doubtful husband, but Alice was done with them. Knowing her time was short, she searched the crowd for she who had pained her most. "Where is she?" Alice shouted at Reverend Trask. "Where is the girl?"

"Did you really think I would allow her to come?" Trask smiled. "I know you well, Goody Alstead. Your tongue can slice a melon. Why would I bring my daughter here for your abuse?"

"Abuse? 'Tis I who's been abused. Bring her to me so I can—"

"Enough!" roared Mayor Bedford, his hands clenched into fists. "You have said your piece. Sheriff, send her to Hell!"

"Finally," muttered the sheriff. He touched the flame to the bottom layer where the branches were thinnest. They caught quickly.

The opportunity to speak had riled Alice's spirit, making her more and more courageous with each word spent. But as the flames spread, all that courage drained away. She gripped her skirts with both hands and gaped at the flames transfixed as, twig to twig, the blaze encircled her.

"Help me! I beg thee!" Straining against her chains, her tear-filled eyes darted from face to face, calling each person by name. But no one stepped forward, and the conflagration grew.

"The Lord's hand is all that's left to you," said Reverend Trask, his voice raised so she could hear him above the crackling wood. "Pray, Alice Alstead. Pray for his aid."

So she did.

"Lord, I beg thee!" she cried, her voice quivering. "Release me from these chains! You know their charges are false!" As the flames rose, a gust of smoke wafted up into her face, replacing her entreaties with a hacking cough.

"So be it," she croaked, once the coughing had subsided. "I've never dealt with him before, but if God wishes to ignore me, then what have I to lose?" She peered up at the sky, now black with clouds. "Satan, I beseech thee! Smite these people! Send down a torrent of fire upon them! Burn them as they wish to burn me!"

As if on command, lightning lit up the sky, followed by bone-rattling thunder. "He comes!" She cried. "He comes, and you will all burn with me!" As her words ended, a bolt of lightning struck a lone oak tree at the far edge of the green. Sparks and flames flashed.

Hysterical, the crowd scattered like the vermin they were. In her haste to get away, Theodosia Milton shoved past her husband, sending him sprawling to the ground. Mayor Bedford's wife tripped on her skirts as she raced down the platform steps, taking her husband with her. Alice cackled as lightning flashed and thunder roared. Screaming townsfolk ran in all directions. But to her dismay, the flames surrounding her still grew, and her laughter soon became shrieks.

By the time the square had cleared, the fire had encircled Alice and quickly towered above her. Like hungry wolves, the flames lapped at her legs with scalding tongues, blistering her skin. Soon, even her screams were agony. With each breath hotter than the one before, the fire roasted her both inside and out. Ironically, it wasn't until Alice was good and dead that rain began to fall, dousing the flames in minutes.

Once it started, the rain fell steadily for two hours. Mayor Bedford was there when the sky cleared, ready to supervise the removal of what was left. It had been Trask's idea to burn the old woman, a good idea at the time, but the sight of her charred frame sagging against its bonds brought him pause.

With his left hand, his right arm bound in a sling from his tumble off the platform, Bedford directed the pyre disassembled and the scorched wood removed. A half dozen men were set to it, and, armed with shovels and pitchforks, in less than an hour they had filled the very cart in which Alice had been transported to her execution.

That was the easy part. Since no one who had attended the burning would go near the body, he finally entrusted the repulsive duty to a couple of farm laborers who had wandered into town after the rain. After settling on a price, the men heaved Alice's remains onto an old sheet of canvas they'd spread in the back of a dung cart. They were then ordered to wheel it to the edge of town where a shallow grave had already been dug.

"Oy!" groaned the smaller. "She's still steaming."

The leader of the two, a barrel-chested fellow with stiff black whiskers laughed. "Aye, she be black as a roasted boar. A pity the rain put out the fire afore she cooked through, God rot her. Maybe she wouldn't smell as bad."

With their kerchiefs stretched across their noses to keep out the stench, the two men looked more highwaymen than undertakers as they trundled the cart down narrow lane. The road ended at the remains of an abandoned Indian village, as they'd been told. They located the hole easily and tipped up the cart. Their scorched cargo slid into the hole with a gut-churning plop.

"That's the most disgusting sound I've ever heard," said the smaller.

"You'll not hear me disagree. But it's the stink that's got my insides whirling. This kerchief doesn't help at all."

With the odor of burnt meat assaulting their nostrils, after a few half-hearted shovelfuls the men decided their work was done. They tossed their tools into the cart and set off to collect their fee.

A few minutes after the creak of cartwheels had faded, two figures emerged from the shadows: Reverend Trask and his daughter Constance. But the reverend did not come to speak any last words over the grave, at least none from the Holy Book.

"And so it ends," said the reverend.

Constance smiled. "I quite enjoyed our little experiment, Father. Sending me to comfort the old woman was a brilliant idea. She was quite disappointed when I ran off without giving her the bread."

"A wonderfully sadistic touch, I must say. And the look on her face when she discovered you were the third accuser was priceless."

"Thank you." Constance giggled. "Look, Father. There's something sticking out of the dirt." She tapped what appeared to be a burnt piece of wood with the toe of her shoe.

"I believe that is a finger." Trask sniffed and pressed a lace fringed handkerchief to his nose. "No wonder those two clods haven't been able to find honest employment. The quality of their workmanship is abysmal."

"A finger? Really?" Constance bent, draped her own kerchief over the bone, and pulled. It came away with a snap. "I'll save it for later. Several spells require a finger bone, you know, especially one from an old hag."

"Seriously, Constance. Have you forgotten to whom you speak? I was casting spells in these woods long before the first Englishman ever showed his face. The Algonquians too, for that matter.

When the girl's smile turned to a pout, he lifted her chin with his finger.

"There, there. I am quite proud of how well you've played your part these last few days. So much better than Abigail could ever be. You handled yourself perfectly in court, although I must admit, I'm a bit surprised at how easily it all came to pass. Old Alice was much too kind for her own good. She should have turned you and your sister in the moment she caught you stealing those apples. If she'd been the one to point the first finger it would have been much more difficult to accuse her of witchcraft, and the others would not have fallen in line behind us."

Constance dropped the bone into her apron pocket. "It *was* amazing, wasn't it? I should never have doubted you. Sacrificing Abigail, was the perfect way to get the ball rolling."

"Indeed," said the reverend. "A small price to pay, considering. Did you not love it when she invoked my name as the flames surrounded her?"

Constance nodded, her blue eyes sparkling. "You're such a showman. All that thunder and lightning. For a moment I thought you'd actually decided to help her."

"Give her hope, yes, but save her?" He shook his head and chuckled.

"I almost burst out laughing when the mayor's wife knocked

him off that platform. Did you hear? He broke his arm!"

"That was nothing. Did you see the Alstead woman's face when that bolt of lightning struck that oak tree?"

"I'll never forget it. She actually thought she'd invoked the Devil!"

Trask grinned and threw one arm across her shoulder. "And now Alice is in her grave."

They turned back toward the village, a walk of no more than ten minutes. It had been an enjoyable experiment and surprisingly successful. With only the slightest encouragement, purportedly God-fearing people had raced to bear false witness upon an innocent old woman. So, why stop there? The colonies were filled with rivalries, enemies and jealous husbands.

Constance gave him a sidelong glance. "Why are you smiling, Father?"

"Because the world is filled with infinite promise. And I hear Salem is in need of a new minister."

Hopscotch

Cooper O'Connor

verybody knows that there's nothing as truly awful, as thoroughly evil, as a 13-year-old girl. This isn't to say that *all* 13-year-old girls are evil, but pure evil will most often manifest itself in the form of one, and Kelsey Perkins was no exception.

She was thirteen, as thirteen as thirteen could be, with an identity gleaned from every reality show star plastered across her TV screen, her words formed from the mouths of favorite movie quotes and song lyrics, her hair fashioned after the latest, hottest trends, her ideas shaped from the teachings of the wise sages of her life: the high school friends of her older sister, the friends who'd achieved a level of cool she both dreamed of but couldn't imagine, much like a Buddhist monk searching for Nirvana. . .not that Kelsey knew what Nirvana was, and if you *did* ask her, she'd probably say, "Wasn't that like a band or something with that guy. . .?"

You might say that Kelsey never stood a chance, that Kelsey was as Kelsey could only have been, a result a cold world and a cold time, where morals were. . .what were morals?. . .and instant gratification was *now*. Yes. Maybe Kelsey never stood a chance. She never had a chance to grow up, to find out the true meaning of life, that life was more than looking pretty, dressing like the person down the hall, that friendship was more than the letters "BFF" and your mood was something more than what your FacePage account described you as.

Maybe she didn't. But we'll never know.

Because the 13-year-old girl never got a chance to peek over the fence of adolescence into adulthood. Because the evil 13-year-old girl bit.

And a bigger evil bit back.

One day after school, walking home with her friends Serena and Elisha, Kelsey squealed when she read a text message from Kaitlynn that read:

OMG! NAISHA SAID BRANDON LIKES U! LOL!

Kelsey *knew* it but couldn't help the blush that crept into her cheeks. At her squeal, Serena and Elisha looked up from their own text messages and wondered what's up.

"I'll forward you the message Kaitylnn just sent me. You'll never guess!" Her freshly painted thumbnails flew over the keypad and sent the message to her friends. Immediately next to her, she heard two different phone rings chime as Serena and Elisha each received the text.

Soon the world was full of girlish laughter.

"Ew," said Elisha. "Brandon's *ugly*."

"No way," said Serena. "He's dum cute."

But Kelsey wasn't even listening. She was too busy W-ing/B to Kaitlynn.

WHERE DID U HEAR IT?
HOW DO U NO?
R U MESSIN W ME???? LOL

And while she W/B'ed to Kaitlynn, Elisha and Serena started sending their own texts into the world, speaking the language without voice, asking the questions without weight, holding conversations with their fingertips, trying to discover the truth behind this because *this* was Cra-zeeee!

Because the girls were so focused on Brandon's maybe-liking Kelsey-maybe *not*, none of the three noticed Charlotte Charmaigne hopscotching down the sidewalk toward them.

And Charlotte, 11 years old, in her own world of pink grids and cracked sidewalk, didn't notice the three girls.

She was in the middle of her third, right-footed hop when she crashed into Kelsey. Kelsey wailed—out of surprise and frustration this time—as her cellphone flew from her hands. She reached after it, but tripped over Charlotte, and as she fell in slow-motion, she watched her phone tumble and turn in the air as it hurtled closer and closer to the pink-squared grid below. And just as Kelsey's chin hit the pavement, she watched her phone shatter in, like, a million pieces.

Kelsey shrieked, this time in pain as her teeth sunk into first her tongue, then her bottom lip as her chin bounced against the pavement, and howled as the pain rushed in while the pavement scraped away the skin on her chin. She was dimly aware of the muffled cries behind her, the snickers from her friends and the blood filling her mouth, but her attention was focused on the black plastic shards that now littered the pavement in front of her.

And with that, time must have shattered—shattered into as many pieces as Kelsey's cellphone—because as Kelsey's eyes soaked up the sight in front of her, all of those black, plastic pieces, neither she, nor Charlotte, Elisha or Serena moved, not an inch, not a budge, not at all. Time, it froze, but thawed, then trickled as did the words that dropped from Kelsey's mouth, words like bombs from a plane, exploding all over the pink squared ground below her, the pink squares housing the tiny black shards of plastic.

"You. Broke. My. Phone."

Behind, a snicker, a giggle and an OMG.

In front of her, with a look of wild-eyed confusion, for she didn't know what had just happened or what was currently happening, Charlotte sat, mouth agape, she, too, staring at those tiny black pieces.

"I, I, I," she stammered.

"What, are you dumb or something? Say something! You broke my phone!" Kelsey didn't just stand up; she nearly flew up. And she was mad, blood-boiling mad, the type of mad where she felt flames singeing the back of her eyeballs.

"I, I, I," Charlotte continued.

Behind them, Elisha turned to Serena. "Hey, isn't that that homeschooled girl? The girl that lives in the woods?"

"I don't care WHO it is," screamed Kelsey and began jumping up and down. It was typical to watch a 13-year-old girl jump up and down upon a hopscotch grid, but not like this. In the flames of her mind, she caught images of her last text messages.

O No!

Did Kaitlynn write back??

Was there anymore news about Brandon?

What if Kaitlynn texted her that Brandon wanted to meet up later? Without a phone, Kelsey wouldn't know! And if she didn't know, then she wouldn't meet up with him! And if she didn't meet up with her, then, why, her life would be, like, over!

At that thought, her temper tantrum building to its breaking point, Kelsey sucked in all the air she could and let loose a tea-kettle scream so high and loud it very nearly shattered the windows of the building all around them. Her phone! All of her pictures! All of her videos! All of her mp3s! All of her old texts! Her computer wasn't working at home, either so without a phone, how was she supposed to check her FacePage?

And the girl, the little girl, stammering away, looking all sad. Why should *she* be sad? It wasn't *her* phone that just broke! And whose fault was it, anyway?

Without thinking, Kelsey reached down and grabbed the doll that hung loosely from the girl's fingertips.

The girl didn't speak but simply reached out plaintively. A part of Kelsey—some small, distant part of her like a cold star flickering in an infinite sky—felt a twinkle of sympathy, but the enormity of her rage quickly engulfed it and burned it to ashes.

"You broke something of mine, you little freak."

The girl whimpered and reached for her doll.

Kelsey looked down at the gutter and saw the storm grate.

"You want this?" she asked and waved the doll in front of the girl's face.

"Please. Yes. Please."

"Well, go get it," Kelsey said and shoved the doll into the drain. There was a moment of silence and splash far below.

Kelsey expected, no Kelsey *wanted* the girl to scream, to squeal, to cry and stomp much like she had moments before. Instead, the girl's face drained of all color, and she skittered to the edge of the sidewalk and stared into the darkness through the grate.

No, the girl didn't scream. Kelsey started laughing, and when Kelsey started laughing, Elisha and Serena started laughing too, because it was their job to have her back, to pick on others when the situation called for it.

Kelsey wanted tears. She wanted Charlotte to feel what she felt. She wanted her to feel *bad*, all brown, muddy and oily inside. But the girl did not cry. She looked up from the grate and her eyes locked onto Kelsey's own and for a moment, the laughter from Kelsey's mouth wavered, trembled and threatened to quit because there was something in the girl's eyes that she didn't recognize.

This girl wasn't afraid of her.

This girl didn't care if Serena and Elisha were laughing at her, didn't care that it was three on one, and didn't care that her doll was just thrown into the sewer. This girl looked like she had her own flames licking the back of her own eyeballs.

Kelsey almost stopped laughing and that distant star within her, that slim, small part screamed out to apologize, to say you're sorry, to beg forgiveness because it was an accident and accidents happen, and you'll get her a new doll, right? But Kelsey wasn't about to apologize because her phone was broken so why should SHE apologize? Had she apologized, would things have turned out differently?

Would Kelsey have gone home, and Charlotte home as well, without any bad blood between them? Would Kelsey have woken up one morning with that hopscotch grid on her driveway?

"Freak," Kelsey mumbled. She beckoned to Serena and Elisha and they moved on, Serena and Elisha throwing out parting shots to her as they left. Farther up the street, Serena turned to Elisha and muttered, "Seriously? I heard that girl's a witch."

"Get out of here."

"No, seriously. Back in kindergarten. She was in Ms. Ellerbee's class. With Sabrina? Sabrina said all this seriously freaky stuff happened when that girl was around. Books flying off shelves and stuff. Sabrina said her parents were called to school all the time to take her home. Guess her parents are seriously weird, live up in the hills. Anyway, they decided to homeschool her, to keep her away from trouble."

"They didn't keep her far enough away," Kelsey muttered.

"Seriously, though. She's a witch. You should watch out, Kelsey."

"Seriously, Serena? You should seriously be quiet. Seriously."

Serena shut up.

As they moved down the street, Kelsey looked behind only once, but once was enough. She thought maybe she's see the girl looking back into the storm drain, maybe crying. But she wasn't. The girl was standing, arms by her side, hands clenched in fists.

That night, Kelsey ate two bowls of ice cream to soothe her swollen tongue. She watched the latest episode of *Jersey Street* to try to block the day's events of her mind, but that girl and her doll, and the tiny black plastic pieces surrounded by walls of pink chalk kept creeping up and reminding her of all she had lost. Her mom had tried to talk to her but Kelsey could only scream and pound on her bed in frustration. Her mom walked away and hadn't tried since. Her dad knew better than to even try. If she walked into one room with the look with which she currently wore, out he went into the next room. If, by chance, they were forced to share the same space, he would mumble an uncomfortable hello and give her the head nod, but no more than that. It was like he was a prisoner, afraid of interacting too closely with the other inmates for fear of what might happen if provoked.

Eventually, she shut off *Jersey Street*. She couldn't pay attention to Nooky and Louie P and the others. She knew that *The Real Life* was on afterward but she wasn't in the mood. She just wanted today to be over. So she climbed under the covers and reached for her phone.

And remembered her phone wasn't there. She always plugged her phone in before she went to bed and would spend the next 40 minutes in a late-night texting barrage until she fell asleep.

But no phone.

She wondered. Was everyone else still texting? What were they saying? Were they talking about her? Were they going to look strangely at her now? Treat her differently? Kelsey felt a column of flame shoot up inside her.

Below, in the kitchen, her mother and father heard a muffled screech and a pound as Kelsey punched the wall. The father shuddered, looked to his wife and asked, "Did you keep the receipt?"

"For the phone?"

"For Kelsey."

The next day, Kelsey woke up with the strange sound of her mother's voice. What? Oh that's right. Her mom had to wake her up because *she didn't have a phone!* Kelsey's face puckered as if she was sucking on a lemon and her eyes slid to the spot on her nightstand where the phone would normally be. A sleepy part of her half-expected to see it there, half-hoped the Cell Phone Fairy would have delivered her a newer, shinier phone in the dead of night. But no: only an empty space where her phone used to be.

Kelsey got ready for school, screeched at her mother when her mother tried to rush her. Jeeze, didn't she know that it took time to look this good? Besides, she had math class with Brandon first thing this morning and she wasn't going to class looking like a scrub. She didn't care if she was late. She was going to be late! She had to text Serena and Elisha! She reached for her phone. . .

Oh, that's right.

Would they wait for her? Or would they keep moving? Whatever.

Eventually, Kelsey stormed out of her house, mad. Mad at the thought of her friends leaving without her, mad at her mom for waking her up, mad at her dad who hid from her this morning, mad at math for being a stupid class, mad at Mr. Schloozel for teaching it, and mad at that girl, that *stupid, stupid* girl with the doll who made her break her phone.

She wasn't alone, thankfully. Serena and Elisha stood in the driveway. Well, they stuck around, at least. You'd think it would abate some of her anger, but no. She was still a little mad at them at the thought of them leaving her behind. They'd have to make it up to her later.

Their backs were to her. They were huddled close together, looking at something on the ground. Serena must have heard her coming because she nudged Elisha and they both turned.

"What's up?" Kelsey said.

Something was wrong, that much was certain. Serena and Elisha shared a look. What? What was that look? Did Brandon text one of them or something? They weren't even going out yet and he was already cheating on her! The angry pillars of flame scorched her guts again.

"What? What is it? Spit it out."

They looked at each other again and they moved away from each other. As they stepped away, the space between revealed the image at which they had been staring before she arrived, the image scrawled upon her parents' driveway.

There, on the pavement, in thick, pink chalk lines was drawn a fresh hopscotch grid.

"What is this? Did you do this?"

"N-no," said Elisha. Serena shook her head. Why did they both look so scared? Elisha was shuffling from one foot to the next and shaking. When Kelsey looked closer, she saw pink dust along the edges of Elisha's sneakers. She looked at Serena. Same thing. She didn't know what it meant, not at first, anyway.

Why was this here? The girl—that was the only explanation. The freak girl with the doll. She must have come here in the middle of the night and drawn it. But why? What was the point? Was it some weird, freak kind of threat?

"I woke up," said Serena. "When I left, I saw the same thing."

"Me too."

"Saw what?"

"*This!*"

"What? Hopscotch?"

Neither answered. Not with words anyway. But why were they so scared?

"Not just hopscotch." Serena moved out of the way and pointed to the words scrawled in front of the first grid.

It read:

Hop along the numbers
To move yourself ahead
If you walk around them
Surely, you'll be dead.

"I don't like this, Kelsey. Seriously."

"What does this mean?"

"I don't know, but it was in my driveway, too."

"Me, too."

"What, is it some kind of threat? Saying I have to hopscotch my way out of the driveway? Or what? What will happen? I'll *die*? That's the stupidest thing I've ever heard."

Kelsey started moving, away from the number one and she certainly wasn't hopping. Serena grabbed her arm. "Kelsey," she hissed. "Don't."

"Don't *what*? Don't *walk*?" And then she remembered seeing the pink dust on their shoes and she started laughing. "Are you serious? Don't tell me the two of you hopscotched your way to school today."

Both girls looked at each other, then at the ground, ashamed at the fear they felt.

Kelsey continued laughing. "What do you think will happen?"

"You'll die, Kelsey," said Serena. "She's a witch, remember? Sabrina said."

"Sabrina? Remember when I convinced Sabrina that clouds were bird farts? Or when she believed me when I said that if she ripped the tag off of a mattress, she would be arrested? Serena, Sabrina isn't all there in the head."

"It doesn't matter! I've heard it from other people. And it says right there. It says you have to hop on those numbers or you'll die, Kelsey!"

"It's too early for this. This is stupid. I'm going to school, and I'm talking to Brandon. When he asks me out, I'm going to say 'yes.' It's a big day for me. Why are you trying to ruin it?"

"We're trying to save you," said Elisha.

"This is stupid. When I get out of school, I hope I find that freak. Who goes around in the middle of the night, anyway? I'm glad I threw her doll down the drain."

With that, Kelsey made the decision to walk to school. She did not hop and she did not follow the directions. She simply picked up one foot, followed it with the next, and stepped upon the pink grid.

Serena screamed and was soon joined by Elisha. Their screams ripped apart the early morning silence. Within seconds, Kelsey's parents rushed out of the house, faces white, their bodies tense with anticipation. They found Serena and Elisha alone in the driveway—panicked, crying, pointing.

The parents asked what was wrong, why were they crying? Why were they screaming?

At first, they didn't notice the hopscotch grid.

They asked the girls were their daughter was. Where was Kelsey?

They didn't notice the hopscotch grid at all.

Then Kelsey's father saw the girls pointing and what they were pointing to. He turned, and soon after, so did his wife and they stared at the pink hopscotch grid that had been scrawled onto their driveway.

They stared at the center square.

There was a picture made of chalk that had not been there moments, even seconds, before.

In the years that followed, long after Kelsey's parents had

moved out and the house was viewed as part of a haunted ghost tour, people would remark at the details of that drawing, how *lifelike* it looked. The same people would go home that night and be unable to sleep without dreaming of that drawing, of that *face*. In the years that followed, no rains could ever wash away the pink chalk lines. No amount of soap, scrubbing and heavy wash could remove it from the pavement. The hopscotch chalk was bonded there—a permanent prison that trapped a girl—forever thirteen.

That Familiar Feeling

Stephen Blake

arah rushed out of bed and pulled back the curtains. The spring sunshine poured in and warmed her skin. She felt sick—sick with excitement and sick with nervousness. Today was an important day. This was the day she grew up. This was the day she moved on from potions and books. Today, she added the final piece of the jigsaw all witches needed to perform magic. That connection to nature—the guide they all required—a familiar.

She dressed for a day, possibly longer, to be spent scrabbling through the woods. She wore her travelling cloak over her most coarse dress and a knapsack for a little bit of food. She tied her long, red hair back into a pony tail and then paused before deciding if there was anything else that could be done in preparation. She looked around her room one last time. As always, it was full of stuff. Sarah was a hoarder, much to her aunt's dismay.

Her aunt had prepared a simple breakfast; a bowl of hot porridge to help Sarah get through the day.

"Do you think I can find a familiar within the day?" Sarah asked.

Aunt Clare replied, "Don't fret about it. It will take as long as it takes. You've got to remember that whilst you are seeking a familiar, the familiar has to be drawn to you, too. You cannot force it. When I was your age, fourteen, it took me three days to find Thomas."

Thomas the toad croaked in the corner as if joining in on the memory. Sarah looked over to him. He was a fat, oddly-shaped toad. Magically, he had been able to live way beyond a normal toad's lifespan. His body suggested he might well be dead most of the time, given his horrible colour and smell. Just as you thought he had croaked it, a fly would quickly meet its demise thanks to Thomas' lightning-fast reactions.

Sarah closed her eyes briefly and thought, *not a toad, not a toad*, over and over.

They lived a fair distance from the nearest settlement and so it was easy for Sarah to enter the woods without having to explain herself. There was still much fear and misunderstanding about.

Her aunt hugged Sarah tightly and mumbled about how her mother would be proud. Any mention of her mother always had the same effect. It made her think of fire. It made her angry. She decided not to dwell on that. It would not help her today.

"I'll be careful," she assured Aunt Clare one more time.

"I know you will," said Clare. "Just remember, you are a bright, intelligent girl, but if you let that anger and resentment dwell in you, it will attract a different kind of familiar. Maybe even dark entities."

Sarah gave her best reassuring smile.

"I'll be back soon," she said, and headed off.

Sarah knew what it all meant. This was when a witch came of age but it was also when you followed a path to black or white magic. The younger girls sometimes described it as the difference between becoming a pretty witch or an old hag. Some thought of it as a choice of real power or just a little magic. Sarah felt sure those that put it in those terms were already headed on the wrong path.

The journey to the woods was fairly short. She'd been going there for as long as she could remember, collecting herbs and fungi for potions. The place never scared her; it felt natural to Sarah. That was how it should be, she knew.

The sun was still quite low in the sky, so, as Sarah entered the wood, it quickly became dim. There was a morning chill, a freshness that made her senses tingle. The odour of the pine trees held happy memories for Sarah. She remembered walks with her mother, seeking herbs and picking flowers.

A red squirrel scampered past her feet, busily going about its business. Sarah and the little creature barely noticed one another, so focused each was on the task at hand.

Twigs snapped beneath her feet as she steadily moved into the woods. The rays of light piercing the foliage seemed to twinkle as Sarah pushed her way through. So far, she'd felt no great draw, no compulsion to move in any particular direction.

A croak to her right made her stop in her tracks.

Again, she thought to herself, *not a toad, please, not a toad.*

The toad sat atop a tree stump. They each eyed one another for what seemed an age before the toad shuffled its fat body and turned its back to Sarah. Heat flushed Sarah's face as she considered the snub, then quickly she reminded herself that this was exactly what she had wanted. She silently chided herself for letting her temper take hold.

Moving on, she listened to the birds singing and closed her eyes, hoping to reach out to the creatures of the wood. She fell flat on her face as she tripped over a tree root. Sarah brushed herself down and looked around to see if anyone had seen her make a fool of herself. From that moment on, she decided she'd try to connect with her familiar with her eyes open.

To her left, the snap of a fallen branch made her jump. A tall, hooded man strode toward her.

"Greetings, young maiden," he chimed. He pushed back his hood to reveal he was one of the village elders. "What brings you out this fine morning?"

"Just gathering mushrooms and the like," answered Sarah. "I must get on," she added.

He held up his hand to prevent her passing. "Don't I know you?"

"I, I don't think so," stammered Sarah, determined not to make eye contact.

"It'll come to me I'm sure," he continued. "Not to worry, good day to you."

With that, he lowered his arm and Sarah shuffled past. The footpath wound to the right, away from him. Instinctively, Sarah felt the need to leave the path. When she was sure he could not see her, she waded into the undergrowth and pushed in to the denser part of the woods.

He might not have recognised her but she knew who he was. He was one of the men who had sat in judgment of her mother. He was one of the ones who had declared her innocence when the fire had died down. Sarah had not forgotten and would never forget his face.

Sarah's heart raced. It was times like this she wish she'd been born a boy, wished she would grow into a strong man with a thunderous right hook. She calmed herself with the imagined satisfaction that hurting him and the others might give her.

Feeling safer, she came across a small clearing where the sun poured down and the moss upon the ground invited you to sit and rest. From her knapsack she pulled out a small piece of bread. She nibbled at its edges, as was her way, turning it over in her hands.

Looking around, Sarah felt uncomfortable, felt as if she was being watched. She searched the foliage for signs of her observer. She carefully put the rest of her bread back into her bag and slowly rose to her feet. There, on a nearby branch, sat a black cat.

Sarah let out a loud sigh.

"Now this is the kind of familiar that I was thinking of. This is more like it," she said.

The cat began to lick its paws and wash its ears, never once taking its eyes off of Sarah.

"So what happens now?" Sarah called to the cat.

The cat stopped washing and turned its back on Sarah.

"I'll take it that you don't want to be friends, let alone anything else?"

The cat turned back to face her. Sarah reached forward to

smooth the cat. A quick swipe of its claws and Sarah quickly withdrew her bleeding hand.

"Ouch, was that really necessary?"

The cat hissed and disappeared into the undergrowth.

Sarah reached for a stick and went to throw it after the cat. She quickly stopped, thinking better of it.

She sucked the blood dripping from her hand. The cut was minor and the bleeding quickly stopped.

The stick was thick and sturdy. She used it now to push through the tall ferns and make her way on with her journey. The going was slow and hard work. Sarah enjoyed it. It helped to focus her mind, stopped her dwelling on the cat and, in particular, the man that she had encountered.

It had seemed like an age of trampling and Sarah had begun to tire. Unsure of how many hours had passed, Sarah only now noticed that the sky had darkened. It was a bright moon and the stars sparkled with great majesty, but the trees now held back the light and whilst she could still see, Sarah realised it would not be long before the blanket of darkness would descend upon her and stop her in her tracks.

She thought now about where she should sleep for the night. Disappointment washed over her that she'd not found a familiar. She felt resentment and anger well within her. Today of all days was meant to be so special and she'd not found that creature who would make her whole. Instead, she'd bumped into that man and, of course, the grumpy cat.

She dwelled on these thoughts and her mind quickly raced to her mother. As always, she struggled to hold the happy memories, the image of her mother screaming within the flames always came to the fore. Sarah's face contorted into a snarl. How badly she wanted to see that man now. Now that she had a sturdy stick in hand….

Her dark thoughts were interrupted by a shuddering chill that passed through her body. It had gotten darker still and she peered through the darkness trying to seek out what had affected her so. Scanning left to right, she spotted a pair of blinking eyes. It was the cat.

"Come back for a rematch?" growled Sarah.

The cat met her growl with one of its own. Sarah felt as if she was knocked back as numerous pairs of eyes suddenly blinked open before her. The low growls emanating from the creatures seemed to vibrate against Sarah's chest.

"So, Little Cat, you brought friends." Sarah said as calmly as she could. "Perhaps we could all be friends?" She tried not to sound anxious.

The cats moved forward to her slowly. It was then that she realised they were not cats. Their black bodies seemed to be elongated as they stretched forward. They appeared to float like clouds, becoming menacing wisps of smoke. It was then that she realised these were the dark entities her aunt had warned her about.

Fear froze her in place. The entities swirled around her with menace. They did not hurt her, though. Instead, they began to wrap themselves around her. They seemed drawn to her like a moth is drawn to a flame.

Sarah was unsure what to do. Her instinct told her to run but part of her wanted to return the embrace. Her pensive thoughts were interrupted by a jolt to the head. She looked to her feet and saw a pine cone. Then another hit her. And another.

"What is going on?" she managed to say. Looking up, she was just in time to see another cone whistle past her head. The next one hit her squarely between the eyes. It was enough to make her realise she had to get away from the entities.

She quickly ran to the nearest tree. She hitched up her skirt and climbed. She ascended quickly. She'd always had great dexterity, and now it seemed to come with ease as she clambered as high as she could.

It's you. You're drawing them to you.

Sarah heard the words but they were spoken in her head. Still up the tree holding onto her stick she called out, "Who's there? Who said that?"

A chirp and movement ahead of her on the thin part of the branch caught her attention. It was a squirrel. No, she realised, it was the same squirrel as she'd seen earlier.

Your anger; the darkness in your heart is drawing them to you.

Realising she was talking to the small, red squirrel, Sarah cocked her head and spoke aloud. "I'm not angry. Well, I'm a bit angry. You would be, too. Anyone in my shoes would be."

Being angry is fine, but don't let it be all of you. Don't let it consume you, or they'll consume you.

"Then what will happen?"

I don't know. I suppose you'll be a different kind of witch; a cruel kind—rotten inside, like a bad pine cone.

"What can I do? How do I stop this?"

The dark wraiths continued to float around the bottom of the tree. They had not risen, although Sarah had no doubt that they could if they wanted.

You dwell on the bad too much. The squirrel bobbed up and down before her, appearing very animated. *I know that you have happy memories. There are many good people and good things in your life. Concentrate on them.*

Sarah did as she was told and remembered the happy days with her mother. She thought gratefully how lucky she was to have ended up with her Aunt Clare.

The dark entities beneath her seemed to fade into the darkness. Still there, but more a part of the night, more a part of the atmosphere than the wraith form they had held.

"Is it really that easy?" asked Sarah aloud.

They are still there, but that is how it should be. Dark and light make up all things. You don't have to stop being angry; you just need to let in all those other feelings, too.

"I think I get it," Sarah mused. "Or at least some of what you say."

Their conversation was interrupted by a flash of lightning arcing across the sky. Fork after fork pierced the darkness until one hit the tree next to them. The dry bark burst into flames. A large branch fell, burning. It landed beneath Sarah's tree and its flames threatened to engulf her.

This way.

The squirrel scampered up through the branches and hopped into another nearby tree. Sarah attempted to follow but loud cracks confirmed that she was too heavy to take the same route as her new friend.

The squirrel scampered back and seemed to look her up and down, seemingly acknowledging that the escape route would not work. It ran up to the stout pole she had in her hands and nibbled at it slightly. Seemingly happy, it ran off again.

Sarah's mind was wrapped in terror. The fire beneath her brought forward her very worst fears. In her mind, she saw her mother thrashing against the bonds, pleading as the flames licked at her body. Sarah clasped a hand to her mouth to stop herself from screaming out.

Within the flames, the dark entities appeared again. Weaving through the fire, merging with the smoke, Sarah felt as if they were beckoning to her to join them in a dance.

Sarah's thoughts were brought back to the present as twig after twig was rained down on her. She caught them and gathered them together. The orange glow from beneath lit the silhouette of the squirrel above her.

"What are you doing? How does this help?"

Besom.

Sarah realised immediately what was meant. Reaching into her knapsack, she pulled out some string and quickly tied the twigs to the end of her thicker stick. In very little time, they had a broom.

"So does this mean you're my familiar?" Sarah coughed, as smoke pirouetted up to her.

Maybe you're mine.

Sarah put her leg over the broom and leapt out into the air. The descent was immediate and she landed heavily on the ground beneath. Luckily she rolled with the fall and was quickly on her feet.

Rubbing her eyes clear of the smoke she looked up to the squirrel. "What happened? Why didn't we fly?"

Never said fly. Besom. Use.

Sarah immediately realised what the broom was for and began beating at the flames. Again and again she brought the brush down on to the fire, trying to smother it away. Just as she thought she had some control on it, another flame would spring up. Unperturbed, she continued to fight. She barely noticed the entities slither away and it was only when the rain became heavy that she realised help had arrived in the form of a downpour.

The fire died away and Sarah stood in the newly formed clearing looking at the damage.

"Fire always destroys," she mumbled as she let the rain wash her face.

Not true. Fire can be good. It cleanses too.

Sarah felt a connection to her squirrel friend and saw in her minds' eye what she—for she was a girl squirrel—had meant. She understood something more about nature than she had before.

The walk home had been a happy and enlightening one. Sarah and Red, that was now the squirrels' name, had talked constantly all the way. Sarah was learning more about nature and the natural world than she had dreamed. Seeing it all from a different perspective had opened her eyes to a whole new world. Already Sarah felt changed, and if she were honest with herself, she'd say she felt whole.

They rested on the tree stump Sarah had sat on the day before. She placed her besom under her backside so that the brush tail sat sticking out, giving Red a perch to sit on. To anyone passing by they would have looked odd, as they both nibbled in an identical manner at the bread.

Sarah swung her feet beneath her, quietly content. She heard a croak and a voice she recognised. It was Aunt Clare.

"Good morning, Sarah. Oh, I am so pleased you found a familiar; and so powerful, too."

"How do you mean?" asked Sarah. She had not looked up from her bread.

"Down here, my love," Clare called.

Sarah looked up and then looked down, as she realised that her besom had lifted her and Red into the air. The broom lurched and Sarah dropped to the ground.

She quickly stood up in the soft ferns she had landed in and adjusted her cloak. Red sat on her shoulder.

Clare dashed to her. "Are you well? How do you feel?"

Sarah blushed, "Don't worry, we're fine. This is a familiar feeling."

How to be Beautiful: A Witch's Guide

MEGAN NEUMANN

dith sat on the four-poster bed watching her grandmother brush powder across Ruby's cheeks. Edith's jaw was clenched and her arms were crossed. She made no sound during this ceremony. At the dressing table, Ruby sat with a smile on her round face. When their grandmother turned to dip the brush again, Ruby's eyes flitted in Edith's direction, and Ruby's smile grew slyer, crueler.

"This is not what will make you beautiful," Grandmother said, her voice soft and soothing, with an English accent. She had lived in the states for 30 years, but the accent never faded. To Edith's American ears, Grandmother's voice sounded refined, proper, but Edith knew it was a lie. The old woman's true voice carried an accent, but it was not so proper and not so refined.

"It is the charms you put on the powder," Grandmother said, holding Ruby's chin between her fingertips. "The charms will create the glamour, My Dear. Though some women may disagree, I always say there is no magic in makeup alone." Then she laughed a dainty laugh, which Edith knew was false as well.

Edith tried to look neutral, but she scowled anyhow, her lips pulled down at the corners. She was fourteen—two years older than Ruby—yet Ruby was the one being trained by Grandmother. Ruby would carry the magic on to the next generation. Ruby would be beautiful to the world while Edith remained plain and hidden in the shadows.

Grandmother did not seem to notice Edith's presence in the dressing room. She was far too busy teaching Ruby.

Through the windows, the sunlight illuminated flurries of dust floating through the air. Edith watched the dust and imagined herself as nothing more than a bit of lint set free into the world to float aimlessly. Where would she land? What would become of her when she did? She imagined she would be swept under a rug somewhere. Life as lint would not be so different from her real life.

"There are only a few charms to learn," Grandmother said, "but simply saying the words, repeating the words, is not enough. You must have something else behind them." Grandmother paused, set the brush on the dressing table, and touched Ruby's chest. "You are blessed to have this gift. Not all are given the heart to create magic."

Ruby's eyes darted in Edith's direction.

Edith tightened her hands into fists.

I have heart, she thought.

Ruby was the cruel one, the one who found slugs in the garden, smashed them beneath her shoes, and laughed.

Once, when they were little, Edith found a frog near their pond. She wanted to keep it in her room as a pet. When Ruby saw it, she snatched the slimy creature and chucked it hard into the water. Edith cried for hours. Their mother told her the frog probably survived and swam to its home. Edith didn't believe that. She didn't believe most of the things her mother said.

Now Edith didn't play with frogs. It wasn't proper. Not that their household *was* proper. Since their father died in the Great War, they didn't dress for dinner. They had let most of the servants go except for a few trusted ones. And Ruby ran wild. Mother and Grandmother laughed every time Ruby came stomping into the house with mud on her shoes and her hair tangled.

"She has spunk," Grandmother would say.

"She has your spirit," Mother would say.

Two weeks earlier, Ruby came into the house with bright red hair instead of her usual dirty blonde. Mother and Grandmother recognized it immediately—an accidental glamour. They hid her away from the servants and created the necessary charms to undo Ruby's carelessness.

"You shouldn't have caused such an incident," Edith told Ruby afterwards as they went down to dinner.

"Like you've never accidentally created a charm," Ruby said, laughing.

"Of course not. It wouldn't be proper." This wasn't completely true. Edith had never created a charm because they had never worked for her. She had tried. Oh, how she had tried. But she had no magic. She would never be beautiful like her mother and her grandmother. But Ruby would be.

Ruby's training began after the hair incident. With Ruby's training started, Edith believed her own time had passed, and she would live out her life as a normal person. At night she whispered to herself, *I won't be jealous. I won't hate Ruby.*

Of course, she was jealous and a part of her—a dark, hidden part of her—hated Ruby.

When Edith was seven and Ruby five, their mother brought them to the library, sitting across from them in front of the fireplace. Grandmother was there, too, leaning against her cane and eyeing the two girls silently.

"It is time I told you girls of our family," Mother said. "You are both old enough to know the truth now. You know your Grandmother and I came to America before you were born. But what you don't know is we came here to start a new life. We needed to live somewhere where no one would know us."

"Why?" Edith asked, thinking perhaps her mother was a criminal. "Were the police after you?" She had read about wrongfully accused people who had to run from the authorities. The idea excited her and seemed romantic. She hoped this was the case for her mother. Her life had been so dull until then. Comfortable, but so very dull.

Their mother paused and looked at her own mother, who only nodded.

"Almost," she said hesitantly. "We were being chased, but not by police. By your grandfather. He had discovered the truth about your grandmother. He was displeased to learn of what he had married."

"And what his child was," Grandmother said, breaking her silence.

"I don't understand," Edith said. She glanced at Ruby, but Ruby did not seem confused. She smirked and her eyes narrowed as if contriving some scheme.

"You see," their mother said, "we are from a line of…" She trailed off, straightening her skirt with her gloved hands.

"Spit it out, Dear," Grandmother said.

"Witches," Mother said finally. "We are witches." She turned away and her neck and ears flushed bright red.

"I knew it!" Ruby shouted.

"I still don't understand," Edith said. "You can't be a witch. You are beautiful and young. Witches are old and ugly. They eat children. And they're not real."

"Not entirely," their mother said. She turned back to the girls and sitting in her mother's place was a stranger. The woman was plain, older than her mother, with sallow skin and sad, muddy brown eyes, which were so different from her mother's sparkling green eyes.

Edith jumped up. "Who are you? Where is my mother?"

"Oh, Edith," the woman said. "I am your mother. You are seeing me for the first time."

It was her mother's voice, but something was different in it. Her mother's voice had always sounded like honey to Edith's ears, sweet and smooth. It had made Edith feel warm inside, had made her want to embrace and love her mother. The voice coming from this woman sounded tired. Tired and sad.

"You come from a line of witches, My Dear," Grandmother said, stepping from the shadows. It was then Edith saw the old crone her grandmother truly was. "We have survived in wealth and comfort for hundreds of years through charms that, well, make us charming." She let out a loud, throaty laugh—a witch's cackle.

Edith stepped back again, frightened of these two strangers.

"Do not be afraid, Edith," Mother said. "We are the same as before, only we look different. Someday you will be like us too. You will cast your light and create a halo of beauty around yourself. You will be adored in your lifetime and never have to worry about a thing."

"They *are* the same people," Ruby said. She ran to their mother and embraced her. "I could always see a little of the real you underneath."

"You could?" Edith asked. She stood apart from the others, wanting to run out of the room and hide.

"Oh Edith, stop this nonsense," their mother said. She whispered something under her breath, something Edith could not understand. Then her mother was back, beautiful and smiling with white teeth and soft, young skin.

"I'm still your mother. Now, don't you be afraid. We'll teach you both when you are old enough. And you'll grow used to the way we look underneath. You'll be able to see past our glamour when you have your powers. Really, I'm not *that* bad looking, am I?"

Edith said nothing, but thought, *Yes, you are horrible compared to the mother I knew.*

Even after Ruby's training began, Grandmother and Mother pretended as if Edith would eventually come into her powers, but Edith felt it would never happen. She knew they felt the same way. One night she heard the two speaking in hushed voices. They were worried for poor Edith, who would never be like them, who didn't understand their ways.

"She takes after her father," Grandmother said.

"That's impossible," Mother said. "No girl in our family has ever *not* been magic. She's just a late bloomer."

"I've never heard of such a late bloomer. Nearly fifteen! Nearly a woman!" Grandmother said. "In a few years she will need to set out on her own to find someone with a fortune. Your money will not last forever."

"We have Ruby."

"Yes, at least we have Ruby."

As she lay in bed that night, Edith thought of what her mother had said. Perhaps she was a late bloomer.

After Ruby found her magic, Edith imagined herself growing into that ugly stranger of a woman in front of the fireplace or that old crone her grandmother was. The thought terrified her. Since the truth had been revealed to her, she longed to grow from an awkward child to a beautiful woman like her mother appeared to be, not like what her mother really was.

When Edith looked in the mirror, she saw a plain girl with mousy brown hair. Her nose was too large for her face, and her brown eyes were too close together. Ruby looked the same, but soon she'd be like their mother—a goddess walking the earth.

Lying in her bed, Edith decided she would find some way to awaken the magic within her. It was in her blood after all.

I will not be ordinary. I will find my magic.

When she was younger, Edith read a book with stories of amazing feats. One story told of woman who saw her child in danger. The child was going to be crushed by a boulder or a piano or something equally heavy—Edith couldn't remember. The mother lifted the heavy object before it could crush her child to death. She lifted far more than any woman could ever lift. Much of stories were similar: people in terrible situations, exhibiting great strength.

"I will exhibit great strength," Edith said to herself as she sneaked into the maid's room while the maid was in town buying groceries. She found the heavy iron sitting by the maid's fireplace. It was difficult for her to lift, but she managed. She placed the iron in the fireplace, watching the iron begin to glow as flames engulfed it.

She wrapped a heavy cloth around her hands. *No use in burning my hands, too.* She needed her hands for magic, for casting spells on young men. This thought made her smile. She would make her mother proud. She lifted the iron with both hands. The handle was nearly too hot even with the cloth. She wanted to drop it, but she reminded herself this was more important than burnt palms. She raised the iron to the level of her cheek. Her face dripped with sweat as she struggled to hold the iron and felt the heat from the metal. Her breath came out in quick bursts. For a moment, she thought she wouldn't be able to do it, but she reminded herself that her magic would come quickly after this. It had to. Then she pressed the iron to her face.

It seared, and she dropped it, smelling her own cooked flesh and her burnt hair. The pain hit her, and the room began to spin. Before she blacked out, she thought with mild amusement, *smells like burnt pork.*

Edith awoke in her bed with a cloth wrapped around her head. Her mother, grandmother, and sister stood in a semicircle around her bed.

"My poor girl, what have you done to yourself?" her mother said before breaking into sobs.

Ruby smiled and said, "You've really done it now."

"Am I hideous?" Edith asked and realized it hurt to move her mouth. She must have burnt her lips as well as her cheek.

"Oh, you are and will be for the rest of your life," Grandmother said. "You've scarred yourself, you stupid girl. What were you thinking?"

"If I'm scarred," Edith said slowly, trying to speak out of one side of her mouth, "then I will use charms to make myself beautiful. My magic will come under the distress of being ugly." She tried to smile at her family, but her face hurt too much.

Her mother gasped and clasped a hand over her mouth.

Grandmother cackled and said, "You really are stupid. This is not how magic works! Now you will be ordinary *and* ugly for the rest of your life. Let's leave her to rest."

The bandages stayed on for weeks and had to be changed and cleaned often. Her mother did this while whispering soft words of regret. "We shouldn't have doted on Ruby like that." Or "I should have told you it didn't matter. This magic, it's small magic. Nothing worth hurting yourself over."

At night, while bandaged, Edith sat in her bed crying softly. Tears came out of only one of her eyes, and she wondered if she had damaged the other eye, would she be able to see out of it? This made her cry harder until she exhausted herself into sleep.

"Edith! Oh, Edith! You ugly girl!"

Edith awoke to Ruby standing on the bed, bouncing on her heels and grinning. "Mother says it's time for me to take off your bandages and give you a mirror."

"Really? Why isn't Mother going to do it?"

Ruby bounced and then fell onto her bottom, shaking the bed and Edith too. "Mother says I'm to do it. I have scissors." Seemingly out of nowhere, Ruby held a pair of scissors. Edith didn't know where they had come from, but she suspected there was some magic at work.

"I don't want you to do it," Edith said. "I don't trust you."

"Mother says I must. Come on. I'll be gentle. Just hold still."

Edith didn't trust Ruby with or without scissors, but she didn't have a way to fight. Ruby was already close, climbing over Edith with the scissors aimed for the bandages. Her tongue stuck out to the side of her mouth as she concentrated on snipping the bandages away. The blade was cold against Edith's skin, and she supposed it was good she felt the blade at all. Perhaps her burns weren't so bad.

"Now time to look at yourself!" Ruby said. In her other hand, she raised a mirror that appeared out of nowhere. Ruby held it shakily at first, and Edith could only see blurs of flesh color and hair.

"Hold it still. I can't see," Edith said.

"Okay," Ruby said and giggled. The mirror steadied, and Edith saw her scarred half face. It was worse than she could have imagined. She really hadn't known what to imagine. It looked as though half her face had melted. The skin over her eye sagged down, obscuring her vision; the hair from her eyebrow and part of her scalp was gone. The corner of her mouth was completely gone, replaced by shining, colorless skin.

"Oh Edith," Ruby said, "It's better than any glamour I could make. I can only make myself pretty. But you have made yourself a monster!" She threw her head back and cackled as their grandmother did so often.

Tears stung at Edith's one good eye. The other didn't seem capable of producing tears. It was her monster side and monsters did not cry.

Edith kept trying. She spent every day in front of the mirror staring at her hideous face and willing it to become beautiful. When that didn't work, she wanted to leave the house and go to the church and pray for magic, but her grandmother wouldn't allow it.

"You'll frighten the townspeople," Grandmother said.

"I can cover my face," Edith said.

"What will they think when the wealthiest family in town forces their own child to cover her face? It will be a source of gossip. You will not leave. You will not bring shame and suspicion to our house."

Behind Grandmother, Ruby stood laughing silently while wearing her new glamour—cold blue eyes and pointed pixie's nose. Mother stood staring down at the ground in front of her.

Edith's plan had failed. She had gained no magic and now had no hope of ever finding it. At least she took comfort in the thought that she was not ordinary. She would never be ordinary with her face half melted.

In the night, Mother came to Edith's bedroom and held Edith's hands. Her glamour was gone. She was just an ordinary middle-aged woman with bags and dark circles beneath her eyes.

"My Dear," she said. "I wish I had the power to cast a glamour over you instead of myself, but I'm not strong enough. All this mess has made me so weak I can't even keep the charms on myself. I'm just a sad old woman now. Your grandmother may have once been strong enough to do it, but you've seen her true form. She's far too old."

"And Ruby?" Edith asked, knowing the answer before she spoke the words aloud.

Mother shook her head. "Ruby may be strong enough, but you know her. She is not like you. She has too much of our family blood in her. It makes her cruel and hungry for power. We spoiled her in her younger years and made her think of herself as invincible."

Edith saw tears in her mother's eyes, but she could not bring herself to weep. She loved her mother then, in the woman's natural form. How foolish Edith had been to fear looking like an ordinary woman. She had thought the only way to gain her mother's love was to be beautiful, but now she realized her mother's love was there always.

They hugged each other, and as they did, her mother's form began to glow.

"Mother," Edith said. She had never seen a glamour like this before. "What's happening to you?"

When her mother looked up, Edith saw a young woman before her—not as perfect as her mother's usual glamour, but still beautiful in her own way. It was her mother's real face, only younger and stronger, not tired and sad.

"Mother, your glamour has returned," Edith said.

Her mother shook her head and said, "That's not possible. I haven't cast my spell again." She looked at her arms with their smooth skin and glow. "But I do feel rejuvenated." She touched her nose and mouth with her hands. "My skin feels renewed. But this is someone else's magic." She gazed a moment longer at her own skin and then smiled at Edith. "This is your magic! You have cast a glamour on your dear mother!"

She hugged Edith again. The longer they embraced the warmer and brighter her mother grew.

"Everyone!" her mother shouted, "Come quickly!"

Edith's grandmother and Ruby came into the room. Neither of the women wore their spells. Grandmother walked with a cane and a bent back. Edith never noticed how slowly the old woman moved. Ruby's face was twisted into a hateful expression.

"You are doing this!" Ruby shouted, pointing at Edith.

Their mother didn't seem to hear Ruby's words and said, "Look, Mother, Edith has cast a charm on me. She is of our blood and a true talent at that."

"Hmmph," Grandmother said. The effort of making the noise caused the old woman to wobble. She saved herself from falling by grasping onto the wall for support. She pointed her cane at Mother and said, "You look like a bright fool of a light bulb. She may be making you glow, but the two of us cannot cast our glamours."

"What?" Mother said.

"The charms aren't working!" Ruby said. "I'm hideous!"

"You look normal to me," Edith said.

"Something in this house is stopping our charms," Grandmother said. "And I can see now it must be Edith."

"I don't see how that's possible," Mother said. She clasped Edith's hands tightly in her own. Edith felt the warmth inside her again and her mother glowed with warm pulsing light.

"Edith is sucking out our power and giving it to you," Grandmother said. "She is wild and has no control over what she casts a spell on."

"I don't think that's true," Edith said, her voice shaking. "I do have some control over it. Each time my heart feels love for my mother, she grows more beautiful. You two have no love for me, nor I for you. And your beauty wanes as your hate grows."

"Ridiculous," Grandmother said. "You are a wretched and ridiculous thing!" Grandmother tried to turn and leave, but she lost her balance and fell in the hallway. She moaned in pain, but no one moved to help.

"You're horrible!" Ruby shouted, and her skin wrinkled and paled. When she saw this happening to her arms and hands, she screamed and ran from the room. Grandmother lifted herself shakily from the floor, cursing under her breath as she hobbled away.

"My goodness," Edith's mother said. "Now that they know how your magic works, they will have to be kinder. It's good we finally have some good magic in this house. Magic made of love instead of vanity."

"Yes," Edith said. She smiled too, knowing it was she, and not their grandmother, who would teach young Ruby how to be beautiful.

'Til Death Us Do Part

S.K. Gregory

ho knocks on someone's door at 2:30 in the morning? I wondered as I hurried downstairs. It had to be bad news. But bad news about what? Or who? I didn't have any family so it wasn't that. Maybe someone stole my car?

I stopped on the way to the door to look out the side window. My beat-up, black Mustang was still there. I doubted anyone was desperate enough to steal it, anyway. They certainly wouldn't get far with what little gas was in it.

I hesitated at the door. What if there was a psycho on the other side? Although it would be unusual for one to knock. Didn't they just break in and murder you in your sleep? My brain couldn't focus, I was so tired.

Lifting my red and blue-striped umbrella from the stand in the corner, I wrenched open the door. On the other side stood Mary Whittaker. She lived in town and worked as a receptionist in the doctor's office. We have never really spoken before, so why was she here?

"Can I..." Before I could even finish the sentence, she pushed past me into the house.

"Thank goodness you're in," she said, pushing back the hood of her coat. Why was she wearing it? It wasn't raining. She fussed with her curly strawberry blonde hair, and looked around the room, taking everything in.

"Of course I'm in, it's the middle of the night. What do you want?" My manners went out the window the second she barged into my home. I really needed to sleep. Today had been a total nightmare. I got fired from my job at the salon when I accidentally dyed a woman's hair blue. I'd only been working there for a couple of months, but I loved the job. I had no idea how her hair ended up blue, but Jodie, the manager, fired me on the spot.

"Mary?" I prompted.

Finally she looked at me, "Something awful has happened."

A knot formed in my stomach, it must be really bad, "What is it?"

"Jeremy left me," she said, before dropping onto the couch and wailing in despair.

I stared at her in confusion as my sleep deprived brain tried to remember who Jeremy even was. I barely knew Mary.

"Jeremy...is your husband?" I said.

She nodded, her head buried in one of my cream-colored cushions. When she raised her head, I could see mascara streaks across it. I moved the cushion out of her reach and sat down beside her.

"I'm sorry about Jeremy. You know what will make you feel better? A good night's sleep. So you go home and..."

She leapt up from the couch, almost knocking me over.

"Please, do you really think I came here at this time of the night for platitudes?"

"Then why are you here?" I asked, running a hand through my dark hair.

"Why do you think?"

I didn't like her tone. No wonder we never spoke, she was such a cow. Every time I went to the doctor's office she seemed to look down her nose at me. Actually she seemed to do it to everyone.

"Just cut to the chase, Mary," I said.

"I need to get Jeremy back and you are going to help me do it."

Now I knew where she was going, but I didn't let on.

"How?" I asked.

"Cast a spell on him. Make it so he'll never leave me again."

I threw my head back and groaned. The witch thing again. I should have known.

"I hate to break it to you, Mary, but all the witch stuff is a rumor."

"Don't play games with me, Aurelia Graves. I'm willing to pay whatever it takes to get him back."

Whatever it takes? I did need to get my car fixed. Maybe this could be a good thing.

"Okay, a thousand," I said.

"What?" Mary balked.

"You said you would pay anything...or isn't Jeremy worth it?"

"Of course he is, but I don't have that much money."

"How much do you have?"

She unzipped her purse and removed her bank book.

"You can have all my savings. $488.68."

That would still go a long way toward fixing the car. I considered it for a moment.

"Deal."

She looked relieved, "Great, do it."

"Do what?"

"Cast the spell," she said, rolling her eyes like I was an idiot.

"I can't just cast on command. It has to be done in private and I'll need something that belongs to Jeremy, too."

She rummaged in her purse again and produced a blue and white poker chip.

"This is his. He usually carries it everywhere with him, like a lucky charm. But he left it behind when he walked out."

I took the chip from her, turning it over in my hand. The name of a casino was stamped on it—Lucky Streak. It was about an hour away.

"Okay, I have enough to get started. I'll let you know when the spell is complete."

She nodded, "Okay, and it *will* work, right? Jeremy will come back to me?"

"There are no guarantees when dealing with magical forces, but it *should* work, yes."

I managed to usher her out the door. *God, she's annoying.*

I couldn't believe people still believed that the witch stuff was real. It started when I was 13 years old and I went with a group of friends to a local cemetery. It was almost Halloween and we were messing around. Someone printed a spell off the Internet, one thing led to another and I accidentally raised the dead. Or at least that was what it looked like. Obviously I know now that it was our imagination. Zombie guy was probably on his way to a Halloween party, but when you're thirteen, you believe anything and because I read the spell that automatically made me a witch. I lost a lot of friends that year.

A few years later I moved away, then last year I came home and nothing had changed. I was still a witch to everyone. Maybe it was time I used it to my advantage.

I wasn't going to perform a spell; that was stupid, but I could try a more direct route. I could track Jeremy down and convince him to go home to Mary. What did I have to lose?

The following evening I drove to the Lucky Streak Casino. Maybe it was a long shot, but I had a feeling I would find him there. Especially if that chip meant so much to him.

Mary had been calling me nonstop all day. I don't even know how she got my number in the first place. So far, I had been able to put her off by telling her that I must wait for the moon to rise before I could start the spell. Thank goodness for my *Charmed* obsession, at least I sounded like I knew what I'm talking about.

The Lucky Streak Casino wasn't what I expected. I thought it would be like the casinos in Vegas, but this was a seedy little hole in the wall, located down a dark alley.

Staring down the alley at the blue neon sign above the door, I wondered if this was a good idea. Then I remembered the noise my car made on the way here and wondered if it would make it home. I straightened the hem of my short black dress and tucked my purse tightly under my arm.

Head up, shoulders back, I thought. My mother's advice when facing any situation was to go into with confidence, whether you felt it or not. One of the few things I remembered about her. She died when I was ten. I lived with my aunt for a while, but she died when I started college.

There was a bouncer waiting at the door, a huge guy wearing a black t-shirt with tattoos covering his arms.

"Hi, I, um, want to go in?" I said. *That really sounded confident.*

"The cover charge is thirty bucks," he said.

"Thirty? That's steep." I needed to eat sometime this week.

"Then don't come in," he said.

"I'm actually just looking for someone, I'm not here to gamble. His name is Jeremy, he's in his thirties, tall, dark hair." That was about as much as I could remember from seeing him around town. I knew I would recognize him when I saw him, but I was having a hard time describing him.

"No one uses their real names here. Either pay the thirty bucks or get lost."

I pulled thirty bucks from my purse and handed it over. Maybe I should charge Mary expenses, too.

The inside was worse than I thought it would be. Low lighting, a sticky floor and the smell of liquor and stale cigarette smoke wafted through the air. Most of the patrons sat around small wooden tables playing cards or at the bar drinking.

Most of them were men, although I did see two women at the bar, but they seemed to be waiting on someone. I felt so out of place. When people started to look my way, I quickly took a seat at the end of the bar. The bartender approached and I ordered a vodka and tonic.

While I waited, I glanced around the room, searching for Jeremy, but there was no sign of him. The bartender slid a glass toward me and I knocked it back.

"Do you know someone named Jeremy?" I asked him.

He shrugged, "Nobody really gives their names in here."

Short of standing up and yelling "Jeremy" to see who looked, there wasn't much else I could do. This was such a waste of time *and* I was out thirty bucks.

A man slipped onto the stool beside mine. I glanced up and my breath caught in my throat. He was insanely good-looking. Well-built, thick dark hair and ice blue eyes that were staring into mine. I could see a thin layer of stubble across his chin, his full lips and prominent cheekbones. Why would someone like him be in a dive like this?

He smiled at me while I struggled to think of something to say to him.

"Searching for someone?" he asked. I was surprised to hear an English accent, but it made him even sexier.

"I, uh, yeah how did you know?" I asked.

"You don't look like you're here to gamble."

"No, I'm actually looking for a guy."

The smile widened, "One in particular or just in general?"

"One in particular. For a friend."

"Do your friends often send you into dumps like this to pick up men for them?"

I laughed, "It's not like that. I'm looking for a man named Jeremy. He and his wife had a fight and I'm trying to get them back together."

"A matchmaker. Well tell me, do you have a match for me?"

"I don't even know you," I replied, though I wish I did.

"Then allow me to introduce myself: my name is Daniel. I'm in town on business and my ideal woman is young, beautiful and talented. Drives an old Mustang and has the ability to cast a spell on a man."

"That sounds very precise." Who the hell was this guy?

"Don't look so scared; I knew what you were from the moment you walked in. It's good to meet a fellow witch."

"Witch," I sputtered. "This is a joke right? Why does everyone keep calling me a witch?"

"Because you are one," he said simply.

"You are a crazy person," I said, getting up from my stool.

I left the casino and headed back to my car. Why were the hot ones always nuts?

"I'm sorry if I offended you," Daniel called.

He had followed me.

"Leave me alone," I said.

He jogged to catch up to me, taking my arm and spinning me around.

"I thought you were aware of your gifts. It's unusual to meet a witch who isn't. I can help you though. It's what I specialize in, teaching witches about their gifts."

"I'm not a witch." I got the feeling that I could repeat that all day and he still wouldn't believe me.

He nodded, "Okay, take my card anyway, just in case."

I accepted the card and dropped it into my purse, "I won't need it."

But as I drove away, I wondered if that were true.

"You said you would do the spell. Jeremy still hasn't come back, what's happened?" Mary screeched down the phone. I moved it away from my ear so I wouldn't be deafened.

"It's all about timing," I said, "I'll perform the spell now."

"Right now?"

"Yes, right now. Bye."

I hung up on her and tossed my phone onto the coffee table. Lifting my glass, I finished the last of my wine. Maybe I should try a spell. After all I was *supposed* to be a witch. Why couldn't I do a spell?

Opening my laptop I searched the web for an appropriate spell. There were thousands of them. How did I know which ones were legit and which we were just fancy poems? Did it matter? Weren't witches able to create their own spells? Why did it have to be so complex?

After an hour of searching, I chose a spell from a Gothic-looking website. I set up some candles and wrote Mary's name on a piece of paper. Holding the poker chip I chanted the spell:

Return Mary's love, wherever he may be,
Unite them once more for all eternity,
As I will it so shall it be.

If that didn't do it, I don't know what would. A shiver ran up my spine as I extinguished the candles. Imagine having that much power over people. It was a scary thought.

Well at least I wouldn't be lying to Mary when I told her that I had cast the spell. Who knew, maybe Jeremy would go back to her and I could get my money after all.

Frantic banging woke me from my sleep. Someone was at my door again.

Stomping downstairs, I yanked open the front door and Mary almost fell in on top of me.

"Close the door, quick," she cried.

"Why are you here again?" I snapped.

She slammed the front door and locked it.

"Good, now can I do that with you on the other side of the door?" I said.

"He's coming," she whimpered, cowering against the wall.

"Who is? Jeremy?" I looked out the window, but the street was empty.

"This can't be happening. He can't be here. He says he wants me back."

"Isn't that a good thing? Isn't that why you came to me in the first place?"

"Did you do this?" she asked.

I sighed, "I thought you were clear on the specifics. I cast a spell, you get Jeremy back. By the way you owe me money."

"The spell did this? What kind of sicko are you?"

"Excuse me?" I said.

"You brought him back."

A loud thump came from the door. Mary screamed in terror.

"What is wrong with Jeremy?" Why was she so scared of her own husband?

"It's not Jeremy. It's Karl."

"Who the hell is Karl?" I asked as the door was struck again.

"My high school boyfriend. We were going to be married.

He was my first love."

"And the spell brought him to you instead of Jeremy," I said, catching on. "Did the relationship end badly? Is that why you don't want to see him?"

She looked at me as if I was insane, "It ended when he wrapped his car around a tree. He's been dead for the past 15 years."

The lock broke and the door crashed open. Mary and I scrambled into the living room. I grabbed my umbrella as a weapon.

A man staggered into the room. He wore a suit that was in tatters and the earthy graveyard smell from him was over-powering. When he raised his head to look at us, I started screaming. He was a zombie.

"Mary," he moaned, barely able to form the word.

She was hiding behind me.

"Make him go away," she cried.

"I don't know how."

Flashbacks of that night in the cemetery filled my head. Did I raise a zombie back then, too? How was that possible?

Karl lurched towards us, but his foot became detached from his leg and he fell forward crashing right through my coffee table. He lay there, unmoving.

"Is he dead?" Mary whispered.

"Yes. For the past 15 years, according to you," I hissed.

"You know what I mean. Check."

"I'm not checking, you do it."

She took a step towards him, then legged it out the front door.

"You bitch," I said.

Using the tip of the umbrella I prodded Karl with it. It sank into his back and I squealed and dropped the umbrella. This was crazy. I really was a witch.

"What am I going to do?" I whispered.

Daniel. The guy from the casino, he said he could help me. I grabbed my purse, searching through it for the card.

Keeping an eye on Karl to make sure he didn't move, I dialed the number, mindful of the fact that it was the middle of the night. I hoped Daniel didn't think I was making a booty call.

"Hello?" he didn't sound like he had been sleeping.

"Daniel? It's Aurelia. We met at the casino, you called me a witch?"

"Yes?"

"I need your help. I've done something awful and I don't know what to do now. I *am* a witch."

"Okay, just stay calm. Give me your address and I'll be there soon."

I did as he asked and hung up. My heart was hammering in my chest, I didn't want to stay there with Karl. If he moved I was sure to have a heart attack.

With no other choice, I went outside and sat on the porch to wait on Daniel. Every noise made me jump.

Finally, a black Porsche pulled up at the curb and Daniel got out. He wore a suit with a white shirt that was open at the collar.

"Aurelia? What's happened?" he asked.

"In here," I said, leading him into the living room. Karl was still there.

Daniel surveyed the body, then gave a low whistle, "Zombie?"

I nodded, "Zombie. Why is this happening?"

"What kind of spell did you do?"

"A love spell for the friend I mentioned. There was no mention of zombies in it."

"Show me the spell."

I handed him the scrap of paper I had scribbled the spell down on.

"Yeah, I see the problem. You weren't specific enough. You called for this woman's true love. Unfortunately, he was dead."

"This is a nightmare. How do I get rid of him?"

"Well it looks like the magic wore off. I guess the only way to get rid of him is to take him to his grave and put him back where he belongs."

"I was afraid you were going to say that."

He knelt beside Karl. "Do you have an old sheet we could wrap the body in?"

"I can check."

Daniel rolled the body over. Suddenly Karl flayed and lashed out at Daniel. He fell back on his butt as Karl writhed like a worm on the floor.

Grabbing my umbrella, I swung it at Karl's head. It collided with his cheek and his head broke free of his neck and sailed across the room. It hit the wall and dropped to the carpet with a thud.

"Nice hit," Daniel said.

"Is he dead now? You know: *dead* dead, not *un*dead?"

"Yeah, they're not much good without their heads. Get the sheet, we'll get rid of him."

Daniel did most of the work, wrapping up the body. I'm not usually squeamish, but these were unusual circumstances. Once Karl was covered, Daniel hefted the body up over his shoulder.

"We should probably take your car. More room."

I grabbed my keys and we loaded the body into the trunk. It was a tight squeeze. We drove to the only cemetery in town. The same one from when I was thirteen.

Using a flashlight, we spent half an hour walking around looking for the grave.

"This is probably it," Daniel said, pointing at a grave with dirt strewn around it. Dirt from someone crawling out of it. The name read Karl McNichol.

"Yeah, this is it."

"You wait here, I'll go and get the body," Daniel said.

"Please hurry," I said, nervously checking the other graves. I was never rhyming again. Not now that I knew what I could do.

Daniel dropped the body beside the grave and started digging.

"Are you a witch?" I asked.

"Of a sort," he replied. "I'm more of a teacher, really."

"I don't understand any of this. My life was normal before all this and now I'm raising the dead. I thought witches cast love spells and worked with herbs. This is a lot darker than I imagined."

"Well, there are different types of witches. With different

powers," Daniel said. He finished digging and hauled himself out of the hole.

"What kind am I?" We each took a side of the body and rolled it into the hole.

He turned to look at me, "You are a necromancer."

"What the hell is a necromancer?" I asked.

"Necromancer's have power over the dead, Aurelia."

"Seriously? Why couldn't I have a cool power, like the ability to make things blow up with the power of my mind?"

"Trust me: that power is more trouble than it's worth."

"But what use is summoning the dead?"

"There are a lot of uses, actually. You could question people about how they died, create your own undead army, stuff like that."

Okay, my own undead army did sound kind of cool.

We made our way back to the car while I tried to process everything. Back at the house, Daniel followed me inside.

"I can clean up for you, if you want?" he said.

"No, it's fine. You've done more than enough. Thank you, I don't know what I would have done without you."

"It's what I do. This is a lot to take in. Try and get some sleep and we can talk in the morning."

"I doubt I could sleep," I said, but I could feel my eyes closing.

I said goodnight and went up to bed.

The next morning, I woke to the smell of bacon cooking. My stomach grumbled in response. But who was cooking?

I found Daniel making breakfast. He smiled at me when I came in and my stomach gave a lurch. Damn, he was so good-looking.

"Hello? What time did you get here?" I asked, wondering how he got in.

"I never left. I slept on the sofa."

Glancing into the living room, I could see the room had been tidied up and the broken coffee table was gone.

"Are you a neat freak?" I asked.

He shrugged, "Yeah, kind of. Sit, eat."

A plate of bacon, scrambled eggs and toast was set in front of me. It looked delicious and I got stuck in.

Daniel sipped on a coffee while I ate.

"I should probably go and see Mary and try to convince her that she imagined everything," I said.

"Forget about her. I've found over the years that people who witness the supernatural either go into denial or are too scared to come forward in case they are ridiculed."

"I don't think it will be easy to dismiss your dead high school sweetheart showing up at your door."

"She's not your problem anymore. What are your plans now?"

"I don't know. I guess I need to learn more about who I am and what I'm capable of. I suppose I have the time now that I'm unemployed."

"So you have no job and no family here?" Daniel asked.

"Thanks for reminding me, as if I don't feel bad enough."

"No, what I mean is there's nothing keeping you here in town. I'm going across country before I head back home. You could come with me and I could teach you about your ability."

"Just leave? Where are you going?"

"I will be visiting other witches, helping them. You're welcome to join me."

It was quite the offer and a tempting one. I really didn't have anything keeping me here right now and it would be a good idea to keep my distance from Mary for a while.

"Okay, I will."

"Great. I have a couple of things to do first but I'll be back in about an hour and we can go."

Excited now, I ran upstairs to pack a bag. Maybe this witch stuff had its advantages after all.

"It's me," I said, "I've got her."

"Then proceed with the plan. And Daniel, I want no loose ends."

"Don't worry, there won't be."

I hung up and slipped my phone into my pocket. It was so easy luring Aurelia in. A novice witch. They were rare and not much of a challenge. Especially her. She jumped at the chance to go away with me. She had no idea what was in store for her. Having no one that would miss her was an advantage, too. The only loose end was Mary. She was a witness.

I checked her body for any signs of life. She lay on her kitchen floor, eyes open, her mouth twisted in fear.

When her body was found they would think it was a robbery gone wrong.

I let myself out and headed back to Aurelia's house. We had a road trip to go on, one from which she'd not be returning.

Hour of the Owl

KEVIN M. FOLLIARD

mother doesn't want to hear about her son's wedding day after the fact. But Wesley was always impulsive. "The Wanderer," I had lovingly called him. In the months before my husband passed away, he had called our son a few choicer things. It was part of what drove Wesley away for so long. The two had never seen eye-to-eye. We had loaned Wesley too much money, too many times. Wesley's father and Uncle Hal had flown to Las Vegas on four separate occasions to bring him home. But the City of Lights always won in the end. I'm convinced that fourth trip was what killed my husband.

So when I read Wesley's letter, I had mixed reactions. Shame over our distant relationship. Doubt as to why he was really returning. But a glimmer of hope that with his father gone, we might restart our family.

Perhaps the Lord had led him to the arms of an honest woman. A wife that would bring him home to me for more than just a visit.

Wesley pulled up the dusty farm house drive in a black SUV. He parked, rounded the vehicle and opened the passenger door for a slender, long-legged woman. She stalked onto the dirt in a black gown slit to the hip. A feathery grey shawl snaked over her shoulders. She had a narrow, heart-shaped face with unnaturally large brown eyes. Silver hair flowed past her shoulders. Her complexion was pale and perfect.

I couldn't decide how old she was. She was either young and exotic or, I feared, an age-defying predator, scooping up eager twenty-somethings for arm candy. It may not have been a fair first impression on my part, but it was Wesley's not-so-glamorous lifestyle that painted it.

The woman swiveled and examined the grounds: the orchard, the barn, the house. She nodded as if to say, "Yes, this will do." She hadn't so much as glanced in my direction. Wesley closed the car door and hurried between us. "Mom!"

I held him tight and kissed his cheek.

Wesley pulled me closer to the woman. "Mother, this is Ava, my wife!"

Ava scanned the apple trees with stern, arched eyebrows. Her skin gave a porcelain sheen.

"Hello, Ava," I tried. "I'm Jean. Very pleased to meet you." I held out my hand.

"Ava," Wesley cooed. "Ava, my mother." He guided her shoulders and coaxed her to pay attention to me.

"Hello, Jean." Her expression twisted into a sickly sweet smile. She clasped my hand in both of hers. "Wesley could not have prepared me for such a charming country home. I can see how my sweet young man could come from such... humble beginnings."

Ava's voice was husky, sultry. Her diction was peculiar. If she had an accent, it wasn't one I'd heard before. She was subtly emphasizing the wrong syllables. Putting just a bit too much effort into sounding normal.

"Well, thank you," I stuttered. "And...I can see that my son has chosen...a lovely bride."

I was trying not to cry. I was failing. This woman was the opposite of anyone I had pictured walking down the aisle with my only child.

"You are too kind." Ava brushed past me toward the house. "Wesley, bring my bags upstairs. I am fatigued. Enjoy time with Mother."

She entered my kitchen. Her hips swayed. Her long black fingernails curled around the door handle, and she smiled before going inside. But not a kind smile. Those huge, dark eyes seemed to own everything they saw.

I let out a small gasp and wiped my eyes on my jacket.

Wesley didn't seem to notice my tears. He hurried inside after his bride with two purple suitcases under his arms. While they were upstairs, I poured cider that had been warming on the stove. I cut a piece of apple pie for Wesley and set it across the table.

And then I cried.

"Aw, Mom, come on," he said from the bottom of the stairs.

"'Aw, Mom, come on?'" I repeated in disbelief. "Gone for ten years, didn't even attend your father's funeral, and now you show up, married to this...and you expect me to just..."

I threw up my hands: "There's pie."

Wesley frowned and sat across from me. "You don't like her. I knew this would happen. You don't like her, and you've only just met her."

"Well, I don't know anything about her," I said. "She looks like she might be a lot older than you."

"She isn't." Wesley glared.

"How old is she?"

He poked at the pie. "Not much older. It's not polite to tell people's ages."

"And how long have you known her?"

"How long did you know Dad before he—"

"That's not what we're talking about."

"Well, it's not how long you know someone, it's who they are!"

"She barely even said hello. She just floated upstairs, like I didn't matter." I reached for a napkin and dabbed my eyes.

"She's tired. We've been driving all day."

"Where is she from? What's her family like?"

Wesley dropped his fork on his plate. "What is this, an interrogation? I came home! I came home because I love you. Because I love her. Because I wanted you to meet her. And now there's a problem before I can even...."

He bit his lip. Red flooded his face. Wesley's fine brown

hair had receded, just a little, since the last time I'd seen him, and in that moment, he looked exactly like his father. "Mom, I've made mistakes, I know that. But Ava's not one of them."

I nodded. "Okay." I sipped my cider. "Good apples this year."

He took a bite of pie. He nodded.

Ava remained hidden in the guest room for the remainder of the afternoon, through dinner, and into the evening.

Wesley continued to explain that she was tired. I told him it was fine. Truthfully, I was happy to avoid her. We could try again the next day.

Lying awake in bed, I remembered meeting my mother-in-law for the first time. Wesley's grandmother had been a stoic woman of few words, but a good woman. We were never close, but we'd always respected one another. How could I know what she'd thought of me that first time? Had I made some faux pas without knowing? Had my husband made excuses for me, just like his son?

To think that our son—so much like his father—could end up with someone so completely unlike myself truly disturbed me. It was with that thought that I had the distinct feeling of being watched.

A chill autumn breeze rustled the curtains. I pulled the comforter to my chin. For years, the bedroom had felt abnormally large and empty without Wesley's father. Tonight it felt microscopic, like I was a bug in a jar.

Out the window, on the branch of a nearby apple tree, sat a pale, ghostly figure. A white oval with a flat face and huge dark eyes.

A barn owl.

I'd seen them before of course. Normally they're a welcome sight. They kill pests, protect crops, and there's usually something beautifully ethereal about them.

But not this one. Its bulging eyes and narrow beak reminded me of that woman. Wings enveloped its body, like Ava's feathery shawl. I had never seen an owl this close to the house. They're almost always searching the ground, looking for rodents. This one stared directly into the bedroom. We locked eyes.

Outside, strange angelic figures fluttered in the night sky. I climbed out of bed, put on my robe, and approached the window. Cold air pulsed into the room. The curtains wafted. The barn owl stared.

More owls flew overhead. Dozens of them approached from every direction and descended upon the barn like pale specters.

The owl on the branch kneaded its talons. It unfolded its wings, adjusted its position, hunkered down, and continued to stare, as if threatening: *go back to bed.*

More and more white owls descended. They landed on the barn roof, drifted into the hayloft. *Owls don't swarm. They don't flock.* I shivered at the thought of what unusual thing could be attracting them.

My first instinct was to wake Wesley, but I immediately thought better of it. What worse way to get on his bad side than to barge in and interrupt his bride's seemingly endless beauty sleep.

I shut the window and slipped down into the dark kitchen. I grabbed a flashlight, zipped my coat over the robe, and ventured outside.

The owl outside my window slowly twisted its head. Its dark eyes tracked me across the clearing to the barn. The red barn doors had been left open a crack. Pale wings fluttered down and squeezed through.

Voices muffled inside.

Owls don't attack humans, I reminded myself. Normally. But nothing about this situation was normal. I clutched the door. Soft whispers continued inside. Language, perhaps not English. Too low to understand.

I pulled the door back. A blast of cold and a fury of white wings filled the night.

I awoke screaming. The pink light of dawn lit the bedroom.

I sighed, caught my breath, and got out of bed. I gazed curiously out the window at the bare branch where the barn owl had sat in my nightmare. The window was closed.

In the fall, I always slept with the window open, nestled under warm covers. In the nightmare, I had shut it, afraid the owl might fly into the room.

My coat hung on the bathroom door, next to my robe. The flashlight sat upright on the nightstand. These were items I kept downstairs, but now they were up here. What had I dreamt, and what had I actually done? I had never known myself to sleepwalk.

Outside the window, the first rays of orange light glowed through the branches of the orchard. The barn door creaked open. And the woman Ava slipped out.

She adjusted her grey shawl and closed the door. Then her head swiveled, independent of her torso, past her shoulders. She glared at me.

I descended the stairs to the aroma of bacon crisping and coffee brewing. For just a moment, it was twenty years ago. A beautiful fall Saturday morning. Wesley watching cartoons in the living room. His father cooking up a feast and bantering with Uncle Hal who sipped coffee behind the morning paper.

The memory faded when I reached the kitchen. Ava sat at the table. She pinched a strip of limp bacon, practically raw, between her black fingernails. She took small bites and smiled at me when I entered. "Good morning, Jean."

Wesley busied himself at the stove. "I made bacon, Mom!" he said. "You want eggs? French toast?"

"Thank you, Wes." I sat across from the woman. "This is very thoughtful. Just coffee though. You didn't have to go to all this trouble."

Ava narrowed her eyes. "It's no trouble. How many meals did you prepare for your son? He can make one for you."

You don't speak for him, I wanted to say. But I bit my

tongue. "Did you sleep well?"

Ava nodded. "Like the dead. I was up before dawn. I took a walk through the apple trees. Saw the barn. Do you oversee the orchard yourself, Jean? It must be very time-consuming."

"Wesley's father and I used to do it together. Now we...I... have Wesley's Uncle Hal come in during the fall season. He oversees spraying, pruning, picking and distribution. Less money, but I get by."

Wesley placed a cup of coffee in front of me. "It used to be a pretty big operation," he said. "Mom and Dad and Uncle Hal and a bunch of other guys from town. Me on the weekends once I was old enough. We had chickens, sometimes. Ran hayrides in the fall. Had pumpkins a few years."

"How charming." Ava nibbled her bacon. "I would love to see pictures of Wesley when he was a boy. I noticed you don't have any on display."

My face burned with anger. "I have pictures."

"You put them away when Wesley and his father had their falling out?" She arched an eyebrow.

"Ava..." Wesley started.

I glared at the woman. Steam from my coffee wafted between us.

"I'm sorry," she said. "Was I rude?"

Bacon grease sputtered.

"I think I'll go for a walk as well. Thanks for the coffee, Wes." I took my drink outside. The screen door slammed.

Branches swayed and apples bobbed in the cold breeze. I approached the barn door and hesitated. What had that woman been doing in there? I entered apprehensively. Light filtered through notches in the wall and the open loft window.

The grey beams of the rafters were devoid of any sign of nesting barn owls, as was the rest of the barn. Not a dropping on the ground. Not a single white feather in sight. Just bushels of crisp, green apples to ship on Monday, stacked against the walls.

"Jean."

I jumped in surprise. Hot coffee sloshed onto my hand, and

I gasped.

Ava stood still as a shadow in the doorway. Her face was blank, save her perpetually scowling eyebrows. "I didn't mean to startle you."

I wiped coffee off my hands. "Why are you here? What do you want?"

"Only to apologize." She strolled into the barn; her black skirts swept the ground.

"I mean why you are here—at all?"

Ava smirked. "You have a mother's instincts to protect your child. I admire that."

"Do you?"

"Oh yes," she said. "I admire a woman who struggled to mediate between husband and son. Who sacrificed so much to raise a troubled boy."

"What sacrifice? Wesley was never troubled until he left here."

"How true." Ava circled the barn. "How sad for you to lose him. And how fortunate that I have brought him home."

"Have you?"

"Yes." Ava fondled an apple with one hand. She traced her fingernails along a wooden barrel with the other.

"Ava, I simply don't know enough about you. Wesley has kept questionable company in the past."

She took a bite of the apple. A very small bite. She chewed and swallowed. "How can you know anything about me if you don't ask questions?"

"Where are you from?"

"New Mexico. My mother originated from Argentina. My father was French. I seem exotic to you? Is that why you distrust me?"

"I don't judge people because they're exotic," I whispered. "How did you meet Wesley?"

"He has not told you?"

"I'm asking *you.*"

Ava took another bite. The black fingernails of her other hand clutched the rim of the barrel. She closed her eyes. "It may not be my place to tell that story. I know you are worried about your son. I know he made poor decisions. He's fortunate to have found me. To have found acceptance. Guidance. Structure."

"Structure in the form of what?"

Ava's head swiveled almost halfway around. Her eyes opened wide. "Love." Her back remained turned. The position looked painful. Contorted. "You must believe in love to have raised such a passionate man."

My skin crawled. "What do you do for a living? How do you and Wesley plan to support yourselves?"

"I have money. I want Wesley to focus on rebuilding himself—spiritually. He is plagued with guilt. I thought, perhaps, it would do him good to return here and spend time with you."

"So it was your idea to come home?" I asked. "Not his?"

"An idea he embraced." Ava's body twisted forward to match her head. "What else would you like to know?"

"You've barely told me a thing," I said. "How old are you, Ava?"

"How old do I look?"

I struggled for an answer. "I honestly can't decide how old you look. But it's a simple question. Why can't you answer it?"

"Talk to Wesley," Ava replied. "You don't have to trust me, but you should trust him." She smiled and swept her way back to the door. Before she left, she swiveled her head around again. "Oh, and Jean, I really would like to have a picture of Wesley as a child. Where might I find one?"

I scowled.

"No worry if you misplaced them. I will find one." Ava's head turned forward, and she continued on her way.

By 10:30 a.m., Ava was complaining of fatigue. She was back in bed by 11:00.

"Wesley," I asked, once I heard the guest bedroom door shut. "How *exactly* did you meet this woman?"

"I don't want to talk about that, Mom. Ava's helped me a

lot. That's all."

"Did she pay off your gambling debts?"

Wesley sighed. "Yes, Mom. She did. And she took me on this retreat and helped me understand a lot about the way I've been behaving. She told me it would be good to reconnect with my family—"

"What retreat?" I asked.

Wesley grew quiet.

"Some kind of clinic? Something for...something to help..." I didn't want to use the word addict. I could tell by that stern look in his eyes that I was pushing my luck. Probing for too much, too fast. It was that same "don't ask" glare that his father had always used.

Wesley shrugged. "I can't really talk about it."

"Why not? I'm your mother."

"I just can't!" he snapped. "It's a rule."

"Whose rule?"

"That's how a retreat works, Mom! You can't go talking about everything afterwards. It's private!"

"There's no reason to shout," I said. "I'm just curious. And concerned."

"You *shouldn't* be." Wesley massaged his temples. "Where are the pictures?"

"The pictures?"

"Pictures of me and our family!" he shouted. "How come there aren't any? Did you get rid of them all? Were you trying to pretend like I never existed!"

"Wesley, no. Of course not—"

"Then where are they? Ava needs one!" He pounded the wall, and the kitchen shook. Wesley's eyes were wide, wild with rage.

I gasped for air, clutched my heart.

Wesley shook his head. He rubbed his forehead as if coming out of a daze. "I'm sorry, Mom. I didn't mean to get mad like that. I'm sorry."

"It's all right," I said. "Just sit down."

"I think I need sleep," he said. "I'm tired."

That afternoon, I called Wesley's Uncle Hal. I cried out the events of the past few days to him, keeping the more outlandish details about the owls to myself. I still wasn't quite sure what to make of that.

Unlike Wesley, Hal didn't have my late husband's temper. There was something Wes wouldn't tell a mother, but maybe he would trust his level-headed godfather. Hal would be over first thing the next morning.

He'd be on my side.

That night, I dreamt of the barn. Same as before, I wandered into the dark of night. The ghostly barn owl perched outside my window, swiveled its head, and tracked me from the kitchen door across the clearing. Scores of white winged specters floated to the barn.

When I approached, the barn doors creaked open on their own. I entered a dark, ethereal void. But the concrete ground was unlike the barn. In the dim shadows I made out the façade of a familiar building. Blue light illuminated a small, lonely figure: Wesley, age four, dressed in a striped white and blue polo, ready to be picked up from elementary school.

He wore a look of repressed excitement. He'd always had some new treasure of knowledge to share when I'd picked him up. Wesley's eyes lit up.

"Mommy! Guess what?" He was holding something behind his back. A surprise for me.

I ran my fingers through his light brown hair. "What, Wessy?"

"I learned so much today!"

"I'm sure you did! You'll have to tell me all about what teacher taught you." It was what we said to each other every day after school.

"It was so much fun! And I made you something!" Wesley held up a drawing on a piece of dark blue construction paper. My stomach sank. Wesley had traced the ghostly image of a barn owl in white crayon. He'd scribbled big black circles for eyes. Scrawled at the bottom was "From Wes to Momy" in childish red print.

"What is this, Wes?"

His eyes gleamed. "It's the Dark Lord Stryxus, who dwells in the forests of the world waiting to be reborn!"

"The what?!"

Wesley pointed to the drawing emphatically. "Stryxus, Mommy. He lives in the owls and waits night after night, year after year. Waits for a broken soul to nest his essence!"

"Wesley, where did you hear such things?"

"Teacher told me!" Wesley pointed to the shadowy entrance of the school building. Darkness lay beyond the open doors. "Teacher told me that if you let Stryxus in your head and feed him morsels of guilt and pride and pain, he grows powerful. And then he gets reborn!"

"Wesley, teacher would *not* have told you that."

"Yes she did!" he whined. "When Stryxus returns, he'll cover the world in forest and black out the sun from the ground below. And the daylight will flicker away forever like a candle. And the canopy stretches to the heavens and smothers the lowly creatures of the soil. And *we* are his vessel! *We* are his vessel!" Wesley was screaming now, slapping his chest, crumpling his drawing in the process.

"Wesley, stop! Listen to me!"

He screeched and shouted. I held him, tried to steady him, but he pushed against me.

"We are his vessel!" He repeated over and over. "We are his vessel!"

"Wesley, stop it!" I covered his mouth. He gradually calmed. His breathing was heavy, labored.

His young eyes narrowed. I took my hand away, and he whispered, "Ask teacher, Mommy. It's true."

Ava stepped out of the darkness, through the school doors. A white owl perched on her left wrist. She held it high. Her lips tightened into a cruel smile. "It's true," she said. "Close your eyes, my lovely child. Open wide."

Wesley broke away and moved closer to Ava. I couldn't

scream. Couldn't move. I could only watch.

Wesley squeezed his eyes shut and stretched his jaws. The barn owl flapped its wings and rushed from Ava's arm to Wesley's mouth. It burrowed its head through. Wesley's head contorted. His jaw stretched as the owl wiggled its way in. Its feathery tail slipped between his lips.

Wesley twitched. Convulsed. Then he turned to me and opened muddy brown eyes. The whites were completely gone. He spoke with a deep, gravelly voice. "It's safe in the dark, Mother. Join us."

His face melted into pitch black. Horns curled out of his hair. His arms spread into wide, terrifying wings. The dark wings spread and swallowed everything in shadow.

I screamed awake in bed. The window was open. The sentry owl was nowhere in sight. The clock read 4:00 a.m.

I approached the window and stared at the silent barn. For a minute, it seemed that nothing was wrong. I tried to convince myself that these strange dreams and false memories were products of stress. They were vivid night terrors, nothing more. Awake and lucid, everything was normal.

And then the barn erupted in an explosion of white wings. Scores of barn owls poured from every opening. The doors burst apart and a river of feathery white streamed into the night. In dead silence, the swarm advanced over the clearing toward the house. As their numbers grew, a rush of air whispered, almost imperceptibly, past the house, over the roof. I pushed the window shut and held my back against it. Wings beat the glass.

I prayed to God to make them go away until at last the horrible thumping against the windowpane ceased. The quiet returned. I turned to find the night empty. The barn doors wide open.

I locked the window with trembling fingers and collapsed to my knees. As I crawled toward the bed I felt lightheaded. The blood drained from my face. Whiteness blurred my vision. And I lost consciousness.

"How are you feeling, Jean?" For a split second, I thought it was my husband's ghost. My eyes cleared to reveal his brother Hal, sporting a concerned smile. The clock read 10:30 a.m. I hadn't slept so late in thirty years.

"Lousy." I sat up.

"Wesley says he found you at the foot of the bed."

"Something happened last night."

"What?"

I hesitated. It would sound crazy. I didn't quite believe any of it myself. Wesley in the barn had definitely been a dream, but the owl swarm, going outside the night before—I knew I had been lucid.

"I haven't been sleeping well," I explained. "Let's leave it at that for now."

"Wesley says he's been worried about you since he got back. I told him this is just very hard for all of us."

I nodded. "You've spoken to him."

"Yeah," he said. "I talked to them."

The word hung between us. *Them.* Hal hadn't been talking to Wesley one-on-one. That woman was orchestrating everything Hal heard.

"And?" I prodded.

Hal sighed. "Ava is strange, but…"

"But?"

He looked away. "She seems to sincerely care about Wesley." He caught my icy glare. "This isn't going to be easy, Jean. I know how you feel."

"I don't think you do," I said. "If you'd been here the past two days. If you'd seen the way she creeps around. The way Wesley erupted into anger. The way they both dodge even the simplest questions about who she is and where she comes from—"

"She told me a little about her family. Very multicultural.

Traveled a lot. Lived on six continents."

"She's so vague about everything, though," I whispered. "They won't even say how old she is."

Hal nodded. "I didn't think it would be polite to ask."

"I'm done with politeness," I hissed. "What does she want with him, Hal? You can't be so blind."

"Wesley spent time in some kind of clinic," Hal said. "I'm guessing she was a volunteer."

"You're guessing?" I repeated. "Don't you see what she's doing? She's suggesting things, and you're assuming it's all normal. Where *is* the clinic? What *kind* of clinic? Why can't they tell us about what they did there?"

Hal took my hand. "I think Wes is embarrassed about that chapter of his life. She's probably trying to protect him."

I snatched my hand away. "Apparently, I'm the only person who's trying to protect him!"

Hal grew silent.

"Hal, this woman is stranger than you know. She's doing something in the barn. It's hard to explain, and I don't know *what* exactly, but she's up to something."

"How do you know?"

"Mother's intuition," I answered without hesitation. "Gut instinct. Call it what you want. I'm seeing things, Hal. Strange things."

"What strange things?"

I didn't want to say I was seeing owls. I knew how crazy it sounded. "I've seen her sneak out to the barn late at night. She's hardly ever awake during daylight."

"Maybe she's just a night person."

"Obviously, she is!"

"It sounds to me like you're stressed," he said. "And you have every right to be. How about you take it easy today, and I promise I'll be around all week. I'll help keep an eye on things."

I sighed. "Fine."

"I'll stick around today, okay? Ava and Wesley were talking about making an early dinner for the four of us. I think that's a

good idea. It'll give me a chance to see more of what's going on."
I nodded.

Before Hal left, he turned and added, "Also, I think you should know, Ava was encouraging Wesley to go to his dad's grave today. They're going together."

He offered the information as if it was supposed to redeem her. But I knew instantly the act was something perverted and strange. "Why should she want to go there?"

"It's for him," Hal said.

I shook my head. "It's for her. I'm sure of it."

Ava's early dinner was set for 3 p.m. For her, that was breakfast. I did my best to avoid her all day. I busied myself outside and in the barn. Once again there wasn't a single trace of owls nesting in the rafters. Whatever she was doing in there, she was cleaning up after herself.

Wesley fetched me in the orchard mid-afternoon. "Dinner's ready, Mom." I followed him back to the house and gasped at the sight of a bloody tarp, draped over the old wood table from the barn. A bucket of blood and entrails sat outside the kitchen door.

I studied the remains, slack-jawed.

"Ava didn't think you wanted us slaughtering things in the barn with all the apples. So we did it here," Wes explained. "We're having wild turkey, Mom."

"Wild turkey?" I shook my head. "Where on Earth did you find one? In three decades, I've never seen—"

"Perhaps you don't know where to look." Ava stood in the kitchen doorway. The sides of her white apron were spotted with bloody fingerprints. "Wesley and I discovered our scrumptious little delicacy wandering the woods this morning. It's my specialty and my treat for you all. Have you ever eaten fowl hours after its death, Jean?"

"Farm-raised, yes," I said. "Never straight out of the wild, I have to admit."

"It's a different experience when it comes from the forest floor." Ava smiled. "You'll enjoy it."

I took another look into the bucket and spotted the turkey's head. Wet, red down clung to what remained of its neck. My stomach turned. I met Ava's eyes again. The corners of her mouth inched upward. Was this a message for me? *I will cut you up and roast you*, that smirk seemed to say.

"Why are you saving these remains, Ava?"

"Blood pudding." She opened the door and gestured for me to enter. "Tomorrow. It's delicious."

The house smelled like Thanksgiving dinner. Ava had set the table with my grandmother's embroidered tablecloth and fine china. Wes pulled out the head chair for me, and then proceeded to seat his wife across from me. Steam crept from beneath the foil covering my good serving dishes.

Hal entered, swirling a glass of red wine. "Where did you say this bottle was from, Ava?"

"Tuscany. I could order another for you easily."

"It's excellent!" Hal sat to my right. He smiled and squeezed my hand, glassy-eyed and red faced. My ally was turning to the other side. I couldn't deny that Ava knew exactly how to charm the men of this family. It didn't take her long to figure out the way to Hal's good side was through his drink.

"Ava," I said. "Please ask permission before you use my things. This isn't an everyday tablecloth. It was my grandmother's. In fact, everything here is for special occasions."

Ava let out a soft "Oh." She covered her heart. "I apologize so deeply. I only wanted to make this meal a special one."

"Mom," Wesley whispered. "Please. She meant well."

"This *is* a special dinner," Hal said. "And I think we should say grace. Ava, as the chef, I think you should lead us."

"I couldn't," Ava waved her hands. "The honor belongs to you, Hal, as the head of this family. I insist."

Hal smiled. "All right, then." We all held hands. Mine in Hal and Wesley's. Theirs in Ava's. "Bless us our Lord, for these thy gifts, which we are about to receive, from thy bounty, through Christ our Lord." Hal tightened his grip. "Amen. Let's dig in!"

Hal passed the sides my way. I took modest portions of Ava's mashed turnip and potatoes, vegetable medley, and sliced turkey breast—fresh from the forest. The skin was roasted to crisp brown perfection. Wes and Hal sang praises as they gorged on everything.

"Ava, this is amazing!" Hal declared.

"You are too kind, Hal." Ava's large eyes zeroed in on me. "Jean, is this to your liking?"

Stone-faced, I took a morsel of potatoes on the edge of my fork and tasted. They were creamy and flavorful. I cut off a piece of meat and sampled it. It was juicy and tender. "The turkey is a little gamey," I said. "Unusual, but very interesting. Thank you for cooking, Ava."

Wesley and Hal said nothing. Ava smiled politely.

Hal took another sip of wine. He slurred, "Okay, um…I think maybe we need to discuss the elephant in the room."

Or the bird of prey, I thought to myself. *Maybe we should discuss her.*

"Ava, the past few years have been hard on everyone in our family," Hal said. "Jean especially. We are thrilled that Wesley is home. And we're honored to have you as our guest. But your marriage…" Hal glanced to me, trying to gauge my reaction. "Was very sudden and unexpected. So this transition is not an easy one."

It seems easy enough for you, Hal, I wanted to say. *A little wine, a handful of lies, and a heaping pile of flattery. That's all it took.*

"I know what you're thinking, Jean," Ava said. "It's perfectly natural—mother's instinct—not to trust me. That is why Hal has taken to me easily, and you remain suspicious."

I scowled. "That's not what it is, Ava. Literally everything about you is suspicious."

"Jean." Hal reached for me. "Maybe we can listen to Ava for a while, and then you can have your turn to speak."

"I've given Ava every chance to speak. I've given Wesley every chance to tell me how they met, who she is, and what strange things she's doing at all hours of the night—"

"Strange things?" Ava smiled. "What strange things, Jean?"

My heart pounded. She had me trapped. The truth was not

going to set me free. It would make me sound crazy. *You've been conducting weird rituals with owls, Ava. You've been giving me nightmares.*

"Jean?" Hal asked. "If you saw something strange. You need to…say what it was."

She's bewitching my son. She's some kind of monster.

"I can't believe you, unless you tell me," Hal whispered.

"I don't know," I said softly. It *was* crazy.

Ava broke the silence. "Jean, I think perhaps I understand more than you think. You have stoically survived severe grief over a living son and a dead husband for a very long time. To see your son return to you with me has made you feel like you have lost him once again. But he will only ever be my husband, and he will only ever be your son. There is room for both of us in his life."

"Ava's right, Mom," Wesley said.

"Okay." I sighed. "If my instincts about you are wrong, Ava, then…I'm sorry." I stood to leave.

"Mom." Wesley reached out and grabbed my wrist. It reminded me of tucking him in at night. When I would leave, he would clutch my nightgown. He used to need me. He used to want me there, and now he didn't. He never would again.

Maybe Ava *was* right. Maybe I was mistaking mother's misery for mother's instinct.

"Mom, I love you," Wesley said. "And I love Ava too. This will all work out." Something was wrong with Wes's wrist. Inside the sleeve of his dress shirt, long dark marks showed.

I reached down and took his sleeve. I started to peel it back. "Wesley, what's—"

He snatched his arm back.

"Do you have scars?" I looked to Hal for support. His face was sallow. He shook his head as if to say, *Don't ask about that.*

Ava's polite smirk persisted. And I had nothing more to say.

I went up to my bedroom and stared out at the barn. Years ago, I could sit upstairs in the afternoon, take a break, drink my tea and watch everyone working hard. The orchard had been a well-oiled machine then. Everyone had loved maintaining it.

Gold leaves rippled in the wind. Fall would end soon. Hal headed into town in the late afternoon. My ally was gone. Around 6:00 p.m., I watched from the window as Ava's black SUV disappeared through the grove in a cloud of dust. Hal had said they were going to Wesley's father's grave, but sunset was fast approaching. The cemetery was a good drive away, and it closed after dusk.

I put it out of my mind. I would have at least an hour to investigate that woman. I entered the guest bedroom. Ava's purple suitcases were stacked on the dresser, but a small leather-bound journal with gilded pages rested on the nightstand.

Inside the journal, gorgeous curved script looped in stark black ink. The words looked like they could be Spanish, some Latin, but I couldn't translate anything interesting. One hauntingly familiar word caught my eye: *Stryxus.*

The name repeated over and over, in what looked like poems, or possibly prayers. *Stryxus. Stryxus. Stryxus.* Finally I found a line that triggered my high school Spanish: *Stryxus Dios De La Noche.* God of the Night.

I placed the book back where I'd found it. My hands shook. Wesley had named Stryxus in my dream, but I had never heard the word before then.

I hurried to the computer in the office downstairs and searched. The results included strange pictures and stories from fantasy and science-fiction websites. But above the results was an alternate search option: "Strix."

I clicked the word, and the page filled with owls. White owls, grey owls, spotted owls. *Strix* was a scientific classification, a genus of owl. The angry red and black eyes of a wood owl glared at me, and I shut off the monitor.

There was no way I could have subconsciously known the connection between owls and the name that haunted both my dream and Ava's journal. Wesley's voice echoed in my head. *Stryxus, Mommy. He lives in the owls and waits night after night, year after year. Waits for a broken soul to nest his essence!*

Hal would not believe me. But it was clear that Ava was doing something evil to my son. And I would have to stop her.

Out of the corner of my eye, I noticed the office closet was open a crack. My heart filled with dread: the family pictures. I'd tucked them away in a drawer after my husband's final visit to the City of Lights.

I entered the closet and opened the chest drawers. A three-photo frame was on top of a mussed-up pile of photos. The first frame had a picture of Wes as a baby. The third, his 8th grade graduation. I knew the one that was missing from the middle: preschool, the blue and white polo. The one Wesley had worn in my dream. Ava had it for some perverse purpose.

I raced back upstairs to Wesley and Ava's bedroom. I opened the first purple suitcase and rummaged through her clothes. I tossed velvet gowns and feathered shawls over my shoulder, but I couldn't find the picture.

I tossed the first suitcase onto the bed, opened the second one, and gasped. A black wallet full of knives and sharp metal instruments, hooks, pins, and scissors lay atop a pile of strange tarps and blankets. A canister of dried, mummified mice was tucked to one side. Metal charms shaped like owls, feathers, trees, and talons were strung to a silver chain. Two mason jars were half full of blue and black ink.

My heart hammered. Why leave all of this unlocked unless she *wanted* me to find it. It was as if she had nothing to fear from me whatsoever.

I shut the suitcase and zipped it. I tried my best to stuff her clothes back in the other suitcase and put things back the way they had been. But I couldn't get those sharp instruments and knives out of my mind. What had she used them for? What kind of retreat had Wesley been on?

If Ava was a cultist, how deeply had her claws sunk into Wes?

A white feather boa had flown partially under the bed. I stooped to retrieve it and discovered an unusual shape under the bedframe. Something had been pinned to the bottom board.

I wiggled my way beneath the bed, yanked the object free, and pulled myself back into the light. It was a bird's foot with four curved talons. Ava had driven a silver pin through a dried owl claw and stuck it to the underside of the bed. I was too furious to be afraid or disgusted. I clutched the owl claw and took it into my room. Beneath my bed, right where my head would normally rest upon my pillow, was the owl's other foot, pinned in place. I knew then what was clouding my mind at night.

It was checkmate for someone. Ava would see that I'd removed her voodoo trinkets, but I wasn't about to put them back. I called Hal and got his voicemail. "Hal, I need you here as soon as possible. I have evidence that Ava's trying to hurt us. We have to confront them. You need to get here before they return from the cemetery. Please hurry."

My heart pounded. Trying to reach Hal in the afternoon was always a gamble. He could be at any one of six different taverns. He might not get the message until late. I couldn't call the police because—so far as I knew—Ava hadn't technically done anything illegal.

I burned the owl claws in a metal bucket outside, and waited for Wesley and Ava to return.

By the time the SUV pulled into the driveway, I had tried Hal's phone five times without luck. The sun had long since set. Curiously, Ava was behind the wheel this time.

She rounded the vehicle, opened the door for Wesley, and helped him out. My son's eyes were dark and sunken. His skin was pale and waxy. I rushed outside.

"Wesley!"

Ava whispered in Wesley's ears. When I got close, she patted his back and said. "Go to Mother, my love. I will handle things."

"What happened?" I shouted. "Wesley, what's wrong!"

Ava's dark eyes narrowed at me. "It was difficult for Wesley to see his father. Please take him inside and get him something to drink."

"Wes?" I held his face. His eyes were glassy, unresponsive. "Wes, come inside. It's okay."

"Good, Wesley. Go to Mother," Ava repeated.

Ava's nurturing tone unsettled me. After finding her arsenal of pins and blades, I had no idea what to make of it. I just helped my son.

Ava climbed back into the SUV. She started the engine and drove toward the barn.

I guided Wesley into the kitchen, sat him at the table, and gave him a glass of water. He gulped it down. His knuckles were caked with soil; black grit showed beneath his fingernails. "Oh God, Wes," I whispered. "What have you been doing?"

He shook his head. "Mom," he whispered. "I don't know."

"What don't you know?"

Tears carved paths in the dust on Wesley's cheeks. "Who she is or how I met her. I don't even know how we got here! I don't know how old she is!" He sobbed.

I held him. Cradled his head. "It's okay, Wes. It's okay."

"I'm sorry, Mom! I had no idea what I was doing until it was over!"

"No idea what? What did she make you do?"

Wesley sobbed harder.

"It's all right," I said. "We'll get to the bottom of it. We'll get rid of her."

He sighed. "Okay."

The phone rang, and I answered it. "Jean, I just got your message," Hal sounded alarmed but sober, thankfully.

"What's going on? Is everyone okay?"

"Just get here as soon as you can. Talk to Wesley, keep him on the phone."

I handed Wes the phone. "Tell Uncle Hal what's been going on. Just keep talking to him, about anything, until he gets here. I'll go outside and keep her busy until he arrives, okay?"

Wes nodded. His face was red and wet, his hands dirty. It reminded me of his first time at bat in little league. Wes had been afraid of the ball. He'd struck out and one of his teammates made fun. He cried in my arms in the back seat all the way home.

Wesley lifted the phone to his ear. "Uncle Hal...I don't know if it's okay...all right...thanks."

I approached the kitchen door. Wesley started to mumble under his breath. I reminded myself again that he might tell Hal something he wouldn't tell a mother, and I ventured outside.

Ava had backed the SUV halfway through the open barn doors. She was unloading something. I approached the barn. My heart pounded. I would talk to her about Wes for as long as possible. I would pretend to be apologetic, grateful. Just buy time. Make sure she didn't go back inside near my son until Hal arrived.

I entered the barn. Ava stood with her back to me.

"Ava, Wesley's doing okay. I think we should leave him alone with his thoughts."

Her head swiveled. She nodded and smiled.

"I...um...I wanted to thank you for..."

Her sick smile widened. Her eyebrows arched, but she wasn't looking at me. She was looking behind me.

I slowly turned. The back hatch of the SUV was open. Upon a brown tarp lay a pile of yellow bones. My guts quivered. I stumbled. Leaned upon the barn door for support.

Ava's body turned to match her head. She folded her clawed hands together in satisfaction. "Wesley has brought his father home. So you can all be together one last time."

I screamed and ran toward the house. Wesley stood outside the kitchen door. He didn't have the phone. His eyes were vacant, his expression stern. I didn't have to hear him speak to know that in that moment, he wasn't my son. Something had changed inside him.

Wesley strode toward me, and I veered toward the orchard. I raced down a row of trees and tripped on a stray apple. My shoulder hit the ground hard. I cried out and turned onto my back. A dizzying frenzy of white wings churned in the sky.

Owls whooshed like ghosts over the trees. One landed on a

nearby branch; its obsidian eyes pierced through me. Somehow, I knew it was the one that had been in charge of watching me at night.

The others crisscrossed the air above the golden canopy. I struggled to my feet and ran again. I didn't get far before a massive force battered me from behind onto my knees. An enormous brown and white speckled owl flapped its five-foot wingspan right in my face. It was a great horned owl with stern, yellow eyes and dark, feathery horns, three times the size of Ava's barn owls.

Powerful talons clutched my wrist and yanked my right arm backward. A second great horned owl was dragging me toward the barn. Its brother snatched my opposite wrist and pulled. Claws broke skin.

I struggled and screamed, but their grip was iron tight. More barn owls swooped between the branches. They scratched my face. Tore my clothes. The pair of great horned owls forced me back. Scores of near silent wings swirled the air.

I struggled to breathe, went limp, and fell into darkness.

Two voices chanted:

"May Lord Stryxus spread his wings
And cast shadow o'er the Earth
Let the treetops fill the sky
Snuff the fires of human hearth."

Wesley and Ava repeated the chant over and over.

I opened my eyes. The two of them blurred into focus. We were in the barn. Wesley wore only a pair of blue jeans. Black and blue tattoos covered his bare torso. Designs of trees and talons ran up his sides. Branches and wings carved their way down his arms. The dark, inky eyes of a horned owl covered his heart. My son's eyes were cold and expressionless. Mud smeared his cheeks.

Ava wore an evergreen gown. Her collar was slit down the center to just above her navel. Her silvery hair was woven into a long, thick braid, crowned by a feathery wreath. She craned her head toward me. "Mother is awake." A circle of torches flickered, casting lanky shadows against the apples.

I tried to move, but ropes bound my waist and wrists against the barn's center pillar. Soft hooting floated from the rafters. I looked up to find scores of Ava's white barn owls perched across the wooden beams. The pair of great horned owls flanked the ridge over the barn doors.

"Wesley, help!" I pleaded. "Don't listen to her!"

"Shh." Ava glided to me. She clutched my chin with black fingernails. "He cannot hear you anymore. His mind has been emptied of all troublesome things. His old world of chaos, sadness and disappointment is gone. His emptiness shall be filled with the dark truths of Lord Stryxus."

"You're insane!" I spat right between her eyes.

Ava casually wiped her face. Her body revolved, and she walked towards Wesley. Her head remained a perfect 180 degrees backward, facing me as she spoke. "You were a good mother, Jean. I owe you, at the very least, a lesson on why I am not insane."

"Do tell." *Keep her talking*, I thought. Maybe Hal was still coming.

"Before there was light, there was darkness. Before man or woman or animal, there was beautiful chaos. The world you live in today is not the realm of harmony that your people and your god have deluded you into believing. It is a shroud that smothers powers long forgotten. A veil that conceals the chaos beneath."

Ava circled a pile of dry, gold leaves and branches, apples were still attached to some of them. At the bottom of the pile I could make out long, yellow shapes: my husband's bones.

"Before man, the most terrible and respected power was Lord Stryxus. Stryxus was the darkness. Stryxus was the night. Stryxus was the shadow, glorious and eternal. But the lords of light created that first spark in the darkness that led to war. A struggle that lasted eons. A tiny flame grew to a beacon, to stars and sun. Soon the darkness fell to gods of selfishness, greed, and destruction, and the path was paved for men and women.

"Lord Stryxus was defeated, but not destroyed. He can never be destroyed. He survives in the night, the ever-living darkness which clings to one end of the Earth. Stryxus dwells in the hearts and minds of his loyal servants."

Ava raised her arms to the rafters. Pale owls glared down, hooted, and splintered the wood beneath their claws.

"I have searched this world of men and women for close to a century in the service of Lord Stryxus, with complete faith that someday I would find a man, broken and desperate in spirit but strong in courage, who would host the return of our Dark Lord."

I gritted my teeth. "I'm only going to tell you one last time: Leave my son alone."

Ava smiled. "That is the very spirit we require, Jean. You and your husband clearly loved your son. You raised him to believe in good things. And yet without you, in the throes of chaos, Wesley crumbled and broke. When I met him, I knew instantly that he was the perfect candidate. I secluded him for months. Starved him. Warped him. Remade him into this empty vessel."

"Stop it," I hissed.

Ava's fingernails traced the blue and black ink on Wesley's torso. "I branded him as my Lord's property. Conditioned him for—"

"Stop!"

"Good, Jean! Feed the tragedy." She wrapped her clawed fingers around Wesley's neck and kissed him.

I wanted to scream, but I choked it back. That's what Ava wanted too. I was part of this. She was breaking me as much as she was him. Anger would not save us.

Ava's lips released Wesley's expressionless face. She approached me again and produced the photograph of Wesley in preschool. "Remember him as he was." She held the photo inches from my face. Wesley's young eyes sparkled, his pearly teeth showed through his wide grin.

Ava held the picture over a flickering torch. It caught orange and yellow flame. She carried it to the pile of branches, leaves, and bones and placed it atop. Flame swept over the crackly brown foliage and wrapped around the wood. The fire spread quickly. The sickly sweet smell of charred apple filled the barn.

"Despair breeds despair," Ava said. "Know that your child is gone. Burned up in the light of your world. And when the light of this fire dies out, so too will all hope for mankind. All creatures of daylight."

Ava raised her arms and proclaimed: "May His Dark Lord's Vessels release His Essence! And may ever-living Darkness prepare His rebirth!"

Ava's eyes darkened to pitch. The owls above began to screech, louder and louder. I stared up in horror as the barn owls raised their heads, flapped their wings and stretched their narrow beaks wide. Inky rivers of shadow snaked from their mouths and pooled in the ceiling. Darkness swirled above, turning the barn roof into a chasm of shadowy nothing, blacker than outer space.

The streams of darkness emptied from each owl. And then one by one, each bird dropped. They plummeted from the rafters and thudded on the ground all around us. The thuds overlapped, bashing the ground like bags of sand. After the final owl fell, darkness engulfed the ceiling and a pair of round, red eyes opened in the abyss.

When they opened, every bone in my body hardened to ice. My heart sank away. My mind clouded into fog. I couldn't begin to explain what lurked behind those eyes. But they informed me instantly that I was meaningless and pathetic. They swallowed my every hope and desire with a glance, and drowned them in a blood-red ocean.

Ava extended her arms at the shadowy, red-eyed mass. "Lord Stryxus has returned! Enter the vessel I have prepared for you and fill this void with limitless power!"

Even broken beneath the crimson glare of her god, all it took for me to resist was that woman's voice.

"He's not a void," I said.

Ava's black eyes turned on me.

"He's not a void!" I shouted louder. "He'll never be empty! He'll always be my beautiful, wonderful, inquisitive child. Wherever he goes, whatever mistakes he makes. Whatever wicked people abuse him, or mislead him, or take advantage of him. You'll never empty him. You'll never destroy him. Because I'll always have him with me. And you'll never break me."

And then I saw it. The faint trace of recognition in my son's eyes. A blink. A scrunching of his forehead. Wesley was listening.

Ava scowled. She gestured to the ceiling. "You delude yourself with a mother's lies before a god more powerful than anything on this Earth! You are *nothing* to him. A speck of dirt on a meaningless world."

"If I'm nothing, then why am I here? If your god is so powerful, then why does he need us?" I laughed. "Who's deluding who, Ava?"

Ava stalked across the floor. She slapped me. Her claws scraped my cheek. The darkness in her eyes swelled. The bonfire flickered. Branches cracked and leaves crumbled into ash.

I smiled in spite of the pain. I was getting to her. Ruining the ritual. "Wesley, listen to me. Your father and I will always love you. And no matter how far you wander, you'll carry us with you."

Ava slapped me again.

"Even if we're mad or disappointed, we're on your side!" I shouted. "You'll always be full of light."

Ava's hands clutched my neck. She squeezed my throat. The darkness from the ceiling seemed to cave in on us. The circle of torches snuffed out. Smoke lingered in the air. The bonfire died down. I struggled uselessly. Ava's claws tightened.

A strong hand grabbed Ava's shoulder and yanked her away from me. I gasped for air.

Wesley clutched Ava by the upper arms. He hurled her to the ground, and she tumbled toward the bonfire.

"Wesley," I choked. "I knew you'd come."

Wesley worked quickly to untie my bonds. "I'm sorry, Mom," he said. "I couldn't think straight."

Ava lay face down in the dirt. Her head swiveled 180 degrees. A devilish, toothy grin crossed her face. Her dark eyes gleamed at the ceiling. "You're too late!" she shouted. "The fire is lit! Stryxus awaits!"

The bonfire was dying out. Ash and glowing logs remained, but the flames were sparse.

Wesley freed my hands, but an invisible force knocked him away. He flew ten feet onto his back and convulsed. Shadow spilled from the ceiling and swirled into a dark oval. A creature with huge red eyes and shadowy horns loomed over Wesley. It spread its terrible wings and opened its hooked beak. The same river of inky darkness that had poured from the barn owls now swirled into Wesley's face.

He cried out in agony.

I worked myself free of the remaining bonds. The firelight was almost completely gone. The blood red eyes of the creature grew brighter than anything else in the barn. I raced to the work shelves in back, stumbling over owl carcasses. Even in complete darkness, I knew where everything was. After thirty years, I could harvest and sort apples blind in that barn.

My hands discovered the plastic handle of a rectangular container. Gasoline sloshed inside it.

Wesley's screams were unbearable. I rushed past the wings of the horrible thing and found the last glowing embers of Ava's bonfire. I hastily unscrewed the gas cap.

Ava appeared out of the darkness. She screeched like an animal and knocked me over. The noxious odor of gas met my nostrils as liquid spilled into the dirt. Ava's claws tore at my clothes. She bent over to bite my neck, and I kneed her in the stomach.

She doubled over. I groped for the spilling container. Ava

moved for me again. This time I punched her right on the jaw. She shrieked and collapsed.

Wesley's cries were scratchy and inhuman now. I ignored the shadowy mass behind me, found the gas container, still about half full of fuel, and sloshed it onto the bonfire. Yellow flame shot into the air.

The dark creature howled.

I poured the remaining fuel all around the base of the fire. Hot white pillars illuminated the barn.

Ava screeched. She lunged for me, but I stepped aside. Her gasoline-soaked gown caught fire. She fell to her knees and reached for her god in futility. Her dark eyes melted. Blue fire swam over her perfect, porcelain skin. Her face winced and crackled into a black husk.

The monster over Wesley screamed as well. The river of shadow ceased to flow from its beak. Ava's Dark Lord flapped its shadowy wings and squinted its red eyes against the intense light of the bonfire.

I took one of Ava's torches and held it in the fire until it caught. I thrust it towards the shadowy god until it retreated from my son. Stryxus backed against the wooden support pillar. His cries were unearthly, monstrous, but still they oozed fear.

I shoved my torch through the dark mass, and the shadows burned away like paper. Its red eyes bled into orange and yellow fog and faded into nothing.

Smoke filled the barn. I coughed and covered my mouth and nose with my shirt. Wesley struggled to his hands and knees. We helped one another outside. After we pushed through the barn doors, I took one last look over my shoulder.

Ava collapsed. Her bones crumbled into a pile of dust. I smiled.

The old barn burned. The flames grew bigger and brighter over the next hour. Firelight flickered against the golden yellow trees. The night was cold. But we didn't care. We watched from a safe distance until the first rays of dawn broke over the hills. The barn collapsed into a pile of charred wood, and a cloud of orange sparks exploded against the rising sun.

Wesley slept the following day away. Hal arrived early in the morning. He had plenty of questions that I couldn't bring myself to answer. I told him Ava was never coming back. The insurance company would have to be satisfied that the barn fire had been an accident. It would be nice to have a new one anyway. A new chapter in all our lives.

Hal wanted to see Wesley, but I asked him to come back later that week. I wanted Wesley to sleep. I wanted him to myself for now. Soon we'd have to assess all the damage that woman had done to him, physically and mentally. But in that moment, I was content to have my sleeping boy back.

Hal didn't argue. In fact he said he was tired himself. But as Hal left, I spotted tattooed talons curving up his neck. Feathery patterns showed through the cuffs of his sleeves.

The Hedge

Tiffany Morris

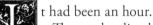t had been an hour.

The patchouli at her temples was burning into her nostrils. The thick myrrh incense smoke felt like it had unravelled directly into her lungs. Rosemary's voice grew hoarse. She paused for a sip of water and glanced around the Barrows' darkened kitchen. The candles cast strange shadows on the dated oak cabinets.

Mrs. Barrow opened one eye, then the other.

"Is it working?" she asked Rosemary, her face wan. Her blonde hair glowed white against the candlelight. Rosemary saw Mr. Barrow furrow his brow, eyes still closed. At the other end of the table, their teenage son's fingers tapped frantically against his phone.

"Jeremy," Mrs. Barrow hissed. She looked embarrassed.

"I'm liveblogging this," he said, his mouth twisted with glee.

Rosemary glared at him.

"No phones," she said, her voice still gruff. "It's part of the contract. The signals create disruption between the spirits and me."

"I'm sure," Jeremy said. "That sounds like a Real Thing."

Rosemary closed her violet-coloured eyes again, hoping that the Barrows would follow suit. Their house was indeed haunted. She had seen an old lady and a little girl at the bottom of the stairs when she arrived, but they had simply smiled at her and walked away. The disturbances this family had reported—things falling from shelves, malevolent whispers at night, knives floating in mid-air—suggested a different sort of spirit.

Rosemary hummed to herself.

"It might be better if your son leaves," she suggested.

When she opened her eyes, the Barrows looked at her, aghast.

"He can't leave, he's experienced things, too," Mrs. Barrow said, an edge of hysteria in her voice.

"We should've gone with Julie Weathers," Mr. Barrow muttered.

"She was booked, Harold," Mrs. Barrow said.

Her face reddened even in the candlelight. She turned to Rosemary.

"Sorry, it's just, you don't have a website, we had to go by your Yelp reviews."

Rosemary sighed deeply. She felt an itch at the small of her back. Her knee already ached from sitting for too long. This kitchen, large and immaculate as it was, felt stifling. The air was thick with teeming suburban rectitude and familial resentment. She wanted to be in her tiny cottage on the outskirts of the city, the small thicket of wilderness before entering suburbia. Maybe she'd make a soup tonight, stop by the grocery store on the way home. She needed to check her balance. She needed to find out on what day her cat, Basil, would have to go to the vet.

She heard three loud knocks on one of the kitchen cabinets. She opened her eyes to see the silhouette of a tall, large man.

"Step into the light," she demanded. Mrs. Barrow jumped. Even Jeremy had stopped playing with his phone, a dim look of apprehension spread across his face.

"Step into the candlelight, please," Rosemary said.

Even to herself, she sounded like a bored TSA agent.

The man stepped forward and revealed his tall, gaunt, charcoal-coloured frame. A malevolent smile stretched too widely across his translucent face.

"Why are you here?" she asked.

"I live here," the man said. His voice sounded like rustling straw.

"You need to move on," she said.

The man stood still. His large, blank eyes peered through her.

"These people," she said, as she gestured with both hands, "are not leaving. You are not among the living. Let this family be and move along."

A low rumble erupted as a plate flew past her face and smashed on the wall behind her. Mrs. Barrow screamed. Jeremy and his father both jumped.

"Sir," Rosemary said. She heard the little girl giggle. The table began to rattle. One by one, the candles blew out. Darkness swept over the room. Faint streams of streetlit night poured in through the window above the sink. All three of the Barrows screamed.

Rosemary's stomach growled. She shifted in her seat, stretching out one leg under the table. Pain radiated from her knee. She massaged it with a sigh.

"May I please speak with the woman of the house?" she asked.

Mrs. Barrow began to speak.

"Not you," Rosemary said.

The old lady reappeared in the dim light of the window.

"What is going on here?" Rosemary asked.

The old lady clucked. "He's so angry, that one. He doesn't scare me. Darn nuisance."

Rosemary nodded. "Can you convince him to leave?"

The old lady pursed her lips.

"I don't want to leave," she said.

Rosemary looked at the Barrows. They stared at her, their mouths agape. She wasn't sure if they could hear the old lady.

"You don't have to," she said in a low voice. "Just get him out."

The old lady laughed, her voice a trickle of water.

"Okay," she said. "I don't much like him, anyway."

Rosemary reached in her pocket for her lighter and lit the

rows of candles once more. The haze of incense smoke had grown even thicker in the dark.

"Is-is it gone?" Mr. Barrow asked with a swallow.

She listened to a low argument in a neighbouring room, followed by the sound of breaking glass. The floor moaned and shuddered.

The lights came back on with a loud pop.

"Yeah," Rosemary said, as she pushed a grey lock of hair behind her ear. She didn't know for sure, but she had faith in the little old lady to finish the job.

Relief spread across their faces. Mr. Barrow grabbed the myrrh incense stick and dunked it in Rosemary's glass of water.

"Terrible smell," he explained. "It's going to take weeks to get it out of here."

He walked over to the kitchen window and opened it. Rosemary breathed in the cool air.

"Did you already get the fee?" Mrs. Barrow asked. She hesitated over her purse.

"No," Rosemary said.

Mr. Barrow shrugged. "I didn't want to pay for something that might not work."

Mrs. Barrow gave him a dirty look and fumbled through her wallet.

"Two hundred?" she asked.

"Two hundred and twenty," Rosemary said. "I quoted that when you booked."

"Yeah, but your reviews said you charge two hundred."

Rosemary sighed. "The twenty is a transportation fee. I don't charge it for people in the city."

"Well, maybe if you had a website where you outlined—"

"Two hundred is fine," Rosemary interrupted, taking the cash from Mrs. Barrow's outstretched hand. "Thank you."

"Really, there should be a discount for clean-up," Mr. Barrow said. He frowned at the wall where the plate had smashed.

"Probably could've just Googled this anyway," Jeremy muttered.

"Jeremy, this is a discussion between your mother, Rosalie

and me," Mr. Barrow warned.

Rosemary didn't bother to correct him.

"I must be off," she said, stepping over the porcelain shards on the laminate floor. "Thank you for your business."

Rosemary walked briskly to the foyer, not pausing over the studio portraits of the smiling family or the thick cinnamon smell of the potpourri on a side table. As she pulled open the door, she glanced behind her. The old lady stood at the bottom of the stairs, a frown spread across her face. The little girl was nowhere to be seen.

"Where's the little girl?" Rosemary asked.

The old lady looked confused. "I don't know a little girl," she said.

Rosemary paused, but didn't know what else to say. She nodded and closed the door. She prayed that her car would start without a fuss.

The grocery store lights buzzed fluorescent as bright food packages screamed from the shelves. Even at 10 pm, the store was full of hurried bodies. They slammed into her elbow, jostled her out of place to reach past her. She hated the grocery store, the aggressive masses of people. She paused over the vegetables in the crisper section and got a faint whiff of their earthy smell. Her knee continued to throb as she waited in the seemingly unending grocery line. The customers ahead of her bickered with the cashier over coupons and discounts. She felt her patience and energy draining. Rosemary wordlessly paid the total and stepped out into the dark expanse of parking lot.

A faint giggle echoed in the darkness. A child.

Not now, she willed the spirit with her mind.

The giggle cut through again, louder this time. Small footsteps sounded behind her. Her heart beat faster and she picked up her pace on the way to the car. The jostle of traffic had died down.

Her hand shook as she opened her trunk and threw the groceries inside. They tumbled over in a haphazard pile. A white silhouette darted past her car. The giggle had grown into a full laugh. It billowed like wind. Rosemary stared straight ahead as she got into the car. The white silhouette—the little girl—ran past the hood. She started the ignition and backed out, more than ready to finish the exhausting night.

The cottage was chilly, a draft set in with the early autumn cold. Rosemary reminded herself to winterize the cottage sooner rather than later. She'd probably have to do more spirit work in order to afford the repairs.

She pushed her worried thoughts out of her mind and felt happy as she heated up some soup stock. She snapped and rinsed the vegetables, chopped them into large chunks and threw them in the large metal pot. She smiled as she ate and read the news from the day.

Her belly full of hearty soup, Rosemary curled up under the quilts on her bed. Basil jumped up and purred. Rosemary was too tired to do her usual night incantations. Instead, she opted to read a book by candlelight, her body covered in her homemade lavender salve for relaxation. She felt her head grow heavy as she nodded off. Her reading glasses slid down her nose and onto the patchwork.

A giggle jostled her awake.

Rosemary started. Her bleary eyes darted around the room. She heard the giggle once again.

"Cut it out," she yawned. She did not want to deal with this spirit. Rosemary realized that she hadn't grounded herself before leaving the Barrows' and groaned. That must have been why the girl followed her home. She was getting clumsy in her old age.

"Leave me alone," Rosemary said as she blew out the candle. Basil pounced off the bed and hissed into the darkness. The rest of the night passed in quiet and sleep.

Rosemary awakened with pale daylight streaming through her window. She dozily looked at the alarm clock. The green digital letters bounced as they read 11:09. She sat up with a jolt, remembered that it was her day off. No wage slavery in the city. No spirit work to be done. She went to the kitchen, heated up some coffee and opened her laptop. Her eyes scanned her e-mail for potential clients. Nothing but spam. With an equal mix of dread and relief, she turned off the computer. She gazed out her window, into the grey day. It would be a great day to forage—not too hot with the last remnants of summer, not too cold with the onset of fall.

Rosemary's whole body ached as she got ready, but she refused to stay in for the day and take it easy. She needed willow bark, an odd assortment of mushrooms, cedar scrapings. She couldn't kneel before her altar on the way out, but instead tossed a loose scatter of tobacco onto the offering plate and asked for a good day's harvest.

Dark wicker basket in hand, Rosemary waded into the woods. The scent of pine was thick in the air. She breathed it in deeply. Her heart surged with joy. There, in that small thicket of wilderness, was where she belonged.

Her hands shook slightly as she hunched over. She scattered needles on the forest floor, looked for fallen bits of moss and bark. She steadied herself. Behind her, she heard a shriek. Probably a fox, she thought, ignoring it.

The shriek grew louder. Rosemary pulled herself back up with some effort and felt dizzy. A deer appeared thirty feet away. A horrible screech wailed from its mouth. She stood still, her whole body frozen, as she watched it stop. It turned its head toward her and sniffed before it turned and walked deeper into the woods.

Rosemary decided to walk in the opposite the direction of the deer, just in case it was sick with some sort of disease. Her heart rate returned to normal as she walked. The sweet sounds of birds trilling filled the air. She went to her favourite tree, a black willow, in a clearing not too far away. When she climbed under it, she felt the leaves brush against her hair. Happiness swelled in her again as she ran her hands along the knobby bark. She pulled a small knife from her pouch, ready to scrape a small sliver.

A giggle darted around her.

"Go away," she said, her annoyance clear in her voice.

A white silhouette darted between the branches. Rosemary looked around the side of the tree.

"Up here," a tiny voice said.

Rosemary gazed up into the branches. Irritation and fear ran through her veins. A little girl in 1940s clothing smiled down at her. She looked familiar, but Rosemary couldn't place her.

"Do you hear the bells?" the girl whispered. A smile broke across her face. She hid her face and let loose another titter.

Rosemary listened. The breeze swayed the leaves and carried the faint sound of church bells.

"What do you want?" Rosemary asked.

The little girl was gone.

Rosemary had to do a ritual when she got home. The little girl would have to move on, or at least go bother someone else. She scraped the bark into her plastic container and snapped the lid shut as she finished. She backed out from under the tree and walked into the woods, now thick with fog. An owl hooted. A chill clamped itself onto her skin. Her steps grew laboured as she walked along the forest path and back into her cottage. Weariness climbed from her spine to her neck.

Inside, Basil refused to move off his perch on the table. He hissed at Rosemary as she threw down her kitchen keys. She set her basket on the floor.

"Basil," she cooed. "What's wrong?"

She cautiously held her hand out to the cat. His yellow eyes stared up at her. She put her hand closer to him. His teeth clamped down on her bony hand.

"Ow," she said. "Basil!"

Basil had never bitten her before. Her eyes welled up with pain and betrayal. He'd broken the skin, she realized, as she ran her hand under the tap. The cold water offered no relief. The chill settled into her bones. Her good hand scrambled through her cupboards. She pulled down her jars of white sage, yarrow and elder. She laboured over a poultice and felt resentful as she wrapped the wound.

Rosemary heaved her exhausted body onto the bed with a long exhale. Maybe I'm getting too old for this, she thought, with a grimace. The day to day grind, the rituals, the foraging. She didn't want to go to the city, a seniors' home. She wasn't enjoying anything anymore, but she definitely wouldn't enjoy that. Her hand throbbed as she drifted into an unintended nap, full of fitful sleep.

Her phone rang. And rang. And rang. Rosemary pulled herself awake.

"Hello," she grumbled into the phone on her bedside table. Her head spun and throbbed.

"It's almost time," a tiny voice said.

"Fuck off," Rosemary snarled. She surprised herself with the venom in her voice.

The voice laughed and the line cut.

Rosemary turned over in her bed. The sky outside had grown dark. She sipped some old water on the side of the bed. Her lips trembled under the weight of the glass. She struggled to remember her friend Diana's phone number. Diana was a diviner, she trafficked in symbols. She would know what was going on. Rosemary fumbled through her black address book. Her eyes strained to decipher the blue snarls of handwriting. The tones thundered in her ear as she dialled the numbers.

"Hello?" Diana asked.

"Diana," Rosemary said. "Hi. I need your help."

"I can't make it out there, dear," Diana said. "My grandson's coming to see me."

"No, it's not that," she said, her head pounding. "I've been seeing this spirit, she's following me."

Diana chuckled. "That's nothing new to you."

"No," Rosemary said, with a hint of smile. "But it's different. She-she called me. I heard bells. An owl hooting in the day."

Diana's silence at the other end was deafening.

"Diana?" Rosemary said, a note of panic in her voice.

"It's nothing, Rosemary," Diana said. Her voice was uncertain. "I'll come see you tomorrow morning. Don't strain yourself."

"Okay," Rosemary said. A knot of fear formed in her chest. She knew Diana refused to give people bad readings and would give them vague answers instead.

Rosemary pulled herself off the bed. The muffled sound of a child running came from the hallway, behind her closed bedroom door. She hesitated before she pulled the knob and opened it

Nothing.

Basil hissed at her as she walked out. She looked down at her swollen hand as she padded into the kitchen to fix herself a drink. The glass of the bottles and jars rattled with her shaking good hand.

The computer, Rosemary thought. *I could look it up on there.* She pulled herself over to the laptop and turned it on. The light of it felt blinding. She clicked on the internet symbol and pulled up the search engine.

Owl hooting day omen, she typed. A list of links pulled up. Words like "disaster" and "death" appeared in the text of each option. She clicked the first one.

The hoot of an owl during the day is believed to be an omen of imminent death, the article read. Rosemary felt her blood run cold as she closed the laptop. *Yeah, right,* she thought. She forced herself into disbelief. She'd trust Diana before some website.

Rosemary grabbed her glass of iced tea. She pulled a black shawl over her shoulders and walked out onto her front deck. The wood splinters grabbed at her bare feet, but she barely noticed. *Light a fire,* she told herself. *Light a fire, drink your drink, and get your head together.*

She walked out to her fire pit. Her head was spinning. She threw a few logs onto it and struggled to get it lit. She shivered, her muscles strained from the movement. The embers finally grew into crackling flames that licked the cold air.

Rosemary sat. She heard voices in the distance. They echoed, unearthly. The spirit of a man she'd sent away last week walked up to the fire, a ghastly grin on his face. A young woman walked up, eyes wide. A silent baby was cradled in her arms. Rosemary's eyes darted around her. A family stood at the edge of the flame. Their tattered clothes hung off of gnarled limbs. Two old men stood beside them. They nodded to her. She was circled by a large crowd of dead, their eyes blank, their mouths smiling.

She held the glass of iced tea to her mouth and sucked in the sweet smell of the sugar, spices and lemon. She felt the coldness of the brew, the smoothness of the glass, the tart jolt of the whiskey and ice cubes. She savoured the taste. Her hand shook as it held the glass aloft. The world tilted. She placed the glass on the arm of her chair. It clattered sideways onto the grass as the remnants spilled across her feet.

The little girl walked up to her. She placed a hand on Rosemary's shoulder with a sad smile. Rosemary looked into the child's eyes. Up close, she was able to see their faint violet glow. Her heart fluttered with recognition.

It had been such a long journey.

It'll be time, then, Rosemary thought. She stared out into the ink-black sky. After so many years of spirits coming to her, she now awaited her trip over the hedge, to join the world of the dead. Embers danced from the flames like fireflies, like spirits freed from the mortal plane, drifting toward the aether.

Vial With Her Cure

Jo Wu

here was no sand on the island where we lived. Instead, the ground fluttered with paper. Milk-white paper, parchment paper, coarse news sheets, they all rustled along the ground like stalks of grass, shuddering and shuffling the way wind blows through pages of a book. These pages were scribbled with ink drawings of skeletons, botanical studies, notes on seasonal herbs, and recipes of soups to cure anything from aches, fear of courtship and recurring nightmares.

On these paper shores of my home, I would try to fly, like my mother. However, unlike her, I could not grow wings. So, on my sixth birthday, she built me mechanical ones constructed of aluminum and titanium feathers that strapped to my arms. Yet, even now, at age ten, no matter how hard I tried to flap my arms, no matter how quickly I ran, nor how high I leapt, I always came crashing down onto my knees and stomach.

Moping in defeat upon rustling papers, I would watch Mother soar through the blue skies and the rolling clouds. Wide-spread wings grew from her back, and the feathers glistened like gold and amber. In the sky, she would collect wisps of clouds, like cotton candy whispers, for the airy texture of cakes she may bake. Then, as she dove head-first toward the water, her feathers would scatter off her body like leaves in the wind, revealing porcelain skin as the ocean waves exploded upon her entrance. Right as she dove into the water, her legs fused into scintillating scales, hues of emerald and amethyst. I never went into the sea with her. She feared I would drown. Not only did I lack her gift of growing wings, I could not grow a fin. On many occasions, she would hold my hands as I waded. But I flailed when I started sinking, screamed as the waves stung my eyes, and vomited salt water in a sopping mess. Relegating myself to sitting on the shores, I lived vicariously through her stories of collecting pearls and conversing with sharks and octopi for the spiciest algae under the sea.

Whenever the sun descended, Mother reached for my small hand. "Time to go inside, Ernest. We can't have you under moonlight."

"Why?"

"When you were a baby, I brought you out to see the moon. Rashes tore open all over you. Your cries were so loud, before you nearly suffocated." She nuzzled her cheek against mine. "You'll never know how terrified I was. I would be so lost without you."

When the setting sun painted the sky with fire and lavender, Mother usually ushered me to bed, where she would read me stories or sing lullabies. Other times, she brought me to her boudoir, where I would watch her sit before her golden vanity and paint her face with sable brushes. Tonight, she swept violet and silver powders over her lids, highlighting how her silk gown was as crimson as her lips.

"Mother, where are you going?"

She met my eyes in the mirror and smiled that bloody-rose smile. Her eyes, as black as polished pebbles, always had a cold glisten, like ice reflecting moonlight.

"I'm going to sing tonight."

"Like your lullabies?"

"No. It won't be lullabies."

After a final stroke of kohl, she followed me to my bedroom. It was windowless, safe from any needle-thin slant of moonlight that would try to peek through a curtain. The ceiling told the time of day: a painted, smiling sun up on the ceiling slowly shifted across the domed ceiling to ultimately to make way for the serene moon with red lips. This was the closest to real moonlight I could encounter.

Tucking me into bed, she read me a book about a maiden who wielded the powers of a bear, a wolf and a firebird to save a prince trapped in ice and eternal slumber. Once my door clicked shut behind her, I rolled onto my side, drifting in and out of sleep, like trying to wade into the sea, only to be shoved back to shore by rushing waves. What did she do at night?

I snuck out of bed. In case if I was caught, I would make up an excuse that I just wanted warm milk with honey from the kitchen. She wasn't in her boudoir, nor her bedroom. I thought of the other room she would like, because it was my favorite.

In the library, through the stained glass windows depicting mermaids sitting on rocky shores, ships sailing through clouds, a winged man flying towards the sun, and dragons made of clockwork, there was Mother, sitting upon the balcony outside. The waves of her black tresses, the same color as mine, tumbled past her waist, and her fair skin glowed like starlight. Her midnight-black lace dress fluttered in the breeze as she sat in an iron-wrought chair and scribbled notes in her journal with her small, looped handwriting.

I stayed in the shadows, staring at the moonlight that stretched along the floor. I did not remember the pain she told me I suffered as a baby. Perhaps if I just pushed my big toe into a corner....

It hurt! Blisters erupted on my big toe, and I had to bite the inside of my cheeks to keep from screaming.

Minutes passed before she set down her pen and raised her face to the moonlight. From the way she smiled, one would think she was the happiest woman on earth. Closing her eyes and breathing deeply, she held out her arms to the moon, as if greeting an old friend. As she stood up, her wings grew from her back, stretching in a great span, glowing gold and amber, and catching shards of shadows for black accents.

She tore the page she had just written on from her journal.

Smiling, she watched it flutter from her fingers, joining the pages on the ground below.

Then, she flew off, vanishing into the stars in the night sky.

After drinking warm milk and honey, I sat at the top of the stairs. When would Mother come home? Where was she flying to? What for? How would she react if she knew I was not in bed?

I slumped against the bannister. Closing my eyes, the sharp angles of the stairs almost felt as comfortable as my bed. All was dark and tranquil. The rolling waves outside hummed like steady breaths.

Laughter suddenly rang like bells.

Creeeeeeaakk.

I shot up. The open door of the manor revealed ocean waves that rustled like black clouds at night, fluttering the pages all along the ground of our island, like dragon scales. Mother's wings folded and vanished into her back as she swept into the foyer, followed by a man whose long auburn hair rained puddles onto the carpet.

"It's been a while since you've been at sea, hasn't it, Ambrose?"

"Yes, Lady Velma. I've forgotten what discomfort it brings me!"

As Mother threw back her head in a haughty laugh, I shuffled deeper into the shadows and stared. Who was that man?

Watching them walk toward the study, I tiptoed after them, keeping a distance and ultimately crouching in a dark corner of the hall, staring through the open door.

"It's been so long, Velma," said Ambrose, one leg crossed over the other, holding a glass of wine. "I remember when you willingly went along with his studies."

Mother slammed down her glass. Garnet droplets projectiled against Ambrose's chin. "It was terrible. Caging and chaining me. It was a pure aphrodisiac to be exoticized, but it did not take long for the treatment to become toxic and degrading."

Ambrose looked sheepish. "We *were* fascinated by your powers of the sky and the sea. We wanted to learn from you."

Mother scoffed. "As if I was an object. As if I wasn't alive."

With one arm crossed over her chest, she buried her face in the other hand.

"Velma, you're beautiful." Ambrose, unsure of what to do, stroked her bare arm, which she shook off, like shaking off a fly. "In a situation like that, a man can't resist you."

"I had hoped to marry him. I thought being his subject would make him love me more. I'm happy I destroyed all his works."

"He was a fool. Any man would be proud to marry you." When she didn't respond, hesitation trickled off his tongue. "Don't you have a son?"

Mother glared at him from between her fingers. "You will never meet him."

"So you do have one. We've heard rumors. Is he like you? Able to fly and swim?"

Shooting up from her seat, Mother slammed her fist into the table. The wine glasses smashed onto the floor, and the alcohol spread like pools of blood. As she stabbed her eyes into Ambrose, scarlet shards glowed in her dark eyes, like flickering embers. "You want to take him away, don't you?"

"The facilities would handsomely compensate you."

She slapped him. "How dare you! My son is not a pig for slaughter!"

"Does he look like you?" He smiled as he rubbed his cheek. "Or him? Does he remind you of him?"

She clutched his neck. He gritted his teeth, but a grin clawed at the corners of his lips. "He's a handsome young boy, isn't he? Like his father?"

Malice on Mother's face grew into a wide smile, too large for her face. Her voice dripped like poison. "Yes, he's handsome."

Sharp clenches gave way to caresses as she curled her long fingers beneath his chin. Pursing her lips, she began to sing.

When she sang me lullabies, her tones were more hushed, more gentle. When she sang to him, she filled the entire manor with her vocals. It was sweet, like dark chocolate spreading over a decadent cake. It was warm, like huddling under blankets by a fire on a cold winter night. It curled up against me like gentle tendrils, stroking my heart and filling my ears and trailing down the back of my neck, right over the bony protrusions of my spine. It made my blood rush through my veins and bask in her glory. It beckoned me to forget my worries and fears. But most importantly, it made me smile as I closed my eyes and let her sweep me away into the crevices of bliss, if only for a few minutes. I'm sure Ambrose felt the same.

Spellbound, Ambrose's throat throbbed as his eyes fluttered from her lips, to her eyes, and back to her lips.

He leaned in.

She barricaded his mouth with her fingers. "Now, now, you're so impatient. Haven't I taught you to beg?"

Her eyes reddened, brighter than before. I thought I saw her shadow swirl on the carpet, molting feathers. The room grew darker, and she seemed to grow taller.

"Please, Velma—"

"No." My mother's grin grew, as if a knife slit into the corners of her smile and sliced her cheeks. "Not my name."

"Please, My Lady...kiss me."

Her tongue stabbed into his lips as she dug her nails into his scalp. In his eagerness, his hands slid down her waist, fumbling with her corset laces.

She whipped out an arm. It didn't look anything out of the ordinary—just a smooth, slender, white arm. But I saw her shadow: the black shapes were nowhere near as lithe as her arm. Sharp feathers sprouted from it. It did not have fingers, but long, jagged claws.

Ambrose jolted backwards, like a dummy shoved off a cliff, as blood spurted from his throat. Clutching a glass flask, Mother collected his blood, as if collecting water from the steady spray of a fountain.

Despite my hands clamped over my mouth, my gasp must have been too loud.

Her head shot at me, her eyes as sharp as the claws that her shadow now retracted. A fresh wave of shock slapped off the sneer smeared across her face.

"Ernest…"

This was my mother. She couldn't hurt me. Wouldn't. Then why would the body on the floor, becoming colder by the second, challenge my conviction? Like a hammer shattering glass?

My ankles snapped into stiffness. From fear? From the belief she wouldn't hurt me?

As the red glow of her eyes dissipated, she collapsed to her knees, throwing her arms around me. Tears rained down my back. Listening to her sobs, I wrapped my shaking arms around her.

Picking me up as if I was still an infant, she carried me back to bed. The grandfather clock in the corner read 1:39. I clutched my stuffed rabbit, and gawked at her. "Why did you kill that man?"

The bed creaked with her weight. "Because I love you."

"That makes no sense." Fear rushed up my body, like a rapid river swallowing me. "Would you ever do that to me?"

"Never!" She threw her arms around me. "Ernest, you are my son. I could never, ever do that to you."

"Who was that man talking about? You said you wanted to marry someone."

Mother shook her head. "It was a long time ago. Something that does not involve you."

"Do I have a father?"

Her face was half-cloaked by the shadows of my room, half glowing in the light of the candelabra she set on my table. Her soft lips curved upward.

"Am I not enough, Ernest?"

I squirmed. "When you take me for trips to the City, I see other children with both mothers and fathers."

"Yes. Some children are happy. Others are not so happy. There are fathers who ignore their children. Or beat them. Maybe even kill them. You don't want a father like that, do you?"

"No. I would want just you, then." I clutched my rabbit more tightly. "Why do you like moonlight?"

"It calms me. Soothes me. When I'm under moonlight, I feel stronger and rejuvenated, as if I can do anything I wanted."

"Why am I allergic?"

She shook her head. "I don't know. I hope to find a medicine to cure you. One day, you can join me. We'll have a moonlit tea party. Jasmine green tea, macarons, petit fours, mooncakes, all the fruit tarts you could ever want."

"Will I really join you?"

"I hope so. One day."

"You promise?"

"I promise." She ruffled my hair. "Ernest, you have no idea how happy I am to be here with you."

"I make you happy?"

"Of course! This beautiful home of ours, seeing you grow up, doing well with your lessons…you make me proud. I wish this could last forever."

"It can last forever, can it?"

The corners of her lips curved down, like folded corners of solemn pages. "You're now ten, Ernest. Your home studies are too easy. You know all the answers to my multiplication and division questions, and read all the books on the shelves in your room. Don't you get bored here?"

"No."

She chuckled. "You may not know now, but one day, you'll become a young man and resent me. Become bored of me. I've decided to send you to school in the City. You'll learn much more there."

"I can still come home, can I?"

"Of course. Come straight back home after school every day."

"Will you sing me a song? Now?"

She chuckled. "I was hoping you'd ask."

Pulling my blanket up to my chin, she then straightened her back, folded her hands on her lap, and parted her scarlet lips.

Shivering in your shell
The stars are glowing, even as you hide here
When the morning arrives
Still you remain blind in your heart
Every painted lie

Every stitch of truth
Weaves a cold, cruel mask of delicate lace
If you never see
Beyond the blackened veil
Your bones will turn to dust

If your sorrow pierces you
Would you bleed and tear shards of glass?
Or would you clutch your sword
Raise it to the moon, crying and swearing honor for once?
At the shores of memories
Whispers dance in bittersweet farewells
Your ship sets to sail, deep in mysteries
No time to cry nor lament
Wake up and journey the dreams

As the final note of her voice rang in my ears, she embraced me. Clutched me, as if fearing I would disappear in the morning. Upon kissing my cheek, I thought I heard a small cry. She hurried out of my room, her rushed movements extinguishing the candelabra she left by my bed.

When I started school in the City, our automaton butler would escort me there in our submarine, and then bring me back to our island once the bell rang at three o'clock.

"Why are you always going home so early?" drawled John, who sat a few rows before me in class. "You never stay after school to play ball." He petted the white dove-like bird that sat on his shoulder. Enjoying the caresses of its owner's fingers, the bird opened its beak. Green tentacles came wagging out, like multiple tongues, and licked John's cheek.

I grimaced.

"What's the matter, Weirdo? Papa created my precious pet for me in his lab. Want to pet it?"

I reached out. Fixing its eyes on me, the bird opened its

beak. Along with the tentacles lashing at me, it screeched. I backed away.

"Why don't you come play with us after school?" asked John as his cohorts behind him snickered. The bird licked each of their hands with its tentacle-tongues.

"I...uh...want to do my homework."

"You must be so stupid to do all that homework," snickered John's twin sister, Edna, who had his bright copper hair and green eyes, and a white bird of her own on her shoulder, which flickered its tentacle-tongues to lick her neck every few minutes. "Come with us. We need someone to sneak us taffy from the corner store."

"No, thank you."

Their friends crowded around me, jeering, "Wimp! Wimp!" Upon seeing my submarine rise from the water, I covered my ears and ran towards sanctuary. The white birds would fly after me, pecking my cheeks and fists.

Despite the bullies, the first year of attending school was tolerable. I did well enough to move on to the secondary school guarded by ivory gates. But Edna and John also made it into this school, and the course load became heavier. Even when I was bogged with the number of electrons on each noble gas, the study of light and shadows with a piece of charcoal, and the overlapping years of different wars spanning continents, Edna, John, their lackeys, and stupid tentacle-tongued birds still followed me, calling me names. The brown noser. The bookworm. The no-good stupid kid who couldn't stay out during the night. The baby who had to sleep early.

At first, I was happy to come straight home, to be greeted by Mother playing the piano, to see sunlight slanting into the study where I did my homework. But now, I felt isolated. Belonging to nowhere. I failed to befriend classmates, even if I offered them bars of chocolate, carried their schoolbags, or let them copy math answers that took me hours to solve. John and Edna made sure I was alone. I could not join Mother in the sea nor the sky. As time passed, the longing gazes I gave her when she flew or swam twisted and churned into envy.

Resentment. Anger.

As I grew taller, she adjusted my strap-on wings for my lengthening limbs, and added more aluminum and titanium feathers. I ran along the shores of our home, trying to jump, to leap from a ramp, to flap my arms harder and harder. Eventually, I could raise myself by a few centimeters, but only for a few seconds before I stumbled back to the ground. It came to the point at which I neglected my homework to spend hours collecting bruises.

Schoolwork slipped from my focus like fine sand blown by the wind. No matter how hard I tried, it was never good enough. I became lost among the tangles of exponents, integrals, covalent bonds and essay citations.

Unable to meet Mother's eyes, my hands shook as I held out the latest density calculation test branded with a crimson 46/100. I needed her signature to prove to my science teacher, Mr. Bertholdt, that she was aware of my abysmal performance.

She slapped my desk. "You're just like your father!"

The test tumbled to the floor like a fallen feather. Both of our widened eyes met, and her hands had slapped over her mouth.

"I really do have a father?" I stood up from my chair. "You denied that I had one all this time?"

"Ernest—"

"Where is he? Dead?"

I expected her to say yes. But she kept her eyes on me as her hands lowered to her chest.

"So he isn't. Where is he?"

"He won't see us."

"Why am I like my father? Because I'm stupid? Weak? Because I can't fly? Can't swim?"

"Because you won't stop hurting me!"

"Hurt you?" Hurt. The word slapped me like ice. Then, it gave way to flaring anger. "Is that why you keep me trapped here?"

"I have not trapped you! I send you to school every day!"

"But you always tell me to be back before sunset. I don't have friends because of this!"

"I'm protecting you from moonlight!"

"Why am I allergic to moonlight?"

Closing her eyes, she lowered and shook her head. "Your father was allergic. You even look like him."

"So I never inherited your wings, nor your fins, but his illness?" I clenched my teeth as I turned to run. "I hate you!"

Grabbing my wings from my bedroom, I strapped them to my arms and rushed to the library. There, I flapped my arms, pleased that I could raise myself up by a few centimeters off the floor for longer this time, about half a minute. Flying across the waters to the City was a possibility! Perhaps moonlight wouldn't be so painful now that I was older. Maybe I could join the boys from school, see what they did at night. Running up the stairs to the stained-glass windows, I opened one of the panels.

The roses that flourished in the garden almost looked silver with the moonlight filtering through the steel-grey clouds. My eyes strained against the soft light, but I fixed them on the glittering City across the waters. If I was lucky, perhaps the moon would never come out.

Pressing myself against the wall farthest from the window, I stared at the sky, daring it to buckle against the intensity of my stare, of my mind bracing myself to aim, aim....

Launching out the window, I glided for a few seconds before shuddering and dipping into the air. Flapping my wings and jolting upwards again, I grinned. I was flying!

That was when the moon emerged.

Screaming as blisters opened on me, I flailed as the wind skidded through my metal wings, even tearing off a few titanium and aluminum feathers.

A pair of arms caught me.

Flapping her wings, Mother flew me inside through a window. Laying me on the carpet, she pressed an oxygen mask over my face.

"Breathe, Ernest. Breathe."

I expected anger to pour out of her. Instead, she stroked my hair, and patted cold ointment into my blistered face, neck, hands, and arms. When I could breathe without the mask, she brought water to my lips. At first, I welcomed the rush of cool liquid. Then indignation bubbled through me.

"You embarrass me," I spat.

Her face was a placid mask. "Why?"

"I can take care of myself! I'm not a baby!"

Her face remained expressionless. Frozen. She stepped away, the wings on her back fluttering before they folded and vanished.

"Very well."

In the morning, I went to the kitchen to make a measly sandwich, only to realize by lunchtime that the bread was stale, and the lettuce had wilted.

On Wednesday, after finishing fistfuls of dry nuts, I went to my science classroom. Mr. Bertholdt sat at his desk, grading papers. Ever since I met him, I thought he looked familiar, with his dark hair and green eyes, but I couldn't place where.

"Hello, Ernest." He placed down his pen with a smile. "What brings you here?"

"In class...y-you always said you had an office hour d-during lunch. I was w-wondering if you c-could—"

"Slow down, Ernest." Mr. Bertholdt patted the wooden chair by his desk. "No need to be nervous. This is what I'm here for: to help you."

Grateful for the seat, I exhaled. "In class, it's so hard for me to keep up. Could you help me understand just how electricity and magnetism are related?"

It didn't help that Mother kept interrupting my focus as Mr. Bertholdt galloped into a storm of words such as *field*, *wire*, *coil*, *amplitude* and *tangents*. Disappointment staining her eyes. The sound of slapping my desk hurting almost as much as slapping my cheek. Turning away from me as her wings folded into her back. She hadn't read me a story or sang a lullaby after I turned thirteen.

"Ernest?"

I jumped. "I-I'm sorry, Mr. Bertholdt!"

He placed a hand on my shoulder. It was large and warm, like a bear's paw. "You seem to be easily distracted in class. Is there anything you need help with?"

I was dying to tell someone, anyone, about Mother.

"My mother hates me."

"Nonsense. Why do you think that?"

Tears sprang out.

"I hurt her. I'm not like her. I'm not smart, I don't have wings or fins, and she says I'm like my father because I'm allergic to moonlight, and I look like him, so she keeps me hidden away and tells me to come home straight after school every day."

Mr. Bertholdt's brows raised.

"Wings? Fins?"

"I haven't told anyone else. She can fly and swim, and has the most beautiful voice. She also makes medicine and heals people when they need her. I wish I could fly and swim like her, but I can't grow wings or fins. And she can see the moon, but I can't because my father was also allergic!"

Before I knew it, I pressed my face into Mr. Bertholdt's shoulder. Sobs tore out of me as tears stained the thick fabric of his blue coat.

Rocking me in his arms, Mr. Bertholdt asked, "Ernest, does your Father help you?"

"I never had one! If she hates him, she must hate me, too!"

"Do you have friends?"

"No. We live alone on an island, and she makes me come home every day, so I never make friends. I hate her!"

"Do you really?"

"I do! I hate that I never can be like her. I hate her!"

The bell rang, howling along with my declaration.

John and Edna stalked into the classroom. I shriveled under their disgusted glares.

"What's this crybaby doing here?"

"John. Edna." A scolding tone in Mr. Bertholdt's voice. "Don't call names."

Edna flipped her braids over her shoulders. "Well, Father, we just want to let you know that the watercress sandwiches that Mother packed for lunch were terrible."

"Just horrible. What the Hell was in that?"

"Don't be so rude. Your Mother works hard."

"What are you doing here with this stupid boy?"

Mr. Bertholdt shot an apologetic look to me. "He isn't stupid. He's a hard-working young man, which is why he's visiting me during his lunch break."

"Psh. Only stupid people need help."

"Well, if you visit your teachers' office hours, perhaps you'll both start seeing higher scores on your tests. I wasn't very pleased with the D's you both brought home two days ago."

Their faces blazing with anger and humiliation, the twins stormed out of the classroom.

My jaw hung. "You're their father?"

He chuckled. "They try to pretend I don't exist. My wife does her best to be a good mother, but they can be so defiant."

"I wonder what it's like to be part of your family. To have both a mother and a father. I wish my life was normal."

"Well, you'd better head to your next class. See you tomorrow morning, Ernest."

My 14th birthday was two weeks after that office hour with Mr. Bertholdt. When I returned home, deadly silence greeted me. Even though we hadn't spoken, Mother had continued to play piano when I returned, so that at least music would be there for me. But not this time. Perhaps she was out hunting for oysters and salmon to prepare a birthday dinner for me.

On my desk in my study was a small vial, filled with an amethyst-colored fluid. The accompanying note had once-wet blotches blurring a few words:

Happy 14th birthday, Ernest.

I know you're angry at me, but this is for you.

Do you remember the night I killed that man, Ambrose? I admit, I had killed several men over the years, taking their blood to finally create this difficult cure for you.

They weren't innocent men.

They wanted wings and fins of their own. I loved your Father, but right before you were born, I ran away. While you were in school, I have been able to lure almost all of the men here and kill them. There is one last man.

Should anything happen to me, whatever you do, keep this vial hidden and safe with you. You need to kill your father and take a drop of his blood into this vial. Then, drink it. It will cure you of your moonlight allergy.

Remember I love you.

—Mother

A screech stabbed through me, making me jump and drop my bookbag in a crashing thud. Through the window, I saw what looked like a swarm of large white birds, larger than Edna and John's pets, chasing my mother through the sky. After tucking the vial into the inner breast pocket of my coat, I threw open my window.

"Mother!"

She soared through the sky, but not as majestically as I had always seen her. Flapping her wings in frantic speeds, she careened through the sky in fast dips at steep angles, only to shoot straight up again. No matter what sharp twists and turns she took, they always pursued her.

Strapping my metal wings to my arms, hiding them under my coat, I ran outside just in time to witness her taking a nosedive into the water. The birds dove after her.

Birds can't swim, I thought.

Minutes passed. She must be fine. She must be enjoying her swim down there, where her pursuers must have drowned. Perhaps she killed them herself in the depths.

I glanced down at my feet. The pages that fluttered on the

ground were ones I had not noticed as a child. Either that, or she had added more. Drawings of...Mr. Bertholdt? Words like *Kill, never forgive, hate, marry, wish* and *kissed.* Another page fluttered into view, chilling me: *I'll kill myself if I return to him.*

She sprang from the water—no! Tentacles yanked and twisted her hair, clenched her thrashing arms. White, rounded bodies of the birds, like monstrous and gargantuan doves, emerged as well. Their beaks were open, with long tentacles sprouting from them, binding her. Her struggles ceased as a giant tentacle slapped over her mouth.

Her eyes fixed on me. In that moment, our eyes met, as if a morsel of eternity froze between us.

"Mother!" I stepped into the water, but gasped at how it ate me up like cold, icy teeth. Mother frantically shook her head. I had never seen her so frightened before, so feral.

I ran back inside our home. Who was that man standing there in the foyer, his back to me?

He turned.

"Mr. Bertholdt?" Cold shock flooded me, like the hungry waves that tried to devour me a minute ago.

The sunlight illuminated Mr. Bertholdt's warm and paternal smile. He opened his arms. "Ernest. *I'm* your father."

In the mirror before us, I studied our resemblance—our green eyes, our thin lips, the way our dark brows fanned out at the corners.

His arms remained outstretched. "Ernest, is this how you greet a father?"

Backing away from him, I clenched my fists. "What took you so long to meet me? Why now?"

"To claim what is mine."

"What?"

"Velma has been hiding from me all these years. She's stolen so much from me. My riches, my research...and you."

"Me?" I recalled the conversation she had with Ambrose years ago. "You're the one who studied her in flight and water! You chained and caged her!"

"Looks like you haven't inherited her freakish traits. You're like me." He held out his hand. "Come with me. To my ship."

With Mother taken away, where else could I go?

"Where are you taking me? I want to see Mother." Boarding his ship, I tried to hide the tears that pricked my eyes. "What are those creatures out there? Edna and John have smaller versions of those birds for pets."

I didn't like his laugh: cold and stiff as a stone slab. "One question at a time, My Boy."

"So where are you taking me?"

"To see your mother."

I looked up. "Really?"

"Yes. As for those birds, I engineered them to take your mother back. My experiments for my plan produced collateral results. If you live with me, you'll have pets of your own."

"I don't want pets. I want Mother."

It didn't take long to reach her. I grew cold upon seeing her bound and gagged by the giant birds' tentacle-tongues to a rocky cliff, where they also perched.

"Hello, Velma. Pleasure to see you again."

Mother glared at Mr. Bertholdt, as if trying to set him aflame with her red eyes. I had never seen them burn so brightly, not even when she murdered Ambrose.

"You've hidden away from me long enough. I want one thing, Velma. I want to take Ernest with me. He'll live a normal life, and see the moon."

The tentacle-tongues squeaked as she squirmed and shook against them. When she bit down on the tentacle-tongue that gagged her, another bird slapped her with its tongue. Tears shot down her face, and a shadow grew behind her, molting sharp feathers. It jerked and swayed, but because of her bound arms, it wouldn't swipe at Mr. Bertholdt.

Mr. Bertholdt gently pushed against my shoulder. "Go on. Say good-bye to your mother."

"Why should I say good-bye?"

"If you want to save her, come with me."

"No, Mister—"

"*Father.*" He ruffled my hair. "Call me 'Father.'"

The word tasted sour. "Father. Why should I come with you?"

"Do you want to save her?"

"Yes!"

"Of course you do. To save her, come with me. Now say good-bye before I decide to turn this ship."

I turned to Mother. She had never looked so vulnerable. I always thought of her as an omniscient figure who could never be captured nor understood. Always so free and powerful. Tears fell down my face as I hugged her.

"Mother, I'm so sorry...for everything. For being so rude. For hurting you." It wasn't until I pulled away that I saw her eyes no longer glowed red. Her dark eyes traced over my face, as if trying brand her memory with me.

I whispered in her ear. "I'm coming back. Thank you for the birthday present. I have the vial in my coat."

Even through her tears and gag, the corners of her eyes crinkled so I knew she smiled.

Mr. Bertholdt steered his ship away. The shores of my home, the island that rustled with paper instead of sand, sailed far behind us. Crossing my arms over my chest, I felt my metal wings pressing along my arms, poking inside my coat like feathers wishing to sprout. Could I fly? Could I try? Would I fall into the sea and drown?

What would happen if I couldn't fly? Even if I did kill Mr. Bertholdt, I couldn't steer this ship.

Mr. Bertholdt held out a finger before my face. Blood welled on the tip, and my eyes widened at the crimson-stained knife in his other hand.

"Your mother gave you a vial, didn't she? The last ingredient is my blood, isn't it? Well, I'm going to give it to you."

I stared at his eyes, so much like mine. Then, at the blood droplet on his finger. Then, back to his face. He seemed earnest. The lines around his eyes were soft, the smile on his face gentle. I unstoppered the vial and held it out.

He pulled his hand back with a wry smile. "What a spoiled boy she's raised. I won't give it to you for free."

"*What?*"

"I need you to promise me something."

"What is it?"

"You'll never see your mother again."

"But you said that if I went with you, I'd save her!"

"True. She won't die. She'll be kept alive in a lab. You can live a normal life. Pretend she never existed. You'll live with me and my family."

Dumbfounded, with the vial still in my grasp, I shook my head.

In my shock, he grabbed the vial. I screamed, jumping and swiping at him to snatch it back, but he was taller than me.

"If you don't want it, then I'll drink it," he told me after I stumbled onto my knees, panting.

Paralyzed, I watched him squeeze a drop of his blood into the vial, and then raise it to his lips. Images of Mother flashed through my mind. Mother in her black dress, like a shadow rippling through the wind. Her wings glowing amber and gold. Her scales like emerald and amethysts. The streaming blood she collected from Ambrose's neck. All of mother's murder victims, all her attempts to keep me safe, would be in vain!

Right when I lunged for him, the moon emerged. Falling to the floor, I writhed and screamed, as if I was on fire.

But then, gentle hands lifted me and raised the vial to my lips. It tasted bitter, like iron. Nonetheless, grasping the vial, I drank it all up, like a greedy suckling.

Pressing my hands to my throat and chest, I coughed and hacked. "You...gave me your blood?"

"It is what I do as a father, isn't it?"

"But you drank some!"

"Only a third. That is sufficient for me. The rest was for you. You're cured. But you'll never see your Mother again."

"Who are you to speak to me like that? It doesn't matter if you cured me or not. If I made a promise to you or not. Even if you don't kill Mother instantly, she'll die if she's with you. She'll even take her own life. She *will*."

"If she dies, it will be for the greater good of science."

"How can I call you a father if you're letting Mother die? She raised me. You never did."

"I'm giving you what you want. A normal life."

"How do you know what I want?"

"You said you wished your life was normal. You also said hate your mother."

"I didn't mean it!"

"With me, it will. You'll have Edna and John as your siblings."

Not Edna and John! A normal life now seemed to be, at best, a banal existence, far removed from Mother and her magical world.

The moon grew brighter. I looked up at it, watching the clouds part like curtains at the theater, marveling that moonlight no longer stung. A cool breeze swirled around me. When I closed my eyes, each inhale felt like a powerful surge through my lungs. The weight on my arms from my mechanical wings felt lighter.

Was this what Mother meant when she said that moonlight made her feel stronger and rejuvenated? As if she could do anything she wanted? Although I couldn't grow wings, nor was I even sure I could breathe underwater, I felt as though I could be one with the moonlight.

I turned to Mr. Bertholdt. "If living a normal life means losing Mother and having to live with Edna and John, I don't want it."

"Oh really?"

"It doesn't matter how much you study her. You can never fly or swim like her. I have only one parent, and it is my mother!"

Tearing off my coat and raising my arms...I flew.

I gasped, trying to flap my wings, and flailing my feet as I tried not to touch the cold water. Dammit, it flooded my shoes as I skidded across the surface. I could not, would not let myself be dragged down by the weight of fear.

The sea swallowed me up. Thrashing and gasping, I thought I would drown. But as the salty water rushed into my mouth and nose, I blinked in surprise.

It didn't hurt.

I exhaled, watching bubbles shoot up before my eyes.

Instincts kicked in. Circling my arms and rising out of the waves, I shot into the sky, feeling the wind lift beneath my wings. I gazed up at the glorious moon shining high above me, encouraging me to lift higher and higher. I was soaring! I did it! I really did it!

"Ernest! Come back!"

He fell back, farther and farther behind me as I sped away.

There was Mother, still gagged and bound by the birds' tentacle-tongues, being shoved into a cage. Landing next to her, I tore off one of the metal feathers from my wings. The birds shot their tentacle-tongues at me, but with the intensity of their movements, my metal wings served as sharp edges that slashed them. Using the metal feather I wielded, I chopped at the tentacle-tongue that gagged her.

Opening her mouth, she sang. Honey and poison blended in her voice as her shadow grew behind her, swiping its claws at the birds' throats so that they sank into the sea.

Trails of smoke from smokestacks caught our attention. Mr. Bertholdt's ship came sailing towards us. She sang to him, and the anger in his face yielded to a glazed expression. Imprisoned by her enchantment, the ship veered, tilting and nearly toppling into the waves. But it rose back up, and in jagged twists and turns, it careened towards the sharp rocks of the cliff we stood on. Mother's song grew louder, stronger, excited for his impending doom.

Pity pricked my heart. Edna and John were my half-siblings. Did they love him as much as I love Mother?

"Mother, stop singing."

Her voice cut off. With wide eyes, she gawked at me, like a surprised child.

Opening my wings, I flew down and landed before Mr. Bertholdt. He blinked, dizzy from her song.

"Leave. Go back to that family you abandoned us for."

He looked hurt, almost like a stricken puppy. "You don't want me?"

"No."

"Ernest, I'm not proud of what I've done. But can you accept me?"

Disgust bubbled in me, and hatred shone in my eyes, the same color as his. "*Never.*"

"I cured you!"

"Mother cured me. You only added your blood, and cured yourself. She had intended it only for me."

"But I'm your father."

"She was the one who has protected and cared for me. Now leave. Before Mother decides to sing you to death once and for all."

Hanging his head, he shrunk into his rejection. With a small nod, he steered his ship away, becoming nothing more than a speck in the horizon.

Mother and I launched ourselves into the air to fly back home. Once we landed on the paper shores, Mother threw her arms around me. I realized I was now tall enough for her head to fit in the curve of my neck beneath my chin.

"Ernest…I never thought I would see you again."

Tears that I tried not to shed in front of Mr. Bertholdt welled in my eyes. "Do you remember telling me that I would one day be bored of you? Become a young man and resent you?"

"I do."

"Even if I were to one day move away, to not live on this island, I'll never leave you."

The papers on the ground rustled. They floated up and whirled all around us. Mother's drawings and writings, all her hopes and dreams, all her hatred and pain, fluttered around us in circles. They folded into roses, and joined the red roses that already bloomed in our garden. I looked forward to a moonlit tea party that Mother promised so long ago.

Roots

FLYNN GRAY

lyssa watched the brittle brown leaves turn green again, lush foliage unfolding at the touch of her finger. Nobody had remembered to water the poor plant for quite some time, judging by the state it was in. She gazed around at the other patients in her dentist's waiting room to gauge their reaction, but they were all firmly absorbed in their old celebrity magazines, conspicuously ignoring the minor display of witchcraft being performed on the potted fern in the corner of the room.

Alyssa leaned back in her chair with a sigh. She really should know better by now. Picking up the nearest magazine, she slunk down behind it and prepared for a very long, boring wait.

Afterwards, on the short walk back to her apartment, Alyssa contemplated her surroundings. Life in the city was usually considered unbearable by her kindred, but she liked it well enough here. Times had changed and life had moved on, the traditional role of the witch now obsolete. There were no more monsters left to fight, no people in need of their protection. The monsters had all been banished, and humanity was more than capable of defending itself against any non-supernatural phenomena. Though who would save them all from humanity was anyone's guess.

Alyssa typically preferred not to dwell on such thoughts, the past, the future, it was all meaningless now. That was precisely why she liked the distractions and fast pace of the city. The very sights, sounds and smells that drove others of her kind insane left little time for contemplation and introspection, neither of which ever led anywhere good.

She had just popped an instant meal in the microwave when there was a knock at her door.

Opening it, she found herself face-to-face with a young police constable, blond, blue-eyed and attractive, his hat in his hands and a distinctly uncomfortable air around him.

"Drew the short straw did you?" She asked.

"Sorry?"

"To be the one to come and see me?" He blushed and scrambled for something to say. Alyssa took pity on him. "Never mind. What brings you here?"

Still struggling to reclaim his equilibrium, the young officer began explaining. "There've been a few…odd deaths around the wharves over the past couple of weeks. We can't get any solid leads and there's a new body showing up along a certain stretch of the waterfront every few days. The boss thought that you might be able to help. Since you're, you know." He gestured vaguely. Alyssa raised an eyebrow, crossing her arms across her chest. "The only registered witch in the city." He finished in a rush.

Alyssa regarded him coolly. "That may be, but I am neither a police officer nor a detective, and I am definitely not a consulting *psychic* of some kind. Natural deaths, even murders, are not my department." She went to close the door and was surprised when it was blocked by the young man's foot. Also a little grudgingly impressed. She pulled the door back open, turning her dark eyed glare on him. He paled a little, but forged on.

"That's just the thing, Ms. Carlton. We think these deaths

may not be exactly natural. That there might be something else out there again." He cut her off as she was about to speak. "I know they're supposed to all be gone, but there's something really strange going on." He looked her dead in the eye, imploring. "Please. Please come and have a look."

Well. Alyssa hated to admit it, but she was impressed. And a small part of her was hopeful, despite her efforts to squash it ruthlessly back down. She vaguely heard her microwave ding in the background, and made her decision. "Fine, there's nothing decent on TV tonight, anyway. Wait here."

Ducking into her room, she grabbed her coat and bag, quickly tying her long dark hair back in a messy ponytail. The constable was still waiting patiently at the door, not crossing the threshold and intruding on her personal space, not trying to pry out her secrets from her living area with his eyes, simply waiting. Good. She might actually like this one. Stepping out into the hall as well, she locked the door of her apartment behind her and indicated towards the stairwell. "Lead the way then, Constable."

The body was a mess, could barely be recognised as human.

The constable—whose name turned out to be Tim Watkins—had given Alyssa an overview of the more perplexing aspects of the case during the drive down to the docks. There had been four bodies discovered along the shoreline so far, including this latest, found by some dock workers just a few hours ago. All of the remains had been discovered within 24 hours of the people going missing, sometimes even before it had been noticed they were missing. And all of them displayed the effects of being dragged rapidly about five kilometers below the surface of the ocean, remaining there for a few hours and then being returned to the shore. The effects of which were most certainly fatal and messy.

Alyssa had remained dubious about the story right up until she witnessed this corpse, the fourth victim, with her own eyes. No wonder even the police had realised there was something supernatural at play here. As she grew closer, all of her senses screaming at her left no doubt that they were in fact right, and her heart sang a little, despite the horrible, bloated and discoloured visage of the most recent victim at her feet. She wasn't obsolete. Maybe there was a place for her in this world still.

Crouching down by the body, Alyssa looked around for someone that appeared to be in charge, finally making eye contact with a weary-looking detective who moved to join her at the body, somewhat reluctantly, crouching down beside her. Alyssa decided to start with some simple background questions to break the ice, though Constable Watkins had given her most of the information they had already.

"What made you decide to seek me out, Detective—?"

"Tanner." He hesitated, before holding his hand out politely. "Liam Tanner."

She shook the proffered hand. "Alyssa Carlton," she replied, "Constable Watkins described the conclusions you have reached concerning the victims cause of death, but I would like to hear more about how you reached those conclusions. Surely there are alternative explanations?" She knew there weren't, of course, but she wanted to hear just how a perfectly rational and science-based investigative team had arrived at this extraordinary conclusion. Human beings hadn't actually encountered a supernatural threat in generations, had all but forgotten them.

Along with those that have always protected them, she thought a little bitterly.

Detective Tanner appeared to collect his thoughts for a moment before he began. "We initially thought that someone was recreating the effects of exposure to extreme ocean depths artificially, using some sort of equipment from a research laboratory or something. But then the pathology results kept returning with evidence of sediment and microbial life that only occur beyond depths of five kilometers. Not only on the surface of the body, but inside their lungs and sinus cavities. Well, what would have been their lungs and sinus cavities before they ruptured, anyway. There are clear signs that they were drowned at that depth, and not only that, drowned before they had a chance to freeze to death or be crushed." He sighed, running a hand over his face. "None of this makes sense, and to tell you the truth, I'm more than desperate. These bodies keep showing up, covered in deep sea flora and fauna, both inside and out, and we can't stop it." He turned to her, brown eyes burning directly into her own. "Can you?"

Alyssa paused, impressed for the second time in one day. *This is becoming a disturbing trend.* She decided he deserved honesty. "I don't know. The ocean is not really my domain."

He looked puzzled, and she was reminded that, despite being aware of witches and their role in the past in a hypothetical sense, modern humans really understood very little about her kind.

She sighed. "I'm an Earth Witch. I am neither capable of travelling the depths of the ocean nor do I hold any sway over the waters or their inhabitants."

A look of understanding dawned. "Oh, right, I remember reading something about that. A Witch isn't just a Witch, they are either Earth, Air or Water witches." He considered that for a moment, before something occurred to him. "But you do think this *is* Witch business, right? Otherwise you wouldn't still be here. There's nothing human or natural causing these deaths?"

Alyssa considered the remains before them once more. "No, there is most certainly not."

She stood abruptly. "I'd like to see the other bodies, if possible."

"Um, sure." The greying man stood a little more slowly, knees reluctant. "None of them have been released yet, since this is an ongoing investigation. I'll give you a lift down to the morgue now."

They were halfway to his police cruiser before he spoke again. "Mind if I ask why you want to see the other bodies? I mean, if you can tell from this one that there's something... else out there, why do you need to see the rest?"

"Because, Detective Tanner, it might just tell me some more about what exactly the 'something else' is."

"Oh."

The rest of the walk was passed in silence.

It was nearly midnight when Alyssa was finally dropped back off at her apartment by Constable Watkins, her mind occupied with all that she had found out that evening. She was almost distracted enough to not notice that the wards around her apartment had been disturbed.

Almost.

She paused outside the still-locked door, which showed no sign of break-in, the key still resting in her fingers. Reaching out with her senses she detected another life form within the apartment. Very silent, no indication of hostile intent. The ability to breach her wards unharmed indicated a skilled magic user. The scent of a fresh ocean breeze wafted into the hall.

Water witch.

Interesting.

Sliding the key into the lock, Alyssa stepped into the apartment, finding the lights already on and her couch occupied by a younger woman, barely out of her teens by appearances, though appearances were inherently deceiving when it came to their kind. Alyssa tossed her bag and keys onto the kitchen table, shedding her coat and tossing it carelessly over the nearest chair.

"Why are you here?" Alyssa decided to get the conversation started, since the other woman was still regarding her silently from the couch, aqua green eyes startling against pale skin and black hair in a messy pixie cut. "If this is about the deaths, you obviously must know what is happening, what's out there, you must know far more than I do, in fact. So why are you here, and why have you waited until now?"

The other woman finally broke eye contact. "I can't fight it alone."

"What?"

She rose from the couch and began pacing. "Of course I realised that something was wrong, I felt it as soon as it arrived. The water for miles around it feels tainted, echoes of malice and cold and darkness stretching out like tendrils trying to wrap around anything it can grab and...and.." The green-eyed woman paused and took a shuddering breath, and Alyssa realised with a start that the other witch was terrified. Well. That changed things, then.

"Would you like a cup of tea?" Alyssa whirled and stalked into the kitchen, mind spinning around this new development. This day was growing more interesting by the moment. She barely managed to keep the gleeful expression from her face.

"What?" The abrupt change of pace had the other woman floundering, for lack of better expression. Alyssa snickered internally.

"Tea, Dear. A hot beverage. How often do you actually come onto land? I'm Alyssa, by the way, what's your name?"

"Um, Mariana. Just Anna, really. And I spend a great deal of time on land, I know what tea is." A hint of annoyance crept into her voice. "I'm just not sure now is the best time for a cuppa and a chat, when people are dying and we're the only ones who can stop it. Also, you seem downright cheerful about the whole situation. What the hell is wrong with you?"

Oops, she'd spotted that. Time to come clean, I suppose.

Alyssa fussed with the tea as she spoke. "It's not that I'm happy that people are dying; of course not. It's just that, there's no place for us in this world anymore." She paused and glanced at Anna. "You must have noticed. We're obsolete, we have no purpose. Nobody needs us, anymore." She collected the cups of tea and placed one in front of Anna, seating herself in her favourite armchair with the other. "This is what we're here for. Can't you tell me you're a little excited?"

Anna looked her dead in the eye. "I'm terrified. I have no idea what this thing is, where it came from, how it got here, or how to fight it. So no, I'm not excited. I think there's something very wrong with you. But I need your help. So, it looks like I'm stuck with you."

Alyssa arched a brow at her, hiding a smile behind her tea cup. *I like her.* "Very well then, so why didn't you come and find me sooner? Why wait until now to seek my help?"

"I didn't know you were here."

"You do realise there is a register precisely for emergencies such as this, not that it has been used for its intended purpose for decades." A tinge of bitterness coloured her tone briefly. "But the information is there for anyone to see. That's how the police found me."

Anna flushed a little. "Most of our kind tends to avoid the cities, particularly Earth witches. Not that there are many of you left, from what I understand. I've never met one of you." She sipped her tea. "I've been following the police investigation, I realised what you were as soon as they brought you to the scene today. I tracked you back here. So, what do we do?"

She really must be very young, thought Alyssa. *She really has no idea what to do in this situation.*

"We gather more information, keep an eye on its hunting grounds to prevent it taking any more victims, and then we either kill it or send it back where it came from and seal the weak spot before anything else manages to come through."

"The police have already secured the waterfront area they think it's been taking victims from. Nobody is allowed near the water down there."

Alyssa nodded. "Yes, Detective Tanner informed me of that this evening. Now it just remains to be seen whether this creature can leave the water, and if it can, how far it can move from the water in search of victims. It may simply move to a completely different section of shoreline once denied access to its preferred hunting ground. We'll have to wait and see on that front. In the meantime, you can find whatever information you can in the water. We need to know the nature of this beast before we can fight it. And you need to find out where it slipped through into our realm, before anything else follows it through."

Anna nodded and they finished their tea in vaguely uncomfortable silence, Anna clearly wary of the older Witch, and Alyssa attempting to contain her curiosity about the younger woman, curiosity which she sensed wouldn't be appreciated at that particular moment.

Alyssa was back at the waterfront the next morning, chatting with Constable Watkins while reaching her senses out over the water for any sign that the beast was nearby. There was no hint of it yet, however she couldn't help being distracted by the scores of friendly seabirds that seemed to flock in Watkins' wake.

She turned to him in amusement. "You really shouldn't feed them, you know. They'll never leave you alone."

Watkins flushed a little. "I haven't been feeding them! They just kind of follow me around. Birds have always liked me. My grandad had an aviary when I was a kid, and I'd spend hours in there playing with them. They'd just climb all over me like puppies or something, which was weird because no one else could get near them."

"Hmmmm." Alyssa contemplated him for a moment. "Do you have an Air witch in your ancestry? It would explain it."

He gaped at her. "Um, no, I don't think so. It's never occurred to me to check."

"You should. You have the general physical characteristics of an Air witch, and an affinity with creatures of the air is an almost certain sign."

Watkins still looked a little shell-shocked at the idea. "Oh. Okay, yeah, I will."

They were silent for a while after that, watching the water while leaning side-by-side against the scenic walkway railing companionably, when a ripple out in the water caught Alyssa's attention. Moments later, Anna emerged from the shallows, short black hair slicked back and flimsy, dark green dress clinging as she sprinted up the beach toward them.

All of the police officers on sentry duty panicked at the sight of the woman emerging from the water, caught between the urge to rescue her from the monster and the decision to shoot at her in case she *was* the monster.

"Everyone calm down!" Alyssa's voice carried easily across the waterfront. "She's with me."

The officers subsided with a little grumbling, watching suspiciously. By this point, Anna was only a couple of metres away from Alyssa and Watkins.

"It's coming," she gasped, indicating out towards the ocean. "I think I provoked it when I found its hiding place and went snooping around."

"Good for you." Alyssa grinned. "Time to see what we're dealing with."

Watkins gaped between them. Alyssa took pity on him. "Constable Tim Watkins, this is Anna. She's a Water witch, and she's helping us with this investigation."

"Oh," he said, "I've noticed you around before, didn't realise you were...you know." He frowned. "You're not on the register."

"Really Constable? I think that is the least of our concerns right now." Alyssa could sense it approaching now, could see the growing ripple that was disturbing the otherwise glass-flat water, heading for the shore. Waves of malevolence preceded it.

A shape began to form, water flowing and twining around itself in a way that it shouldn't, forming a large, squirming shape with tendrils fanning out from it in all directions, constantly mobile. The overall effect was that of a writhing, tightly-packed pile of squirming water that wasn't really water, emerging from the sea and slinking its way sinuously up the shore.

After a breathless moment of palpable disbelief, pandemonium broke out, with almost every officer at the scene opening fire in blind panic, shooting as they retreated farther up the shore as the thing approached.

"Well, it appears that it can leave the water completely," mused Alyssa.

"Yeah, that's great." Anna looked on the verge of the same panic that gripped the nearby police. "Now what?"

"We see how *far* it can go from the water."

"What?" The exclamation comes from Watkins and Anna simultaneously, as they both turned from the monster long enough to give her an incredulous look.

"What if it attacks someone?" Watkins asked.

"Then we stop it,' Alyssa replied calmly, gaze not leaving the creature. She noticed that it seemed to be losing structural integrity the farther it moved from the water, seeming to unravel a little. It was a potentially vital piece of information that they didn't have before. It was also perfectly obvious that bullets had about as much of an effect on it as trying to shoot a waterfall to stop it running.

Her interest quickly turned to a fascinated horror as the beast shot out one long fluid tentacle and snagged the ankle of an officer who had been hiding behind an overturned dinghy, apparently waiting for the creature to get closer to get a good shot. For all the good all the shooting so far had done. A little brave, but mostly incredibly foolish, noted Alyssa.

The young man was being dragged rapidly towards the bulk of the creature, which was itself retreating back into the water, pleased with its prize.

Watkins began running towards his entrapped comrade, Anna hesitating a moment before following. Alyssa simply watched, partly out of further curiosity about the beast's methods, but also sending tendrils of power into the earth, seeking out the complex networks of roots and life forms that reside below even the most urban of backdrops.

The captured officer had been drawn into the writhing bulk of the creature's body now, encased in the watery mass, which edged ever closer to the waterline. She didn't have much time left. Her concentration was disrupted briefly, however, as Watkins neared the beast and was also snared by its tendrils, which sought to absorb him, as well.

Before it had the chance, over a dozen birds began diving from the sky—gulls, a few kingfishers and one hawk—slashing at the beast's hold on Watkins with beaks and talons until the Constable was freed, the monster abandoning him in favour of retreating with its first prize.

Now, though Alyssa. She gathered her power around her, drew it up from the earth and *pushed*.

Thick, powerful roots and vines erupted from the sand around the creature, tearing through it mercilessly and twining around the form of the captured officer, drawing him out of the beast's watery mass and shredding it in the process. With a furious howl reminiscent of a whale call crossed with an angry bear's roar, the disassembled tendrils fled back into the ocean and vanished.

With a deep breath, Alyssa carefully uncurled the vines and roots from around the coughing and gasping officer, and closing her eyes to turn her focus inwards, returned them to their rightful places, releasing the energies that she had drawn upon.

Opening her eyes again moments later, she surveyed the scene on the shore with some amusement. Anna seemed frozen on the spot between Alyssa and Watkins, head swivelling back and forth between them, mouth gaping soundlessly and looking completely lost. Watkins' knees seemed to have stopped working, and he was sitting on the sand, absently patting the back of his gasping colleague, his gaze alternating between the birds still circling above and the places around him where the ground had erupted in a flurry of activity only moments before. The rest of the observing police officers seemed to be frozen, barely capable of breathing, let alone comprehending the events they had just witnessed. Anybody would think they had never seen a sea monster defeated by an overt display of witchcraft before.

She snorted with amusement, beginning to stroll down the shore towards Watkins and Anna, who seemed to finally regain her senses and took the few steps required to reach the now freed officer, assessing his vitals efficiently and calling for someone to send for an ambulance.

Alyssa chuckled as she watched them fumble to try and regain enough senses to remember how to use a phone, still exhilarated from channelling that level of power for the first time in too many years. Watkins finally seemed to be returning to himself as well, and he met her eyes for a moment before he began snickering as well. Anna glared at both of them and Watkins just shrugged at her helplessly, before almost collapsing in another fit of chuckles. If there was a slightly hysterical edge to his mirth, Alyssa wasn't going to point it out.

She reached them as sirens began to wail in the distance, performing her own quick assessment of the previously captured officer's vitals, judging that he would be fine apart from the psychological trauma of his ordeal. She clasped Watkins' arm and dragged him to his feet, clapping him on the back as he was left breathless and gasping from the giggling fit, still gazing towards the sky every few minutes in wonder.

Alyssa pulled him close and spoke near his ear. "Definitely Witch ancestry, Constable. No doubt, now. You have power, Tim Watkins." She paused, for effect, before continuing, "Search your feelings. You know it to be true." She slung her arm around his shoulders, announcing to Anna. "The Force is strong with this one." Anna just looked confused.

Watkins groaned. "No. You did not just quote *Star Wars* at me. Because that would actually make this day more bizarre, and this day just cannot get more bizarre." He looked her dead in the eye. "Got it?"

"Fine." Alyssa rolled her eyes, but gave his shoulders a reassuring squeeze, anyway. "You guys are no fun."

The sirens grew deafening as two ambulances pulled up to the shore, along with another two squad cars, one of which was carrying Detective Tanner.

He drew Alyssa away from the paramedics swarming around the officer that had almost been the next victim and Watkins, and from the rest of the onlookers, which were mostly other police officers hovering uncertainly, not exactly sure what to do next.

"What the hell happened here?" He asked in a hushed tone, looking back towards the chaos.

"Well, the beast came ashore looking for victims, it found the unfortunate officer there, and then left after we stopped it from taking him."

Tanner looked at her. "That's it?"

"Pretty much."

He sighed. "You know what, I don't want to know. What happens now then?"

"You keep your people doing what they were doing, keeping the public away from this part of the shoreline. You'll have to warn them to stay farther back themselves as well this time though, and avoid the automatic reaction to shoot blindly even though it has no effect at all. You're quite lucky that none of them managed to shoot each other."

Tanner chose to ignore that last comment. "And what if it decides to move to a new hunting ground after failing here? It's going to be pissed about that, right?"

Alyssa nodded. "That is a concern. We'll have to move quickly."

"So, after all of this, do we actually have a plan to get rid of this thing?"

"Yes, Detective, actually, we do." Alyssa smiled as she turned and wandered back towards Anna and Watkins. She would need both of their help to put her plan into action.

The next morning, Alyssa, Anna and Watson were back at the shoreline, the heavy grey sky and early fog adding to the foreboding atmosphere that pervaded the beach. The three of them had assembled at Alyssa's flat the previous evening, outlining their plan of attack, and now it was show time.

"You ready?" Alyssa asked Anna, who looked the most nervous of all of them.

"I think so." Anna took a deep breath. "But what if I can't

do this? I've never attempted anything like this before."

"You have support. It is truly amazing what we can do with the combined power of the elements, you'll see." Alyssa turned to Watkins. "Have all the low-lying areas been evacuated? Including the police? There is going to be a serious risk of tidal waves and flooding if this goes well."

He snorted. "Right. Tidal waves and flooding are the good option here. Yes, everything has been cleared."

"Okay, then." Alyssa nodded and squared her shoulders. "You're up, Anna. Make sure it chases you but don't let it catch you. It's going to be very upset with us after yesterday, and it may not be able to drown you, but there are plenty of other things it could do."

Anna shuddered. "Got it. Don't worry, I'll keep well clear." She headed toward the water's edge, slipping into the icy sea until she dove under and disappeared.

"Why doesn't she wear a bathing suit?" Watkins question came out of the blue.

"What?"

"Anna. She always wears a dress. Aren't they awkward to swim in?"

Alyssa smiled. "Not really, not for her. And it's a matter of practicality. Most other garments get in the way of her tail."

"Tail?" The expression on Watkins' face was priceless.

"The natural form of a Water witch while in the water is what you would call a mermaid." Alyssa responded, amused. "A dress doesn't get in the way of the transformation."

"Oh." He shook his head. "Just when I thought things couldn't get any weirder."

"You ain't seen nothing yet, Tim."

Just then, Alyssa sensed the malevolent presence approaching once again, far stronger this time.

"Oh, yes, it is definitely upset with us. Hurry up, Anna."

The younger witch emerged as the ocean's surface began churning behind her, forming into a writhing mass much as it had the day before, but this time much larger, and much more agitated. Anna sprinted up the shore and it followed close behind, a gurgling, thrashing form the approximate size of a bus.

Alyssa nudged Watkins forward. "Off you go, then. Time to be a diversion."

Tim had gone rather pale at the sight of the enraged monster, but moved forwards nonetheless, ready to intercept it and distract it from Anna, hoping that the local avian population would be ready to help him out again.

Alyssa moved forward as well, already sending tendrils of power into the earth, preparing to make her move.

As predicted, the beast turned its attention to Watkins quickly, spotting one of the prey that had escaped it yesterday, one which would be far easier to kill than another creature of the water, such as Anna was. It engulfed Tim with frightening speed and Alyssa took just a moment to worry that she had miscalculated before springing into action.

As she had yesterday, she called forth roots and vines to anchor Tim and prevent him being dragged into the ocean. The beast refused to release him, however, and she realised it was still intent on drowning him, even if it couldn't drag him down to the depths. She raised more vines, these ones adorned with large spikes, slashing though the creature repeatedly until it began to howl and deform, seeming to unravel as it lost structural integrity.

She withdrew the spiked vines as the local bird population took over the attack, swooping and snapping and clawing at the already damaged beast in an attempt to force it to release Watkins. Seeing that it was almost about to start retreating into the water again, Alyssa called out to Anna, who had regained her breath and was watching the fight with horror.

"Now, Anna. You have to do it. Remember what I told you."

As the creature destabilised and began writhing back towards the sea, Anna gathered all of her focus and forced the waterline backwards, drawing the water back out into the ocean until there was a wall of water several meters high about 50 meters further down the beach than the waterline had been before. She was shaking with the effort, and even with the extra energy they were generating by being in each other's proximity, Alyssa knew she wouldn't be able to keep it up long. She had to act fast.

The creature grew more desperate as it realised that its escape route had just been made so much farther away. Alyssa wasn't even sure it would survive the trek back to the water if they did nothing else at all, but they couldn't risk it.

She focused on a point on the ground halfway between the beast and the water and made the earth move to her will. A huge sinkhole appeared, and the creature stumbled straight into it. Alyssa focussed further, tapping into the reserves of magma flowing deep below and forcing it upward until it flooded the crater that she had just created. The crater that the creature had fallen into.

There was an immense sizzling sound and the beast let out a curdling, gurgling wail before all became silent save for the hiss of cooling lava. The stench was revolting. Alyssa hurriedly buried the whole mess back beneath several tonnes of rock, earth and sand, moments before Anna let out a pained cry and collapsed, losing control of the water.

The small tsunami came rushing at the three of them, and Alyssa lunged toward the vines still wrapped around Watkins and grabbed one for herself, holding on and coiling it around her wrist as the first rush of water hit, swirling around and dragging at them.

Alyssa felt like her lungs were about to burst when the water finally receded around her, and she realised that Anna had cleared a patch of dry land around the three of them, before beginning to coax the water back into a calm state, the waterline gradually smoothing out at its original level.

Turning her attention back to Watkins, Alyssa carefully withdrew the vines and rolled him over, realising that her fear had materialised. He was unnaturally still, with no pulse, cold and blue around the lips and fingers. She barely noticed Anna race to her side and dropping to her knees, desperately starting CPR.

"He's not breathing, Alyssa, you have to help me. We can't

just let him die."

"He's already dead." Alyssa heard her own dull voice as though it came from the distance.

"What? No, you can't just give up! You have to help. What's wrong with you?"

The assorted birds stood sentry in a solemn circle around them, at a respectful distance. Alyssa looked back at them, as though in a trance, before turning back to Watkins. Tim. Brave. Attractive. Funny. Witch. Leaning over him, she placed her palm over his heart, and gently shoving Anna out of the way, placed a light kiss on his cold, blue lips.

She felt the warmth begin to gather at the two points of contact, a reddish glow emanating from her palm and sinking into Tim's chest. His lips warmed beneath her own, and she leaned back as his eyes flew open and he took a gasping breath, immediately leaning over to the side to cough the seawater out of his lungs, heaving and gasping for a long time before flopping on his back, exhausted.

He squinted his eyes open a crack and looked at them. Alyssa smiled. "Hi."

"Hi," he croaked back, throat still raw. "What happened?"

"You were dead." Alyssa's matter-of-fact tone betrayed nothing of her inner turmoil.

Anna looked awed. "Wow, I'd heard some Earth witches could actually manipulate the life force, but I've never actually seen it done before."

"Takes it out of a girl, though." Alyssa slumped a little on the sand next to Tim, allowing some of her exhaustion to show.

"I bet." Anna eyed her with some admiration.

Alyssa continued. "What I really need is coffee. Black, two sugars. Be a dear, would you?"

Anna rolled her eyes. "Afraid I've got a portal to seal. So, no." She hauled herself to her feet and headed slowly back into the water.

Alyssa looked at Tim. He held his hands up weakly. "Hey, I just died."

"Loafer." Alyssa flopped on her back on the sand next to him dramatically. They both appreciated the warm glow of the early morning sun as it began to break through the clouds.

"You know, Tim, we could whip up some awesome superstorms between the three of us."

Tim opened one eye to look at her. "Um, no. Not a good idea."

She waved a hand at him dismissively. "Out in an unpopulated area, of course. Like the desert or something."

"No."

"You guys are so dull. I'm –"

"If you say you're bored right now, I'm going to make every bird on this beach attack you. Somehow."

Alyssa snorted, holding her hands up in surrender. "Fine."

Sirens started wailing in the distance.

Alyssa contemplated the man next to her. "So, we're just staying here, then?"

He shrugged. "I'm comfy."

"All right, then. I hope someone brings coffee."

Night's Favored Child

Silas Green

he girl ventured deep into the wood, riding upon the shoulder of a dead man. It was fully night. The moon was a slice of silver light in the sky, barely giving any illumination at all. Dark and wicked things were about, but none would dare approach her. Death clung to her like a perfume, and even the creatures that thrived in the deepest part of the forest knew to stay away.

Her goal was a grove of trees where a makeshift grave was planted. Her thrall carried her there and gently set her down in front of the grave. A lantern glowed softly in her hand, throwing a flickering orange light on the gravestone, nothing more than a smooth rock with the name "Elaine" scratched onto it. The child stood over the grave and stared down at the name for a long time.

The child's name was Nim, and she only *seemed* a young girl. Once she had been, long ago. How many years was it now? She could not remember. She had been such a bright child. It was Elaine who had been the dark one, the one who wanted to brave the dark wood, to find the children of the night, to learn the secrets of magic. Nim had been the one who was full of light.

No longer. She was still a child in appearance, still wore a frilly pink dress and a ribbon in her raven-colored hair. But if you looked closer, you could tell that something was not right, the same way you could tell that the man who carried her was not right, even before you realized that he was dead. It was in the way they moved, the way they carried themselves, the very way they *stood*. It was as if they were always listening to music that only they could hear.

The man, of course, was lifeless, a walking corpse. When you got up close, you could see. But Nim was alive. What was wrong with her was harder to define. Her skin was chalk white, and there was an alien *stillness* to her, an unchildlike calm.

"Elaine," she spoke.

The spirit of a young woman rose like vapor in front of her, a glowing phantom that bathed the entire grove in watery, green ghostlight. It turned Nim's pallor a sickly color. This was the ghost of Elaine, the one whose death had summoned Nim to this place.

The ghost and the child considered one another in silence. It had been years since they saw each other last, when the strangers had come to the village and taken Nim away. She was special, they had said. She was *chosen*. And Elaine had been left alone. Now Elaine looked down at the young girl before her and marveled. *She looks exactly the same*, the ghost thought.

"You came," Elaine said.

"It's what I do, now," Nim said with a shrug.

Her voice sounded cold, unfeeling, drained of all emotion.

"So you're here because it's your duty?" There was disappointment in the ghost's voice. "This is just part of your job, servant and master of the dead?"

Nim seemed to soften, but only a little. "I came to help you. I was... saddened when I heard you had died."

Saddened? Elaine frowned. The spirit had hoped for something more like *heartbroken*. Or *devastated*. But "saddened" would work. At least she was here. That was all that mattered. Elaine needed her, and Nim was here.

"I was murdered," Elaine said. "My life was taken from me for the selfish desire of someone I loved."

"Do you know who killed you?" Nim asked.

A strange thing happened then, and Elaine almost gave Nim her killer's name. She wanted to blurt it out, to tell her everything. It was something about necromancers; the dead could not lie to them. If Nim asked her directly, Elaine would tell her the truth...

"Yes—but do not ask me!" Elaine implored. "I...still love this person."

Nim paused as if she were considering this, as if something as human as *love* were beyond her understanding now. "I will need the name of your killer if I am to bring you justice and peace."

"Of course...but not from my lips." Elaine pointed in the direction of her old house, which stood a stone's throw from the grove where she was buried. "Over there is my home. Ask my family what happened."

She vanished.

Nim stood there a while longer. "Elaine," she asked the darkness, "what happened to you?"

The dead man carried Nim to the house that Elaine had called home. It was an old place. It was not big enough to be called a mansion, but there was something about it that brought that word to mind. It was two stories tall, but somehow seemed to squat, clinging to the earth. All of its windows were barred, boarded up or both. It had no paint to speak of. By the light of the stars and moon it was colored in shades of grey.

Nim's thrall set her down and watched its master eyelessly as she strode up to the front door and knocked, using the ornate iron knocker. Then she waited. There was no answer. She knocked once more, and waited even longer this time. Still no one came to greet her. Finally, she called her thrall, who beat against the door until the whole house shook.

A voice floated down from a window above her. "Who goes there?"

"A servant and master of the dead, and she is tired and cranky," said Nim.

The door opened and a man stood before her. He had

cloudy grey hair and wore a dusty suit that had been out of style before Nim was born. His face was ageless, at once ancient and young.

"Welcome, young necromancer," he said. It was the same voice that had called down to her from the window upstairs only a moment ago. Nim knew at once what the ageless man was. There was only one creature of the night that could move so fast. She could feel it about him, too. Living on the life's blood of others, he himself was only half alive. Like all of his ancient race, he straddled the border between world of the living and the world of the dead, which was Nim's domain.

"Save it," said Nim, waving away his pleasantries. "I am here on errand, sent by the dead. Someone in this house has blood on their hands."

The ageless man gave her a sly smile. "We're all children of the night here. Most of us have blood on our hands."

Nim eyed him coldly. What was Elaine doing living with a creature like this? She had always been interested in dark secrets, even when they were children. It seemed her fascination with the darkness had brought her to a bad end at last. But Nim could not judge her. Not anymore. She was beyond judging people. "The only blood I am here for is Elaine's. She is dead and someone in this house knows why. Now wake your house and bring everyone to me."

It was a strange little family that gathered in the sitting room of the old house and made nervous introductions. There was a young witch in a black dress, who sat in a soft chair with her arms crossed over her chest. She wore an expression of contempt. Next to her the ageless man in the dusty suit stood with casual ease. Across the room, a scrawny boy sat with his knees drawn up to his chest, his sunken eyes darting around the room in furtive glances. He seemed wild, restless, like an animal trapped in a cage, even though the moon was far from full tonight. Above the fireplace sat a black cat with a white patch of fur on its chest. There was far too much awareness in the creature to mistake it for a pet.

So, this was Elaine's odd family. All of them were creatures of darkness now, people who were shunned by fearful humanity, usually for good reason, but able to live in peace in the wood. These dark outcasts were the ones Elaine had loved. Nim looked around the room.

And one of them killed her. But which one, and why?

"This is the first time a necromancer has visited our home," said the cat. Nim was not surprised that it could speak. "What is the occasion?"

"The only occasion there ever is," said Nim. "Death."

"This is about Elaine," the wild boy told the cat.

"Yes," said Nim. "I am looking for her murderer."

"But she died in an accident," the wild boy said. "She fell down the cliff at the edge of the wood."

"No." Nim shook her head. "She was killed on purpose. The dead cannot lie to me."

"And you think one of us did it?" the witch asked, her eyes narrowing.

"Are you her family? Are you the only ones she loved? Because she was killed by someone she loved."

The wild boy murmured something.

"What was that?" Nim asked.

"I said there is also Roderick. Elaine and Violet both loved him."

The young witch glared at the wild boy. "What would *you* know about it?" she spat.

Nim turned to the ageless man. "I thought this was everyone."

"Roderick couldn't have done it," said Violet. "He is…not alive."

"Good," Nim said. "At least there will be one person here who cannot lie to me. Call him."

The young witch spoke a few quiet words and a wisp of pale green light spiraled into existence above the couch next to Nim. It slowly took shape until it appeared as a handsome young man. He wore ghostly clothes that were from another time.

"Servant of the dead," he greeted Nim, bowing to her.

"And master," Nim said. "Did you kill Elaine?"

"I am not without blame. But no, I did not kill her," he replied.

"Do you know wh—"

"Please forgive me," Roderick interrupted her. "You know I must answer whatsoever you ask me, but I beg you not to ask me that. If you are a servant of the dead, give me this. Please."

Nim stamped one small foot. "Hollow hills and starless skies!" she cursed. "Do *all of you* know who killed her?"

"Well, *I* certainly don't," Violet said.

"Nor do I," said the ageless man.

"I don't, either," said the wild boy.

Nim looked over at the cat.

"Oh, I know who killed her," he said.

"I don't suppose you will tell me."

"That is correct."

"Why not?"

"Because I am bored, and watching you is interesting."

Now a necromancer could demand the truth from ghosts and ghouls with ease. With some effort, she might even be able to compel a vampire, since they were only half alive. If she searched out some terrifying black device of her Art, she might even wring an honest answer from a living child of night. But this was a cat, a Servant of None, and you had to know when you were beaten.

"Fine, then!" Nim turned on the ageless man. "You know something. Tell me."

He actually took a step backward from her. "She was like a daughter to me! I could never have…not when she…why don't you ask Violet? She *hated* Elaine!"

"You hated her?" Nim asked the witch. If she hated Elaine, could she really be her killer? Only if Elaine loved someone who hated her. It was not impossible, and it would give her a motive. But why would anyone hate Elaine?

"*Hated?*" Violet rolled her eyes. "Not *hated*. We quarreled, but it was like sisters. We competed. We practiced magic together. We raced to see which of us would be the first to perform the Ritual of Three, and gain the Power. It was I. But Elaine followed quickly. *Too* quickly. We were dead even in our race to see which of us would perform the Ritual of Five first and become a witch in full."

"You don't have the power to complete that spell," Nim said matter-of-factly. So, Elaine was practicing witchcraft. Trying to collect souls touched with different kinds of magic. That was a dangerous pathway to power. If Elaine was doing that, then she was as much a child of night as anyone in this house. Nim smiled faintly. It was what she always wanted, wasn't it? Her brief smile faded. Except for the part where she ended up dead. "You need to gather five different children of night to perform the Ritual. And you need the power to compel them. Unless they are willing…which I would guess they were not."

Violet's face darkened. "You are right. Neither of us had the power, or the right five souls. But we kept practicing, waiting for another child of night to turn up."

"And in your competition, you never tried to cheat her?"

"Never!"

The wild boy grumbled something in his low voice.

"Huh?"

"I said she's lying."

Nim beamed at him.

"I am *not* lying!" Violet jumped to her feet. She took an outraged step toward Nim…and made the mistake of looking the girl in the eyes. An understanding passed between them. All the blood drained from the witch's face and she staggered backward, collapsing in her cushioned chair.

Nim's voice was sweetly menacing as she asked, "What. Did. You. Do?"

"I enchanted her," Violet confessed. "A harmless sleeping spell, just something to keep her from studying at night so she wouldn't get ahead of me. But that's all I did, I swear. I did not *kill* her."

"Elaine…sleepwalked," Roderick supplied.

Nim turned to the ghost. She had almost forgotten he was there. He was not looking at her. His emerald gaze was far away.

"Sleepwalking…" Nim mused. "She could have gone outside, ventured into the deep wood." She faced the wild boy. "That would be *your* domain, would it not?"

"I did not kill her."

"If you were dead, I would believe you."

"I did not…"

"The moon was full that night," said the ageless man. It looked like the members of this little family were beginning to turn on each other. "You could have chased her without even knowing it. Did you hunt near the cliff where we found Elaine's body?"

Nim pursed her pale lips as she considered this. "A full moon, it is possible…"

"No…"

"*Something* happened that night," said Nim. "What do you remember?"

The wild boy turned his head. "The moon…it was so bright that evening. I chased…something. It was fast. Faster than Elaine could have ever been. I almost caught it, but it got away. I scratched it though, tore a piece of its dress. The fabric, it was…hers. But the thing I chased…it could not have been Elaine. And it escaped from me."

"I see," said Nim. She sighed. The pieces of the puzzle were falling into place, and she did not like the shape they were taking. "And now I think I understand." She faced the ageless man once more. "You lied to me before, now tell me the truth."

"I was telling the truth. I did not kill Elaine."

"No…but you did bite her."

He looked around the sitting room. All the denizens of the house were staring at him. There was no support on any of their faces. "I did not know it was her! What was she doing so far from the house? In the deep wood! It was dark when I came upon her, the moon was not out yet. Her blood was sweet…it was singing to me. I recognized her afterward, but it was too late. I had already bitten her. All I could do was leave her alive. It took all my strength to do that. But I *did* do it. I left her alive."

Nim closed her eyes and massaged the bridge of her nose the way an older, much wearier person might.

"Poor Elaine," she whispered. "A triple-cursed child of night. Go on, Roderick. I'm ready to hear your part in this. I can already guess who finished her off."

Roderick's ghostlight dimmed.

"She looked so lost. I knew that something was wrong, that she was hurt, but when I called to her she would not answer me. I tried to reach out to her. Then I knew. She was so *wrong.*"

"Dark powers do not mix well," said Nim. "Elaine was enchanted by the touch of black magic, then cursed with the bite of the vampire—that is what made her so fast, she was already starting to change—then poisoned by a wound from a child of the moon."

"I did not know how to help her," mourned the ghost. "I did not even know what she *was* anymore. What name could I have given it? Is there a name for it? It was *terrible.*"

"It has a name," said Nim softly.

Everyone was watching Roderick with wide, haunted eyes.

"She looked up at the moon, then she looked me in the eyes. She knew me. I loved her. I begged her to come with me, promised I would find a way to help her. But she...we were on the edge of the cliff and she..."

Nim knew. She knew everything now.

"She jumped," Nim finished.

"I wanted her to," Roderick confessed. "I wanted her to be with me on this side of death."

"I am sorry," said Nim.

"Why are we not together? You are a necromancer. You understand death. You have spoken with her, haven't you? Where is she?"

"You loved her, and maybe she liked you, but she did not love you..."

"What is happening?" Violet whispered. The air around them was growing colder. The fire in the hearth died down to embers. Most of the light in the room came from Roderick's dim ghostlight.

"The one Elaine loved," said Nim, "is the one who killed her."

"But...she *jumped*. It was a *suicide*."

"Exactly," said Nim. Then she called, "Come on out, Elaine. You have what you wanted."

She did indeed.

Elaine descended as if from on high, floating down through the rafters, clothed in light. She shone like a poison star. Her voice shook the house when she spoke.

"Five souls of night's children, and one of them a necromancer...

One for the blood,
One for the moon,
One for life,
One for death,
And One, a door between the two."

"What are you talking about?" Violet shrieked. "You're *dead!* A ghost can't gain the Power of the Ritual of Five!"

Elaine looked down on her rival with pity.

"Not a ghost," said Nim. "You three saw to that. She is a child of shadow, one who has been ruined by the Night. A *lich.*"

"You mean undead royalty?" said the ageless man. He strained, trying to flee with his great speed, but couldn't. Elaine's power held him fixed to the spot.

Nim felt it, too. It was like being underwater, hard to move, hard to even breathe. She felt her soul move within her. It was an unpleasant sensation.

"The magic of the dead is as powerful as that of the living," Nim said. "But it's not every day that the dead ascend to full magic."

She was not panicking, which unnerved Elaine a little. *Does she not realize what is happening here?* It seemed she did not, or was not worried by it.

"How can you be so calm?" Violet demanded. "If it is poisoned by death, the Ritual will kill every child of night whose soul is used to power it! She is going to destroy us!"

"Don't be afraid, Violet," Elaine cooed. "Death really is not so bad. Well, not for me, anyway..."

Everyone in the room strained against the force of Elaine's spell, but none could break it. Nim's thrall roared and moved to help her, but Elaine lashed out with her power, severing its soul from its rotting body. The corpse hit the floor with a meaty slap and something dark splattered out of it.

Nim cursed. Those things were really hard to make. "Stop this, Elaine," she sighed.

Elaine did not stop.

"Why should I? The Power is within my reach. And it's not like anyone in this house is innocent, is it? Just look what they did to me. And as for you...where is the bright girl I used to play with in the village? You reek of death, Nim. You are every bit the monster the rest of us are. You, me, every child of night, none of us deserves more than death. So, no, I will not stop this."

Nim looked at Elaine then, and her black gaze was gentle. "Elaine, give it up," she said. "There are things you do not know. Even you. Even now. Death is not a toy for you to play with. Do you really think that touching the Power will satisfy you? You always did believe in your secrets. But look at me, a necromancer now, one who they say holds the secrets of death. But I know better. Do you want to know what secrets I have found? I have traveled death's dark passageways, I have walked down the Pale Road, the path that winds through the Endless Fields in the lands of shadow. I have walked it right to the end, and do you know what I found there?

"A door. One final, simple door, with no markings on it, no secrets, no clues as to what lies beyond. It is always shut and everyone that goes through it does so but once. I stood before it in all my power. And I feared. I was afraid, Elaine, the same way everyone is afraid. No one wants to die. Don't make that choice for anyone else."

Elaine shook her head sadly. *It's too late*, she thought. Nim could never understand. That night, staring up at the moon, no longer mortal, no longer bound by the chains of love and life, she had realized the truth. An awful truth, one that Nim could never accept. Maybe there was in this pale creature still too much of the bright girl she used to be, and she could never truly fit in among the children of night. *What a pity.*

Elaine shrugged. "I do not care," she said. "I've come too far to give up now. The Final Power is mine by right, and with it all the secrets of magic. All I ever wanted…"

Nim turned away from her. She looked around the room at the spellbound children of night. Then she exchanged a look with the talking cat, which was watching the whole scene with shameless interest. She asked it a question with that look. It stared back at her and seemed to dip its head in a nod. Nim looked back up at Elaine, her youthful face set in grim defiance.

"Then you aimed too low."

"What?"

She spoke a few soft words that Elaine could not understand. "You have only played at the Art, like a child with a toy she can't understand."

"A child?" Elaine laughed musically. "Me?"

"The First Power will open mortal eyes to see our world," said Nim. Her voice was grave. "The Third will grant the power of magic, the beginning of the Art."

"And the Fifth will make me a master of the Art!"

Nim shook her head. "The Fifth *will* make you a witch in full…but what of the Seventh?"

Elaine's emerald eyes narrowed. "There is no Seventh."

"The Ritual of Seven opens wide the door between life and death. It's the first test in necromancy. I was only a child when I performed the spell and opened the door for the first time. It is powerful enough to stop you." And here Nim's chalk-white features split in a fanged smile. "And I have seven souls of night's children here before me."

It could not be. *She must be lying*, Elaine thought. But her pale lips began to move. Elaine met her eyes, her cruel black eyes. Meeting her gaze felt like looking out a door that someone had left open to a place no one could go. It was a dark place, and cold. It went beyond death, above heaven, beneath hell, outside the universe itself. It went on forever.

"No…" Elaine breathed.

Nim intoned,

"One for the blood,
And One for the moon,
One for the living,
And One for the dead.
One for night's power, twisted.
One for the power to make it straight again.
And One for a Servant of None."

There was a noise like a thunderclap, or maybe a great door slamming shut. A flash of light and awful power. The rush of a great wind. Like a speck of dust blown away with a breath, the world vanished. Elaine thought she heard the sound of two girls, so different, even then. They were laughing. The wind caught their laughter and drowned it out.

Then all was quiet.

It was nearly dawn when the dust and ash settled. Nim stood in the ruin of what used to be the old house. Around her stood a group of bewildered ghosts, glowing like lanterns in the twilight. It was unfortunate that her spell killed them, but it was better than it would have been if Elaine had been allowed to complete the Ritual with her twisted power. Still, most of the new ghosts were quite unhappy with how things had turned out.

"I can't be dead!" Violet whined. "I never even got to perform the Ritual of Five!"

"It wasn't all it was cracked up to be," Elaine said. She examined her ghostly hands. There was something different about her, she could feel it. She was only an ordinary ghost now, not an undead horror.

"This is *your fault!*" Violet accused.

Which was mostly true, so Elaine held her peace.

The wild boy was no longer a slave of the moon, which

was a rusty sickle, sinking over the horizon. The ageless man no longer heard the musical call of blood, though Nim's was pumping loudly in her ears as she struggled to flip over the corpse of her thrall so she could reanimate it. And Roderick, now with two ghostly maidens in his reach, discovered that neither of them were very interested in him.

The cat. It licked its ghostly paw and flicked its ghostly tail. It was the only one of the house that did not seem to mind being dead. But then, he was a cat.

Nim carefully restored the soul of her thrall. The corpse climbed to its feet and picked her up. She rode on its shoulder once more. They left the wreckage of the house, heading into the wood.

"Wait!" a voice called after them.

Nim's thrall stopped. The girl looked at the ghost of her friend, her expression unfathomable.

"What is it, Elaine?"

"What am I supposed to do, now?"

Nim shrugged. "I tried to tell you that I didn't have any answers. Eventually you are going to find your way to that door and go through it, same as me."

Elaine looked away. "I'm sorry, Nim."

Nim put a small hand on Elaine's shoulder. The ghost found it strange that it did not pass through her.

"It's okay. Life is like that sometimes."

A ghost cannot cry, Elaine realized then.

"I wish I had more time," she said. "I wish *we* had more time."

"You had more than me."

Elaine did not ask what she meant by that.

"What will you do now?"

Nim started to shrug again, but just then she cocked her head to the side, like she was listening to that music that only she could hear.

"Someone is calling me. There has been a death."

"Are you going to go to them?"

"It's what I do now."

She patted her thrall and pointed to a spot on the horizon. Elaine stood there and watched them go. The sun was coming up, a thin line of gold burning over the wood. It was dawn, no time for a child of night.

Except, perhaps, one.

All Sales Final

TANYA BRYAN

udra and her daughter, Lettie, entered the tentacle-like gates as soon as they opened. Audra didn't want to lose her nerve like she had the past several times she'd intended to do this abominable thing. But what choice did she have?

The streets were crowded with merchants and thieves, oftentimes one and the same. Audra held Lettie's hand snug as she dragged the bewildered young girl through endless swarms of people, smells and sights she'd never seen on their farmland.

Lettie didn't have the words to describe any of this, but she soaked it up, wanting to remember every detail of the piles of meat stacked up like bricks, to the smell of the too-ripe fruit making her salivate and realize they hadn't eaten in over a day. Even the piles of grey dust, pestled from hundreds of feet grinding against cobblestones and concrete, seemed to sparkle and look like nothing Lettie had experienced before. The City was full of secrets. She could feel eyes on her as they walked, but when she turned, never found anyone's stare.

Audra hadn't walked this way since she was a child not much older than Lettie, holding her mother's hand just as she held her daughter's now. She remembered the beggars tugging at her sleeves, asking for change or something to eat or favors she didn't understand. But on they went, as they had nothing to give. Now she was the mother tugging her daughter to the place to which she herself never wanted to return; she

saw the frightened awe on her daughter's face, but knew there
was no other choice. They plodded on through the throngs of
people, avoiding the biddings of rebels and buskers all wanting their attention and time. Audra tried to shield Lettie's eyes
from looking up at the gallows, but she insisted on seeing everything. *Conspirator. Looter. Regicide.* She didn't know what
many of the words on the signs meant around the necks of
the hanging dead. The putrid smell of their rotting corpses
told her to learn them quickly, lest she be joining them there.

Through the froths of shoppers bartering for food and
clothing, Audra looked for the signs that would tell her where
to find the one peculiar back alley where the lesser known,
more *complicated* shops were located.

After a few twists and turns down narrowing alleyways, they
arrived at the dilapidated shop with the crooked old sign: *Not
Just Toys!* it announced with false enthusiasm in faded paint,
chipped at the edges. They climbed the rickety stairs, the middle one slumping the same as it had when Audra was a child.
The door was ajar, as if time itself had permanently wedged it
open to ease the comings and goings. Audra went in, Lettie
following close behind. Inside, it was musty and poorly lit.
It took a few moments for their eyes to adjust. When they
did, they saw Old Man Alden sitting behind the counter, his
bat-like mask barely peeking above the toys teetering in front
of him. His blond-red hair shagged around his face, bushing
down to cover his chin. Ageless, or rather, ageful. Always the
same, never getting any older as far as anyone could tell. No
one ever saw him outside the shop. His permanence there was
one of many mysteries surrounding *Not Just Toys!* sitting along
that narrow alley, on the edge of time.

Alden inspected the mother and daughter, noting their
empty hands and boots crusted with mud from the long journey to town. "Hello," he said. "What do you have for me
today? Toys, perhaps?"

Audra shook her head, steeled her nerves. "I came to sell
you my childhood memories," she said, not letting her voice
waver even though she was trembling inside.

"Ah," he said, scratching his beard thoughtfully. "Do you know the rules? And the consequences?" he asked.

"Yes," she said, squeezing her daughter's hand, hoping forgiveness would come with understanding years later. She recited: "Recent memories don't count for much. They're unfinished. Time hasn't moulded them into a softer, more delectable palate. They still have sharp corners that bite, instead of cotton candy-fuzzed edges you can sink your teeth into." She looked at her daughter, who was looking up at her with confusion. She had to look away before she stopped and left. "Happiest childhood memories are worth the most, since they're rare. And the customer doesn't get to choose the memories. They are already chosen as soon as you enter the shop." Audra sighed before she added: "All sales final. No refunds or exchanges."

"Good," Alden said, squinting at her. "Say, aren't you Audra, the one who gave me this?" He brought out a cup with wildflowers in it. The wildflowers were alive, thriving, in the cup with no water or dirt. He handed the cup to Lettie, who relaxed as she plucked at the petals, which drifted to the dusty floor and scuttled away out of the open door, with no discernable wind to help them along.

"That's the present I gave to you for helping us," Audra said, bewildered by how they were still alive despite the fact she'd picked them over 15 years before. "I didn't know what your kind of help meant back then."

"And now you do?" he asked.

"I accept it," she said.

He sat there silently for a while with his eyes closed. Audra was wondering if he'd fallen asleep when he spoke: "There is something else you can do." She looked up at him, still hopeful despite everything she'd been through to avoid coming back here. "You can take my place instead." She frowned. "You can run the shop. There's space in the back where you and your daughter can live, no rent required, which I'm guessing is better than the homelessness you're facing."

She looked at the toys spanning many lifetimes spread

out along the walls. Considering the alternative, the wooden games and dolls with wonky eyes looked ready to welcome her and Lettie home. She looked at her daughter. "What about Lettie? Does she have to stay here until someone takes my place?"

Alden shook his bushy head, the bat mask staying perfectly in place. "No, she'll be free to leave once she turns 18. Earlier, if her father returns for her."

Audra knew her choices were nonexistent. The shadowy version of her mother after selling her memories still haunted her. After their visit to this place, her mother had never been the same. Her best memories sold, there wasn't much left of her. She didn't want Lettie to shudder every time she looked at her. That was too much for anyone to put on a child. She also knew Lettie's father wasn't returning. He'd made it clear he wanted nothing to do with either of them before he joined the rebels and headed north. For all she knew, he'd died in the last uprising. No one had heard word of him for years now.

Audra knelt down and asked Lettie: "What do you say, Sweetness? Do you want this to be our new home?"

Lettie knew they were here out of desperation. Her mother had worried over this voyage for months, trying everything she could to get them out of the trouble they were in with back taxes and constant pillaging of their land until almost nothing was left to eat, let alone sell. She knew they wouldn't be here if there was any other choice. She looked at the hundreds of toys around her, wondering how long it would take to play with each of them. "Yes, Mama," she replied. "I want to learn all the secrets these toys have to share. I'm sure they have plenty. Look at them all!" She smiled her best smile, trying to reassure her mother that this was all right.

Audra took a deep breath and stood, comforted by the ebullience only youth could bring to such a bizarre turn of events. Lettie could experience the childhood she deserved instead of having to grow up too soon and become the caregiver. Turning to Alden, she said, "Yes, we'll stay."

He smiled sadly, bent over and took out a book, which he

pushed across the counter towards her. "This is the ledger of all the sales going back, oh, longer than anyone can remember," he said, brushing the thick coating of grey dust from its cover. She opened it and flipped pages, finding different languages and handwriting throughout. The last 50 pages, at least, all contained the same scrawl she remembered when her mother signed away her memories. She found her mother's X and put her fingers on it, choking back a sob. That was the last time her mother had sought out and held her hand, tightly, as if that touch could tie them together as she signed herself away. After she marked the ledger, her grip slackened. There was a crackle in the air, a flash of light and the smell of sulfur and her mother's eyes went vacant. She dropped Audra's hand completely. Her head bobbed, but she remained standing. "Mama?" Audra said softly, but she didn't respond. Audra tugged on her sleeve and she looked down, not even seeming to recognize her own daughter. Audra wanted to cry, but instead took the bag of coins Old Man Alden held out to her.

"Don't forget this, Audra," Old Man Alden said back then. "You don't want to keep repeating this pattern."

Audra promised Old Man Alden that she would never forget. "Thank you," she said, handing him the cup of wildflowers. She pulled her mother outside and set out to find someone to sell her some farmland.

Audra snapped back to the present. Alden marked the ledger with his loopy signature, now on the customer side, and turned it towards her. She signed her name in the merchant column and felt tingles all along her body.

Alden gave her a slip of yellowed paper, old and tattered. "These are the instructions on how to run the shop. She'll keep you safe, even when you think she won't."

With a nod of his head, Alden walked to the door, letting his bat mask fall to the ground. Outside, he turned to them, waved his hand in their direction and said with his voice suddenly crackling with age: "Take care of her." They weren't sure if he meant the store or each other. The door stayed open so they could watch him age with every step away from the shop. By the time he reached the first bend, his blond-red hair and beard were white and his tall frame looked crunched and withered. And then he vanished into the crowds.

Lettie picked up a doll from a low shelf. Holding it to her ear, she nodded and smiled. "It's going to be okay, Mama. We're going to be okay."

The Whispering Trees

D.T. Neal

n the town of Overwatch, far to the east of the Kingdom of Mandria, there was the Red Wall, the Wall Without Gates, said to have been mortared with the blood of its builders. And beyond the Red Wall, looming over Overwatch itself, was the Red Mountain, a spar of iron-rich rock that pointed like an accusing finger to the northernmost star in the sky.

The Dragon forbade His people to visit the Red Mountain, and had built the Wall Without Gates to keep His people away from it. To pass the Red Wall was to face death—violators who were caught were burned as witches.

Overwatch's seasonal ritual, the Festival of Fire, at the height of summer, had the townspeople gather and wheel one of Overwatch's catapults to the Red Wall and place a burning brand in the catapult's cup, which already contained an incendiary liquid—Dragon's Venom—provided by the Temple.

Sibyl, nearing her 13th year, was transfixed by the Festival of Fire, watching the Dragon's Venom launch over the Red Wall in an incandescent arc, while her father, mother and two older sisters looked on, and the townspeople cheered. Sometimes, the fires would burn for days in the Forbidden Forest that grew beyond the Red Wall, sometimes for weeks. Sometimes they would not burn at all. When it did not burn, it was taken as a sign that the witches beyond the Red Wall had put out the fires of the Faithful. It was considered a bad omen.

When the Forbidden Forest burned well, it was taken as a good omen. Mandria had many enemies abroad, and a constant need for good portents.

To the east was Imperia, the heathen empire of the Preserver, a rival god who was the Dragon's sworn enemy. Although it had been many years since Mandria had last gone to war with Imperia, the history of antagonism between the Kingdom of Mandria and Imperia was a long one, one of unrelenting bloodshed.

Sibyl knew that she would soon be taken to the Temple, and like all Mandrians, become one with the Dragon, their god. She would, like her parents and sisters, become suspicious, superstitious, obedient and utterly devout—the Blood of the Dragon would claim her as it had claimed all Mandrians. Any who had drunk the Blood of the Dragon became His eyes and ears, hands, fists, teeth and claws.

"Will it hurt, Father?" Sibyl asked later, after the Festival of Fire had passed. The fires had burned out almost as soon as they'd been launched, the Dragon's Venom quenched in the darkness of the whispering trees. This was taken as a terrible omen among the townspeople, and had led the priests of the Temple to sermonize against the wickedness of witches and to exhort the townsfolk to pray for their salvation and deliverance from evil. There was also suspicion that there might, in fact, be witches afoot in Overwatch, flown over the Red Wall to plague the Mandrians. This was taken to be one of the reasons why the Dragon's Venom did not burn the forest that year.

Sibyl helped her father organize the aromatic oils that underpinned his trade as a perfumer and poisoner—both occupations were in high demand at the court of King Orelian. Both trades required a ready access to exotic and rare herbs, which made Overwatch a natural place for him to move his family, with all manner of botanicals available nearby.

"No," Father said, his eyes aglitter. "The Blood of the Dragon is like fiery nectar. He becomes one with you, and you come to know Him as He knows you. You will never, ever be alone.

You will become one with all of us. You will know His wrath and glory, His ageless wisdom, and His power without peer."

"Why does He wait until our 13th year?" Sibyl asked. More than her sisters, Sibyl learned her father's craft. Her sisters were more drawn to the seamstress trade their mother pursued, sewing elaborate gowns for the ladies of the Court.

"He waits until you are no longer a child," Father said. "So it is written."

"So it is written," Mother and her sisters echoed, and they all made the Sign of the Dragon, which Sibyl mimicked, because it was all she had ever known.

Her mother was particularly proud of Sibyl's golden locks, for in Mandria, where the Dragon's careful shepherding of His people's unions led to so many with red hair, Sibyl's golden tresses were seen as the Kiss of the Dragon, a sign of special favor. Indeed, to Mandrians, blonde hair was referred to as being "Dragon-kissed" and signified great potential. King Orelian himself had golden hair. Sibyl's mother, Sigrynd, would speak to it sometimes while braiding it.

"The Dragon has special things planned for you, My Dear," Sigrynd said. "He has told me you will have a favored place at Court."

The Mandrian Court was the very center of political life in the entire country, and was what all who served the Dragon aspired to, for in Mandria, the Dragon was supreme, and there was no one closer to the Dragon than the King, and no one closer to the King than his Court.

"Have you ever been to Court, Mama?" Sibyl asked.

"No," Sigrynd said. "I've made dresses for courtiers, but I'm only a seamstress. Your father has been there, a time or two."

"Is it beautiful?" Sibyl asked.

"It is. Beyond measure," Sigrynd said. "And the Dragon wants you there as one of His ladies of the Court."

"What will I do there?" Sibyl asked.

"You will serve His will, as do we all," Sigrynd said. "You will be beautiful and you will be seen, and you will bear beautiful children with golden hair like your own."

"Who will be my husband?" Sibyl asked.

"Why, maybe King Orelian himself will take you as his wife, if you do not embarrass us at Court, Sibyl."

"But what will I *do?*" Sibyl asked. "I'm no noblewoman."

"The Kiss of the Dragon is not lightly turned aside," Sigrynd said. "You are a gift to our family, from the Dragon Himself. We are blessed."

Sigrynd just brushed and braided her hair, a soothing rhythm that Sibyl always enjoyed, while her sisters looked on with open envy laced with barely-hidden hatred.

"It doesn't matter what you do," her oldest sister, Nalla, said. "To be at Court is its own reward, you little fool."

"Truly," said Maryl. "We aren't highborn, Sibyl. For the Dragon to offer you a place in His Court is not to be questioned, you stupid, stupid girl."

Sigrynd stilled her daughters with a stern look. "Don't envy your sister because the two of you are not Dragon-kissed. Although your spite and envy have, no doubt, prepared Sibyl well for what awaits her at Court. From what I've heard, the intrigues are spread thick there."

"It's not fair," Nalla said. "*I* should be the one at Court."

"I'm smarter than all of you combined," Maryl said. "It should be me."

"I don't even want to go to Court," Sibyl said.

Her mother and siblings gasped at that, and her mother tugged on her hair to emphasize her disapproval.

"This is for our family, Sibyl," Sigrynd said. "You will go there, and you will do His bidding. You will do whatever He requires of you. You will not embarrass us."

"Sibyl only thinks about herself, Mama," Maryl said. "She sees things and talks to crows."

Another tug of her hair from her mother's brush.

"No more of that," Sigrynd said. "Believe you me, we'll have none of that. You've seen the firepit in the center of town, Child. You know what happens there."

And Sibyl did, for the center of every town in Mandria had a firepit, which wasn't so much a pit as it was a circular space in the center of town marked off by carefully placed stones, with a charred blackwood pole in the center. It was in this place that enemies of Mandria burned, sacrifices to the Dragon.

Anytime a transgressor had been found—whether through obscenity, blasphemy, heresy, apostasy, iconoclasm, sacrilege—they would be tied to that blackwood pole, kindling piled around them, and some of the Dragon's Venom that the Temple kept poured upon them, and the presiding priest of the Temple would offer them up to the Dragon, and they would burn.

In her young life, Sibyl had seen a dozen burnings at the pyre, had heard the screams of the damned and saw them consumed by the Dragon's holy fire. Most often, it was witches who found their home in the pyre, for the Dragon would not abide witches in His kingdom, and they were rooted out wherever they were found. There was no greater wickedness than witchcraft in holy Mandria, a contravention of the Dragon's will and testament.

"Why does He burn witches, Mama?" Sibyl asked.

"Because they threaten His order," Sigrynd said, her eyes turning golden and her voice changing to a faraway, tinny rasp that was echoed by her sisters, who had been taken by the Dragon as well, and spoke in unison:

"I will not suffer a witch to live in My Mandria, little Sibyl."

"Mama?" Sibyl asked, turning, terrified at the manifestation of the Dragon in her home, seeing all of them gazing at her with golden eyes.

"Witches are kindling to Me," they said in unison, in that serpentine rasp that was the Voice of the Dragon. *"They have no place in My kingdom beyond fuel for My holy fires. Know that I am watching you, Child. Always."*

Then the Dragon left them, and her mother and her sisters swayed, sweating and dizzy, the manifestation gone as if it had never been, and Sibyl was terrified at the golden gaze of the Dragon, for she had heard of it, how the Dragon sometimes entered His people and spoke through them, but she had never directly seen it, and never thought it would be directed at her, that the Dragon had seen her. It left her shaking, afraid.

"You see?" Sigrynd said, mopping her sweating brow. "Do you understand?"

To have a visitation from the Dragon was a miraculous moment, and her mother called out to her father, and all of them threw themselves on the ground and prayed.

"The Dragon came to us," Sigrynd said. "He spoke through us. Spoke to Sibyl."

Her father's face was filled with envy, and he grabbed Sibyl with both arms, made her look him in the face.

"What did He say? What did He say to you?"

"He warned me about witches, Papa," Sibyl said. "That's all."

Her father released her and paced around, trying to divine the meaning of it. "I'll go to the Temple and ask. They'll understand."

And he ran out of their home, toward the Temple, which loomed over Overwatch like a great, golden, spired sentinel.

Watching him go, Sibyl cried, ran free of her mother, and ran outside into the chill morning air, hands shaking, tears running down her face. She had never been more afraid in all of her life. Sibyl dropped to her knees into the feygrass that grew nearby, sweet-smelling fronds brushing at her cheeks in the breeze, as she turned her gaze to the Red Mountain, the insolent incline that it was, affront to the Dragon, pinnacle that even He could not dispose of, it would seem. The Red Mountain was forever a thorn in the Dragon's paw.

Why the Dragon had not razed it, had not destroyed this place, was unknown to Sibyl. But she was not the fool that Maryl thought she was, for even in her childish mind, she understood something—the Red Mountain stood walled because it was somehow beyond the Dragon's power. There was some ineffable quality to the place that exceeded His capacity to control and destroy. It was as simple as that, for everyone in Mandria knew that when something displeased the Dragon, that thing was destroyed.

But there was a wall separating Mandria from that mountain, and a wall could serve only two purposes—to keep something in, and to keep something out. So, to her mind, the Red Wall reflected not the power of the Dragon, but His weakness. She did not understand why, but it was clear to her. Clear as the caw of the crows that flitted about whenever she went outside.

Her father had brought Father Crennwyn from the Temple, and the old priest gazed at Sibyl with his hawkish eyes, his wild hair bright red, wearing his gilt robes and bearing the bejeweled Book of the Dragon.

Sibyl saw them approach and wanted to flee, but stood her ground, looked the priest in the eye, while crows cawed from the trees in the distance.

"We know the Dragon spoke to you," Crennwyn said, taking his seat across from her. "It was a warning He shared with you."

"A warning?" Sibyl asked.

"Beware the whispering trees, Child," Crennwyn said. "They call to the unwary and the innocent, lure you from safety. This place, your home, your country—this is safety. Beyond that Red Wall is only pestilence, death and damnation."

"Why does the Dragon not raze the Red Mountain, Father?" Sibyl asked.

"He leaves it as a monument to malevolence," Crennwyn said. "A warning to all who would dare to transgress against Him. If He wished it, He could smite the Red Mountain and turn it to rubble. Yet He does not. Tell me why."

"Is it a test, Father?" Sibyl asked.

"Yes," Crennwyn said. "It surely is. He leaves it there as a temptation. It is like when the Golden Dragons make war on an enemy—they do not cut off means of retreat. For if you back someone into a corner, desperation helps them find their courage. So long as there is a means of escape, the weak will seek it out. So it is with the Red Mountain—He leaves it there that it might tempt the weak-willed and sinister souls who might be drawn to it, to better help Him draw out those among His flock who are fit only for the fire."

Sibyl considered the priest's words, and looked at her parents and her siblings, for they were all looking at her, now. Crennwyn spoke again.

"The Dragon knows who you are, Child," he said. "He knows what you might become. He offers you a proper way, a sanctioned path for your talents. One of honor and service to the Kingdom. There is no other path but the pyre. Do you understand me when I say this? Do not trust the whispering trees—they only serve to lead you astray, far from hearth and home, and from light and law."

Sibyl nodded, and Father Crennwyn left her in the care of her parents. Sibyl wanted to see beyond the Red Wall more than anything, but she knew also that she could not tell a soul, because the Dragon's spies were everywhere. In Mandria, every adult was an agent of the Dragon, as the possession of her mother and sisters so clearly demonstrated.

But she had told Anders, a boy she suspected Father wanted her to marry, who had not yet drunk the Blood of the Dragon, but would a few months before she would. Red-haired and roguish, Anders laughed at her, and laughed with her. He trained as a warrior, a squire who aspired to become one of the fabled Golden Dragons Crennwyn had alluded to, the order of knights who defended Mandria from infidels. No one was more gallant and brave than the Golden Dragons.

"Why would you want to go over the Red Wall, Sib?" Anders asked. "It's death to any who do. You know that as well as anyone."

"But I want to see," Sibyl said. "I have dreams of it. I dream that I'm a crow and I fly over the wall. Father Crennwyn came to warn me about it. The Dragon spoke to me about it, after a fashion."

"A warning. That's what the Festival of Fire is," Anders said. "Or should be. This year was certainly a disappointment, wasn't it?"

"But why the wall?" Sibyl asked. "What's He afraid of?"

Anders looked around them, even though they were alone

together on a hill. Like most Mandrians, he lacked much imagination, simply laughed at her, pawed at her mane of golden hair, like buffed brass. "Only infidels and apostates and heretics would ever dare to cross that wall."

"But it surrounds a forest," Sibyl said. "I've seen it. Though we try to burn the woods every summer, the forest remains. The trees never cease their whispering."

And she had seen it. Like much of the land in the east, there were hills and mountains aplenty, not just the Red Mountain alone, and from those places, she'd been able to look over the Red Wall from a distance, and could see the thick forest that grew around it, and the massive lake that lay at the foot of the Red Mountain.

Contrasted with the farmland around Overwatch, the tamed land, the land beyond the Red Wall looked lush and inviting, a sea of green in summer, and a dazzling blend of red, orange, and yellow in the fall.

"You might as well put that out of your head now, Sib," Anders said. "I'm for the Golden Dragons soon enough, and you'll be my wife. Our parents have practically betrothed us. Once married, we'll leave Overwatch and head west to the capital, and I'll have made my name as a Golden Dragon, and you'll be my lady at Court."

Sibyl could not imagine herself a courtier, least of all in the court of King Orelian, where she was likelier to end up as one of his many lovers, for the King's appetites were well-known, although no one dared question them. Indeed, it was something of an honor for a woman at Court to bear one of the King's bountiful bastards.

"Don't you wonder what's past the Red Wall?" Sibyl asked.

Anders, as ever, was unfazed. "I don't care. Trees. Squirrels. Nuts. Are you a nut, Sib?"

"I'm not insane," Sibyl said. "Only curious."

"Curiosity has no place in Mandria," Anders said. "Curiosity kills."

He toyed with her bodice as they sat together in a field of fireflowers, a sea of red that rivaled the red of the Red Mountain. Sibyl kissed Anders, and he kissed her back, long and hard, with the fitful ardor of the man-child that he was.

"If you were a knight, I'd ask you to find me a way across that wall," Sibyl said.

"If I were a knight, I'd never let you go," Anders said, clutching her hand in his.

Sibyl plucked a handful of fireflowers, a bouquet, and sniffed at them. Thanks to her father, she knew every wildflower, every plant and weed, every tree, and what they could do, and how to draw forth their essences into essential oils that could create intoxicating scents.

"Soon you'll be the Dragon's," Sibyl said. "And I'll not be able to trust you."

"You can always trust me, Sib," Anders said, taking the fireflowers from her and lobbing them over his shoulder, scattering them in the breeze. "Forever."

Yet, when his 13th year came, Anders went with the others who shared his birthdate to the Temple, in the Red Procession, and drank the Blood of the Dragon, overseen by Crennwyn, who was rumored to crush feyberries into a paste that he applied to his white hair to turn it bright crimson.

Sibyl watched Anders drink of the Blood of the Dragon, saw the golden flagon that was in the sinuous shape of the Dragon pour forth the red elixir, and saw Anders, like all of the others, transformed, saw him flush, saw his eyes grow fervent and far-seeing, as he became one with the Dragon. It was a frightening change he underwent, a communal gasp echoed by all of the onlookers, the adults who had undergone the ritual of binding.

"One of us," the people of Overwatch said, in unison, of one voice, a golden-eyed chorus of the faithful, their eyes like coins. "One of us. One of us."

Anders and the others held hands and received the chorus with zealous enthusiasm, and, in the celebration that followed, he sought her out, a man, now, no longer a boy.

"Sibyl," Anders said, golden-gazed. "I see you with new eyes. I look upon you with the eyes of the Dragon."

Sibyl was afraid, for the zealous fire in his eyes had doused the impish spirit of Anders. He had become someone else. She'd never known her family to be any other way, but with Anders, she could see the difference in him, and it made her sad beyond belief.

"You cannot know how it feels," Anders said. "But you will. He is with me. He is with all of us. He is watching. He sees you, Sibyl."

"Call me Sib," Sibyl said, upset at the formality that had crept into his voice.

"You are Sibyl," Anders said. "He knows that you seek to cross the Red Wall. He forbids it, Sibyl. Only witches dare to cross the Red Wall, and you are to be no witch. He knows what I know. I have told Him everything that I held in my heart. You'll see, Sibyl. Soon, you will know Him."

Anders reached out and took her by the wrist, gripping her tightly. His hand was hot to the touch, as if he were feverish.

"You are to be mine," Anders said. "You are to be His. You are to be ours. A Daughter of the Dragon."

Sibyl pried her hand free of his, for he was hurting her. The lust in his eyes was not like the playfully amorous looks he'd given her before. She could see his plans for her, giving him child after child, delivering them unto the Dragon in their 13th years, and he, a great knight of the Dragon, armored in gold, in service to King Orelian. In that moment, she could see the fate he had in mind for her, and she recoiled from it.

She could see the red print of his fingers on her wrist, could see the hardness of his gaze upon her, and felt so afraid.

She would not allow this to come to pass. Even if she were to die in the attempt, she would resist this fate. A crow cawed from an ironwood tree, and then another. Sibyl turned her gaze to the great black birds, who seemed to regard her a moment before flying east, over the wall, and into the Forbidden Forest, without a care, to find concealment amid the whispering trees.

"Filthy blackbirds," Anders said. "I'll bring my bow next time and stick them with arrows."

Sibyl watched the hate crease his young face, and felt a sorrowful loneliness overtake her. Anders was gone, wrapped tight in the coils of the Dragon.

Sibyl slipped out on a rainy night shortly thereafter, when her family was asleep, and she stole out to the Red Wall, walked it in the dark, felt the stones of it with her hands, trying to find a way past it. She carried with her some bread and water, and several of her father's precious vials of perfumes and poisons she'd taken with her, and some of his little recipe books, scrawled in his deft and darting hand.

"Please," Sibyl said. "Let me through."

But the Red Wall did not answer, and it did not open for her, and no one came to deliver her across it. Sibyl drew forth a length of braided silk she had made out of the sight of her family, upon which she had tied a grapple made from a horseshoe, and hurled it overhead. It took her three tries to get it to catch over the wall.

Then she wound the braided line over her fists and pulled herself up the wall, winding the line around her wrists and arms as she forced her way up, pausing, hanging while she caught her breath, until, after an agonizing ascent, she had reached the top of the Red Wall, and collapsed upon it in the rain, her wrists and arms throbbing.

She could see Overwatch in the rain, the few watchlights that were lit, for in Mandria, no one ventured out in the dark; the Dragon forbade it, enforced a curfew among His people.

Only the Golden Dragons ventured out after dark, along with other appointed agents of the Crown. Had she been caught, she'd have been detained, and had she been detained, Sibyl would have paid dearly for her transgression. She could have been branded. She could have been burned. She could have been sent to the Red Abbey, forced to atone for her transgression.

Sibyl understood that when she crossed that wall, she would never be able to return to Mandria, had crossed into another place, a place beyond the Dragon. To her family, none of whom suspected that she sought to pass over the Red Wall, there would be the momentary mystery of her absence, until Anders, or even the Dragon Himself, spoke to them about what had happened, that their youngest daughter had sought to travel over the Red Wall.

It would be incomprehensible to them, she knew. They could not hope to understand why she would have done it, for they lived in service to the Dragon, and would live and die within the borders of Mandria, their fates decided. There would be an investigation, but her family had nothing to hide. Perhaps that was why Sibyl refused to tell them—she did not want them to pay for her own transgressions, or worse, to try to stop her.

Looking into the wilderness of trees that grew thick and wild, contrasted with the denuded landscape of her home, it could be no clearer than this. She would not drink the Blood of the Dragon. She would dance in the heart of a sacrificial bonfire before she ever succumbed to Him. In the darkness, crows cawed, a chorus of them. Sibyl was sure they called for her. It was an omen, as surely as the dousing of the Dragon's Venom during the Festival of Fire.

Drawing a deep breath, Sibyl leaped into the dark of the whispering trees, trusting the grasping branches of the Forbidden Forest to break her fall.

And they did.

Grey Magic

J.T. Lawrence

When people ask me what I do, I usually lie. I used to tell the truth, when I was young and had an exoskeleton woven from life-spirit and arrogance, as most young people do. Before that threaded shell was gradually eroded by the hurt in the world: the violence, the bad luck. Now only middle-aged, liver-spotted skin remains, which is no adequate barrier to life's bashing. Now I have to protect myself in other ways; age and wisdom bring another type of armour.

I used to tell the truth, but now the lies slide out of my mouth like spotted eels. Easy and familiar. When I get bored of the untruths, I make up more, to keep things interesting. A year ago, I would have told you, if I had bumped into you at a conference or a cocktail party, that I was a botanist. The trick to believable deception, as I'm sure you know, is to keep it as truthful as possible. I have trained in botany, so it is an obvious one, one that springs quickly to my just-licked lips. But I am also qualified—fib-wise—to be a doctor, an astronomer, a zoologist, an archaeologist, a chemical engineer. Sometimes I surprise myself: my subconscious becomes adventurous, wants to pursue less lofty careers. I become a marketing consultant, a sous-chef, a yoga instructor.

When I was starting out, I thought I had to tell people what I did—what I really did—in order to get work, but I have since found that when you do the work well, the work will come. The universe, after all, supports action. Now, I only accept referrals from close friends and previous clients (the ones that are still alive, anyway).

The reality is there is never any shortage of demand for the kind of work I do. Telling strangers about my vocation hardly ever translates into real jobs, anyway. I find time-wasters incredibly annoying. I picture them as velcro-legged parasites that cling to my aura until they have unloaded their whole Sorry Story, only to refuse my offer of professional help. It takes all the self-control I can muster to not place some kind of small, irritating hex on them, a monkey on their back, just to cause them the same amount as chagrin that they have caused me. That kind of tit-for-tat may seem childish to you, but it keeps the cosmos nicely balanced. "An eye for an eye" out of the old book was never meant to be vengeful or malicious; it was instead to keep The Balance. If The Balance is off, bad things can happen. Some people call it karma, others say that "the wheel turns." It's all true, no matter how you choose to dress it up, with gory stories of biblical eye-gouging savagery or with glittering, ice-cream-coloured animal gods. The wheel just keeps on turning.

Worse than the time-wasters are the impromptu sermons delivered to me in inopportune places, like on the train, or standing in line for my daily fix. It's awkward. I'm always amazed at how many religious fanatics there are in our midst, dressed like ordinary people, slacks and crumpled tees, or polka-dotted summer dresses and glass beads, doing things that ordinary people do: eating processed-cheese sandwiches and listening to music on their phones. Using greasy hand cream that smells of roses. They seem so normal from the outside. It's only when they start babbling about necromantic prophets and being "saved" that you realise they have demons in their heads. When you look closely you see black scribbles on their auras. In my opinion, religious fundamentalism is a psychological disorder that has yet to be officially classified.

It's easy for me, in this day and age, to sit in the branches of my oak tree, feeling the light dapple my cheeks, the breeze lifting my hair, as if flying—when all feels right in the world—

and ruminate about these people, but my predecessors weren't that lucky. There were no tree-dreams for them. No leisure to sit in a leafy bower and shine acorns, contemplating the spinning cycle of life. Just a couple of hundred years ago I would have been dragged down and lit up. Sometimes I wake up in a fever, as if I am on fire. It spreads from my feet upwards, like I am burning on a stake somewhere in a parallel (or previous) life. The first time it happened, when I was a little girl, I just lay there and blazed. I remember feeling paralysed by the fear of my destiny; perhaps even wished to burn up altogether. Wished to be nothing more than a glint of sad ashes in the creeping morning light. The next day, my legs were covered in blisters. The time after that, I ran an ice bath as soon as I felt it start, which I have been doing ever since. I lie in the arctic water and listen to my heart slow: run ice cubes over my flickering skin, absorbing the cold; the opposite of a sun lizard. Sometimes the fever brings with it auditory hallucinations: chanting, shouting, the sound of an angry mob. The crackling of a spiteful fire. I don't know if I experience these episodes because my energy has an intense empathy for my foremothers, or if they are echoes of my previous, or future, lives. Whatever the reason, I thank the universe daily for the Age of Enlightenment. Of course, I use the word "enlightenment" loosely. I'm also grateful for my ice machine.

So I lie about what I do because of the fundamentalists and the time-wasters, and also to preserve my psychic energy. I've had enough of the rubbernecking. This fox mantle of dishonesty, this deception, can be lonely, but in my experience—and as parents warn—no good comes from talking to strangers.

At the moment, if anyone asks, I'm a shopkeeper. In a way it's true: I sell all kinds of ideas scratched on paper. I've always liked the idea of owning a bookshop.

It's not only strangers I lie to. I am less than honest with my clients, too. I guess you could say that I place less emphasis on the truth than most people, but only ever for the right reasons. I find honesty for the sake of honesty naïve and often unnecessarily harmful. Sometimes a profoundly dishonest act can have a major positive affect on someone's life. For example, a client of mine—let's call her "Betty"—was having trouble getting pregnant. I could sense, in the first consultation, that she was perfectly fertile (her energy was the colour of a ripe mandarin) but despite this, Betty's womb remained stubbornly barren. I told her I'd have her pregnant within three new moons. All it would take was some skilful spell-crafting, an eggshell sail, and a little resourcefulness on my side. In the Dark Ages we were called "the cunning folk" for good reason.

It was clear to me that her husband's sperm was the problem, although Betty wouldn't entertain this idea, wouldn't even "insult him" by having him tested, as if he was some kind of caveman with the emotional intelligence of a Sumatran Orangutan. The matter of their infertility was not even discussed in their household, apart from their monthly ritual of him shooting reproachful looks at her tear-stained face, raw and bruised by her steady disappointment.

They had been trying for six years, which was good news for me: 6 is an incredibly fertile number, as you can probably guess from the shape. It also told me that if it hadn't happened by now, it probably wasn't going to happen unless I took some drastic action.

Once I was prepared, Betty was mid-cycle, and the moon was full, it was time to cast the spell. She had invited her sister, Danielle, for moral support, as she was keeping my services a secret from her Orangutan.

"I just want you to know that I don't approve of what you do," were the first words the sister said to me.

"Okay," I said, and continued to unpack my things. I would have preferred "Hello."

"I just don't think it's right," she insisted.

"Oh, Danielle," sighed Betty.

"In fact, I think…" she started. I could tell that she was

about to hit her stride if I didn't interrupt her.

"You are more than welcome," I said, "to wait outside."

"Out-side?" she said, as if it was the first time she had ever heard the word. I found myself wishing that she would close her gaping-fish mouth. If we were characters in a comic book I could have waved my wand—abracadabra!—and turned her into a puffer fish, bouncing and flapping on the kitchen floor.

"There is no place for negative energy here tonight," I said, slowly and clearly, to the sister. "If you have a problem, it's best to go, and leave this sacred space." I was hamming it up a bit, for effect. Perhaps I am less mature than I give myself credit for.

"Sacred?" she gasped. "Sacred?" It took remarkable restraint on my behalf to not ask her if English was her first language. If her reaction weren't interfering with my work I would have found her outrage quite entertaining.

"Look, Dan, this was a mistake."

"Yes! That's what I was trying to tell you!"

"No, I mean, I think you should go," Betty said to her, gently.

"I'm not leaving you with this...this..."

What would she think would happen if she left her sister in my supposedly evil clutches, I wondered? That I would possess her, kill her, steal her soul? I wasn't surprised by Danielle's attitude. You are bound to bump up against some people in my business, people who believe that witchery is wicked. Little do they know that they cast spells themselves, when they curse other drivers in traffic, touch wood, or blow out birthday candles.

"I need this to work," said Betty.

"Listen to me," whispered her sister, bunching up her fists around the gold crucifix that dangled from her moist and unpleasantly chunky neck. "You don't need to do this. Come to our church! Our cell group has been praying for you..."

"And she has yet to conceive," I said. "You say you don't like spells, what do you think prayer is? You just haven't been saying the right ones."

Blasphemy! her aura shouted.

"And I suppose you know the right ones?" She eyed me: a wolf in wolf's clothing.

"Yes," I said. "It's my job."

I began the ceremony by smudging the room with the sweet smoke of lavender and white sage. With a piece of chalkstone I drew a circle on the pine floorboards around Betty, on which I placed six green candles. I anointed the candles with vanilla oil, lit them, then began my fertility incantation. Betty was instructed to close her eyes and sit as still as possible, as if meditating, and just allow the spell to wash through her. Her hands were placed over her abdomen, sending warmth and acceptance deep into her pelvic chakra. Afterwards, we sailed the eggshell by moonlight while Betty recited a poem she had written, inviting the soul of her baby into her body. I found her vulnerability touching, and couldn't help thinking that she would make a tender mother. I gave her a silver bracelet with a charm of a carnelian-eyed hare—I had charged the crystal with pentacle-cast spells—as well as a gift of bespoke tea: stinging nettle, red clove and raspberry leaf, which she was to drink every day. She held my hands and thanked me. On my way out, I gave her a syringe I had been keeping warm between my breasts. I told her it was a potion to open and soften her cervix, and that she should keep it at blood temperature and use it before making love to her husband that night.

Six weeks later, Betty was pregnant, as I knew she would be. She has since given birth to a bonny little boy with a full head of hair and an easy smile. Her Orangutan will never know that the child is not biologically his.

The timing of Betty's lunacycle couldn't have been more perfect. I had been consulting that day with another client of mine who was having trouble sustaining his phallus. Feri, or sexual mysticism, is a speciality of mine, and I had been training him in the art of Tantra. This client wasn't dissimilar-looking to the man in the wedding photo that Betty had given me. Without going into too many details, this client had inadvertently given me the means to help Betty. The universe had been particularly supportive that day, as it can be, when you are following a beneficent course of action. Neither client was aware of the transaction, and they were both extremely pleased with the results. Had I been honest with either of them, the outcome would not have been nearly as satisfactory.

The thing about earth magic is that it can go either way. We are all under the influence of so many factors at any one time that it's not an exaggeration to say that anything can happen. Without even knowing it, our destinies are pushed and pulled by the sparkling cosmos, kneaded and knocked back like baker's dough. You can try your best to stake out your life's path—or others' lives, as I do—but our humanly influence is limited. There are people—women and men—who become taken with a neopagan lifestyle, study Wicca, indulgently call themselves White Witches, but if they truly knew their craft, they would know that there is no such thing. These dabblers are the moths of the sorcery world, not unpleasant to have around unless they get confused and start battering themselves against a light-source that is not the moon. Some are elegant and pretty to look at, others leave moth-dust and holes in your winter underwear.

There is no such thing as white magic. Real magic is a wide spectrum encompassing good and evil, and there are very many shades of grey in-between. The reason a spell can never be pure white is because of the cosmic baker's influence. A sorceress may start out with a clear, benevolent purpose, unalloyed ingredients, and a pure heart, and perform the incantation as close to perfectly as she can manage, but after that, she has little influence. Once it is out of her mouth, the spell is out of her hands, and cannot be kept un-grubby.

As with magic, as with witches. Just as a person cannot be 100 percent good, a witch, as pure-thinking as she may be, cannot achieve Perfect Snow. Witches are human, after all. She may be milk, ivory, or limestone, or one of the hundreds of shades between them, but never fresh snow. You have this trembling human spectrum overlapping and interweaving with the sure orbit of magic, and it becomes evident—despite the illusions of the giggling Wiccans—that a White Witch is nothing but a fairytale.

I am under none of the pagan pretences. I practice grey magic; more dove-grey than charcoal. Or more accurately: the colour of a raincloud as it swells and shrinks and flickers between shades of pearl and slate. I have to be careful of slipping towards the sooty part of the spectrum. The darker the magic, the quicker the flame takes, the more powerful you feel. You have to be on your guard and think things through: sometimes you set out to do good and the result is murky, or worse. I once killed someone with a simple love spell. That may sound like I'm just not a very proficient witch, but the opposite is true. The spell was one of my best: refined over and over again to be as simple and striking as possible. But setting out, I wasn't told the whole story. A woman had left a man, and the spell was to reunite them. What I hadn't been told was that the woman had left the man for someone else. That someone else happened to meet with an accident the day I triple-cast the reunion conjuration: an innocent bystander, he was shot in a cash-in-transit heist. My client, his grief-stricken lover returned, had been delighted, and paid me double. It had not been my intention. Apparently they are happily married now. He still sends me fruit baskets.

Taking lives is not always dark sorcery. Counterintuitive as it may seem, killing people is sometimes the kindest, and most important work I do. In a topsy-turvy society such as ours, where your life is not your own, a sensible outsider—

not bound by popular morality—is sometimes required. On occasion, a client needs to be supported in their decision to perform certain actions that are usually frowned upon by the bleating world at large. This is where my services come in, as a non-judgmental advisor, helper, sponsor, drug dealer, psychologist, relationship counsellor, prostitute, or mercy nurse. Being a witch isn't about spells and trickery—not really— more than anything else, it's about having a completely open mindset, and having the courage of your convictions. In short, to be a consummate witch, you have to have a titanium spine.

I help the client take a psychic step away from their supposed reality, and offer them a perspective that is unconstrained by the values of others. I coax them out of the dogma-box. Although most people seem happy to be trained and controlled by banks, employers and television, it is only when we are unfettered by indoctrination that we can live our free and true lives. I help people with this awakening, but often this bitter-bright truth comes too late, when they are in an acute crisis, or are dying.

The client I am busy working with has stage 4 pancreatic cancer. He joked when he called me, saying: "there is no stage 5". He needed someone who was willing to end his life for him, when the time came, and he found that time rapidly approaching. Just a month ago, he told me, he was driving his Porsche Carrera with the top down, meeting friends for lunch, drinking Scotch, and following the Premier League. But now he finds his appetite vanished, his balance is off. He can't hear properly, doesn't have the energy to drive.

"Could it be true?" he asks me, "That my drive to the café around the corner, for the paper, was my last? That I'll never drive again?"

It wasn't just his beloved car he was grieving, of course, but his independence. His life as he knew it. He is plagued by a constant "empty" pain in his abdomen that gnaws at his mood. He has no children, his wives are all estranged. His doctor says her hands are tied, there are no more treatments available, that she can only make him "comfortable."

"Comfortable?" he demands. "What the hell is comfortable about dying?"

I wouldn't say he is at peace with his impending death, but he doesn't want to live like this. Not when we know there will be no improvement.

"I should be grateful, I suppose," he says to me, "Going downhill so quickly. It's what every terminal patient hopes for…once you reach the top of the hill, that is."

It's difficult to be grateful when you feel your life is being snatched away. He is not the kind of man who will accept being bedridden, or fed chicken broth with a spoon. He has lost 8 kg in the past two weeks. When he can no longer walk, I take things to cheer him up. He still likes iced coffee but refuses berry pinwheel pastries, his former favourite combination.

On the third day, the heavens open up and blast us with a dramatic thunderstorm. Once the rain slows I follow the sound of mewling outside to discover trees stripped by wind and a skinny-ribbed kitten with opalescent eyes. I rub her dry with a tea towel to reveal tiger stripes and chinchilla-soft fur. I place her on my client's chest, and she soothes him with her loud purring.

I read the newspaper to him as his consciousness swims in and out of shallow sleep. I tell him the football score, who has saved a goal, who has been carded. I am with him for five days and five nights. Every hour drains me, although I try not to show it. We do this pretend-dance of patient and nurse until today when he takes my wrist in his cool bony fingers and says he is ready.

The truth is that nothing is being snatched away from him, not permanently. Once his heart stops knocking and his cells power down, his energy will move on to a better place. Not heaven (or hell), not a resting place, but a living place. I have told him that energy cannot be destroyed, only converted, but his imagination cannot stretch that far. It's not a "better place"—not necessarily, just different—like a new day. You don't know exactly what it will hold, but it will surely be kinder to him than this suffering. We are all souls surfing through history. This moving on, this energy conversion, is why I have no problem with ending someone's current life. It is no more sinister than putting a child to sleep.

There is a common misconception that ending a terminal illness requires active euthanasia, but this is most often not the case. The majority of the time, all that is needed is for the patient to sign a living will that refuses any further medical treatment, and for the caregivers to respect his or her wishes. The very last thing a terminally ill patient wants is to be fussed over with antibiotics and feeding tubes in order to prolong his pain, but this is often what families insist on. They panic and press red buttons and jam oxygen masks over their loved ones' faces, despite their clear DNR stickers, because they are the ones afraid of death.

In most cases I have found that if you cut off all access to medical treatment and are liberal with the painkillers, nature takes its course easily, and the soul is allowed to ascend, un-barbed, to its beckoning place. Sometimes gentle help is needed: extra analgesics, if you can get them, or a steady pillow over a slumbering face.

"I'm ready," he says to me now, clear-eyed. "I'm ready to go."

With a long match, I light the nine black candles in the room, and smudge with sandalwood and willow. I put a smooth Obsidian stone in his palm. I recite the Druidic Death Hex under my breath. The kitten's purring gets louder as the magic electrifies the room. I load up a syringe with morphine, nine times the prescribed dose, and push the needle into one of the beetroot-purple veins that snake over his arms. I can see the effects of the drug cascade over him; his relief is instant. I hold his hand as the spirit leaves his body. I feel a pull, a falling away, and then it's gone. The room exhales. The wheel turns, the cycle spins. There is no need to check his pulse, or put a mirror near his mouth to search for breath. Nothing remains but a sad skeleton in skin. The kitten cries.

I blow out the candles and pack my things, including a fat envelope of cash with my name on it. I wipe the house down to vanish any fingerprints. After a moment's hesitation, I put the moping kitten in my basket, too. I have always resisted having a cat, given my occupation. It seemed a terrible cliché, like sporting a wart on my nose, or flying a broom.

Today, however, I no longer mind the idea. I let myself out of the house, and leave the polished key under the doormat. The wind has picked up, and dead leaves flutter and swirl across my path like ugly butterflies. The moon is waning, and I'm feeling a bit older, colder, bashed-about.

Burnt out. Ashes to glinting ashes.

It will be nice to have a warm creature at home. We can sit in the oak tree together.

The Robbery

CYNTHIA WARD

Chicago Suburbs, Summer 1995

arah Martin unlocked the front door of her tract house and stood staring: the kitchen door had been broken open. She'd been burglarized. Again. A month after she'd bought this house in a "safe suburban neighborhood," someone had broken in when she'd gone to Chicago for the weekend. They hadn't taken anything except the coins on her nightstand, but still she had felt furious and violated.

This time Sarah had told no one she was going away except her neighbors, the Armstrongs: a friendly, nervous blond housewife named Trisha and her pompous lawyer husband, Carmichael. They'd known about her previous break-in, and they'd agreed not to tell anyone she was going away. They wouldn't have told anyone. Except, Sarah suddenly realized, their son.

She'd never met the boy, but when she'd invited the Armstrongs to dinner, Carmichael had boasted at length about his only son, Thomas. About what a great athlete and terrific quarterback, what an over-achieving student and well-behaved Christian his son was. Because Thomas was so good, Carmichael Armstrong had bought his son a Corvette and, if Thomas didn't get a full scholarship, he would pay his son's way through college and law school. "I had to drive a dangerous junk car and pay for my education with lousy back-breaking labor," Carmichael had told Sarah over dinner. "Why should my son suffer through some low-paying menial job when he doesn't have to?" Sarah had said nothing, though she'd been angry at Carmichael's scornful dismissal of labor—all her relatives back East worked hard jobs, lobstering, logging, driving trucks, waiting tables, and they deserved respect. Sarah had held her tongue and, remembering the brawny, sullen youth she'd seen working on the sports car in the Armstrongs' driveway, she had thought that Thomas would benefit enormously from working like every college-bound teenager she'd ever known—including herself.

But they seemed to do things differently in the Midwest. Especially when the kid was the star quarterback of the high school football team.

She'd lived here a year now, and Sarah still couldn't believe how *big* football was in the Midwest. God, the high school teams played in stadiums of NFL dimensions! Schools in eastern Maine couldn't even afford football. The boys played soccer, and often the spectators didn't have a bench to sit on.

Sarah Martin realized she was still standing in her doorway, staring into space. Shaking off her stunned reverie, she reached down and picked up the rope that had lain alongside the inner sill of her front door. The rope was slightly longer than the doorsill, and tied along its length in four complex knots. Sarah stepped into the house, closed the door, and untied every knot in the rope. She went to each window, removing the ropes from their sills and undoing their four knots. Then she went to the half-open kitchen door that opened into her tiny back yard. The doorjamb had been splintered by blows to the latch and deadbolt. Hammered open by someone strong, just like last time. Sarah looked down. The knotted rope had been slightly disturbed. She picked up the rope but did not touch the four knots.

The utility drawer was open and in disarray, but nothing appeared to be missing. Sarah dropped the lengths of rope in the drawer. Had it worked?

She called the police.

While moving through the house she'd noticed that she

hadn't lost any big-ticket items; she still had the stereo, the TV and VCR, the CDs and videocassettes, the computer and printer. When she hung up the phone, she checked her medicine cabinet and her yanked-open closets and drawers. The thief had gone through her jewelry box but taken nothing—had busted open her strongbox but ignored her stock certificate for the private medical clinic where she worked; however, he had taken the silver dollar her father had given to her before he'd died.

Sarah's fists clenched with rage.

He'd gone through her underwear drawer. He hadn't done anything except search for money, but she still couldn't bear the knowledge that he'd fingered her panties and bras. She emptied the drawer in the laundry basket.

Two officers and one detective arrived in response to her call. The uniforms dusted for fingerprints. The plainclothesman asked questions and Sarah answered.

Then she said, "Detective Adams, can I tell you something in private?"

"Pete," he said. "Sure."

She stepped into her home office and Pete Adams followed. She closed the door and spoke softly: "I've only been gone two nights. And I'm a doctor, so I keep weird hours. Someone who knows my movements did this. It was a neighborhood kid."

"Definitely," Adams said. "This has all the earmarks of a juvenile perpetrator. Ninety percent of these crude B-and-Es are committed by kids looking for money."

"I'll bet," Sarah said. "Pete, I know my neighbors' son broke in here."

"He's under eighteen?" Adams asked. Sarah nodded. "A juvenile. If he has a record, we can bring him in."

"What?" Sarah cried. "Under those conditions, no juvenile thief could get a record!"

"I'm sorry, I was unclear. If we lift fingerprints that match a convicted juvenile's prints, we can make an arrest. But we can't go and fingerprint a juvenile without a record purely on your say-so. We'll question your neighbors—if someone else witnessed the crime and recognized the perpetrator, or gives a description matching your neighbor's kid, then we can bring him in. But a hunch isn't enough, Dr. Martin."

"Christ," Sarah said. "I know it's the son of my neighbors across the street. I asked them to keep an eye on my place and not to tell anyone I was gone. I know their son did it. I know he did both break-ins here. The thief is Thomas Armstrong."

"Thomas Armstrong!" Adams exclaimed. "The star quarterback of the Lincolnville Eagles. Ma'am, no one will believe the biggest celebrity in town broke into your place."

Sarah's eyes narrowed and her mouth opened.

"Oh, I believe you, Dr. Martin," Adams said. "Thomas is a spoiled, swell-headed brat. I think he's broken into some other houses on this street. But you keep your suspicion to yourself. Telling anyone else won't do anything but make you enemies. Anyway, it is possible Thomas didn't break into your house this time. Yesterday he woke up in such terrible pain he could hardly move. His parents took him to the hospital. He's developed such a bad case of arthritis the doctors can't believe it. They can't do anything except give him tests and pills and a wheelchair. They can't even figure out how it developed so fast."

"My God," Sarah said. "I've never heard of such a thing!"

"No? And you're a GP. Jesus!"

When the police left, Sarah went across the street. Carmichael Armstrong was at the law office where he was a junior partner, but his wife, Trisha, was home, taking care of their son. Sarah told Trisha how sorry she was to hear about Thomas's illness, and asked if she could speak to him; she was a general practitioner, maybe she could think of something that might help. It was a long shot, but surely worth trying. . . .

"Of course!" Trisha said, nodding several times. She looked more nervous than ever, and seemed brittle; Sarah guessed another blow would shatter her. Sarah suppressed a sigh. She liked Trisha. "Please, Sarah, come in—this way"

The Armstrongs' house was laid out exactly like Sarah's.

Sarah hated suburban housing, but she couldn't afford anything old enough to possess individuality.

"His room. . . . " Trisha pointed to an open door. One of the two bedrooms, Sarah knew from her own tract house.

"I think it would be best if I spoke to Thomas alone."

"Oh, of course." Trisha drifted away.

Sarah closed the door and turned around to see a riot of color; the bedroom walls were covered with glossy posters of NFL stars. Sarah didn't know their names, but she recognized the logos of the Chicago Bears, the Denver Broncos, the San Francisco 49ers.

Thomas wore a Minnesota Vikings jersey. He sat rigidly in a wheelchair. His face was even more sullen than Sarah remembered.

"What do you want?" he demanded. "Did you come to pity me? You can't help me, Dr. Martin. The experts said nobody can help me." His voice rose, harsh with rage. "You doctors are all useless bastards!"

"I understand your frustration," Sarah said, glancing over the powerfully built, utterly motionless body. "But sometimes a clear conscience can work wonders, Thomas." She kept her voice calm. "While I was away, you broke into my house. If you apologize and return the silver dollar you stole, I will forgive you and you may feel better."

"You lying bitch!" Thomas's tone was furious, but his voice was soft. "I didn't break into your house!" His voice rose: "Get out!"

Sarah stepped out of his bedroom and softly closed the door. She saw Trisha rushing toward her. She apologized for disturbing Thomas, and said, "If there's anything I can do, Trisha, please don't hesitate to ask."

"You're so kind, Sarah," Trisha said.

Back in her house, Sarah took the knotted rope out of the utility drawer. She'd learned how to tie a knot practically in infancy; her father and grandfather had been fishermen, in the days when fishermen made their own nets. But the foreign trawlers stripped New England's ocean waters, and most of Maine's fishermen were driven ashore, or turned, like her father and grandfather, to lobstering. Sarah heard tales of the old days on Dad's or Grampa's knee, and she heard that there was power in the knots a fisherman tied: power to summon the fish, to summon a wind fair or foul, to summon trouble for a troublemaker. When she grew older, Sarah realized no amount of knots could regenerate the schools of fish captured in miles-long nets and eaten by foreigners; she realized her father and grandfather were superstitious old men embroidering tales of past glory.

She studied science, she was going to be a doctor; she knew better.

But when someone broke into her new house, Dr. Martin found herself feeling vulnerable. Unable to afford installation of an alarm system on top of her mortgage and medical-school loan payments, she thought about buying a dog. But she worked such long, odd hours, it would be cruel neglect. So she found herself thinking about what her father and grandfather had told her. Dad and Grampa were dead. She called her grandmother, said she was just curious about it—couldn't quite remember what she'd heard when she was a kid, you know how that goes, Gram....

"Oh, ayuh, there's power in knots," Grandma said in her age-weakened voice, "if someone's troubling you, Granddaughter."

"That's just it, Gram," Sarah had said, dropping the pretense of idle curiosity. She'd listened carefully to everything her grandmother had told her.

Sarah looked at the rope in her hand, the rope that had caught the unwelcome intruder without his noticing; she looked at the four knots, one for each of the intruder's limbs. If she untied the knots, she would unbind the intruder's arms and legs, free him from crippling agony.

Her grandmother had told her the best thing to do would be to tie a slipknot. Make a noose. But Sarah was a doctor. She worked to save lives, not end them. All she wanted to do was stop the thief from breaking in.

The idea of causing such pain was disturbing enough. But this pain could be stopped. Death could not be reversed.

But if the crippling pain were stopped, it was clear Sarah would be right back where she started.

Sarah sealed the knotted rope in a Ziploc bag. She took her trowel out of the utility drawer and went through the broken door into her back yard. She struck the earth of her tiny flowerbed with angry blows of the trowel. She buried the rope.

She would give the boy one more chance. Perhaps another week of pain like ground glass in his joints and he would confess, return the coin, and allow her to heal him.

If not?

She had sworn an oath: she was a member of society with special obligations to all her fellow human beings. Thomas was like a disease that, if not stopped, would worsen and adversely affect—no, infect the lives of many more.

Sarah returned to the kitchen and rinsed her trowel off in the sink. She dried it and replaced it in the drawer, hoping she would soon need it again.

But if Thomas did not wish to be cured, the rope would remain buried, the bag would corrode, the hemp would rot, the knots dissolve without unbinding. Thomas Armstrong would remain crippled for as long as he lived.

Little Red Witch

SPINSTER ESKIE

he wolf will smell your blood," Red's mother told her the day she bled for the first time. And she explained that this was why she had strict rules about Red leaving the house. The young, freckle-faced girl was not allowed to go into town or go to church. She did not have friends, nor did she participate in village life. Her mother was a seamstress and they had little money, but they lived quietly and peacefully within the confines of their small, discreet cottage in the woods.

Red's real name was Miranda, but her mother called her Red because of her copper curls. On the day of her first blood, Red's mother, Gwendolyn, finally presented her with the cherry-stained, hooded cloak she had made years ago and had been waiting to give her. She told her daughter it was a very special cloak and that it would keep her warm and protected always. Red was thrilled to wear such a fine, noble garment, and she would dance around and twirl in it as though she were royalty. All she had, really, were her cherished dreams and fantasies. She was grateful to her mother, but felt sheltered and locked away. She did not understand her mother's fears and mistrust of mankind. Gwendolyn was a young woman, younger than most mothers, even, but she looked as though she had lived a long, hard life, and every night she would barricade the doors and leave the lanterns burning, for fear that something would somehow get in.

The only brief freedom Red had was when her mother would allow her to pick berries by the stream. It took months of persuasion to get her mother to allow her to venture off, but the stream was a short distance from the cottage and Red agreed to not take too long and to not talk to strangers. However, the real reason Red wished to explore the stream was to watch some of the village children play. There were at least six of them, all different ages, and they would frolic in the cool water with their toys and their games, and Red would sit on the hillside and wish that she could join.

"Play with us!" The youngest one, Victor, pleaded invitingly, but Red regretfully shook her head and headed home before her mother became concerned. She learned that one of the boys was named Peter. He was tall and skinny and had a pleasant face. He sometimes took off his shirt in the water and Red liked the way he looked and the way he smiled at her, but she dared not speak to him. Her mother had warned her about the dangers of boys. More importantly, nobody could know about her strange, ungodly gifts. Such things were meant to be hidden or it would be the end of her.

Red could make things happen. She wasn't sure how she was able to it, but ever since she was a toddler, unusual events would occur. Once, she made all the leaves fall off the trees in the middle of the summer. She also revived the dead rabbit her mother had caught for supper, and it hopped out of the basket and back into the fields. Red's abilities were by no means controlled or intentional. She didn't quite know how to make these things happen; they just happened. If she thought about something long enough, or wanted something badly enough, she could manifest the idea into reality, but it was never accurate or without consequence, and Gwendolyn made her promise not to use her powers if she could help it. Red would try to keep her powers maintained, but it was difficult. She didn't want to be different, but she knew that she was and the older she got, she realized her mother was, too.

Firstly, it was not common for women to live and raise children alone. Red never knew her father and her mother refused to speak of him. The Reverend Harrington would occasionally visit to make sure that Gwendolyn and her child were safe and well, and he was always relieved to find that the young mother was indeed resourceful and a worthy caretaker of her daughter. She knew how to hunt and how to build and Red was even surprised to learn that her mother knew how to read. Yet, when she inquired about her mother's education, Gwendolyn dodged the subject and explained that she did not like to talk about her past. She'd simply say that life had taught her many survival skills.

"I could teach you how to use your powers properly," a sly whisper spoke through the crack of her bedroom window one night. Red glanced through the glass and saw a dark grey wolf with sharp, glowing green eyes.

"How? Who are you?" Red wanted to know,

"Someone who has waited a long to time to know you, Sweet Red. Someone who can free you from these prison walls. You're a very special girl, Red. More special than you realize."

At the stream, the children continued to beg Red to play with them, until she finally shrugged and figured that there would be no real harm in participating in one short game of tag. Of course, she had never played tag before, so Peter had to provide the rules. It was wonderful to feel like a typical girl for once, as Red and the kids ran about in the grass, taking turns being "it," tripping and stumbling, and splashing through the flowing water. Red felt like she had friends for the first time in her entire life. When Peter became "it," he darted toward Red and pushed her to the ground, falling on top of her. They locked eyes for a moment and she could feel his hands ride up her dress. "Only harlots wear red," he said into her ear, and the warnings of her mother echoed through her mind.

"Peter, let her be! She's a whore and a witch, just like her mother!" said Cynthia, the pretty one with the blond hair. The other kids laughed and started chanting "red whore, red whore" over and over. Red dashed home as the sun began to set, her heart sorely broken.

"Red, it's nearly supper! Where on earth have you been?" But Red did not stop to talk to her mother. Instead she hid away in her room and cried miserable, devastated tears. She then took out her dagger and tore into the scarlet garment, causing massive gashes and rips along every edge of the beautiful fabric. Gwendolyn entered the girl's room to find the cloak destroyed at her feet and she smacked her daughter hard across the face and held the wreckage close to her, also in tears over the sight of it.

"I don't want to be different," Red told Gwendolyn.

"You're not different, Red. You're the same as everyone else."

"But I'm not. Why do I do the things I do? Who is my father?" Gwendolyn said nothing and left Red to be alone.

"Your father was a very powerful man," the wolf by her window told her that night. "His name was Lord Hector. He was brilliant and as close to a god as any mortal could be."

"Why won't Mother speak of him, then?" Red questioned.

"Because she killed him and she killed your real mother, the true owner of the red hood you wear. Her name was Miranda." And with that, the wolf offered Red her cloak back within its mouth. The fabric that had been shredded and damaged was restored without an extra stitch or hint of its former condition. Somehow it had been miraculously repaired.

"Red, who are you talking to?" Gwendolyn asked as she entered the room and the wolf was gone. The woman then noticed the red cloak in her daughter's hands and was overjoyed to see that it had been put back together. She assumed that Red had done it herself, but was surprised that her daughter had succeeded in what was clearly a challenging project. Such an effort would take great precision. "Well, normally I would not permit you to use your powers this way, but you've done a nice job making the repairs, Red."

"I didn't repair it myself," Red admitted. "The wolf did."

"The wolf?" Red then remembered that the wolf had specifically instructed her not to tell her mother about its nightly visits. "What wolf are you referring to?" Gwendolyn pried, as she peeked out the window. "Who were you talking to in here?"

"Nobody. Myself."

"Red, if there is something you are keeping from me-"

"Who is Miranda?"

"What?" Gwendolyn seemed alarmed.

"Did you kill her? My mother? Did you kidnap me? Is this why you won't let me outside these walls? Is this why I cannot show my face?"

"I will not tolerate this disrespect. You may speak to me again once you are ready to treat me with kindness." But when Gwendolyn returned to check in on her daughter the next morning, she did not find Red in her quarters. The girl's bed was empty and a terrible fear overcame the young woman. She suspected the wolf, or whoever it was that Red was communicating with, might have snatched her away.

However, Red had escaped only to head toward the stream that morning. She was not exactly sure what compelled her to see the children that had tormented her again. Perhaps she wished to prove to them that she was not what they said she was; that she was just like them and she wanted to be friends.

Innocent Victor was happy to let the girl back into their game, but Cynthia, whose eyes for Peter were apparent, scowled at the very notion. "My father says her mother is wicked! My father says any girl who wears such a garment must be married to the Devil!"

"I think she looks nice," Victor said coyly.

"It matches her devil hair." Peter remarked and the other children snickered.

"I think she's ugly!" Cynthia insisted. "I think she's the ugliest girl I have ever seen in my life!" And Red glared at the girl, and the girl glared back. Then pieces of Cynthia's blond hair began to tumble from her brow, strands at first, then clumps. Her lovely, golden locks loosely fell off her scalp as she brushed her fingers through her hair, screaming. When the girl was completely bald, Red gave her a satisfied smirk, until suddenly Cynthia's flesh began to melt off her face, as well. Blood, muscle and bone could be seen and Cynthia cried out in pain and collapsed. The rest of the children shouted "witchcraft!" as they ran into the woods toward the center of town.

Red arrived home in a panic, unaware of how she had caused such a violent accident. She thought to tell her mother, but Gwendolyn shook her and hugged her and sobbed fretful tears. The reverend was standing nearby. He had been informed of Red's disappearance and told Gwendolyn that he would let the villagers know that she was safe. As the gentleman let himself out, Gwendolyn thanked him for his company and turned to her daughter with a deep inhale. "Daughter, sit down. I want to tell you about your real mother. I want to tell you about Miranda. She was my sister and my best friend. Before you were born we were travelers, gypsies, your mother, myself, and your grandmother. My father had passed away and so we learned to fend for ourselves. We stole what we needed, but we were educated, so we used it to our advantage. Luxuries were plentiful until your grandmother met Lord Hector. He was handsome and charming. She fell in love with him and he taught her the dark arts. We all learned from him, and he seduced us all."

"What of Miranda?"

"She became with child. She was young and confused and Hector was mad with obsession. He told her that if she didn't love him back, he would kill her. My mother grew jealous. She had me make for Miranda a red cloak to wear in shame. Miranda was unhappy. She wouldn't eat. She became ill, and I urged her to run away with me, but the trek was too much for her to bear. She gave birth to you in the woods. I was trying to protect her. I was trying to protect you both." Gwendolyn's voice trailed off, recalling the blood from her sister's womb gushing out onto her hands as she caught the baby's crowning head. She had then wrapped tiny Red in her sister's cloak and wandered for weeks, seeking shelter from the ravenous beasts of the woods, before coming upon the abandoned cottage she would make a home in.

"And Lord Hector?" Red further questioned.

"Lord Hector was a monster and I'm glad he's dead." At that moment, banging could be heard at the front door, and a crowd of angry villagers with torches stood outside the cottage. Gwendolyn reluctantly lifted the barricade and opened the door to cries of rage. "What is the meaning of this?"

"Madam, we're here for the girl!" Demanded one man.

"My baby's been murdered!" Cried a distraught woman among the group, "Hand over that witch in the devil's cloak!"

"This is absurd!" Gwendolyn said, holding her daughter close.

"Madam, hand the child over! Several youths witnessed her evil doing just today!" It was then that the Reverend Harrington pushed through the crowd and spoke with the reasonable calmness the villagers had come to expect of him.

"My Good Folks, I have known this family since they came to our village 11 years ago. Madam Gwendolyn is a hard-working and simple woman and I cannot imagine her being in any proximity to the Devil. However, if the Devil lives here, let me be the one to find out. Let us not go making accusations before any proof. We are a civilized people." As he entered the cottage, the villagers slowly dispersed. Gwendolyn told her daughter to fetch the reverend some wine and to gather eggs from the chicken coop for their morning meal. She sat with her friend, her hands buried within his, as he compassionately listened to her worries and dread.

"These are all lies, Reverend," she told him, "You know that."

"I know your daughter was missing earlier today, and now the butcher's daughter is dead. Her skin had somehow corroded off. This deed is unnatural, Madam."

"They can't take my daughter, Reverend! She's all I have!"

"Then marry me, Gwendolyn. It isn't right for a woman to be on her own. If you marry me, they can't touch you." Gwendolyn suddenly felt more burden than relief at this abrupt offer.

"I am not a woman of God, Reverend. I have done things. Awful things."

"Then let me redeem you." The Reverend could never truly know or understand the kinds of heinous acts she had done.

He may have believed he loved her, but he could not love the actual woman she was. She was not unlike her sister's daughter. She, too was a killer, having caused her mother's lover to break out into a fever so high, boils surfaced all over his body and his insides burned to a crisp. She was a woman who had dragged her 14-year-old, pregnant sister into the woods late at night, which made the sickly girl go into premature labor and bleed to death before ever getting to know her young. She was a woman whose own mother would annihilate her if she had the chance.

As Red gathered eggs, the wolf appeared from the darkness and advised her to flee. "They will be coming for you, Child. You are not safe here."

"Are you Lord Hector? Are you my father?"

"Lord Hector is dead, but his legacy lives through me and through you." The wolf's body shifted and morphed into that of statuesque older woman dressed in colorful attire with auburn hair pulled back in a plum velvet sash. "My name is Dorothea and I am your grandmother. Come with me, Red. Learn the art of magic and be who you were born to be. Together we will make the weather do as we say!"

Though still uncertain about the idea of marriage to her pastor, Gwendolyn showed her appreciation for his good will by allowing the Reverend into her bed. It was impulsive and against Lutheran teachings, but they were both so alone and desperate for one another. And while Reverend Harrington was not an attractive man, being much older than she, Gwendolyn had never before felt the touch of a man so gentle, sincere and devoted. Other men had pursed her and her sister years ago, but these men were not unlike Lord Hector: cruel and deceptive. And as she and the Reverend made love, Gwendolyn considered a better life for her daughter with the Reverend as her husband. She had let her guard down with this man and indulged in a basic pleasure that felt oddly freeing.

The Reverend held her as they slept together and the wolf quietly crept into their quarters and onto the bed. As it sniffed the man and gazed down at him, the Reverend turned and opened his eyes to find it growling above him, and before he could scream, it bit into his throat and pulled out his arteries. Blood splashed everywhere and Gwendolyn, naked and covered in it, flung herself out of bed and grabbed a knife, as she watched the savage creature turn into the familiar form of her estranged mother. "You demon!" Gwendolyn shouted.

"An eye for an eye, my dear daughter," Dorothea confidently replied. "You took from me everything I ever cared about, and now I will take from you, the same."

"You will not take Red!"

"I don't have to take her. She will come willingly, since you have imprisoned the poor child." Gwendolyn raised the knife toward her mother, but froze and was unable to move. Then, at Dorothea's powerful hand, Gwendolyn placed the knife at her own throat and began to cut. She tried with all her might to resist the force that gripped her, but it was too strong and Gwendolyn was unable to refrain from slitting open the base of her neck.

"It's time to leave," Dorothea told Red, who waited for her grandmother in her bedroom.

"I should say goodbye to Mother, first," Red spoke softly.

"There's no time, Red. You come with me now."

"Mother will worry."

"It's time to embrace your independence, Child. Go after what you want! Your mother has done nothing but lie to you your entire life!"

"She's still my family."

"I'm your family. I have told you the truth. I have earned your trust and I'm the only one that supports your special talents. Your mother never did; she only suppressed them." Dorothea's words were honest, but Red still forgave Gwendolyn, even if she wasn't her real mother. She had raised her and cared for her, and kept her safe, and while she didn't always make the right decisions, Red believed Gwendolyn had only her best interest in mind.

"I want to see my mother," Red said firmly. "I will go with you, but I want to say goodbye."

"You can't do that!"

"Why not?"

"Gwendolyn is dead." Red paused and stared at her grandmother in disbelief.

"That can't be," She protested and headed toward her mother's quarters. "Mother!" She called out, as the slaughtered, lifeless bodies of Gwendolyn and the reverend came into view. "Mother!" Red threw herself to Gwendolyn's side and bellowed storms of tears.

"She was so guilt-stricken over what you have become, she killed the Reverend and took her own life."

"You're a liar!" Red seethed.

"I have done nothing but enlighten you to truths. It is your mother who has shielded you from them."

"I'm not going anywhere with you!"

"Red, I'm all you have now. You are all I have. We belong together. Whatever it is you think I did, one thing you should know is that without me, you will never learn to refine your gifts. How many more people are you willing to accidentally kill before they hunt you down and stone you to death?" Red considered this, but with Gwendolyn's dead body lying limply in her arms, she quickly became skeptical of the sorceress she had come to trust, admire and feel drawn to.

"This thing you think you could teach me, whatever it is, I will have to learn on my own," Red expressed to the old woman, and Dorothea yanked onto the soft, thick fabric around Red's collar and lifted the girl off her feet. But as she did, Red's cloak began to shine like the burning sun. It became hot like fire and Dorothea dropped Red to the floor. When she went toward the girl again, the cloak burned even brighter and Dorothea's hands stung with agony. Behind Red, the old woman could see Miranda, standing protectively over the child. Dorothea's eyes filled with grief as she watched the daughter she had shamed and rejected appear, mouth inaudible words, and then fade. "She said I belong to no one," Red informed her grandmother and she morphed and shrank into a red-winged bird, and flew away.

Red traveled for years, and embraced the kind of life the women in her family had once lived. A life filled with enchantment, wonder, discovery, and knowledge. This was the life Gwendolyn had sought to escape, but Red knew she did not belong anywhere else. She met others like her and studied with keepers of the great gift to hone her valuable skills. Sometimes she felt lonely, but her red cloak reminded her that the sisters, Gwendolyn and Miranda, were always watching over her. In time, Red gave birth to her own daughter, and the cloak was passed along to her at the arrival of her first blood. "Trust is earned," she told her child, "don't ever let the wolf deceive you." And she prepared for the inevitable day that her grandmother would return.

Baba Yaga

MIKE PENN

Melinda screamed and her cries of anguish echoed throughout the entire brownstone.

Her gown was saturated in sweat. Flanking her, the midwife and doctor tried to offer comfort.

Her husband, Charles, stood in the corner of the bedroom, beside an open window, a pipe in his hand left unattended as he stared at his wife. Down on the avenue, a horse and carriage passed by. Releasing a soft whinny, the animal tossed its mane, attempting to shake off the dusting of snow.

Melinda screamed again and Charles' brow furled. "Should I call for the carriage to be brought around?" he asked yet again.

"No, Mr. Grimes," replied the doctor softly as he applied a cold compress to Melinda's forehead. "Your wife is going to be just fine. There is no need to tax her with a bumpy ride to the infirmary." A smile crossed his tired face. "I just hope your baby does not exhibit the same stubbornness as it is showing inside the womb."

"Charles," Melinda weakly raised her head. "Cha…aaagh!"

Slumping back into her pillow, she clutched at the bed linens, balling them up with her hands.

Somehow the doctor was able to determine that this scream was different from the dozens that had come before. He quickly moved into position. "Push, Melinda!"

Charles' pipe slipped from his grasp. It struck the window-sill and tumbled to the street.

Melinda screamed again, this time so loudly, those passing by outside took notice.

"Once more, Melinda!" the doctor commanded as the midwife stepped up beside him. "You're almost there!"

Charles tried to take a step closer but found himself unable to do so, as if his feet had been cemented to the floor. The few scraps of food in his stomach began to churn dangerously. He was certain to make a fool of himself if he ventured any closer.

A new scream suddenly pierced through the room. The midwife, holding the blanket, bent down beside the doctor. A moment later the doctor was grinning and the midwife faced him, holding a small bundle. "Congratulations, Mr. Stevenson. It's a girl..."

Melinda screamed out.

"Doctor...?"

"She's going back into labor."

"The child has been born, Doctor!"

"One of them...push, Melinda! We cannot wait another ten hours for the second child!"

Melinda outstretched her hand and Charles, fighting back the nausea, rushed over to take hold of it.

"Twins!" he gasped.

She smiled weakly at him, but her eyes were full of concern. "Dearest..." Charles felt her hand go limp. Her eyes rolled back into her head.

"Doctor!"

"She's going into shock," he replied. "Melinda, don't give up. Not now. I can almost see the..." The doctor slid his chair back with a start. His skin was as pale as Melinda's. "Good lord."

"What is the matter?"

"This cannot be."

Charles, still gripping Melinda's limp hand, looked to where the twin should have been.

Lying on the linens, no larger than a man's hand and covered in blood and afterbirth, lay a small doll.

Eight years passed.

It remained a mystery as to how Melinda had come to bear the doll. After delivery, Charles had walked over, scooped it up in a spare blanket and had taken it to the fireplace.

Neither the maid nor the doctor ever mentioned the incident again, for fear of bringing any shame to Charles or the baby.

They simply assumed Charles had burned the doll.

The baby was named Vassilisa, after Melinda's mother, for the same bright blue eyes and her golden. That night, Vassilisa cried as if suspect to what she had lost. However, once the sun surfaced over the Palisades, her tears dried and her wailing ceased. From that day forward she never cried again, neither for her mother, nor anyone else.

The doctor soon moved to another city and the midwife succumbed to age. Unbeknownst to either of them, Charles had never destroyed the little doll. That night, as he was lighting the fireplace logs, sleep overcame him. While he slumbered, Melinda appeared in his dreams. She looked radiant and youthful, as when they had first wed. "The doll, Charles. You must hide Liandra," she whispered as if lying beside him. "She will protect Vassilisa. Just feed Liandra a bit of food and ask what it is you need of her."

Charles awoke and did as Melinda instructed, wrapping the doll in soft linens and placing it in the farthest recesses of his closet.

It was not until Vassilisa's fourth birthday that Charles presented her the doll, omitting how it came to be. "Keep it with you always and never tell anyone."

The girl took the doll and made her promise to Charles.

"Vassilisa!"

The scream barreled down the hall and into her bedroom. The trio of pigeons huddling outside Vassilisa's window abandoned their crumbs and took flight. Vassilisa watched them sail across the avenue and over the park.

She could hear the rhythmic *clopping* of shoes on the floor below.

Lenora was home.

Her father had remarried several years after Melinda died. Lenora Hingis, widow. Both she and her daughters, Caitlin and Rebecca, had treated Vassilisa with kindness during her father's courtship. It was not until after the wedding that their true personalities surfaced.

An elegantly dressed woman appeared at the doorway. Hands on her hips in disapproval, she glared at Vassilisa. "Correct me if I am wrong, young lady, but were you supposed to have washed the kitchen floor before dinner? Flecks of mud cover it! Is that your idea of cleaning?"

"No, Stepmother," she fell quiet. It was futile to tell Lenora that the floor had been scrubbed hours ago. Futile to tell her that Caitlin and Rebecca were the culprits. Lenora was wise to her evil daughters, but as long as Vassilisa was made to look bad, she would always condone their bad behavior.

"I expect the floor to be re-washed before you go to sleep."

"Yes."

"Yes...*what?*"

"Yes, *Stepmother.*"

A faint grin appeared on the corner of Lenora's lips. "Good. But before you do that, there is an *errand* I need you to perform for me. The man who manages Bruttanio's has a package waiting for me. I need you to pick it up."

"Where is his shop?"

"On the east side of the park."

"Of course, Stepmother. I will go with Roderick immediately."

Lenora shook her head. "No. I have instructed Roderick to put the horses down for the night. I do not wish for the animals to be disturbed until morning."

"Then I will have the doorman summon a wagon."

A scowl washed over Lenora's face. "Do you think money simply grows on trees, Vassilisa?"

"But the shop is on the other side of the park, Stepmother.

It will take me at least an hour to reach it, and the sun has already begun to set!"

"That is not my concern."

"Father will…"

"Your *father* is not due back until Saturday. Until then, you will not question my authority. Am I clear?"

"Yes, Stepmother."

Lenora stormed from the room.

Vassilisa turned back to the window. With the sun dipping below the trees, the park had been transformed into a gloomy monolith. It was far too large to walk around.

She would have to go through it.

Pocketing the crust of bread she had been feeding the pigeons, she left the room.

Stepping out into the cold dusk air, Vassilisa looked up to see Rebecca and Caitlin at their bedroom window, snickering and giggling. Inside, one of the servants rang the bell for dinner and immediately they slipped from sight. Already, Vassilisa's stomach began to protest.

Thankfully, the moon was unsheathed enough to provide a feeble light as she walked along the wooded path. The clamor of people and carriages on the avenue were replaced by the soft winds passing through the leafless trees. It only took a moment for the street to disappear entirely from view. Though she played regularly in the park, the night had the power to transform even the most familiar paths into the unknown.

The wind increased and Vassilisa pulled the coat tighter around her body. She could feel the cold beginning to seep through her shoes, numbing her toes. Making sure the brownstone remained behind her, Vassilisa trudged directly through the brush, risking the damage to her coat, for fear she would lose her sense of direction.

She emerged from the thicket to find herself facing a cluster of trees. Their branches stretched far and wide, creating a canopy, blocking out the moonlight. Strangely, Vassilisa's vision was not hindered. With each step the surroundings became more defined. Orange mushrooms peppered the forest floor. It was from these mushrooms that the light radiated. A sweet perfume lingered in the air, smelling like squashed berries.

Vassilisa was so intent on avoiding the mushrooms she did not notice the gate until she had collided with it. Taking several steps backwards, she clasped her hands over her mouth to muffle her screams. Atop each of the posts that made up the fence was a skull, facing away from her.

A cackle sounded from within the trees as she turned to flee. From between a pair of birches an old woman appeared. She was garbed in tatters stitched together haphazardly. In her right hand was a large staff.

"What is your business here, Young One?" Her voice was raspy and crackled, as if it had been several days since she had last spoke. Amidst the wrinkles there was a glint in the woman's eyes that made her appear more youthful than she seemed.

"I am traveling to the east side of the park," replied Vassilisa in the most commanding voice she could muster. Her courage quickly shriveled as her eyes fell upon one of the skulls.

The woman's face held so many wrinkles and folds that when her expression shifted she seemed to change in appearance. "To the east? Such a long distance, and at this late hour," she said. "My name is Baba Yaga."

Vassilisa wondered where the woman had come from. She didn't think it possible that she lived nearby. Not in this part of the park. Not when they were still so close to the avenue.

But then, as if suspect to her thoughts, Baba Yaga, with her bony hand, beckoned Vassilisa forward. "Why don't you come to my home for something to eat? Surely you must be hungry?"

She said *no*, but her stomach betrayed her, grumbling loudly.

Baba Yaga smiled. "Excellent. My home is just up the way."

The trees shifted, allowing Vassilisa to see beyond the branches. A small hut was nestled there atop a huge stump. Looking carefully, Vassilisa was surprised to see it slowly rotating.

Baba Yaga noted her astonishment. "It is so there is never any part of my park I am not facing."

"How does it work?"

"A spell. A very old spell."

"Don't you get into trouble living here?"

"I suppose it would cause concern if my little house was discovered. That is why my trees do such a good job protecting it, Vassilisa."

She looked at the crone uncertainly. "How do you know my name?"

"No need to be alarmed, Child. The forest has many ears. Many eyes." She again outstretched her hand. "Now - let us go inside and have something to eat...ah, the skulls trouble you?"

"Who do they belong to?"

"Animals. All manner of dangerous beasts lurk within these woods."

"What are they for?"

"My protection. Death to those who stare at the eyes."

The old woman began walking towards the hut and Vassilisa hesitantly followed. As they approached the stairs, the house ground to a halt, allowing them entry.

Stepping inside, Vassilisa was surprised at how large it was. She had assumed Baba Yaga's hut to be cramped, but the room they entered seemed twice as large as the entire hut. It was brightly lit, illuminated by the numerous candles and lanterns that dotted the room. A large cast-iron cauldron stood in the center. Thick trails of steam wafted upwards and out through the slats in the roof.

Vassilisa heard the door click shut behind her. "To keep the cold out," the old woman said. Walking to the cauldron, Baba Yaga poured out two bowls of porridge and tore a chunk of bread from the loaf that lay in the wicker basket beside the pot. She handed Vassilisa her share before settling down to eat.

Vassilisa sniffed the soup in the clay bowl. It smelled heavenly. Baba Yaga had begun eating so Vassilisa discounted any possibility of it being dangerous.

Baba Yaga watched Vassilisa finish her portion. "Very good." The crone placed her bowl down onto the straw mat that covered the floor. "Child, do you see that pile of poppy seeds over there?"

Vassilisa turned and saw three large baskets nestled beneath one of the windows.

"Would you be a dear and separate the black-eyed peas from the seeds for me?"

"But, Ma'am. To do that would take most of the night and I must be going before I am missed."

"My Dear, did you enjoy your meal?" asked Baba Yaga.

"Yes, thank you."

"Are you full?"

Vassilisa nodded. "Yes."

"Good. Now it is time to repay me for your meal." Baba Yaga rubbed her hands together. "I have to go out. If you finish before my return I shall allow you to leave."

"You promise?"

"Baba Yaga always keeps her promise."

"What if I am not done?"

Baba Yaga said nothing. Instead, the cauldron emitted a low *burp* as a large bubble burst on the surface.

The wooden door reopened with a gesture of her hand. Baba Yaga looked at Vassilisa. "Trying to escape would not be wise, My Dear."

The door closed behind her with a resounding *thud*.

Looking out the window, Vassilisa watched the old hag disappear into the surrounding trees. No sooner had she lost sight of Baba Yaga than the skulls that surrounded the house slowly rotated towards her. A reddish glow emanated from within the sockets.

Vassilisa moved back from the window. She was trapped - alone in the middle of the woods. If she did manage to escape the witch's lair, Lenora would certainly punish her for being so late. Sitting down on the floor, she drew up her legs and thought of what to do.

Looking down at her old coat, she saw a familiar lump in

one of her pockets. *Liandra.* Removing the doll, she smoothed out Liandra's blonde hair and flattened her dress. Her father's words passed through her head. Getting up, she walked to Baba Yaga's cauldron. With the wooden spoon, Vassilisa gingerly poured a few drops of the porridge into Liandra's little mouth.

She placed Liandra on the ground, not knowing what to expect. However, no sooner had Vassilisa done this than her eyes grew heavy. Lying down, she was suddenly fast asleep.

She awoke to Baba Yaga's staff prodding her. "Get up," the old crone said. Another jab followed, more forceful than the rest.

Vassilisa rubbed her eyes. Baba Yaga was standing over her, a scowl on her face.

"Who are you, Child?"

Vassilisa did not know what she meant.

"Who are you?" Baba Yaga repeated, the anger evident in her eyes. She then stepped aside, allowing Vassilisa to see beyond her.

Neatly stacked were a pile of unshelled black-eyed peas.

"How did you do that in the short time I was gone?"

Vassilisa shrugged her shoulders innocently. Her hand rubbed gently against the lump in her coat pocket. *Liandra.*

Baba Yaga looked at the girl suspiciously. "Well, choose not to tell me. I suppose we will now move on to your next chore."

"But, you *promised* to free me if I completed this one!"

"I said no such thing."

"Yes, you did!"

"Are you calling Baba Yaga a liar?"

"No…" Vassilisa felt her pocket grow warm.

"Good. Now, for your next chore. I shall need you to…" Baba Yaga began rubbing her wrinkled forehead. "I need to…sit down…" Baba Yaga made her way to her chair and slumped down into it. "Remain there. When I awake I shall instruct…." She closed her eyes and was silent.

Vassilisa watched as Baba Yaga's chest rose and fell in rhythm. She was fast asleep, placed under the same spell by Liandra as Vassilisa had been. Looking at the door, she saw that Baba Yaga had not locked it. She remembered the skulls, but realized her only opportunity to escape was now.

Moving silently, she made her way from the hut. The sentries were facing outwards, keeping watch for trespassers. Walking up behind one of the skulls, she yanked it from the post. Making certain the eyes faced away from her, Vassilisa placed the skull in her coat.

Though the light was poor, Vassilisa began to run. The cold night air made her chest burn and her calves ache. Tree branches lashed at her face, and the lichen-covered stones beneath her feet threatened to dislodge themselves. On several occasions thorns from the surrounding thicket latched onto her coat, as if threatening to hold her firm until Baba Yaga awoke.

A *gurgling* from ahead made Vassilisa stop. A babbling brook crossed in front of her. It was not wide, but in the dim light she could not determine how deep it ran. She touched the current and her fingers burned from the chill in the water. She had not passed the stream earlier. Vassilisa was certain she was lost.

A tree branch rustled behind her. Not bothering to turn her head, Vassilisa shut her eyes, believing she had managed to awake and find her. However, instead of Baba Yaga's cackle, she heard something unfamiliar. Opening her eyes, she was shocked to see a large dog standing before her. Its coat was snow white and seemed to glow in the moonlight, so much that for a moment she did not see the two others flanking it. They were identical to the white dog, except their pelts were red and black.

The White Dog leaned forward and sniffed her.

"Fair Vassilisa," it said in a quiet, somber voice. The animal's jowls did not move, and for a moment Vassilisa thought she had imagined it. However, the animal continued. "What are you doing alone so late at night?"

The Black Dog took a step forward. "She comes from the witch's lair. She carries her smell."

The three dogs looked up to the sky and howled. Vassilisa covered her ears to muffle the noise.

"How did you manage to escape, Little One?" asked the White Dog.

Vassilisa quickly relayed her story, taking care to leave out any reference to Liandra.

"No one has ever managed to escape from Baba Yaga. She hunts the forest, capturing and killing all those who are lost." said the Red Dog. "Once, our kind filled this area Now the three of us are all that remain."

The White Dog walked up until his furry pelt brushed up against her. "Come. Climb onto my back. We shall take you to the edge of the park."

"Am I too heavy?" she asked, for fear she would hurt the animal.

"No, little one," he replied as the other two dogs followed behind. "Though, once I begin to tire, my brothers will carry you."

Arriving at the brook, the dogs seemed to know every loose stone in the bed, every pitfall. In a matter of moments they had crossed the water and were bounding through the woods. Vassilisa held onto the dog's mane, hoping that she wasn't harming the animal but at the same time fearful she might tumble off.

A scream bellowed up from behind, echoing through the forest.

Vassilisa swallowed hard.

Baba Yaga had awoken.

It didn't take long for the White Dog and then the Red Dog to drop off, exhausted from her weight. As they raced past the trees and bounded over the bushes, she could hear the gasps coming from the Black Dog. Of the three animals, it seemed the oldest. The dog's face was weathered as if the animal had never known the comfort of sleeping indoors. A grey goatee surrounded its mouth and long, straggly whiskers protruded from its cheeks. Just when she was certain the animal could go no farther, Vassilisa heard the sound of hooves striking cobblestones. A moment later she saw her brownstone appear from beyond the trees.

"At last," panted the Black Dog as they reached the edge of the tree line.

Vassilisa climbed off the animal. "Will you be all right?" She glanced back into the dark woods.

"I will be fine, Little One." The Black Dog answered. "As for yourself, do not worry about the witch. Once you leave the woods and dawn arrives, Baba Yaga will have forever lost her opportunity to capture you."

Vassilisa rubbed the dog's chin affectionately.

"Goodbye, fair Vassilisa."

"Well, Young Lady, it is *certainly* about time you decided to return."

Entering the house, Vassilisa had tried to be as quiet as possible. However, her attempts were futile as Lenora was standing at the top of the stairs, her hands at her hips. "I trust you have a good excuse for taking so long?" Rebecca and Caitlin appeared behind her, dressed in their nightgowns, which made Vassilisa glance at the grandfather clock in the hall. It was close to midnight.

"Is that the parcel?" she asked, pointing to the bulge beneath her coat.

"Parcel?" Vassilisa repeated, following her stare. "Yes. Yes, it is."

A smile crossed Lenora's face. "Good." She began walking down the stairs, her daughters following behind her like wraiths. "For your sake."

"Were you concerned I had not returned on time?" she asked. "The park is a dangerous place at night."

"You are not a young child anymore, Vassilisa. It is time you acted like an adult."

"But my sisters are older than me."

"How dare you question my judgment!" Lenora's eyes flared

wide. "When you wake in the morning I will have a full list of chores for you to do. And don't expect to go to sleep without attending to the kitchen floor! Now, give me the parcel!" Behind her, Rebecca and Caitlin began to giggle.

Vassilisa removed the small bundle from within her coat. Lenora looked at her curiously. "*That* is what was given to you? It seems so small."

"Yes, *Mother*," replied Vassilisa as she unwrapped it. "I think you should take a good look at it, just to make sure it is what you wanted." Grabbing the skull by its base, she turned it to them.

Lenora's and her stepsisters' eyes grew wide as they looked upon the death's head. "What is that wretched..." Beams of crimson light burst forth from the skull's eyes. It struck them, its crimson aura enveloping them. Their screams were brief, lasting only seconds, as the light incinerated them.

The following morning, just before sunrise, and well before any of the servants were scheduled to arrive, Vassilisa buried the skull in the far corner of her back yard. No sooner had she patted the soil firm with her little shovel than the beginnings of a rose bush burst forth.

Then, using a broom and dustpan, Vassilisa collected the remains from the staircase, walked to the uppermost room of the house, and released the ash from the window. She watched as the small cloud drifted across the avenue and out over the park before being dispersed by a strong current of air. Then, just as Vassilisa was about to close the window, she heard what sounded like a scream coming from deep within the park.

But it was just the wind.

The Heart of a River

Virginia M. Mohlere

he thing that had been the Witch-Empress of Iley twitched in the oily mud. It convulsed, then breathed a rattling sigh.

The horizon flickered with the bonfires of the army and pyres of the defeated. The thing that had been the Witch-Empress rolled over onto what had been its front, once making a sound like a baby rabbit in the jaws of a cat. The thing reached out one crisped stump of what had been an arm, then the other.

The thing pulled itself forward. Its breath wheezed and gurgled, and the keening cry sounded out several times more. Once the cry startled a crow, which rose up from the face of a dead soldier and flapped into a nearby tree.

Long after midnight, a deep-soaking rain fell. The priests down on the battlefield praised the rain even as it put out their fires. The rain was an omen, the people said, of good times to come, of the evil of the Witch-Empress's reign washing away.

One thing definitely washed away was the track of the burned thing, gouged into mud from hilltop to forest. By morning, no trace remained.

Under a low holly tree the burned thing rested. It held its mouth open and waited for raindrops to filter down through the leaves.

The thing that had been the Witch-Empress lay under the

holly tree for perhaps weeks, though it felt more like decades. It wheezed, and slept, and wished to die but did not. The thing smelled its own roast-pork scent. The thing cried out in the agony of a million bits of skin no longer there but still hurting. Nothing of the forest would approach it.

The thing had no words, only burning. Only pain, and the shudder of a world too cold, even though fire still burned inside it. Its mouth tasted of smoke. Its lungs could barely take in air.

When there was rain, the thing opened its mouth, and sometimes water fell in. When there was sun, the thing turned what had been its head away from the light.

The thing grew bored by pain. Boredom made room for a thought: *how am I not dead?*

Then, much later, *how am I alive, stripped of magic?*

The thing probed itself, under roasted meat and screaming nerves.

And then, *oh hells.*

The trickle of power left to her would not let her die. The ooze from her blackened skin dried until she crackled. Eventually the burned thing inched her way out from under the holly bush—slowly, to avoid ripping open the newly-hardened flesh—and then pulled herself up branch by branch, until she stood (hissing, hunched) and shuffled from tree to tree. Each pattern of bark pressed a new configuration of hurt into the shiny, dark meat of her shoulders.

Her chin had pulled down to her chest, her arms curled in, stubby hands clawed over her melted breasts. The bit of power let her navigate by witch sight, eyes glazed blind.

It would have been so much better to die, but the dribble of magic insisted. She walked.

Rushing water eventually crowded out her rattling breath and the shuffle of her feet through leaf litter. A little river tumbled prettily over mossy boulders. The burned thing leaned against a tree and breathed cool, wet air that eased the smoke taste in her mouth. In her witch sight, the water glowed with health and life. She could sense crawfish in the shadows. The dimpled paths of water striders flickered yellow and pink across the surface.

The magic prodded. The burned woman trudged upstream to a sheltered place—a shallow pool behind two large rocks, where the current slowed to a lazy swirl. Yet another holly bush grew out from the bank, so the pool was black with shadow.

She could sense a fat, ancient trout snoozing under one of the rocks.

The burned thing wished for enough breath to sigh, enough face to roll her eyes. If magic had been a stone in her hand, she would have thrown it into the current and walked in the other direction.

Instead, she climbed down into the water, and the magic let her sleep.

Whole seasons could have passed while she slept. Until the burned thing heard a sigh, and a rush like water suddenly set free from a dam, which in her sleep sounded like a triumphant shout. From that moment, she dreamed.

She stood on her own battlements, staring down at the city she had had built: people packed into the streets, small and busy to make gold for her treasuries and weapons for her armies. They moved in dark lines, like ants. Watching them made her foot itch, as if an ant crawled there, across the arch, where it tickled. She tried to stamp her foot.

She woke, and her foot still tickled. The pool's chill had extinguished the shriek of her roasted nerves. Low light suggested early evening or the time just before dawn.

The tickle continued, a little touch on the sole of her foot. She tried to move but could manage only a vague jerk—currents swirled around her, tiny variations in temperature. The tickle disappeared.

She lay several inches under the surface of the water. The dribble of magic had stiffened her and pulled air through her ruined skin, like a fish gill.

If it plans to keep me stuck like this forever, magic is shit.

The paladin had used a holy sword filled with relics and dripping with his own blood to strip her power. He had broken the bond with her demon, and magic had peeled away as painfully as if he'd flayed her with a bamboo knife. She had had that done once, to a priest with a big mouth, so she knew something about it.

At least the paladin had been quicker. But he must have left behind one last miserable surprise: a seed of magic to keep her alive, awake, stuck. Worse, stuck in water, when fire had been her element and friend until the very last.

That monstrous boy could not possibly have thought up such a move himself. No, it had to have been someone close to her, because it felt so much like her own magic: familiar, though she was cut off from it, an observer of and slave to it. She was actually impressed by how well and truly they had defeated her.

The maddening tickle returned. The little touch repeated at intervals that were not *quite* regular. Tickle, pause. Tickle, pause. And then the tickle was more like a gentle pull. Current moved around her foot. She felt a painless tearing, heard a faint splash, felt a cool spot along the bottom of her foot.

Her gorge couldn't rise, her eyes couldn't widen. She couldn't scream and jump away.

The trout.

The trout was eating her foot.

The long scream in her mind was soon silenced by unconsciousness.

She awoke next at night, cool up to her ankles. At the back of her right ankle she felt the knock-tickle that had so terrified her before, but with the moon peeking through pine boughs, she couldn't muster the same horror.

Her feet having become fish food made the ghost of them

comfortable. It was a strange fate to be consumed in a quiet river pool. A very calm punishment, compared with those she had dealt out. Maybe things would get worse as the trout ate its way upward.

The spot behind her ankle cooled. Black water was soft as velvet under her, surrounding her, and the jewels in the sky would not crack and burn, could never be plundered by an enemy.

The burned thing would have smiled if she could. How different from before. She felt she could never be greedy about the stars.

Next: silver pale light of early morning, the forest distorted by a thin layer of ice, shot through with opaque feathering. Her little pool was so quiet, cut off from the current's hum. She hadn't noticed the thrums and plinks of the river around her until she could no longer hear them.

She could, however, hear the trout. The tickle had moved up to her right calf, and in the quiet, she could hear tiny smacking sounds, like a baby blowing kisses. She groaned inside, and the tickle stopped. She wanted to pant—or better, to vomit—but she still could not move.

The trout's mouth smacked against her, and this time her mind screamed. The trout shot backward, quickly enough that she felt its current. After a pause, the trout swam slowly toward her head, hugging the bank away from her.

"Regret," spoke a voice in her inner ear—a deep voice, but quiet and hesitant. "Hurt?"

The former Witch-Empress held herself as still inside as out. Not since childhood had any being been strong enough to breach her mind and speak thought to thought. *She* was the one who broke barriers, the one who split minds until they cracked into madness. She was the giver of never-ending whispers, of words that sliced like knives from the inside.

She thought back to finding the pool. The trout's energy had been strong and old, but she recalled no magic in it.

To be strong enough to hide itself from her, then speak in her head, marked it as a dangerous creature. Perhaps it had called her here, to steal the echoes of her power.

Perhaps it could be tricked into giving up its own.

"Hurt?" the trout asked again.

"I am very hurt," she said. "Would you cause me further pain?"

No words, only confusion, until the trout-voice said: "Good meat. Pale underneath."

The burned thing hissed, her mind taken over by the image of leg bones thrust white out the ends of her charred limbs, foot and toe bones already resting at the bottom of the pool.

What kind of spell was this that held her conscious in her body as it fell apart?

"My bones will curse you," she growled at the trout.

Her mind pinged with surprise.

"Bone?"

The trout flashed back toward her feet; she felt its mouth, heard the faint kissing sound.

"Bone bone no bone no bone," the trout hummed.

The trout's cheerful voice sent her back into the dark.

Ice lay thick over the water—above her she saw only blurs of light and shadow. Her right leg was cool to the knee and her left leg past the ankle. The trout hovered at the bottom of the pool. She felt it listening.

"Not asleep?" the trout's deep voice whispered in her mind.

"I am awake, fish," she thought to it, trying to curl anger out with her mind like a whip.

But the fish radiated only excitement. It swam toward her head until she rocked a little with the movement of the water.

"Bone, you say, long before. Went looking. Bone good to eat, bone with meat, like outsides of insects, but inside. Went looking, no bone. No anger! Is no bone. Only new meat underneath. Like skin, but no scales."

The Witch-Empress tried to process this and could muster only shock. The trout's excitement stopped abruptly, replaced by a sad worry. It said, softly:

"Is strong skin, cannot eat. But fins broken. Split, many times. Eating in between, take out old black meat, make new. But fins stay split. Cannot make whole. Tail split also, one time, tail and tail. Will try! Will take black meat, eat, good to eat. Is making large, is making voice to tell you this. Is showing remembers, see days are different, day and night and day and night. Maybe if growing, if eating more black meats, is speaking learning remembers, can make tail and tail fixed. Maybe if tail fixed, fins fixed too."

The trout paused. It wriggled.

"Will try to fix for swimming. Will try. No angers! Will try."

The Witch-Empress held her mind quiet, tried to parse the fish's strange speech. Tried not to let the thing quivering in her chest resemble hope, that a trout could describe something that sounded very much like healing.

"No anger?" the trout whispered.

"I...no," she said in her thoughts.

And there was the trout's excitement again, its eager wriggle and simple happiness.

"Is good! You are sleeping, trout is eating! All happy, and ending is all strong and swimming and king trout of river! Is good *good*. Very happy for eating and new skins."

The burned woman remembered ambition. Hers had been boundless. From the moment she arrived at school and saw how her talents surpassed those of even most of her teachers, she had craved being envied and feared. It was an efficient way to ensure that she wasn't relegated to the lonely back table in the food hall.

Power gave her contempt for others: her teachers, her first employer. Hired at nineteen to join the court magicians, she had been awed briefly by their wealth and hereditary sense of privilege, but soon she saw that the other magicians despised her for her youth and farmhouse origins, not because she was less talented than they.

The only advantages they had over her were experience and knowledge of theory. So she flattered them one by one into giving up their secrets. Two she blackmailed; seven she took to her bed, rolling her eyes in the dark as they jiggled and rattled atop her. For the others, it was as easy as smiles and the odd enthusiastic nod.

After six years of flattery and note-taking, she began to test her new knowledge. She siphoned power from the strongest of them, sent nightmares to the most high-strung. Placed temptations before the weak ones.

A scandal broke out when a young prostitute was found dead inside the palace, stabbed with a dagger known to be personally sealed to the queen's personal oneiromancer. The pressure of the investigation caused the king's weather-worker to crack, and two of the earth-workers showed obvious signs of a sleep-smoke habit.

More quickly than she expected, it was done: she was the king's chief magician.

The queen was pious, and the king was a dirty old man. The king's sons were dirty young men who exhibited a sudden, startling tendency to find the wrong end of a hunting spear, the bottom of a ravine, or that one pesky bone left in a serving of…

Trout.

The ex-Witch-Empress laughed herself back to oblivion.

She woke again to a thin layer of ice through which she could see the linear black shadows of leafless trees. The trout snoozed at the bottom of the pool, and she could almost read its dreams. She could feel insects in her mouth, crispy wings and a too-many-ness of legs. It made her sick.

In her days of fire, she had dismissed the strength of water. She had thought of it as easily conquered—boiled, turned to mist. But the trout dreamed of the unending flow of current, minute after minute, day after day without cease. Under the thin ice, she could hear the river rushing from its source to the sea. She could feel how it bent smoothly over rocks that it had shaped and gouged until they were smooth as pearls. But the water had no voice of its own. The river had no heart.

Even with the river-spirit missing, her fire could have no power in this pool, constantly replenished by new water, always cool. She had always sought warmth, with fires kept high autumn through spring. But having been burned to her core, now she relished the chill that kept her still and without pain, that gently stroked her lower legs.

She slept and woke again and the ice was gone from the water's surface, the trees were outlined by pale green. Her legs felt cool up past her knees. The trout still snoozed, snoring inside its own mind, and she wondered whether the snoring was something it had pulled from her memories, because she couldn't imagine that a creature with no nose could snore.

She tried to smile, but her frozen face would not permit it. The fish was silly, enthusiastic, like a child eager to please, and the longer she lay in its pool, the more it helped her. She could stretch her toes now, almost wiggle them, feel the water's fluid embrace. Sometimes her knees itched as if she might soon be able to bend them.

Down at the bottom the pool, the trout dreamed of snoring like a human. She felt a throb in her chest that reminded her of finding kittens in the barn as a girl, their tiny cries and fat, warm bellies, their whisper-soft fur.

But Father had always drowned the kittens. And if she protested, he made her go with him, held her hands around the sack to throw it in the pond.

The sack would roil with movement and cries before it sank, before it was still.

She dreamed of her harem—a whole wing of the palace filled to bursting with political hostages: princesses, generals' sons, siblings of minor kings. She had loved to walk in unannounced, to see which of them drew back in fear, which of them abruptly ended conversations, which of them looked eager.

Most often, after such visits she spent time with the second group, until they belonged to the first.

What consternation it had been to ministers and subjects that she kept a harem just like a king. Worse still that she kept concubines of both sexes. It had been deeply satisfying to take from whomever she wished, to watch pious old farts stare at her in horror and wonder what she would do with their daughters or their tender little sons.

Sometimes she sent them back.

Leandra had been betrothed to the Earl of Strixelm, who paid his tributes but whom she knew was quietly supplying bands of rebels up in the mountains of his territory, one of which had a vexingly powerful wizard. So she had traveled to Strixelm for the wedding, and at the pre-wedding feast she had announced the bride's unfitness for such a worthy ally. With her demon shadow flickering around her and a fire lance growing from her fingertips, no one at the feast had dared protest her offer to take the bride for "training." Even Leandra's response had been merely a sobbing collapse.

She had kept the girl chained to the bedroom wall by a length that stopped her short an arm's length from the door. For several weeks she ignored the girl except to strike her for making noise. The girl was fed and allowed to cleanse herself but to wear only a sheer blue tunic and the gold collar and cuffs of her chain.

Every night of those weeks the Witch-Empress had entertained one of her concubines: all the ones with the darkest cravings and most robust appetites. At first the girl shut her eyes and cringed, but within days she watched the activity on the bed, first gawping and later with slit-eyed interest.

That evening she walked in from her bath, still damp and scented with jasmine. She let her robe puddle around her feet and lounged on her bed.

"Whom shall I call tonight?" she said to the girl.

Leandra stood slowly, cheeks bright but her jaw set in a stubborn pout.

"Me," she said.

The Witch-Empress of Iley had smiled. Leandra was inexpert but eager, and the burned woman in her river-sleep was caught up for a long space of dreaming by the memory of the girl's busy mouth and her slim hands.

On the day when Leandra sprawled on the bed, at home as if she belonged there, the Witch-Empress set her free from her chains. As the cuffs and collar fell away, the girl sat up, arms curled over herself, unsure again.

"I must return you to your bridegroom now," the Witch-Empress had said, pitching her voice full of regret. Leandra's mouth dropped open, but the Witch-Empress rebuffed all her protests and tears, inwardly grinning the whole time.

"Dear girl," the Witch-Empress said finally, "perhaps, if the tribute is sufficient, you will be able to return with it to me."

Three months later, Leandra showed up at the palace with a cylindrical box finely lacquered in orange and gold. Inside, packed in salt and herbs, was the head of her husband.

She did not return to the harem. Leandra went willingly to the reeking room in the foundations of the palace, where the walls shivered between this and the demon realm. She and the demon Ekhnazz had pieces of one another's flesh sewed into their own abdomens. The Witch-Empress made her a general.

She had been the last thing standing between the Witch-Empress and the paladin, at the end: a whipcord-thin woman covered in blood and scorch marks, naked but for cuffs and collar, with a shuddering shadow around her that had two sets of arms and wide-curving horns. Her human throat had bellowed curses in the demon's language. The paladin's two cats—knee-high, white-furred monsters raised in the Temple of the Just Winds and given to the boy with his other protections—had pulled Leandra down, both of them stinking of burnt fur until she overreached her own power. The fire went out. The demon-shadow faded, and there was merely a bloody body on the ground, a dead cat on one side and a barely-living one on the other.

The burned woman woke with a jolt; the trout was working at a piece of flesh at the base of her stomach. Cool water reached up just past her hips.

"Humans have odd mating habits," the trout hummed at her.

The river's current pulsed like a heartbeat.

"Is much heat in your dreaming," the trout said. "River is better. Water nicer, cool, make good skins."

"Yes," she said.

What would she do with a Leandra now, crisped and curled from the waist up, with no lips or eyelids, and who knows what from the waist down? Her inner circle had no place for weakness. The weak were ground up or sacrificed on altars to the demons with whom they allied.

Any of them would take advantage of her weakness, especially without Ninshur to protect her. To what end might she be renewed? She could feel the places inside her where magic had been burned away, like hollowed-out coal tunnels. With practice, she might be able to light a candle some day, or keep milk from souring for an extra week.

Without power roaring through her, the ex-Witch-Empress of Iley had no idea who she would be. She told herself the ache in her chest was cold and stiffness.

"All in river is what is," said the trout.

And she remembered her first teacher, when she was a young girl just away from home, angry with fright, furious to still have to haul water and stack firewood when she had imagined an entirely new life. Not just a bed of her own and a full belly for once.

He would say to her, "your best magic is that which can flow only from you and none other," which at nine years old was the stupidest comment she had ever heard. She had clung to fire because it was quick and strong. Simoneus had groaned with annoyance at her hopelessness with earth and water magic, without ever noticing that it wasn't lack of talent but boredom. Earth and water were slow, heavy-footed things. She liked the size and speed of air and fire.

It took time to crush a man, to drown him. The air in his lungs could be burned up in an instant. As Simoneus learned when she was thirteen.

"You must learn control," he had said to her constantly. "Not every working should be a blast of your full power."

Reaching inside to kindle the air inside him with a spark had been an interesting lesson in how he was right. Once he died, exhaling smoke, all the books were hers, and she could not be told anymore that certain ones were above her head, that others were full of magic not to be attempted.

"Then why put it in a book?" she had asked.

"Not everyone works on the side of the gods" had been his supremely stupid answer.

She had wished to bring him back and kill him again once she got started on those forbidden books. She had never known such things were *possible*—to creep into dreams, to make voices in the air that would speak even when one wasn't around, to rewrite a person's history inside their own mind.

To make a pact with another type of being and gain access to their power.

She couldn't do any of it at first, of course. Simoneus had been right that some things were beyond her. But he had taught her how to study, how to practice through the part where it seemed a spell would never work, until suddenly it did.

The fish paused in its nibbling. It laid its mouth to her side, then paused again.

"Bad spot," it hummed at her. "Bad meat."

The healing thing could not move her hand to the spot, though the memory was vivid in her mind: a black blotch larger than her hand, often hot to the touch, ridged and hard. It had been a habit to run her fingers over the spot at night before she went to sleep. On quiet nights, she could hear the echo of the clank and hiss of the demon realm through the piece of Ninshur lodged in her gut.

She had just turned twenty-two when she pulled out old Simoneus's book and performed the ritual. In the oldest section of the palace, where the stone was so old that it hummed to itself of the days when Iley had been merely a small fort on a trade route, she found a room coated in dust. She read a fire to determine a fortuitous day and spent the time between cleaning out the room and stocking it with supplies.

The first ritual was simple, much different from later, when the room had been expanded, when reality had a hole in it leading to the demon realm and there were attendants on both sides of the hole to assist the participants. The bond was weaker when the transfer was done by foreign hands; the Witch-Empress had let no one but herself perform the rite solo.

She made a large fire and burned in it things known to be attractive to demons: brimstone lumps, goat tongues, the left foot of an infant. She never did learn why the left foot in particular. She dosed herself heavily with a bitter tea of hallucinogenic and numbing herbs. When she felt the fire shiver with foreign attention, she took a knife to her belly and called out the harsh syllables written in Simoneus's book.

Ninshur came through the fire. At first she was disappointed. Ninshur was small for a demon and almost pretty by human standards, all high cheekbones and muscle definition. Then she felt its ambition—hunger like hers to rise and devour. Ninshur spoke the returning syllables. She carved a piece of flesh from inside herself and handed it into the fire, received back a similar piece of flesh.

She bit down on her urge to scream (to vomit to run to weep to fall over dead) and took up a sharp tanner's needle and linen thread. She and Ninshur stared at one another while they sewed, and she learned that demons produced oily tears.

When the wounds were sewn, they reached for one another, grasped hands, and the bond kindled. The demon's language unfolded in her mind, just as she felt hers unfold in Ninshur's. The fire expanded, then went out, leaving behind the hole between realms and the two of them kneeling, hands linked.

Judging by how her legs felt when they finally released their grasp and staggered upright, she and Ninshur knelt for a very long time, staring at one another, their brains and bodies reassembling into a bonded pair. Both bodies tried to reject the foreign flesh, but magic slapped back the spasms (vomit pain infection) with a painfully accelerated healing process. Both brains tried to reject their new knowledge and the new shape of reality, and in this they each bore the other through screams and tears.

At the end, she had a magic that could not be countered by much of anything in her world, as Ninshur had for its. Their strength was magnified by that of the other. Ninshur was as clever in the ways of demons as she was of humans. And neither of them was ever alone.

The boy with his sword and holy blood had broken the bond, but Ninshur's flesh remained—could it be "tainted," when she had coveted that bond, welcomed and used it? There was an empty spot in her mind where the demon had lived.

She remembered, suddenly, the paladin—his solemn, hairless face and hazel eyes. To her demon's eyes, his feet stood on the very roots of the earth, and the air around him shimmered with water. Where had they dug up such a boy, unsullied and willing to go through the training and the rituals needed to make a young man so holy? They would've needed a whole temple's worth of priests, a bottomless chest of gold, and a river willing to sacrifice its heart.

When she had laid her hand on his face, it had felt like trying to hold a chunk of ice. His sword had pulsed with the sanctity of age and more blessings than she could count in that moment, which she had dismissed as useless until the mechanism in its handle pierced him and his blood ran down the blade to mix with hers. The steel could not be corrupted by her heat; something held the sword solid in the world. And the boy's blood had been so *clean*. Ninshur had found nothing in him to grab onto in the time it took for the boy to snap loose the alien flesh inside her belly.

Ninshur had been a part of her for so long that she no longer remembered how to tap her own talents, and its loss had left her flailing, stripped bare, unable to tamp down her own flames. It was an awful thing to burn.

She seethed down to a point far inside her own head,

dreaming a hundred revenges that would never come to pass. The boy, the priests, her army that too quickly scattered and fell. She had always been good at inventive punishment.

"Anger is like the skins of trees," the trout said in its deep voice. "The skins that fall to the bottom and make water dark. Makes my mouth feel small."

Damned darkness again, dreams. She wanted to stay awake and feel herself cooling, releasing. She wanted to wish herself whole, rising like vengeance from this small, cold pool. Instead, she dreamed of a winter night, the end of a ball, and stripping her tight, sweat-soaked dress from herself to feel the welcome chill and the smooth comfort of mint-scented sheets.

Caught in this new dream, she went deep into her own childhood, to a memory she did not want to have. A harvest of barley, a sickle swung by a large, dark-bearded man, and she was too little, too inattentive, and it caught her.

Deep in the chest she felt it, too tight to breathe, her arms stilled by pain. Cold in her legs, not enough air, the world gone black. Just like the first time, the sense of stillness lasted forever, and her panic occurred in instants punctuated by long breaks of nothing.

Then a tug at the place where the sickle had gone in, where her skin had parted with a tiny sucking sound and turned the metal red at the edges. Just a pull—not painful—that she grabbed and pulled hand over hand until the blackness around her lightened to grey.

A voice called her name. A far-off part of her that had been majesty and empress leaned forward at the memory of it.

"Come on back to us, Doneen." So many years since hearing that name.

Gee's voice was low and warm, like a candle, and Doneen could follow it as if it were light. Gee sang one of the songs they would sing together on the rare occasions Father allowed her to visit her grandmother. Gee sang the song about bringing the chickens in for the night, gather up the biddies and bring them safe a-home.

The little girl swam up and broke the surface of the darkness, into light and pain.

Gee was a witch, and Father was afraid of her, though Doneen had never understood why. Gee's tiny house under the edge of the forest was the whole of heaven.

Doneen stayed with Gee for the rest of the season, at first lying in bed, weeping with pain. But she would watch with interest when Gee held her wrinkled hand over the white bandage on Doneen's chest and made the air shimmer in between, which pulled some of the hurt and heat out of the wound.

And when she started to feel able to sit up, her eyes grew wide when Gee unwound the bandage and peeled a little sheet of mica off the narrow pink wound.

"Why that, Gee?" she asked.

"To keep your air inside you, so you could breathe."

Doneen curled her hands in front of her chest.

"Will it stay in now?"

"Yes, dear heart."

The air stayed in, and Doneen graduated from sitting up in bed to sitting on the floor by the grate with a dolly made of scraps, an empty cookpot, and a spoon to play with. Gee even let her stir the porridge, and later to hit the bread dough. Doneen shrieked with laughter every time, to hit the dough and watch it collapse around her fist. Gee would pinch off a bit and let Doneen knead it until she learned how to make the dough so it was neither shiny nor sticky.

"Just right," Gee said.

When Doneen felt mostly better, and the pink line on her chest no longer pulled at her unless she was *very* tired, Gee taught her how to make the end of a wisp of straw catch on fire to light candles. Doneen liked being able to make the air shimmer like Gee did, and to call little bits of fire from all the corners where they were hiding and bunch them together on the straw.

"Can you make bigger fire, Gee, just by calling louder?"

Gee had laughed.

"Yes, that's it, sweet girl. With practice, you can call louder and louder."

"I want to shout!"

"You will, sweetheart."

But Father came to fetch her soon after that, and Doneen was so excited to show him what she could do that she missed Gee's warning glance. Doneen made the straw light up. Father smacked the straw out of her hand and stomped on it. He grabbed her arm and dragged her home without her dolly or any of her clothes. He beat her until she promised never to call fire, and she never saw Gee again.

It took five years of wishing until a cart finally overturned on Father. Doneen ran away from the funeral and found Gee's cottage empty, dusty, with one corner caved in. She howled and wept, and figured out how to shout loud enough to call a big fire that burned the cottage down.

Then she went home and pestered her grey-faced mother until she was apprenticed out to Simoneus.

The ex-Witch-Empress did not want to remember Gee. She did not want to remember Gee telling her where each scrap in the dolly came from.

"This was my wedding dress. This green bit here was from a dress your mother wore when she was your age. This blue was once a curtain."

The burned woman could not turn her face away.

"Stop, trout," she thought finally. "Please stop."

"Sweet memories," the trout said. "Sweet as fry in spring."

But it stopped, and she stared at the water's surface until she was allowed to sleep again.

The woman, almost an ex-burned thing, practiced her will while the trout finished its work on her. Unwelcome memories pressed at her, but she shut her mind to them, listening instead to the trout's mind as it chewed at her. Its thoughts were full of things like "all the river is my pool" and dreams of eating—cold, wriggly fry; the hard-and-soft of crayfish; the smoke flavor of her own flesh.

When it wasn't pulling at her (arms, now, with insistent visions of the uses to which she had put her hands: bloodstains and whip handles), the trout rolled the flavors of the river through its mouth. Oak bark, pine, stone, silt. The ghosts of these flavors trickled through her mind. She wondered where the river spirit had gone, that the trout could eat magic from her flesh and become the river's heart.

"Mountain to sea," the trout hummed to itself.

She had never known delight like the trout's, even far back in the days she did not wish to remember. The trout would wriggle with joy merely from a cold current; it loved to watch light change above the surface, proud that it could mark time. The trout saw nothing but beauty, even in the ragged leaves rotting at the bottom of the pool. The woman tried to think "like a child," but she had been nothing like it, even when very young.

Through their connection, she felt the strength that surged through the fish each time it swallowed a strip of her burned flesh, which it thought of as strong currents. The trout was becoming the River, turning inexorably into a Thing no longer quite a fish. The trout was making plans—to travel the river, to make baby fishes, to eat everything it could catch. Its cold little will was drawn to a dark pool far upstream it had never seen before that must have been the home of the river's previous heart.

The trout would be the river spirit now, thanks to her. Her magic circled through it, and it would be the head of its own empire.

She lay cold as the water and silent while the trout hummed, rejoiced, peeled the final strips of burned flesh from her face, up to the top of her head. Down in her own core, she refused to look at the visions given to her or to listen to the fishy song around her.

Then it was done. The trout pulled a final strip from her head, and her body moved with a stiffness borne of her many months under the water. The bit of magic left propelled her up and out of the pool to slide and struggle onto the damp ground. The trout rose to the surface, and the woman blinked her new eyes at it, practically shining with the magic it had consumed from her flesh.

Taken from her. And left something so small.

"You are back in your air," the trout said. "We are both made new, now. You in the air, and I am King Trout of the river."

The trout wriggled and hummed. Its magic—her magic— made the water around it ripple.

She bent toward it, smiling, and the trout was overcome with a happiness that made it forget the language it had learned from her. The woman's mind was filled with sunlight-water strider-current-joy that rushed at her like spring floods, and if she hadn't been so *angry,* it would have been enough to stop her.

But she grabbed the trout, hooking one hand in its open mouth and wrapping her other around its tail. She pulled it from the water and slammed it hard, headfirst, onto the hard ground. Her hand scrabbled for, and found, a rock.

Just as her mind heard, "what," she brought the rock down hard on the fish's head. It flopped once, then lay still. The woman panted, staring at its dark back, spotted silver belly, and the tender blush of pink just below its head. She growled and split the trout with her rock. She remembered the old forms, had enough magic to make them work. She ate its liver and a double handful of its raw flesh. It wasn't the whole of the trout's magic—some of that was too alien, her own digested and transformed to something cold-blooded and wa-tery—but she could feel a new strength course through her. It curled chilly through her torso even as her stomach awoke and remembered its job, sending a more basic strength to her body.

She kicked the rest of the trout into the water and knelt on the bank. The trout's power swam through her, carving new channels where fire had run. Chill infused her center like a cramp; she bent double until the scent of water surrounded her face.

Has water always had a scent?

Now it smelled like home.

The woman stared into the water and realized that she could see the current, the layers separated by temperature. Water magic seeped into all her corners and crevices. Every effort she made to block it was useless—the water magic slipped past her, flooded her.

Her heart had just begun to beat again. Now its rhythm changed from a dual thump to a rush and flow. So stupid, she should have known. Her body tipped itself back into the river, where she settled at the bottom of the pool, down among the tannin-dark water and rotting leaves. Her traitor's hand reached out for the trout's remains, her betraying mouth chewed them, and all the while the water moved through her. She was a channel that the river's power cut to suit its own currents. She was a stone being smoothed.

Another dark pool awaited her, far upstream. She would rule another, smaller realm: no longer Doneen, no longer Empress, but the river's creature. Something new.

Miscellaneous, Spooky, Weird

Liam Hogan

mergency. Which service?"

This is what you'll hear if you are unfortunate enough to need to call 999.

There are, of course, many more than three options.

The AA—the car breakdown company, not Alcoholics Anonymous—once claimed it was the Nation's 4th Emergency Service. But that was just self-serving, aggrandising claptrap.

After Police, Fire and Ambulance come other services you might know to ask for by name: the Coast Guards, Mountain Rescue, Bomb Disposal and the like. And then there are those you probably won't; it is the dispatch operator's job to forward you on to the appropriate people, working from a list which is rather longer than you would suppose.

There are departments that the Government, Freedom of Information Act or not, will point-blank deny exist, until that one time they are needed. Some are the stuff of nightmares: cures as terrible as the disease, only to be contacted in the direst of apocalyptic emergencies.

At the very bottom of the list, there's Mavis Ethelwright. Not by name, she's listed as: "Miscellaneous, Spooky, Weird", but from Land's End to John o' Groats, there is only one phone that will ring if that call is made and it's sitting on a lace tablecloth on a small occasional table in a semi-detached house on the edges of Walthamstow.

There is a reason she lives there and a reason so much of the Hackney Marshes will never be built on and the two *might* be connected, but that is for another story.

Mavis was in her favourite armchair when the red Bakelite telephone rang. It rang 7 times—just long enough for her to finish her cup of tea—before she reached out and picked up the handset.

"Yes, Dear?" she answered.

"Erm…is that…?" the emergency dispatcher warbled.

"This is Mavis Ethelwright."

"Ah. I think I have the wrong—"

"Oh, I don't think so, Dear," Mavis said, peering at the leaves at the bottom of her teacup. "I don't think you have the wrong number at all."

Miscellaneous, Spooky, Weird does not have official transportation, so after taking the particulars from the still wary Dispatch, Mavis rang for a Taxi. Miscellaneous, Spooky, Weird does not, as a general rule, require immediate response, sometime before the next Tuesday is what appears on her rather reluctantly filled-out Service Level Agreement.

She gathered her things and, after performing a quick ward to protect her home, she went out the front and sat on the small garden bench to wait for her ride.

"Alwight, Mavis?" the taxi driver said as he drew up.

"Oh yes, thank you, Alan."

Alan hopped out of the cab and swung open the back door.

"The front, I think, Alan," she said.

He drew in a sharp breath. "That serious?"

"I'm afraid so," Mavis said. "I'll be wanting to see where we're going."

"Right-ho." He wasted no further time, nearly breaking into a run as he rounded the taxi and retook his seat. "Where to?"

"South," Mavis said, squinting at an old iron nail dangling from a piece of yarn.

Mavis Ethelwright is England's only official witch. That England's other witches tend to keep a rather lower profile has a lot to do with the oldest on that list of emergency services, a hangover from the 16th Century and never fully disbanded. Mavis calls them the "Drown 'em and Burn 'em Brigade" and a number of her spells and incantations have more to do with protecting herself from them than the evil power that lurks deep in the marshes.

Their destination became obvious after only a couple of minutes' drive, an ominous black cloud roiled in the otherwise blue sky. That it was centred over an unremarkable row of terraced houses did little to lessen the chilling effect. As they drew to a halt on the opposite side of the road, Alan reached out to close the cab's windows.

"No," Mavis said, putting the yarn and nail back into her large carpet bag. "Let it in, Alan. Best I know as much about it as possible."

The cloud's shade enveloped them, a gloomy darkness fell and the street lamps fizzled briefly on and then, just as quickly, faded back into the black, the amber light sucked dry by smoky tendrils.

But Mavis wasn't looking up, or even down at the blue front door of No. 16 as it squatted deep in the shadow of the glowering cloud. She was facing the other way, eyeing that rarest of mythical beasts, a working BT phone box.

She handed a Thermos flask to Alan and rooted in her bag for a couple of extra cups. "Three teas, please, Alan. One for you, you know how I like mine, and…the third with one— no, better make it two sugars."

She cracked open the cab door and shivered.

"You sure this is your department, Mavis?" Alan asked, his Mockney accent slipping somewhat and showing a hint of his long-buried Armenian heritage.

"No, I don't suppose it is. But we're here now. Best make do."

She edged her way carefully over to the phone booth. An advert for a 'Meat Inferno' pizza hid the interior but beneath the door there was a glimpse of black-laced underskirt over a pair of scuffed DMs.

Mavis pulled the kiosk door open. "Are you alright, Dear?" she asked, as a pair of startled eyes peered up through charcoal eye-shadow streaked by tears.

"Ah…"

"Janice, isn't it? I guess it was you who phoned…this…in?"

The girl, her black hair shot through with purple, silver pentagram earrings swinging in their circular hoops, nodded and slowly relaxed the knuckle-whitening grip she had around her knees.

"Come and have a nice cup of tea and tell me all about it."

The telling didn't take long. She huddled on the kerb, the "safe" side of the taxi, as Mavis perched on a garden wall overlooking No. 16 and Alan stood on the cab's runner, peering over the top.

"It was an accident," Janice mumbled, head bowed.

"You mean," Mavis said, not unkindly, "that you didn't expect it to work?"

The girl looked up through her fringe, her shoulders momentarily bunched.

"Well, at least your primary ward took."

"Primary ward?"

"The thing that's holding it where it is, Love," Alan helpfully chipped in.

"I fear it won't hold for much longer," Mavis said, as the double glazed PVC windows pulsed. The front-door letter flap popped open and something long and purple snaked through, tasting the air.

Mavis pulled a yellowed candle stub from her cavernous bag. She had a half-dozen Ikea tea lights that would have done just as well, but then, she did have an audience.

"Janice, my dear, I'm going to need something from you."

Janice nodded and defeatedly offered up her arm, a fresh white bandage scrappily tied and edged with red.

Mavis shook her head. "Not that; your tea cup, please. I need to see which way it will break."

After peering intently at the pattern of leaves at the bottom of the tin cup, Mavis consulted her iPad. Ever since the British Library had digitised their occult section she had been saved lugging around a half-dozen hefty books, but such easy access was a mixed blessing. Although much of the scanned content was palpable nonsense, there were, scattered amongst the alchemical instructions and obtuse lore, the occasional page of true power. And so, somewhere in the heart of No.16 sat Janice's smartphone, the screen locked onto a page from a dusty French grimoire—a summoning spell.

She lit the candle, sprinkled a few herbs around the base, and chanted under her breath.

For a moment, the fabric of the stone-clad terrace seemed to disintegrate, each brick, each slate, floating free of its neighbour and, through the gaps, the three of them caught a glimpse of something rising up on squat, powerful legs. Through the roof, a pair of torn, reptilian wings flexed, blood red, and eight, or quite possibly a lot more, tentacles writhed in front of a hidden head, rippling hungrily towards them. It was slipping its bonds, shaking itself free both of the physical restraints: the bricks, the mortar, the cavity wall insulation, and also of the magical ward that Janice had invoked in its summoning.

Mavis reached out and with her bare fingers *snuffed* the candle.

There was a noise not unlike that of an elephant, minus the bones, dropped from a great height directly onto the hard concrete floor of the Tate Modern's Turbine Hall.

Mavis ducked behind the body of the cab as a couple of tons of calamari and dragon blood splattered across the road and the stench of the grave passed over them.

The chill, dank air lifted and sunlight flooded blindingly back, as though a total eclipse had finished way before it was due. In the near distance, a bird nervously started up its song, only to peter out into embarrassed silence when it realised it was singing solo.

"May I borrow your phone, Alan?" Mavis asked.

Alan stood rooted to the spot, something purple dripping from his cheek, until she asked again and silently he handed it over.

She tapped quickly away and immediately a voice asked:

"Emergency: Which Service?"

"Eldritch Cleanup, please," Mavis said.

"Eldritch...what?"

"It's on the list, Dear. Authorisation code: Howard Phillips. Better get me an Environmental Disaster Squad as well," she said, eyeing the splattered tentacles and ectoplasmic goo. "And a Media Blackout Squad, STAT."

"What happens now?" Janice asked, her voice small.

Mavis looked up at the gaping hole in the roof as a section of chimney plummeted into the smoking remains. "Normally we go down the 'gas leak' route. Any strange sightings are attributed to oxygen deprivation."

"No...I mean...to me?"

Mavis peered over the top of her glasses. Janice stood, pale, morose, currently rather sticky, although the taxi and Alan had borne the brunt. And yet this curiously-attired slip of a girl had summoned a real stinker of a Class 2 minor demon, with little more than a blood offering and a high resolution smartphone. She'd be dead if her ward hadn't held, but the point was, it had, for just long enough, anyway.

"Ever thought of being an apprentice?" she asked.

"Like on the telly?" Janice said, "'You're fired'? an' all that?"

Mavis smiled. "Yes. Something like that."

The Bone of Magic

Heddy Johannesen

Christiania (Oslo), Norway, Midsummer, 1610

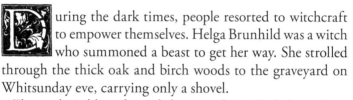uring the dark times, people resorted to witchcraft to empower themselves. Helga Brunhild was a witch who summoned a beast to get her way. She strolled through the thick oak and birch woods to the graveyard on Whitsunday eve, carrying only a shovel.

The cool air blew through her grey hair. Owls hooted on the creaking trees. Twigs cracked under her feet. She inhaled the woodsy scent and studied the ripe, round moon. Before long, she reached the graveyard. She glanced around her, but the only company she had was the quiet tombs. She stopped at the grave of her late husband, Ferdinand.

Helga shoveled hard soil in the graveyard. She dug until she found what she wanted. She scraped dirt away from the skeleton. She gagged from the stench. The shovel clattered to the ground. The skull jeered like a court jester at the sly moon.

She glanced around to see if anyone saw her. She tugged the rib bone until it broke free in her hand. Helga dusted herself off and whispered a prayer. She shoveled the dirt back over the skeleton and left the cemetery.

She was weary from the long journey home.

I hope no one saw me steal the rib bone for the spell. Hail to mighty Odin.

She climbed the wooden steps to the front door. Helga grew an herb garden. There were few windows. The roof was built of grass and thatch. The house was old and chipped. It was her parents' home and she lived in it all her life.

She hid the rib bone in the special spot she prepared. She would cast the spell tomorrow. She shivered as she slipped into her frayed pajamas and, seeking what comfort her thin blanket offered, she sat on the bed. She brushed her thick, grey curls with shaking hands but her cornflower eyes faded under her lids. She placed the brush back near the soapbox and lay on her bed. Despite her shivers, she fell asleep.

Helga admired the bright colors of the mystical stained glass windows in church the next Sunday. She hid the rib bone wrapped in wool in her blouse.

She waited till everyone was gone and approached the altar. She scooped sacred holy water from the chalice using an earthen cup and hurried from the church.

Helga sprinkled the holy water onto the rib bone. It wriggled in the wool in her blouse. The sensation sent shivers up her spine.

The next two Sundays, Helga took a seat in the church. Again, she spilled holy water onto the rib bone. She quivered with fear but she forced herself to look calm. The rib bone wriggled in her blouse as she left. She reminded herself why she was doing this.

She put the tilberi next to a human skull and her wand. The sparkling candles cast an eerie glow on the skull. She tapped the bone with her wand three times. She concentrated on the tilberi, the rib bone of her late husband, wrapped in wool. It quivered, wriggled and blinked at her. It was alive.

Helga cut the flesh of her thigh with a double-edged blade. Blood spurted from the wart on her thigh. The tilberi sucked on her blood and crawled to the floor. She shivered in revulsion then composed herself. She'd forged the pact between her and the tilberi.

"What task do you have for me?" the tilberi exclaimed in a high-pitched voice. It was 16 inches in length, a ruddy, reddish pink color, and a few inches in width. Its eyes were two small slits. A tiny nose perched beneath the eyes. Its mouth was wrinkled and toothless.

"I command you to steal milk for me, tilberi. I command you to steal milk for me." She repeated the magic words over and over again. Her wand circled in the air. The candles flickered. She summoned the tilberi outside.

The tilberi crawled to the cows grazing in the fields. It jumped on a cow's back. The cow mooed in protest as it sucked on the milk. But it persisted.

A few hours later, the tilberi slithered into Helga's house. Its body was bloated with milk.

"Churn lid off, Mummy!" The tilberi vomited the stolen rich milk into the churn. Pleased, she stirred the milk.

Helga's mangy black cat, Magpie, hissed at the tilberi from where she sat at the windowsill.

Helga stirred the stew in the cauldron in the hearth. She savored the aroma. She wiped her hands on her stained apron.

After dinner, she stirred the milk in the churn. There was a knock at the door. She threw the lid onto the churn in her haste and answered the door.

Astrid Lidveig smiled and entered. She wore a brown wool gown, a white cap on her head, and a beige shawl over her narrow shoulders. Her strawberry blond curls were braided with a blue ribbon. Though she smiled, Helga noticed a bruise on her cheek.

Helga welcomed her in and shut the door. She offered her tea.

"How are you, Helga?" Astrid settled into the rocking chair.

"I'm fine. How is the baby?" She glanced at Astrid's wide girth.

"I will give birth any day now. My husband hopes it's a boy." She drank her tea. "Do you have the herbal remedy?"

"Yes, I do. You'll be fine. The herbs should help with the labor. Did you see the midwife?" Helga asked.

"I did. It's a good thing it's not too cold now. The Ice Age ends soon. We've struggled through a hard time these last years."

"Let's see what the runes tell us, if it's a girl or a boy." Helga didn't see the shocked expression on Astrid's face. She cast the runes and glanced up.

"Look," Helga continued and pointed at the rune. "This one, *beorc,* means birth but the rune *othel* means possessions. Erik will be proud."

"You dare to read the runes? The church doesn't like it. Erik knows the priest well. He won't be pleased if he should hear of this." Astrid frowned.

"I honor the Old Ways. I'm sure you will be a wonderful mother. A baby is a blessing."

"Thank you, I'm excited about becoming a mother." Astrid took the herbal sachet from her and left.

The next day, Helga rose and ate her porridge for breakfast. She swept the front deck. With a dismissive sweep of her hand, she commanded the tilberi to fetch more milk. It slithered away to the fields of clover. The tilberi elongated its body to reach across a cow and sucked from two teats at once. The cow mooed and stomped its hooves. The tilberi sucked till it was full. It moved onto the next cow.

A farmer saw the tilberi near the cows. He made the Sign of the Cross on the cows. The tilberi collapsed to the ground. The farmer comforted the cows. He tried to stomp on it with his boot, but the tilberi dodged him. He followed it to Helga's house, and hurried home in alarm.

The tilberi appeared at the window.

"Full belly, Mummy." The tilberi vomited milk into the churn. She smiled at the amount of milk.

Helga prepared to go to the Midsummernight feast. She checked her appearance in the mirror. She donned her black wool cloak. She removed the plain cap around her head. Her hair tumbled past her shoulders. She grabbed her broomstick made of birch twigs and straw.

She patted Magpie's soft head. Magpie purred to let her know she would protect the home while Helga was gone. She twitched her tail and stood guard at the hearth.

Helga's long hair blew in the wind as she flew through the cool air. She joined the other witches at the castle in Hekkenfeld. She greeted her coven members and they all embraced each other. She'd known the coven for nearly a decade. The castle stood in shadow. Black crows and *gejrfugle* (great auks) circled overhead. She strutted down the great hall. Candles glowed at the great dining table. The room was swept clean and the table set for a feast.

She offered flax in the large earthen bowl full of herbs and other offerings. They enjoyed the mead and food.

The Head male witch dressed as Thor played a merry tune on his fiddle. Helga inclined her head to him in greeting. He wore a set of horns on his head, an elaborate oak mask and a brown cloak.

"Helga, good to see you here." A witch appeared at her side. Elsa was the head witch of the coven. She wore a huge, black feathered hat and a revealing black robe. Heavy brown hair tumbled down her back.

She smiled.

"Did you try the familiar spell I told you about earlier?" she asked.

"Yes I did, it worked. Thank you, Elsa." She accepted the token of dead bat wings and crows' claws and stored them in her cloak. Elsa smiled and returned to her seat.

Thor spoke up. He put down his instrument. "I have heard of a man who questions people in the town about witchcraft. I don't like this person. We must be careful. I loathe to think we should dwell in shadow. But for now, it is perhaps wise to heed caution." Thor's wise deep brown eyes met everyone else's. They all nodded in agreement.

After the feast and the music were over, everyone got ready to leave. They all danced around the bonfire on the beach till the sun rose over the horizon.

Wearily, Helga clasped her broomstick to fly home. Midsummernight was the most honored event of the year. She'd enjoyed the flowing wine and fiddle music.

The next day Helga visited the town market.

"Good day, Astrid, how are you?" Helga said. She squinted from the bright sunlight. Her head ached from the feast the night before.

Astrid blushed with pride. She cradled her newborn baby in

her arms. She and Erik enjoyed the adoring glances of people around them. She tucked back the soft blanket to let Helga see the baby.

"Oh, what a bonnie wee baby," she said. She fussed over the infant.

Erik glared at her in disapproval. She tensed when she heard Erik's words.

"It's unwise to join those heathens for those nighttime meetings with the Devil," he said.

"What makes you certain I was?" she said. She looked him in the eye. His words angered her. She bit her lip to keep from lashing out at him.

Erik studied her broad shoulders and aged face. She grew anxious. His snide gaze infuriated her. She felt like she couldn't breathe.

"A farmer told me a sinister creature suckled on the cow's teats. He chased it away through the woods. He said he was sure it was evil. The farmer's cows are sick."

Relief swept over her. So far, she hadn't been accused.

"Oh, I am sure it was nothing."

"A priest of a higher order is visiting the church soon. He cares much about the good will and fate of the people. If anyone can end this heathen pestilence, it's him. I'm sure he will be eager to meet you," Erik said.

"Helga, please be careful," Astrid whispered as she soothed the baby.

Helga paled. When she recovered herself, she managed a small smile.

"I appreciate your concern." Helga was relieved when they left and strolled through the market.

A few days later, three men appeared at her door. They talked in low voices. She watched them from her kitchen window. She hoped they wouldn't find the tilberi.

She studied herself at her bedroom mirror. She smoothed her hands on her apron. She retied the plain white cap she wore on her head. Her long, blue wool skirt and fitted sleeves were stained with dirt. She fidgeted with the apron ties and the laces on her kirtle.

The moment she opened the door, she wished she hadn't. A tall man stood at the door. He wore a black robe. He had a shock of grey hair on his head. He narrowed his eyes and strode with purpose. His frame filled the doorway.

"May I come in?" the priest said in an authoritative voice and French accent. His accent sounded unfamiliar to her. She strained her ears to understand his next words.

Helga's throat went dry. She boiled hot water in her copper kettle and sat next to the hearth. She struggled to talk but her throat was too dry. What was happening?

"What is your name?" he asked.

"I'm Helga Brunhild. What's wrong?" She sipped her tea to calm her nerves. Magpie twitched her tail as a warning to be careful of this man.

"My name is Monsignor Macette. A farmer tells us the cows are unwell. Do you know anything of this, Helga? Did you endanger a woman's baby with an herbal poison?" His voice grew darker and deeper with every word. Helga's blood froze.

She needed to think. She needed to get away from this man. She needed to leave.

His gaze took in every detail: the skirt she wore, the scuffed shoes, her curly grey hair and her threadbare shawl. She hated the way he looked at her and drew her shawl around her.

"They suspect you of witchcraft. Do you not believe in God?" The priest's tone of voice made her cringe.

She stared at him in fear. He loomed over her, a sour expression on his face.

"She asked me for the herbal remedy. I would never harm anyone."

He barked at her. "So you confess to witchcraft?"

"Astrid asked me. If she was harmed, why didn't she tell me?"

"That is not the way of God. You live alone, do you not? You don't have a husband, Helga? You own land?" he asked. He looked around the room and back at her.

She glanced sharply at him. His expression was unreadable. The tilberi caught her eye. It crawled to the front steps. She suppressed a gasp.

"My cows are suffering," a farmer said. "A strange creature stole their milk. I blessed the cows with a Sign of the Cross. Are you responsible for this?" He set the Bible on the table. It landed with a heavy thud.

She bit back her laughter.

"No," she said when she regained her composure.

"My wife's baby is ill thanks to your strange herbs and potions. This is the last time you threaten my family." Erik looked at her then to the priest and back at her.

Helga opened her mouth in protest but before she could speak, Monsignor Macette rose to his feet.

"Witchcraft is a serious crime. I would be more careful if I were you. You could be condemned to death."

Monsignor Macette stood a few feet closer to her. His breath was on her face. She grimaced.

"We will stretch you on the rack, dunk you in the ocean with your limbs bound, burn you at the stake." Helga said nothing. The icy look in his eyes froze the blood in her veins. He turned to leave.

They left. Monsignor Macette's cloak billowed behind him. His beady eyes scanned the yard for anything unusual. She couldn't find the tilberi. Her gut clenched.

When they were gone, relief coursed through her. She found the tilberi under the front steps. It coiled around the churn like a snake.

"Churn lid off, Mummy!" it exclaimed. She lifted the lid. The tilberi emptied itself of milk.

She clenched her hands into fists. It wasn't fair! How dare they storm into her home and threaten her! What did they know of struggle and hardship? She paced across the room, trying to control her emotions.

She tucked the keys into her pocket and left the house. She walked across the field. She decided she was safe for now. A farmer saw her. He wore a suspicious expression on his face.

When he turned his back, the tilberi hid in the foliage under the fence posts.

"What are you doing here, Helga? Weren't you warned about not harming our cows?" His eyes narrowed.

"You have more coin than you do cattle," she said. She laughed. He frowned at her.

Helga walked away. People stared and whispered to each other. She quickened her pace. Her face turned red. She glanced at them as she passed.

She rushed over to the church and reached Astrid's side. They walked away a few feet before talking. Monsignor Macette stared right at them from where he stood.

"Hello, Astrid, can I talk to you about something?" she said.

Astrid frowned but listened. She wore a new dress woven of fine silk. Jewels gleamed on her red linen cap.

"You wanted the herb treatment for the labor pains. I never meant you any harm," she said.

"I know you didn't, Helga." Astrid fell silent.

Erik appeared by Astrid's side with an unpleasant expression on his face.

"Why are you here? Get going now," he said. Helga's cheer vanished. She stared at him in shock. Helga noticed a bruise on her shoulder. Astrid stifled her tears.

"I have to go to church. I'm sorry but I am busy right now," Astrid followed Erik into the church.

Erik shut the door before she could protest. Helga left, stung by Erik's harsh words.

Helga's calloused hands fumbled with the fire in the fireplace. She worried about Astrid, the tilberi, and how she would survive. The tilberi crawled across the floor to its usual spot near the churn.

Magpie lapped cream from her bowl. The tilberi sucked the milk. Magpie hissed. It hid from her. Magpie peered accusingly at her. She petted her cat to comfort her and tucked the tilberi into the pocket of her petticoat.

The next day, the tilberi appeared at the window. It heaved milk into the churn and climbed up to the hearth.

She jumped in alarm when she looked out her window. Erik stood on her lawn with a smug expression on his face.

He entered, followed by the priest in the black robe, Monsignor Macette. A chill came over her.

"Hello, Erik," she said. Magpie swatted her paw at Erik and hissed. If Magpie bothered him, he made no sign of showing it.

"Our baby is ill. You gave her a charm. Our milk is curdled. It's your fault."

"I don't know what you're talking about." She folded her arms across her chest.

Long shadows fell around the cottage. The woods appeared ominous. A strong wind blew through the trees.

Helga cuddled Magpie. She hated herself for feeling this way. She hated him for mistreating Astrid.

Gesturing to Erik, she motioned for him to sit but he remained standing. Monsignor Macette watched her steadily.

"Helga Brunhild, you stole my cow's milk and sent your strange beast to do your evil bidding. I shall have you tried for witchcraft."

Helga reeled in shock.

They forced her into the carriage. A crowd of people stared as she was taken away from her home. The horses' hooves clattered over the cobblestones.

Her bound hands clasped the iron bars. Helga stared at the faces for pity. She found none.

Her heart pounded. Her head spun and she forced herself to stay calm. She read the wooden runes for a sign. Peeved, she hid them in her pocket. Her chin trembled.

She ached for the warmth of her hearth. Her house grew smaller in the distance. Tears splashed on her cheek. What would happen to her cat? She tugged at the folds of her skirt. Her heart lurched. The tilberi was at home.

The carriage halted. Helga's eyes widened with panic. The men led her to the courthouse. She struggled against their grip. The large doors closed behind her.

"Helga Brunhild, what evil spirit do you have?" Monsignor Macette asked her.

"None," she replied.

"Have you made a contract with the Devil?" Monsignor Macette said and scowled.

"No," she said hoarsely.

"Why do you steal milk from these farmers?"

"I am poor. I need to survive, but I mean no harm. I don't steal milk."

"What do you do?" he said.

"I steal nothing," she said and ached for a glass of water.

"What creature do you use?"

"I use no creature."

"Why did you walk near the farms when you were ordered to stay away from them?"

"I went for a simple walk." She swallowed hard.

"Have you made a contract with the Devil?"

"No."

"Helga, why do you torment these people? Can you not see the evil of your ways?"

"I've done nothing, I detest evil."

"Why do you steal milk from farmers?" he said.

"I steal nothing. You are accusing me."

"Helga, we find you guilty of practicing black magic." She shook her head no.

"You will be burned as a Witch. May God have mercy on your soul." She stared at them in horror. Monsignor Macette's expression darkened.

They shoved her to the wall in the far corner and removed her clothing. Her clothes fell to the floor. She struggled against them in vain. They examined her body for the witch's teat, the Devil's mark.

They pinned her arms. Her hair was yanked hard from her head. She cried in pain. She blushed and flinched as they probed her body for a mark. Their rough hands pulled her legs apart. She struggled. They released her and returned her clothing to her. She threw on her clothes.

"I found a Devil's mark on her leg," a man said to the stern priest. The priest nodded in understanding.

They led her to her cell. She peered out the window. A cold, sunny morning arose. Her heart hammered with fear. Her throat was parched. She hadn't slept all night. Her eyes blinked from the morning's brightness. She huddled on the stone cold floor and cried.

Helga read her runes. One rune was *thurisaz,* the rune of vexing thorns. She pounded on the bars. But no help came. She cried till her throat ached. An idea occurred to her.

She banged two rocks together to start a fire. She pushed straw together to form a mound and blew on the sparks till they caught flame. A small fire burned. She warmed her aching hands.

She concentrated hard as the flames mesmerized her. The magic grew within her. She held her hands at arms' length. She concentrated on the tilberi but something seemed wrong. There was no answer. She heard a plaintive faint cry for help. It sounded like Astrid. Alarm washed over her.

She checked to see if the guard was asleep. She chanted harder as she gazed into the flames. She called on her coven members for help, remembering the feast in the castle. The fire grew higher. A single flame caught. Elsa appeared in the flames.

"We will help you, Helga," Elsa said. Her voice sounded far away. She nodded, relieved. Elsa vanished. The flames died. The smell of sulfur wafted through the air.

The guard shifted in his seat. The keys were within her reach. She extended her arm but to no avail. He snored. His head reached his chest.

Flushed with anger, she grasped the keys and pulled. His hand still clutched the keys. She checked to see if he was awake. The guard grunted and mumbled in his sleep. Her hands pried the keys from his hand. Sweat poured on her back as she unlocked the cell door. She was free! When she turned around, the guard was still asleep.

She searched for the guards. No one was there. With her heart pounding, she fled the courthouse. Helga raced home to find the tilberi.

She burst through the door. The house was cold and empty.

A basket of biscuits caught her eye. Where did those come from? Understanding dawned on her. Astrid. She fled.

She hoped she wouldn't be caught. The branches tore at her clothing and scratched her face but she ran harder. As she drew closer, she heard screams.

Helga's face was dirty. Her hair was tangled. She knelt by Astrid's side.

The tilberi sucked on the milk from her breast. Blood stained Astrid's chest. Helga's hands flew to her face. Her eyes widened when she saw the tilberi.

"What-what happened to you, Astrid?" Helga said. Her eyes were full of questions. "I command you, tilberi, to stop." She waved her hand. The tilberi crawled obediently toward her.

"Full belly, Mommy!" it cried. Helga stared at Astrid with a sympathetic look on her face.

Erik pulled her to her feet. He cradled the baby in his arms and stared at her in rage.

Astrid screamed.

"I didn't mean to hurt you," Helga said.

Astrid drew her blouse and shawl around her. Erik embraced her. She looked away.

"Get away, Witch, or the priest shall have you hanged," he said.

Helga held a drawstring bag in her hand.

"How do we get rid of it, Helga?" he demanded. Erik's gaze was fixed on her. His countenance was fierce. "How did you escape?"

"Full belly, Mommy," it said. Astrid shrieked. Erik stared at the tilberi.

"What evil black magic have you conjured?" he said.

"We must save her, please listen to me." She almost tripped in her efforts.

Astrid cried.

Helga trapped the tilberi in the brown cotton bag and drew the string.

Erik wiped off the blood on Astrid's chest.

"I'll create three piles of dung. The tilberi will explode, it eats so much. It will eat till it dies."

Astrid gazed around her. She heard her name being called. She realized she heard Helga's voice in her head.

I will do it. I started this. I should finish it. Run Astrid, run, go home, she said to her mentally. When she turned around, she saw no sign of them.

She released the tilberi from the drawstring bag. It wriggled on the ground. With a heavy sigh, she formed three piles of dung. She commanded the tilberi to eat it. It ate the first pile. She waited.

She stood alone in her garden. The hot afternoon sun beat down on her neck.

The sounds of horses and the carriage grew louder. She stared at the tilberi as it ate. Her hands clenched with anger. She was poor. She needed the tilberi. But it almost killed Astrid. She couldn't let that happen. She pursed her lips.

The tilberi reached the third pile of dung. Helga sighed hard and hated herself. This would destroy the tilberi.

She gazed at her scuffed shoes and her threadbare shawl. Her chin trembled. The tilberi ate so much dung it couldn't eat anymore. The tilberi exploded. A rib bone lay on the ground. She buried the bone in the grave and walked away without looking back.

It was destroyed. Astrid would never be harmed again. Everyone was safe from the tilberi. She gazed at her home with love for what may be the last time.

The sounds of the approaching carriage and horses emerged into view. Monsignor Macette's cruel gaze met hers.

Helga hid her rune stones in her pocket. Monsignor Macette carried a set of cuffs in his hand and came closer. She made no protest when he forced her into the carriage and the courthouse. A few men sat at a long table.

Monsignor Macette spoke.

"Have you made a contract with the Devil?"

She shook her head.

"Have you not sought to inflict much suffering upon your neighbors?"

"No. I was accused by those who hate me."

"Can you name those who hated you?"

"Yes, yes I can. Erik Lidveig. He much accused me. He follows me around and never leaves me alone."

"Do you summon a creature of the Devil, an imp, to do your bidding?" He glowered at her. Helga remained seated though her heart pounded with fear but she remembered Elsa's promise.

"I know of no such creature. I own no creature. I have a pet cat."

"Cats are a Witch's familiar. They are in league with the Devil."

"The gentleman—"

"Which gentleman?" she said.

"Erik Lidveig tells me you stole their milk." They all peered at her harder.

"Erik tells a lot of stories, I think. I see many bruises on Astrid's body."

The priest shrugged his shoulders. Helga pursed her lips in anger. *The nerve.*

Helga smiled as a misty cloud of smoke filled the room. *Elsa helped me!* Hope swelled in Helga's heart.

They coughed from the plumes of smoke. She disappeared from the room. They searched everywhere for her but they couldn't find her.

Helga greeted Magpie at the door. She hung her broomstick, started a fire, and swept the ashes clean. The copper kettle boiled. The cauldron bubbled in the hearth.

Astrid rocked the baby in the rocking chair. Her curls bounced and she wore a smile on her face. Her face and neck were free of bruises. The baby cooed.

Helga clutched her double-edged blade in her hand. She stabbed the blade in the wall and set the empty wooden churn on the floor beneath the knife. Milk spilled into the churn from the knife. Helga smiled secretly to herself. *Hail to Mighty Odin.*

Bruja

Jeff Parsons

ohn was alone in the dark.

The relentless downpour of cold rain kept his skinny body soaked and shivering as he stumbled through the nighttime woods of pine, fir and cedar.

He was a scruffy 12-year-old lost in the remote mountains of California's Klamath National Forest. It had been almost two days since he'd run away from his "blended family" at the park campground. At the time, he'd been terribly angry, resentful that his dad had remarried after the divorce. All of those problems seemed to be insignificant now. He was afraid.

He fell again to the unseen forest floor. His shorts snagged on something thorny as he staggered back up. New blood dripped down his scraped knees.

Thunder boomed and lightning flashed, several times in succession, sputtering illuminations upon the nearby gloomy area. Large raindrops began falling.

He saw that he had tripped on a jagged piece of cut lumber rising from a moss-covered stone foundation.

The derelict ruin was probably once a small cottage. He was lucky that he hadn't impaled himself on an exposed timber shaft.

In the lightning flashes, he had seen the remains of other houses as well. Most of them had collapsed into jumbles of shattered wood and glass edges, but there was one house still standing. About a hundred yards away, in the dark, on his left.

He could barely see his hands outstretched before him as

he groped his way through the tangled, wet undergrowth and around an occasional tree branch.

Why are there houses way out here? He wondered, deep in thought. *Maybe they're from the Gold Rush Era?*

He'd visited ghost towns before—like the term implied. He thought he felt the presence of ghosts around him, like the half-heard whispers of long-dead secrets, waiting to come to life again.

Lightning continued to explode with rolling thunder.

Just ahead, he saw the mansion intact, two stories tall, but modest by today's standards. Undoubtedly, it was an opulent extravagance in its time.

As the flickering light subsided, the house appeared to wobble before his eyes.

That's weird. Sheesh, I'm so darn tired.

He rubbed his eyelids—red afterimages of the house flared in his eyesight. When his vision adjusted to the darkness, he thought he saw a faint glimmer of light coming from ahead. He blinked several times. It was still there. It was from inside the house.

What is that?

He felt his way through the scratching brambles towards the fuzzy mote of light.

Another lightning flash—a quick one that resulted in a long, resounding crash in the woods far behind him. It sounded like a tree had gotten hit.

Now that he was close to the house, he could see that it was dotted with freckles of remaining white paint, standing out like pus on dead grey skin. Boldly climbing a few steps to look inside through the lighted window, he saw a small room with some furniture shapes in it, but that was it. The light source came from an adjacent room, behind a closed door.

Wading through waist-high weeds, his wrinkled fingertips trailed along the rough, weathered wall boards until his sneaker bumped against an elevated flat rock. He stood before the front door. Faint light trickled onto the doorstep from a crack along the door's bottom.

The door creaked when he pushed on it, opening onto a warm, cluttered living room that had three other doors and a stairwell going up.

The light source was a fireplace hearth.

In the hearth, a greasy, black kettle pot was suspended above a smoldering bed of orange coals.

Someone lives here.

A pair of worn plush chairs faced towards the dwindling fire...one of them had a blanket draped over its wide back.

On an end table between the chairs, a stoneware mug of dark fluid sat alongside a huge leatherbound book. Judging from the condition of the once-fancy furniture, decorations and wall sconces, the house had fallen long ago into a prolonged descent of water-rotted decay.

Hmm. Something's cooking...

The aroma was heavenly. But there were other scents present in the house as well. Aside from the pervasive, earthy smell of mold, his stuffed nose could sense something else... distant, subtle and elusive, making him feel uneasy.

Hunger overwhelmed the vague warning from his instincts. He was starving—bubbly saliva collected at the corners of his mouth.

Moving forward, he grabbed the thick pot handle.

He yelped and pulled his hands away. The metal was hot! He waved his hands in the air to cool them. The pain eclipsed his hunger for several stinging moments.

"Are you hungry?" a gruff voice asked from behind.

Startled, he whirled around, drops of water flying off his dirty sweatshirt.

At the open door, an old woman stood tall, dressed in faded archaic clothes, carrying an armload of firewood. She was rail-thin, yet from the way her knobby fingers gripped the wood, she also appeared to be quite strong, in a wiry, resolute way.

"Suh-sorry," John stuttered, forcing the words out, "I'm lost. I'm cold and hungry and it looked good. I'm-I'm hungry."

Water streamed down his body onto the warped wooden

floor while he waited for a response.

A smile slowly crept across her craggy face, revealing teeth arranged like a shattered picket fence, stained black and reddish-brown.

"Of course. Have a seat," she motioned gracefully to a chair. "I'll get the fire going and you can dry off and have some stew. You like stew?"

"Yes!" John replied eagerly, a little more excited than he intended to be, suddenly ravenous.

After closing the door, she placed some split logs onto the ashy coals and dropped the rest of the logs into a wood storage box. Using an iron poker, she dug into the coals and stirred them into a crackling flurry of activity.

He watched the colorful flames as they whipped about in a lively fury that was mesmerizing, hypnotic. Over the last two dreadful days, he'd forgotten the blessed feeling of warmth. Without thinking, he moved closer to the growing fire. Water dripped off him and spattered into steam on the hot hearth.

The old woman chuckled while he blissfully soaked up the heat.

"So, you've been outside for a while," she said casually, with a touch of a Spanish accent.

"I got lost in the woods. I saw your house when the lightning flashed."

He glanced out the window. Outside, rain streaked down, silent as silver meteorites. His ears were still ringing, but despite the raging storm, he was amazed at how peacefully quiet it was inside the house.

"You're a very observant lad—maybe that's why you found my house—lucky you," she said, watching him discreetly.

"My parents will be looking for me. Do you have a phone?" he asked, hopeful.

"No," she smiled again. "Nothing like that here."

Her eyes sparkled like emeralds near the fire. She stirred the pot with a wooden spoon and ladled some stew out into a bowl.

"Here. Sit down, already." She remarked, handing the bowl and spoon to him.

He sat down cautiously—the chair groaned, but didn't break. Its comforting warmth helped to drain away the cold dampness afflicting him.

"Go ahead and eat," she motioned and smiled again. "It's not often that I get visitors. I value my privacy, as you might guess."

He sampled the chunky stew. Turnips, potatoes, carrots and peas gave it a familiar flavor and texture, but the tasty meat within it was unfamiliar to him, and the gravy had a rich, juicy blood aftertaste like drippings from a fresh-cut steak.

He began to wolf it down in earnest.

"Not so fast," she chuckled. "You can eat as much as you'd like. Plenty of time for that." She paused, gazing into the fire. "The storm won't clear 'til tomorrow. No sense going out 'til then. I'll take you to a logging road. You can follow it back to the main road and find your family."

Chewing away with his mouth full, he bobbed his head enthusiastically.

Thunder rattled the windows, but the sound didn't penetrate much farther into the house.

An anguished howl, coming from the second floor, accompanied the thunder.

He stopped eating, or even moving, rounded eyes riveted toward the stairs. After moments of ensuing silence, he looked back at the old woman with a questioning look.

"My dogs don't like the weather much," she grinned, lopsided and uneven.

He went back to finishing off his stew.

She continued to stare at him with her thin, narrow face scrunched up in a shrewd, thoughtful expression.

"Would you like more?" she asked.

"Yes, Ma'am," he said, giving her the bowl.

"So polite. By the by, what is your name?" She handed him another steaming bowl of stew.

"John Ramos. What's yours?" He dug into the delicious stew.

"My my. It's been sometime since I've been asked that. Leticia is my name. Leticia Vasquez."

A jolt of electric sweat prickled like sparks igniting across the surface of his skin.

Around the family campfire, one of the scary stories he had heard was about a witch, a *bruja* in the Spanish language, who had lived in this area many, many hundreds of years ago when the Spanish ruled California. Her name was Lettie....

It's not her. Stop being silly.

She leaned closer to him, looking concerned.

He noticed that she had a multitude of miniscule warts sprouting like mushrooms across her leathery skin. Also, his nose wrinkled at her sour smell; it was as if she never washed herself.

"You're looking a little pale. Are you feeling well, John?"

"Um...not really. I think I have a cold or something."

"Oh dear," she fussed in empathy.

She vigorously stoked the fire again with the poker. The light caught her dirty, dishwater-colored hair, seemingly transforming it into molten silver. He thought that, once upon a time, she must've been exceptionally beautiful.

"I have just the thing for you!" she smiled widely and clapped her hands together softly. "Do you like cider? Just made it, no more than a week ago. I could heat some up for you, if you'd like?"

"Yes, please," he said.

She nodded and went to the door beside the stairs. It was a kitchen door, he saw as she entered, door slapping closed behind her. Tromping about within, she hummed to herself and moved things about, apparently looking for something, with a clatter and bang of pots and pans.

He heard another noise, coming from the top of the stairs.

It wasn't a howl. It was a whimper. And it wasn't from a dog.

Someone's up there!

Curiosity aroused, he left the stew bowl on the end table and approached the steep stairs. The second story landing didn't appear to be as dark as it should be.

The old woman was still humming away in the kitchen.

He crept up the stairs. A few of the steps squeaked as they sagged, adding nervous tension to the anxiety he felt.

Upstairs, there was a short, low-ceilinged hallway that contained a door on both sides and also at the end. The end door was especially interesting to him—lines of soft light outlined the door's edges.

There it was again. A sobbing. From straight ahead.

The sobbing stopped when he pushed open the end door.

The musty room was illuminated by the pale electric-blue glow of weird symbols covering the floor and five large cages.

The metal-barred cages were enclosed within a runed pentagram of grey-white salt, each cage arranged near the tips of the star, closed doors facing inward.

Dark shadows crouched within two of the caged confines—the shadows moved closer to him. They were children, his age: a boy and a girl, watching him wide-eyed, mouths agape, their disheveled, filthy bodies pressed hard against the interwoven cage bars.

"Help" and "Let us go." They simultaneously cried, pitiful and desperate in their pleas.

He rushed towards them, feet scuffing the pentagram, spreading salt across the blood-sticky floor. A sharp, acrid stench of defecation, urine and sweat surrounded the cages—his nose twitched and his eyes watered. He felt like he could sneeze at any moment.

There were no locks on the cage doors.

"What…how do I open them?" he asked, boggled.

"We don't know! Hurry or she'll get you too!" the boy screeched, frantically shaking the bars on his cage.

Then, the girl said something truly awful: "She's going to eat us!"

John felt his body go slack with chilled shock and fear.

In his dazed stupor, he noticed that the children suddenly went still and expressionless, quietly eyeing the door.

John's heartbeat raced as he turned.

The old woman was there, blocking the exit, with a porcelain pitcher hanging loosely in one hand.

"Well now, this does complicate matters," the old woman said. "Most unfortunate…."

She gestured with her claw-like free hand.

The room spun and he lost his balance; he heard his body hit the floor just before he lost consciousness.

He was slowly roused into awareness by the muffled cries of people calling out his name. Many people.

"Mom! Dad! I'm here!"

He bolted awake, realizing that it wasn't a dream.

The room was well-lit by narrow windows. The storm had broken and tree-filtered daylight clearly showed the decrepit state of his nauseating confines.

He was lying inside one of the cages! With a low groan, he shuffled his body to relieve the pain on his backside. The hard metal cage lattice had left aching marks from where he had lain. He sat up and cradled his throbbing head in his hands.

The people calling out his name were nearby!

"John. That's your name?" the boy asked. "Those people are looking for you!"

John let go of his head and shook his cage door. It wouldn't budge. There was a crude lock holding it shut. His rescuers were so close and he was trapped in here!

"Help!" he yelled in frustration. His voice didn't carry very far.

"Stop that!" the girl hissed. "She'll hear you! There's a better way…" She pointed to a sliver of bone next to his cage. "Use it to open the lock."

Squeezing his arm through the cage's bars, he stretched real hard and finally grabbed the bone from beneath a knobby tuft of green mold.

He inserted the bone into the lock's crude keyhole. He had no idea what to do, fumbling around, his hands shaking.

"Move the tip of the bone. Find the lever inside and gently turn it." The girl suggested.

"Okay. Hey, why does my cage have a lock and yours don't?"

The boy spoke, "Don't know. She's crazy. She locked us up in here using witchcraft. Maybe she didn't have a lock at the time?"

The bone kept on slipping whenever John applied pressure to the lock's internal mechanism. He sighed, then slowed his breathing to help calm his trembling hands. It worked—he went back to picking the lock.

"Hurry. Our rescuers are getting farther away," the boy said, eyes darting around desperately. "She's probably outside, casting her illusions to hide the house again. The lightning storm must've…"

The lock clicked, opened and fell to the grimy floor with a dull thump.

John scrambled out of the cage in an instant, crawling to the nearest captive, the girl, when she shrieked, "Look out!"

He turned and saw the old woman striding down the hallway, hands gesturing, arcane energies gathering like dried leaves caught a whirling vortex of fire.

What! Not again!

He dove toward the room's door and slammed it shut.

A feathery gust of wind brushed against the outer surface of the door.

Something heavy hit the hallway floor, hard.

Listening intently, he heard slow, wheezing breaths on the other side of the door.

"You did it!" the girl cheered.

Hesitant, he yanked open the door.

The old woman lay sprawled on the floor, unmoving, except for her wild rolling eyes, which looked dazed until they focused on him.

The old woman's lips oozed spittle as she babbled, "Ooooohhh."

She must've gotten paralyzed by her own spell—it had rebounded off the door!

He was stunned by the sudden, fortuitous turn of events.

"Let us out, quick, while you still can! We'll go find the search party," the girl said. "John! You can be with your family again!"

"Nnn-ooooohhh!" the old woman gasped.

Evil crone.

The hope of seeing his family again spurred him into action.

He pulled open the cage doors—it was ridiculously easy.

The boy and girl eased out of their cages slowly, stretching and grinning widely.

"I told you he could do it," the girl marveled.

"It was wise of you to summon him," the boy admitted.

Summon? What?

"Hmm…first things first," the girl said, directing her brilliant smile towards the paralyzed old woman.

Invisible forces dragged the old woman across the uneven floor into a cage. The cage door slammed shut and flared an incandescent bright white as it welded to the cage.

"Nasty witch. Let her starve," the boy grumbled.

"Now…John." The girl stared at him, coquettishly. "Thank you for setting us free. We've been locked up for ever so long…"

"Centuries," the boy clarified.

"What are you? What are you doing?" John asked, in shuddering breathes, afraid of hearing the answers.

"Oh dear…still confused?" the girl smirked with malevolent compassion. "Poor thing. Who are we? Let's just say that we're your worst nightmares come to life. We love chaos—encouraging it, causing it, savoring the flavor of fear. The witch had imprisoned us. You set us free. How sad. Now your world is going to suffer again…."

The boy and girl laughed as they transformed into…something else.

The air surrounding them began to infuse with writhing wisps of vapor, struggling to push into the boy and girl from all sides, as if insanely enormous entities, monstrous and terrible, had forced their way into this dimension and protruded the images of a boy and girl, images no more real than a child's finger puppet.

"Before we set out, how about a snack?" the girl said, looking at John, hungrily.

John screamed, one last time….

Wasp Wing

COY HALL

he searched the frozen windowpane, clearing frost with her arm, but she found no reflection that grey morning. The cabin, a single room hidden in the forest, possessed no other mirrors. It was a bare room, austere—the home of woodsmen in fairy tales. There was a bed where the couple had slept, and a bed their children—three boys—had shared. The quilts were handmade. There was a fireplace and a homespun rug on the floor. There were cabinets on the walls that housed an assortment of utensils and a few stoppered bottles of tonic. There were two windows. Outside, there was a trail that led into the woods, a dirt trace that, after miles, met one of the state routes. She tried to recall the number. Was it 784? There were so few signs.

The frozen window meant she couldn't see herself that morning, and the prospect of being blind to her metamorphosis seemed tragic. Witnessing the beauty of the changing would, she hoped, lessen agony that had already scissored her nerves and wrenched her bones. It was the pain of mutilation, of primitive surgeries. If she had not been so anchored, so devoted, the agony may well have cost her mind. Lack of sleep did nothing to help. She had done her best to sleep on her stomach that night, but, like so many other nights, sleep only came in rapid fits.

After moving from the cold window, she reached to her back. She stroked the enlarged protrusions at her shoulder.

At both shoulder blades, the skin was flayed, hot with infection, and the wings that partially emerged caused excruciating pain when moved. If the wings shifted (only eight inches had surfaced, the remainder waited below her skin) her spine seemed to twist with the burden.

She got to her knees at the foot of the child bed, an imitation of prayer, gritting teeth at the nauseating pain. The agony was nearly enough to knock her unconscious. She placed her ear against the floorboards. A familiar buzzing came to her, a familiar stench, and then a familiar gravity in her limbs. Ever since the first night, she'd been pulled. She closed her eyes in a moment that was almost sublime. The aura rose like steam through the floor.

An unwelcome but familiar paranoia gripped her.

She opened her eyes and listened. With a grimace, she rose from the floor.

She often heard their voices, as she had that first night, pleasant, a family sitting down to dinner. Now she heard the voices outside the cabin. The same sounds, the same family—the boys, the parents. Had they come back? Had she been delusional all along? Had they simply left and gone away, now to return? She'd taken their space, was using it as her own. No doubt they were angry. Furious. The possibilities made her tremble. However, in the moment before her increasingly fused fingers met the door, she dashed the thought away. The family wouldn't return. They couldn't.

They were below, weren't they?

They were buried in the crawlspace, rotting. She could smell them. If she strained, she could peer through cracks in the floor and see their wasp-covered corpses. She'd put the bodies there herself.

How could they ever return? There were no voices.

She drew a breath and calmed herself. Returning to the frozen window, a more positive thought occurred. The night had been cold and snowy, but sunlight fought the clouds. A couple hundred yards from the cabin, in the opposite direction of the road, there was a small pond with fish. She had been there once before. The only ice glazing its surface would be brittle. What better mirror than water under the sun? She began to search the cabin for a blanket to jacket her body. It took great willpower to keep from blacking out.

She'd found the driver and his fellows at the counter, running forks over their plates. A waitress stood opposite the three men, a smirk and glass eyes, offering coffee. The men declined, then asked for something stronger. The aura made her skin crawl, yet she approached.

Your name? Who are you, girl? What's your name?

In shy tones, she demurred.

We don't talk to strangers, gal. Conjoined laughter, a noise she hated.

She spoke to escape the laughter. "I'm called Dani," she said. "I need a ride from here."

Called? Who calls you that?

Her father did, had, but she didn't answer.

As she left the diner, the glassy-eyed waitress frowned and shook her head in warning. Dani stopped, but the men swept her through the door. A bell clanged, and the waitress was gone. The truck, a boxy Ford with wooden slats enclosing the bed, waited in the lot. Dani had little experience with automobiles. Her father, a demon-haunted preacher, shunned them as "devil carriages." A man once offered to sell her father an open-topped motorcar in 1913, the year before war, but her old man had damned the fellow. He had a mare in the barn, he said, and God gave him legs to move about. Wasn't that enough? But the flash of that car, as dirty as it was, stuck with Dani. She dreamed about it sometimes. So the opportunity to ride in the truck, even with three lecherous men, was alluring. This was her time of rebellion, after all.

How better to continually damn her father?

Once the engine was cranked and running, the men, reeking of body odor, crowded into the cab. They insisted Dani ride up front rather than in the bed with straw and crates. It was much too cold, they said. They would keep her warm and snug. The truck took to the road shakily. The rows of brick buildings disappeared, then the houses and yards passed, and then forest ate up the highway. The men passed Dani back and forth on their laps (even the devil-may-care driver), rubbing their erections against her body. Despite Dani's protesting, their hands explored and groped. She wore a long coat, but her clothes beneath were thin. With clumsy fingers, the men loosened buttons. Finally, the truck stopped. The road was dark and shadowy, lined with bare trees and brown-grey undergrowth.

Dani fought back. She clawed and kicked and hammered. She screamed until her lungs felt like bloody pulp. Bruised, the men relinquished their collective grip and let her flee. They laughed together, watching her go. She did so, dashing lithely between the trees, cutting through the painfully resistant brush.

She looked like a cat, they agreed. She was a weird one, all right. Something not quite right in her eyes. Eventually, the truck coughed and rolled away.

She stepped onto a blanket of snow that stretched over the field and draped trees. It was heavy snow, the kind that clumps and crunches. Sunlight emerged at breaks in the clouds, and warmth caused surrounding trees to drip. There was comforting peace in the forest, peace she couldn't find in the cabin, no matter how she tried.

Revulsion and gratitude made strange bedfellows.

The cleft in her soul was confusing. With the blanket carefully avoiding the protrusions at her shoulders, she distanced herself from the cabin. In the light, she examined her hands. With a process that began nights before, her long, delicate fingers were fusing together, skin melding, nails blackening. The hands were folding in on themselves, thinning without withering. Only the thumbs remained mobile. Her hands, it appeared, were forming into a sharp point. It was grotesque. Nauseating.

Guilt washed over her. Where was her gratitude?

Craning her neck, wincing at the pain, she glanced at her right wing. It was black, hard as bones at the edge, and webbed with membrane thin as cheesecloth. The glint of quicksilver covered it, and when sunlight hit the membrane, the purplish rainbow of oil emerged. It was grotesque, but also beautiful. She knew she needed to find gratitude in that beauty. She found the wing revolting and alluring. How would the wing look when it fully emerged? Possibly, it could be as beautiful as one of her father's angel wings.

Regardless of her feelings, metamorphosis was a fitting gift. Had she not bargained for the ability? The Goddess had granted her such freedom. If not for the pain, she reasoned, she'd be glad. There would be no question then. There would be no cleft, no ingratitude.

The will of her Goddess meant everything to her.

She looked to the cabin, which stood uneven on a slope of earth. At the left of the porch, bound with a rusted latch, a square door enclosed the crawlspace. She had discovered the divine there. The divine, which her father had ranted over, mutilated his mind in fear of, begged on his knees, finally cursed and abandoned, was not sought. The divine had found her. As reinforcement, she considered walking forward and unlatching the door. A mortal fear, however, kept her distant. She had looked upon the shape only once. That was enough. It was a form best kept in the abstract, best restrained in the back of thoughts.

How would her father react to seeing the divine? How would he react to seeing his daughter's change?

He would lose his mind. *He'd call you a witch.*

She resigned herself to the task at hand, which was not to admonish her father, or even remember him, but to find a reflection. Under the warmth of the sun, she started toward the tree line at the rear of the cabin.

Witch. The word settled uncomfortably. She had never liked it. Her father, frowning over an open Bible, the word on his lips.

Witch.

She frowned, but it was at a pain deeper than her bones.

Dani had run for several miles. She couldn't reckon the actual distance, but hours had passed, and she hadn't stopped in that time. The sun had moved, early winter twilight settling over the trees. She stopped now because of two things. She'd arrived at a dirt road, and she'd spied a young boy, bundled against the weather, standing in the road, using a tree limb to overturn rocks. He was lost in play. Breathlessly, lungs cold, Dani approached. Unlike with the men in the truck, she felt no need for caution. She raised her hand to the child and the boy waved back amiably.

It was dark when they reached the cabin. An image of the home nestled in a clearing, smoke enveloping the roof, candles in the windows like jack-o'-lantern eyes, a box of pleasant voices and clatter, would remain with her. The image was deceptive rather than idyllic; it masked what lay below. These were people like her father. As they approached, the boy cheerfully leading his guest to dinner, the cabin's front door opened, revealing a tall, broad silhouette and a swath of firelight. The boy obviously had a fondness for stray animals, because the father chided him for bringing home yet another. When Dani came into the light, it made for an odd meeting. The father, a quietly angry, red-faced man, was distant and wary. He searched Dani's eyes.

Reluctantly, he allowed Dani into his home. He kept the boy on the porch, however, and whispered angrily at the child. It was a family of five, a mother and father and three sons ranging in age from four to twelve. The mother invited Dani to sit down for dinner. The mother did not eat. The boys watched Dani in such a way that she wondered if they would grow to be men like the truckers.

That night, Dani lay awake on the floor, bundled in a quilt, listening to the family sleep. With her ear close to the floorboards, a thump and rattle from below stole her attention from the quintet of shallow breaths. Something large moved in the crawlspace. Dani listened more closely, moving aside the bundled sheet she'd been using as a pillow. Through the wood, she could hear a low but intense buzz, the noise of angry insects. Again, something large shifted its weight. The planks rattled against her cheek. The buzzing grew louder.

Suddenly, darkness grew deeper around her, and Dani looked up from the ground, startled. The man stood tall above her, his stance reminding Dani of her father. His knees creaked when he knelt.

Outside, he whispered.

With attention to the others' sleep, she followed the man out the front door. The night was blustery, moving her hair about, cutting into her jacket. Her feet were bare and hard as ice. The father, after closing the door, handed Dani her worn leather shoes.

You must leave, he told her.

He was so stern in his demeanor, so unmoved, he reminded Dani of the granite Confederate soldiers she'd admired in town. She found herself attracted to him. She reached for his hand and touched the corded flesh. He looked off into the moonlight, but didn't resist. After sliding into her shoes, Dani followed him from the porch.

Once upon the dirt road, he spoke.

Temptress.

There was venom in the word. From an inner pocket, the father pulled a Bible. Without opening the pages, he showed it in the silvery light. The book was well worn, the pages marked at close intervals.

My wife says you're a witch. She can feel it. She says you got a devil in your eyes. You're no better than the waspers under our house. You're a weird one, aren't you?

Dani didn't know what to say. The accusation had a numbing effect, leaving her detached. She stared, and she felt cold.

Be on your way, the man said. *You aren't welcome here.*

He left her at the road. In the distance, Dani spotted candles in the cabin windows and four watching faces hooded by curtains.

Snow hid the trail that led to the pond. She was not so familiar with the land that she could do without a path, so she took a meandering route, winding between trees, looking less at the ground and more at the familiar patches of forest. Thankfully, the pond wasn't far. As she walked, keeping her spine still as possible, a twin memory, although years apart, came to her. She could not explain why the memories were conjoined. The episodes never occurred to her separately anymore.

She crunched through the snow, pushing aside limbs, lost in thought. The sun was pleasingly warm. The trees dripped.

Her father, a shape and a voice in her bedroom, woke her from a dream. She couldn't remember the dream, but she recalled the jarring cut from lucid sleep to fogged reality. She recalled the shape and voice, the genuine concern her father conveyed, which was rare. He had found her altar, he said, the patch of forest she'd cleared by hand, the animal bones so intricately placed, the collection of wasp nests, the teeth, a pile of grey ash where incense and forest herbs had burned so often. He was not angry. He had failed her, he admitted. How could he be so foolish? How could she?

Overlaying this recollection was another, like two pictures on a sheet, one folded atop the other. The Goddess, the mother below the sleeping cabin, had taught her to use shadows. Hurt and eager, she'd learned quickly. She came into the cabin as subtle as a breath, not disturbing the sleeping couple or their children. There were no candle flames, and the fire burned low. She carved shapes from the shadows and brought the shapes to their feet. She approached the beds like her father had once approached her own. Shadows moved over the boys. Shadows moved over the mother and father.

Below her feet, the Goddess shifted her bulk, and her wing pushed against the floor, her barb stabbed the mud. The Goddess was rightfully excited.

In her hands, she held honeycombed nests of myriad shapes and sizes, lifted from holes in the crawlspace. She lay the nests about the boys' necks, and stuffed nests into their mouths. She covered the faces of the mother and father, placing nests on their eyelids. With shadows smothering the bodies, no one awoke, not until the thin-waisted Goddess scuttled and her children awakened.

She'd done well keeping to the invisible path. She looked back to where she'd pocked the virgin snow, then looked ahead to the shimmer of sun and ice. Wafts of steam snaked over the pond. Despite the pain, she smiled. The thought of her reflection brought an exhilarating fear. She felt alive.

She felt grateful.

When the father had returned to the cabin and firelight shrank from the windows, Dani moved from her perch on the road. She could not bring herself to obey the man. More than that, something called to her, pulled her with a whisper. Behind the wind, there was a palpable thrumming in the air, the beating of wings. All of this emanated from the crawlspace beneath the cabin. Bundled, Dani walked gingerly over the grass, her arms crossed atop her stomach. The icy wind sliced in and out, rattling shingles on the cabin roof. One shingle, holding on with a single nail, lifted and fell rhythmically. A weathervane, somewhere near but hidden in darkness, shifted and creaked.

Had she not felt a similar beckoning once before? Of course, she had been a child then, new to the Veil. With a child's eagerness (and ignorance) she'd peered beyond. That was in the forest, when wild things grew over her altar. That night a similar pulsing gravity had called her from sleep. She'd gone and retreated, however, too soon. Her mind was too fragile for the sight awaiting her. She'd glimpsed it only briefly. The wing, she remembered, rumpled like the skin of a vulture claw. Foolish of the opportunity, she'd caught no more.

Tonight was a second chance. No longer a child, she was ready to receive the gift of sight. How would it alter her? she wondered.

With mixed emotion, Dani ran her hands over the cabin's stone foundation. To the side of the porch, her palms left cold rock and patted a wooden door. Her heart quickened. She found the latch, gritty with rust. She pushed the door inward.

The wet stench of mildew and mold roiled from the cabin's underbelly. The air was thick, warmer than the night, and windless. Dani reached through the threshold and planted her hands against a skin of mud. She ducked her head and entered. From mud to floor, the space was only two feet high, less when the ground raised in mounds. With the door open, moonlight weakly reached inside. From above, firelight came through the cracks in the floorboards, pinstripes of orange light. It was enough to keep the crawlspace from having the blackness of a cave, but it was not enough to subdue Dani's growing fear.

I'm not a child anymore, she scolded, but her fear didn't bow to the rebuke. The feeling swelled in her chest, and then became a copper flavor at the rear of her tongue.

A second chance, she remind herself. *You were foolish before.*

The clatter of wasp wings reminded her that she was not alone. She crawled farther. Wasn't it odd for wasps to be so active in winter, to be awake? Regardless, she didn't fear their sting. That was part of the beckoning, a promise of safety from the poisonous barbs. Indeed, even as her groping hands fell into holes and crushed nests, the wasps avoided her touch. Although they sounded angry, they kept distant.

Maybe it was the pressure of the small space and the wind, maybe it was more, but the door slammed shut, cutting away the moonlight. Only slats of light from above remained. Dani felt nauseous, suddenly unwilling, as if she'd awakened from a spell of sleepwalking. More than terror, paralysis snaked through her limbs. She craned her neck, peering into one of the far corners: the space, she thought, above which stood the family beds.

In the faint light, the Goddess revealed a shape. What she had been before, or what she'd be after, Dani could not say, but her current form was that of a wasp. It was inconceivably large, filling the space from mud to floor. The massive wings tottered. The triangular head and swollen hindquarters moved in opposite directions, hinged by a minute waist. Floorboards shuddered at the disturbance.

The Goddess, patient with ages, peered inside Dani. She found no shame in the loosening of her bowels.

Witch. Her father's voice. The voice, too, of the man above. Her voice, wrapping around the ugly little word.

Priestess, Dani corrected.

Watching the dark figure, she felt a completeness she'd never felt before. The connection was overwhelming.

Priestess, she thought again.

The wasp did not move to attack her, although it scuttled closer. The barb probed. The Goddess, like Dani, better approved the nomenclature.

Her father, she reflected, had once taken a shovel and murdered a black feline. When he offered reason, he was terse.

The devil's brood, he said, his eyes distant, plumbing memories. He smeared blood in a patch of weeds by the front lawn, making an effort to clean the shovel. He'd thrown the cat's broken body into a fast-flowing creek, recently engorged by a downpour. She'd captured the animal in the woods as a kitten, a stray, and nursed it to robust health. She'd hidden the cat until now.

Impudently, she asked, *How is killing it any better?*

Who's worse? he said. *The murderer of the body? Or the murderer of the soul?*

He was, she realized, a horrible man. But he had hurt her so deeply and so often that the grudge in her heart would not accept his death, drawn out and agonizing as it was, as payment. His suffering was over. She wished, and not even the Goddess could grant her this, that she could continue his suffering, draw up his ghost and let him watch through her eyes. She wanted to torment the man.

She wanted to tell him that she'd never destroyed the altar, nor had he.

Was he watching? He would say so. But she figured he was still in the coffin, a tangle of mold-encrusted bones.

She pressed through remnants of brown cattails and brittle weed stalks taller than the snow, making her way to the pond. As she approached, she shed the blanket; it fell into a crown at her heels. Above, clouds had dispersed, thinning where they remained, and the sun was bright and large. She felt like a basking cat.

The devil's brood, her father said.

Why?

Vessels, he said. *God knows what they carry. Spirits. Worse.*

Can people change into cats?

He scoffed. It was amazing how he picked and chose his superstitions.

Fairy tales, he muttered.

She dashed the thin coating of ice with a stone. Snow crunched as she knelt. She moved her face over the rippling water. The edges of wasp wings poked over her shoulders. Her hands were blackening, as was the sclera of her left eye. She remained in that position for a good deal of time. With concentration, focusing on the drifting shards of ice and the squirming minnows drawn to sunlight, her hand transformed and became human again. Inkiness swirled and nearly receded from her eye. The wings remained. She flexed her fingers. Painful as it was, and revolting as it appeared, it was a metamorphosis she could learn to command.

History Repeats

Jonathan Cromack

he was bustled into the candlelight, a slight figure held between two black-hooded hulks. They made her stand beside a low table directly opposite a Gentleman seated cross-legged in the centre of the hall. This Judge of Jury beheld her with grave, wearisome eyes. Neighbours and villagers scattered alongside the wood-panelled walls looked on—wide-eyed and open-mouthed. Many of the faces were restless, impatient for a chance to offload their complaints. When the furtive whispering and shuffling had silenced, the Gentleman spoke.

"Dorothy Wallace, you are brought before this court of law to be tried for the heinous crime of befriending the Devil, of bringing ill fortune to the village of Stapeley Hill and of placing upon to William Sampson—a curse—by means of conjuring a Demon, to plague him, thus turning him to madness."

Fifty pounds was a lot of money to Sydney McKinnen. In fact, there wasn't much he wouldn't do for such a tidy sum. His neighbour, Mrs. V. C. Wilovski, had approached him on Tuesday evening with such a proposition while he was dragging out his recycling bin. Standing at her door at the top of the steps, she addressed him as a Victorian lady might make some demand of her gardener.

"Sydney?" she yelled in her cultural tone: "'Seed-nee."

He squinted up, dazzled by the sun.

"Would you be able to oblige me a small favour on Friday evening, if you can spare the time of course? I am required to attend an arts meeting and I don't like to leave Venus and Jupiter alone. Venus is still recovering from her accident, you see."

Sydney winced "Well, erm…"

"I'll pay you fifty pounds for the theft of your time, naturally."

"Certainly. What will I need to do?"

"I'll explain when you call. Shall we say eight o' clock?"

"OK!"

"Excellent, Sydney. I'll see you then. Lovely day isn't it?…"

She slammed the door before Sydney had time to answer or to fully absorb exactly what he had agreed to.

On Friday evening, Sydney found himself climbing the twelve concrete steps—Hobbit-like—to the glossy front door of number 67—next door but one to his own. The building was a grand, five-storey terrace of Victorian townhouses which faced onto a once prosperous, busy street just outside the town centre. Unlike Sydney's rented two-storey apartment, Mrs Wilovski owned her house in its entirety; it had not yet been partitioned into flats.

As Sydney reached for the doorbell, the door opened to frame the occupant in her usual unique style of dress—bold, flowery shirt complemented with a huge, silver star medallion hanging from her neck.

"Ah, Seedernei. Thank you for coming." She stepped back ushering Sydney in with an elegant, cavalier-style gesture.

As Sydney crossed the threshold, his eyes took a while to adjust from the bright spring evening. He was in a long narrow hallway leading to a kitchen at the far end. Through the open door he glimpsed a toaster and some mugs on a wooden tree. A door to his left let into the living room, flickering with light from the TV; on the right, a narrow staircase led into darkness above. The air smelled of cooking, possibly pie and chips, Sydney hazarded, but to Mrs. Wilovski this would undoubtedly be "Flaked Pastry Mousseline and Maris Piper Chippings." He followed her into the kitchen where Venus, a tortoiseshell cat was fast asleep in a fluffy tartan basket hanging from a radiator. A white bandaged front paw extended leisurely into the air in keeping with her other three appendages.

"Jupiter is out somewhere at the moment." began Mrs. Wilovski, "They utilise the cat flap as required. Venus may nip out later if she can hobble that far, but do keep an eye out for her if she does."

"Uh huh," Sydney conceded.

Mrs. Wilovski went to a maple cupboard above the work surface.

"Cat food and treats are in here," came her amplified voice from inside, "they may both need feeding in an hour or so. I'm sure they'll let you know." she produced a strained coughing sound which Sydney took to be a laugh, then she exited the cupboard and gestured her arm elegantly around the room. "Help yourself to a drink—anything you can find. I'm sure you know how to work the TV." The coughing sounded again. "Any questions?"

"I just have to watch the cat...?" Sydney asked. He looked at the Moggy as her four outstretched paws twitched in a dreamy little Mexican wave.

"I'm afraid I simply cannot avoid this meeting. I do worry about poor Venus."

"Ah."

The two neighbours stood awkwardly searching for any overlooked detail before Mrs. Wilovski departed.

"Is there a number I can ring if I need to get hold of you in case of emergency or something?" Sydney asked.

Mrs. Wilovski winced, "I'm afraid not, I don't actually own

a mobile telephone and the group I will be attending wouldn't allow such an…" her brow furrowed, "…intrusion."

"Oh, I see…"

"I must dash now, Sydney. You'll be alright won't you?"

"Well…" Sydney began, but the woman had turned her back on him in order to rub her knuckles on the cat's head. The animal stretched itself tremblingly, then curled into a neat, dormouse-like ball. Sydney followed Mrs. Wilovski as far as the front door, she snatched her keys from a small shelf on the way, then hurried down the steps to the pavement below and to her car at the back of the building. Sydney closed the door on the murmuring traffic.

In the lounge, he first noticed the huge, wood grain-effect television which must have been at least thirty years old. One entire wall was covered with shelves full of books—gardening, cooking, travel, philosophy, Yoga and Wicca. An old brown sofa and two matching armchairs surrounded a coffee table. Sydney sighed and went to the bay window overlooking the street through netted curtains. Mrs. Wilovski's original, bright-yellow Volkswagen Beetle phutted noisily away. Revellers were walking into town for their Friday night out— packs of bawdy lads and groups of tottering, scantily-clothed girls.

Sydney glanced at the Slug and Lettuce on the opposite side of the road, its windows glowed invitingly. He could probably nip over for a swift one, Mrs. W wouldn't know any differently; alternatively there was always the coursework to tackle. Perhaps later.

He ventured into the kitchen. Venus was still comatose and Jupiter hadn't returned. He went to the fridge—coconut water, vegetable juice. He fumbled around for a beer but the only alcohol he discovered was half a bottle of absinthe, bizarrely placed in a magazine rack. In the end he settled for a cup of Nescafe and took it back to the lounge.

Warming to his comfortable situation, Sydney did what comes naturally to bored men of all kinds, that of channel-hopping. But even this activity had to end at some point. The best option, Sydney decided, was a repeat episode of *Only Fools and Horses*. Dell-Boy in a wine bar with Trigger about to attempt a fraternisation with a group of young women. Sydney settled back anticipating the classic scene where Dell-Boy catastrophically leans onto a nonexistent section of the bar...

He never got the chance to see it.

Something huge hit the ceiling above so hard that it rattled the miniature cottages on the bookshelf. Sydney froze and grabbed the remote control to silence the TV. He sat upright, staring at the ceiling. A quiet metallic sound like heavy chains being dragged across bare floorboards gradually became a violent, angry thrashing in the room above. He had assumed that he was alone, but someone was tearing one of the upstairs rooms apart.

Silence again.

Sydney crept out of the lounge to the bottom of the stairs and, stretching upwards with one hand on the bannister, he peered into the gloom but could only see as far as a small landing where the stairs turned to the left, out of view.

"Hello..."

Nothing.

"HELLO..."

Silence.

Sydney began to imagine what might be around the corner—a jealous husband; a secret child; some mad relative kept locked away; or some forgotten migrant, the subject of a hideous experiment.... He dismissed these thoughts and did what any normal man would—should—do, and so to ascend.

Coughing self-consciously as he trod the dust-ridden stairs, he eventually paused at the top, finding himself within a narrow landing lit from a small window at the far end. There were doors on either side but these were all closed.

"Hello." he said, "It's Sydney from number 63. Is anyone there?"

Again, silence.

He carefully opened the first door and stepped inside—a large room, possibly the master bedroom, Mrs W's perhaps? An ancient black cast iron fireplace and a king-size divan bed—quite normal, but then there was the solid oak wardrobe *UPSIDE DOWN* in the centre of the room. Both of its doors were open, spilling a rainbow of knitwear and cotton, strewn around the whole room. As Sydney tried to make some rational sense of this bizarre scene, the wardrobe began to slowly rock back and forth pushed by some unseen hand, building a steady momentum. It then toppled heavily onto its face, snapping one of the doors loudly under it's own weight. The wardrobe then started to shake violently on the floor like it was suffering some kind of convulsion. Sydney yelled out once, fled the room and ran downstairs risking his neck jumping two, three stairs at a time and straight out of the front door.

He stood outside panting. A group of lads drinking from lager cans giggled together as they passed by. Sydney stepped down to the pavement and looked up at the first floor windows—motionless white curtains with dark voids between them. There was movement lower down however as the curtain in the next-door bay window twitched, then a bolt scraped at the front door, which opened with a tacky release.

"I thought it was you, Syd!"

It was Frank from number 69—*Oh no!*

"She got you babysitting her cat's has she?" Frank was already in his pyjamas, the cord of his dressing gown straining to keep in the bulk of his midriff.

"Yeah. How did you know?" asked Sydney.

"Ah, you know." Frank offered a wink and tapped the side of his nose knowingly.

"Did you hear that commotion just now?" asked Sydney.

"No, mind you I do have my telly on loud. Why, what're you up to? You got a girl in there or something?" He chuckled.

"No, there's something in there. Frightened the crap out of me!"

Frank shrugged, "Didn't hear anything myself, but I do hear funny things coming from her house some nights, she seems to talk to herself. Ever noticed the visitors she has from time to time?"

Sydney shook his head.

"Weird looking bunch—wealthy lot, mind you—BMW's, Mercedes, even a Bentley turned up once—took up half the car park! Mind you, I'll bet she's worth a bob or two, herself. Never knew what happened to her husband. Maybe she bumped him off." Frank smiled as another idea came to him, "Can you still do wife swappin' if you don't have a spouse?" He gave another laugh.

Sydney persisted, "I didn't know this building was haunted or anything…."

"Neither did I. Wouldn't surprise me though, she's a weird one—member of some secret cult, so she says, Pagan or something like that. Dancin' naked round a cauldron on the heath at midnight." He barked another laugh.

"Really." said Sydney with disinterest, his mind still reeling, "I'm not going back in now. Besides," he checked the pockets of his jeans, "I've got no key. I'm shut out."

"I don't blame you mate" said Frank "She's had loads of people babysit her cats lately. Young un's like you. Very strange that she never seems to have the same one twice. Does she pay well?"

"Fifty quid."

"She never asked me!"

Sydney laughed, feeling more relaxed, "Look, I'm going home now. I'll see you, Frank."

He turned and walked a few steps.

"Poltergeists! They call 'em." Frank called out to Sydney's retreating figure. "Them noisy ones that throw things around."

Sydney nodded over his shoulder while he walked, determined to make his escape. "Yes, I guess so."

"Not what they appear to be." Frank persevered in a more serious tone. "Very dangerous…"

Sydney continued walking the few strides back to his own apartment trying to make sense of just what it was that he had encountered back there.

Five officials were grouped at a table, shielded directly behind the Judge, each dressed identically in black robes with contrasting stark-white ruffs. From one of their number came a harsh voice, it's tone thick with accusation as it addressed the woman:

"It is the opinion of the prosecution that by means of witchery, though summoned a Demon of most evil to turn the boy to madness. His crime is not his own, or that of God's, but that caused by your allegiance with the Devil himself"

"No, no your Honour, it is I also who was plagued with the Bogie. It started with tapping on the walls of my cottage then I became taunted by evil shapes. In God's own eyes—I am a victim of this Devil and truly innocent."

"And what of your familiars', constantly at your beckoning? Do you deny these also?"

"My lord, they are my friends, my companions. I am a lonely woman. Since my husband left me—he was a wicked man—my Mousers have been company for me."

"Is it not perhaps the harsh—perhaps justifiable treatment of your husband which turned you to Satan?"

"No Sirs. No."

A man standing by a studded oaken doorway, tightly clasping his hat cut in angrily: "She lies! We've all seen her hair turn from raven black to this grey in a swifter time than God's own will."

An agreeing murmur filled the room.

"Aye!" a sparrow-like woman spat from beneath her bonnet, "It was one of her Bogie's who took my William away and bewitched him to Annie Goodson—another Witch!"

A shrill, unseen voice countered, "Your William is bewitched only by his own pizzle..."

The escalating laughter was silenced by the harsh voice. *"And what is your association with the young man who has committed this... ungodly act? He claims it is from you that he became afflicted with this... contagion."*

"The Bogie took to him, it wanted him more so than I. I was glad when it left me, but not so for the boy. It was worse for him. Much worse..."

"And what of your association with this boy?"

"I left for the Mitchell's Fold to attend a friend who was suffering terribly with the pestilence. She is very dear to me, as if she were my own kin. She is young and has no family." The woman looked down and fidgeted with her fingernails. "Only myself. I attend to her comfort as she is in great need. The boy, being a neighbour, he is good and kept watch over my cottage when I was away. I had a fire needing kindling. T'is all I know of this, my Lords."

A lean, bearded man standing to the side spoke; "She was found in possession of a crucifix of which the metal was bent. Surely an abomination in the face of God?"

A number of murmured agreements echoed in the hall.

The man calmly picked at his teeth with a knife between sentences. "It is well known that from long ago, the witch is able to summon such Demon's in return for earthly favours. Once called upon, the evil is transferred like a plague to other folk and so spreads forth bringing suffering and death—the Devil's work amongst us. Is not this what we have here—with this woman?" He turned to the accused. "And how has your Master rewarded you Dorothy? Being never short of a Shilling."

Again, the murmured agreements were voiced.

"No Sir, I weave cloth for my living."

The man continued "I have seen those who have been cursed with such contagions before, it is to my observation that such Demons cause fright and anger within its host. This is its food. It seeks always for more and more, taking on any appearance it desires in order to get that which it desires. Those who fear it most are but a feast for it." he narrowed his eyes accusingly at the woman, "If the host were to find someone young, someone whose fear is fresh—someone like this woman's young neighbour—well, not only does she free herself from its burden, but her master's work is continued and he is thankful for it."

A wave of hushed chatter swelled in the hall. The accused woman shook her head in disagreement.

From the centre, the Judge silenced the disruptions with a lazy raise of an arm, "Let her make her defence in the full light of God."

All eyes turned upon the accused. "No... No I am Godly. I am truly innocent." She gazed, searching into the Judges own moist eyes. Eyes which had grown creased at the edges from happy laughter, long ago. He fingered his pointed beard and thought in silence for a moment then gestured to the two hooded Clerks standing either side of the woman. He then pointed at a plump, ruddy-faced woman standing by attentively. "Goodwife Gwendolin, check her for the mark." he said, before leaning back and stroking at his beard again.

The woman struggled futilely as the two men roughly stripped her under the hostile gaze of the court.

Amanda McKinnen walked quickly. The nights were drawing in and it was so much colder now. Sydney had seemed troubled on the phone; not his usual carefree self. Being based so far away as Edinburgh, it was not often that she had a chance to visit. She recalled, months ago, that he had told her about some strange encounter he claimed to have experienced in a neighbour's house. He seemed obsessed, talking about nothing else for the entire call, even becoming tearful. At that point she had determined to see him in person.

Amanda descended the steps into the basement recess and knocked. After a lengthy wait the door opened, freeing a waft of cigarette smoke, she wondered if the acrid smell of cannabis was there, too. Sydney stood in the doorway with the light shining behind him like a halo. He had dark rings around his eyes and wore a creased grey T-shirt which looked like it hadn't been washed in a while.

"Hello Sis'." he said, forcing a smile, though in his eyes Amanda detected a sparkle of genuine pleasure.

"God, you look like SHIT, Sydney!" his younger sister observed, smiling back.

As the two sat chatting on the sofa surrounded by soiled plates, crushed beer cans and abandoned DVD cases, Amanda noticed that her brother was smoking constantly and that he kept darting his eyes around the room. He fired questions like bullets from a machine gun, regarding her life at university, how her ancient Fiat was clocking up the miles and whether she had found a steady boyfriend yet. All of this, Amanda suspected, to avoid the conversation veering on to his own affairs. She decided to get straight to the point.

"What's the matter, Syd? Look at the place." She gestured about the lounge. "What's up?"

Sydney paused for a moment to collect his thoughts. "That night back in the spring, the business with the wardrobe. I think that poltergeist followed me home."

Amanda kept her expression neutral as Sydney continued. "I hear footsteps upstairs. When I'm in the kitchen cooking or on the sofa reading a book—I can sense it right behind me, I can hear it breathing just a few inches away. When I manage to get to sleep at night, I can never be sure if the bedcovers will be jerked away. This has happened twice, I swear! Sometimes I can smell it—like rotten garbage. I even saw it once…"

Amanda looked around, searching for the right thing to say.

"Amanda, I swear. I've lost my temper and screamed at it, but it throws things around—plates, books, even furniture. Have you ever seen a bed move on its own volition? I think this thing could really hurt me."

"You say you saw something?" Amanda asked.

"I was sitting here about three weeks ago, waiting for my laptop to boot up, just looking into the black screen when I saw something move, reflected in the screen. It looked like a dark figure wearing a cloak or something because I could just see the hazy shape of a man, then it suddenly rushed up behind me really fast. Just before I turned round, I saw a face reflected in the screen, very close. For just a split second I clearly saw—" Sydney closed his eyes and ran a trembling hand over his face, "—like a white leering skull which had somehow melted like wax and wept downwards into the neck and body, the eyes were just black voids, but somehow they were filled with an awful hunger. When I turned around to face it, there was nothing there."

Amanda tried to sound sincere, "Where is it now—this thing?"

Sydney lowered his voice to barely a whisper. "It knows you're here. It won't show itself to you. It's here watching us now, but it only shows itself to me." Sydney's bloodshot eyes darted around the room.

Amanda frowned. "What about work, and the diploma?"

"When I'm away from this place I'm free. Maybe it's bound to this building. I don't know for sure, though."

Amanda searched for suggestions, "OK if this…poltergeist or whatever came from your neighbour's house, have you tried to contact her?"

"Oh Mrs. Wilovski." Sydney sniggered. "Nobody's seen her. She's vanished. I've tried to look her up on IdentiSearch on the internet and I've asked around—nobody knows anything about her, even the Council knew her as 'Mrs. Heather Jones', but it's a dead end on that score, too."

Sydney slumped back heavily into the couch and took a gulp of beer. "I wonder what she knew about all of this— more than she said I'll bet. I heard that she was weird. A witch."

"Look Syd, I don't know anything about this sort of thing but I'll ask around for you, see if I can get some help. Why don't you stay at Mum's for a while?"

Sydney snorted and shook his head.

"Okay," Amanda continued, undeterred, "I'll tell you what, I'll help you get this place tidied up, get some clothes washed, I'll treat you to some Chinese and when I can, I'll see what help I can get."

Later that night, after Amanda hugged her brother goodbye at the doorway, she hesitated. "Promise me you'll do something to solve this, Syd? Make some effort to fight it. Drinking and smoking won't chase it away."

"I'll do something." Sydney promised gravely, his stony silhouette giving nothing away.

The Judge stroked at his whiskers, as he studied the woman intently. Considering. "And what of the madness she is accused of afflicting on the boy. What is the story there?"

"My Lord, he made claim that he was cursed with a Demon, passed from the accused and that it would not leave him. That it struck him and taunted him always. His madness became clear to see—he began walking around the village making talk with himself. His once-youthful stride became a limp. He set it upon himself to burn down his dwelling and that of two of his neighbours by means of setting a tinder to the thatch of each. In the fire, an elder man, being asleep, had the misfortune of becoming overcome and so burned to death in the flames. The boy has since been committed to a house of correction at Shrewsbury. In time, a trephine will be wound into his skull and the evil spirits—whom he claims do speak to him—will be driven out."

The Judge continued to scrutinise the sobbing heap in front of him entwined within her garments. "And what of this Demon?" he asked her. "Speak up, now."

"I know nothing of the Demon, Sir, if God be my witness,

'cept it being most terrifying and evil." The woman hastily made the sign of the Cross. "Satan deceives us all."

The lean, bearded man, still leaning at the wall, toying with a knife broke the tense stillness with a resigned tone of voice. "My God, the stupid youth." he glanced up from his blade to view the dim surroundings, "Such demons are not anchored to any place. It is the victim which it sucks onto like a horse leech. But chaos always ensues in its wake," he looked scornfully at the accused, "even those who summon and nurture it." The man spat his derision at the floor.

"Interview commences at 1530 on November 2nd 2015— Detective Sergeant Ian Farrow. Interviewing Sydney McKinnen on a charge of suspected Arson under the Criminal Damage Act 1971 committed on the night of November 1st 2015 at Abbey Street, Shrewsbury. Solicitor declined by McKinnen and not present."

"Sydney, do you deny this charge?…"

Sydney did not respond but closed his eyes.

Farrow leaned over the table towards his suspect, "I have to tell you that the evidence against you is pretty conclusive, Son. It's as if you wanted to be caught." he paused, "Well did you?…"

Nothing.

Farrow sighed once then softened his tone, "What's gone on here? Personal problems? Girlfriend messing you around? Landlord being unreasonable? Was it a moment of rage? Revenge?"

Sydney shifted in his chair but didn't answer.

"This is First Degree Arson, Sydney. You might be looking at a couple of years inside for this."

Still no response.

"We've done some digging around" Farrow selected a sheet of A4 paper from a file on the table. "Your boss, Phil Edwards, he spoke to us, says you're good, you get on with the other Lads; you're reliable, a good engineer, and you get a lot out of your study for…" Farrow studied the A4 sheet, "an IVQ Diploma in Motor Vehicle Engineering, right? Good future. Only thing is, you haven't shown up to work for the last four weeks and you're not answering the phone. Care to explain why?"

"Kate, ex-girlfriend, good friends now, regularly chatting on the phone, still go out for the occasional drink together. Only, she hasn't seen or heard hide nor hair of you for, again, four weeks. What's troubling you Syd? Why did you do it?"

Sydney hunched forwards, his hands clasped together on the table, showing white around the knuckles while Farrow stared at his suspect for a full minute. "I'm going to get a cup of tea." Farrow said at last, "Do you want one? You look like you need a brew."

He leaned over to switch off the tape recorder. "Interview suspended at…"

"It was the only option I had." Sydney stared at the light reflecting from the melamine table top as he spoke. "It would not leave, so I had to destroy it. Fire purifies—that's what they say."

Farrow slumped back into his seat across the table. "Had to destroy exactly whom?" he asked carefully.

"The poltergeist. It was getting more powerful, more threatening each day. You want to know what did it for me in the end. Knives went missing from the kitchen and reappeared in my bed." Sydney hugged his arms around himself. "What do you think it meant by that? Eh? Where would this have ended?"

Farrow blinked, taken aback by Sydney's sudden conviction.

"I'd do it again if I had to. 'Destroy the seed of evil, or it will grow up to your ruin', that's what someone once said, right?"

"Aesop." Farrow said.

Sydney smiled and began rocking in his chair.

"You could have moved away." suggested Farrow.

"It was growing too destructive." Sydney said as if he were

stating the obvious, "Someone had to put an end to it."

"What was it trying to do to you, this thing?" asked the detective.

Sydney looked up from the table directly into the eyes of DS Farrow for the first time during the interview.

"It wanted to frighten me!" he said.

Sydney began to laugh. He didn't stop laughing, even when the three police officers had to physically remove him from the interview room, drag him through the brightly lit corridors and back into the cell.

The shadowy candlelight flickered around the hall among the whisperings of the Judge and his officials as they huddled together, deep in discussion with every pair of eyes upon them. Eventually the Judge turned and resumed his seat at the centre.

"Dorothy Wallace. The evidence of this court has been presented to the Jury. There is evidence enough, but this is substantiated by a mark found upon your inner left thigh which has been examined by a midwife and by myself. It is determined to be the mark of the Devil. Therefore, you are hereby found to be guilty of committing witchery. It is the will of God and of English Law through King Charles and of my Governance as Judge of Stapeley-Hill and White-Grit to see that you are taken to the gallows of Old Heath and hung by the neck until you are dead."

At this, the sleepy hall awoke to shouted curses and obscenities. Some, mainly the womenfolk, looked silently towards the condemned woman with unconcealed expressions of spite and contempt. The two Clerks shielded the convicted woman as best they could, but some folk managed to land a well-aimed globule of spit onto her. The woman herself stood, still clasping her garments tightly to herself, her face was expressionless, though inside, she was screaming.

DS Ian Farrow turned back from the window, swigged the last drops of coffee, grimaced, then threw the plastic cup in the waste bin and left the office. He returned with a tall, solidly-built man. The two sat at opposite ends of the same table Sydney had been interviewed at two days before. Farrow tapped at a laptop computer at his desk, cursing to himself at some error before looking up.

"Thanks for coming in, Mike," he said, "I just wanted to get a few details from you before we wrap this case up."

"No problem." replied Mike Forrister, Fire Chief.

"You were there just after the call was made. You say it was a neighbour who called 999?"

"A family two doors away. The husband was out back having a cigarette, said he saw smoke, so he came to the front of the building and there were flames in the window."

"What about the extent of damage?"

"Once we got there, it was easy enough to hose the fire out. The basement floor of the apartment is extensively damaged, the floors above seem to be unaffected except for some minor smoke damage. Structurally, a surveyor will have to take a look but I would say it's probably OK. This potentially could've been a whole different story. If the fire had been allowed to take hold, with all the residents in that building, we could've been dealing with multiple fatalities here."

"Any evidence yet of the cause?" asked Farrow looking over the top of his glasses.

"Fire Investigation are still looking into it, but the detectors have indicated a strong presence of hydrocarbons. In addition, the burning was extremely localised. Both of these indicate that petrol was used as an accelerant. Petrol or similar liquid initially spreads rapidly causing sudden heat surges, the plaster on the walls had spalled, yet parts of the room were relatively undamaged."

"So at this stage it looks like Arson?"

"I would say so, yes. That Lad standing on the pavement outside with half a can of petrol points to that also, I would think." Forrister leaned forward tilting his head questioningly, "What was he, a nut or something?"

Farrow sighed "It looks that way, Mike. His sister's been on the phone constantly since the arrest. Shame, she sounds like a nice lass. I think after Investigation finish up, we'll have the evidence for a trial, it just depends on his mental state to determine what happens to him. He doesn't help himself you know—just rants about some ghost in his flat."

"Could be drugs. Some kind of hallucinogenic, maybe acid."

"Maybe." said the Detective as he typed.

Forrister shifted uncomfortably, his memory brought back to the flames. He was aware that patterns of flame can form shapes, strange dancing shadows for those with susceptible minds but what he saw that night. The way the shadow had rushed at him from within the intense blaze. Such an intense but fleeting impression of fury and anger. At no other time in his career had he had to feign illness and get out of the building like a frightened lamb. Strain and overwork, he figured—fighting fire was a younger man's game.

Farrow looked up from his computer and pushed a sheet of paper towards Forrister, "I just need you to sign the initial statement and that's it from you, unless you come up with anything else. You know my number." Farrow flicked a card to Forrister, who pocketed it in his shirt.

"Yeah sure." said Forrister, "I'm going to have a last look around the place. The immediate neighbours have been evacuated, pending a structural survey. The surveyors can't go in without my officially signing the place off, I want to get the job over with, don't want them or the insurance suits' badgering me on Monday morning when I'm supposed to be off." Forrister grinned.

"OK, Mike. Be careful. And thanks."

The two men shook hands and Mike Forrister left the room.

Farrow pondered. The address of this case—Abbey Street.

There was another case being dealt with where the victim of a mugging had coincidentally lived on that same street. A woman who had been attacked at night in an area of woodland outside Birmingham. Farrow remembered the report, as it was a strange case. There seemed to be no obvious motive— the poor woman had been found early in the morning by a dog-walker. Her body was barely concealed in a shallow grave to one side of the main pathway which runs alongside a playing field. The body was naked and had been stabbed 58 times by multiple assailants—as yet to be identified. This was a case which Farrow's West Midlands Police colleagues in Birmingham were dealing with. Farrow remembered the area being notorious for strange cults to gather at night. The upper body of the deceased had been so viciously mutilated that she could only be identified from medical records. It seems, she had a distinct birthmark on her inner left thigh. The victim's name was a strange one too—it sounded Eastern European. Wilovski. That was it.

Forrister walked the short distance from his parked car to the terraces of Abbey Street. He lifted the striped police tape and took the steps down to the surprisingly unscathed door of Sydney's basement flat. Bricks had been licked black where flame had escaped through the window and the iron hand rail had warped from the heat.

Hidden from the street, he opened the unlocked door which led straight into the living room, half expecting to find alcoholics or drug users making themselves at home but the only resident was an overpowering smell of dampness and smoke. Forrister shut the door behind him and took in the scene in the gloomy daylight that the small window afforded. Walls and ceiling were sponged black, strips of wallpaper and burned fabric hung like thin grey icicles; water ran in little streams down walls and still dripped from charred, unrecognisable furniture which had been heaped to one side by the firefighters. Forrister noticed a rack of DVDs or CDs which had melted and solidified like marbled chocolate in a corner of the room. Although well-used to such aftermaths, Forrister felt particularly uncomfortable, so closed off in that quiet basement with only the one doorway in or out.

He reached into his sports bag and fetched out a thermal imaging camera together with a notebook and pen. He took some measurements, pointing the gun-like device at strategic points of the walls and ceiling, he went through into the kitchen at the back, which was mainly undamaged except for smoke having darkened the once-white walls, cupboards and ceiling. He took readings, making notes of the deep internal temperatures. He then mounted the stairs. No visible damage, but the permeating odour of smoke would have taken hold into carpets, clothes, bedding and furniture. He took tests in the bathroom and finally, the bedroom. Satisfied with the job done, he crouched over his bag to return the expensive image-gun.

Forrister was proud that his team had made such a difference here, the Lad had been very lucky. It was just a pity these idiots started....

He froze at a distinct creaking sound in the landing just outside the bedroom door. There was definitely somebody there.

He had just been through the entire flat and it was empty.

He was done here!

Swinging the bag onto his shoulder, he approached the door, readied himself, then swung it open.

Nobody there.

He hurried down the stairs but as he reached the bottom few steps, he heard the creaking sound of footsteps treading the stairs close behind him. At the bottom, in the lounge, Forrister turned around. There was nothing to be seen but he could hear the footsteps, more slowly than before, now slushing in the sodden carpet. As Forrister watched, footprints appeared in the damp, he could see the indentation of the heel and sole of invisible shoes, but something didn't seem right. Forrister stood rigid as the steps materialised around his side and came to a slow rest between himself and the doorway. As he watched, it became obvious. Both footprints were shaped slightly to the left—they were both belonging to a right foot. He hurried around the imprints to make his escape. He flung the door open, feeling the fresh, cool air envelop him. Looking back one last time he saw a very dark, smoky shadow which seemed to fill one whole corner of the room right up to the high Victorian ceiling. Whatever it was, he would later recall, though monstrous in proportion, was definitely humanoid in shape, but, with what seemed to be huge growths curling grotesquely outwards from the skull—like the horns of a ram.

He was convinced from the way it faced him at that point, that it's intelligence, its awareness was directed wholly upon himself.

A crowd had mustered at Old Heath as the cart clattered its way uphill; the Woman was standing inside looking down at her bare feet, trussed and with a thick, heavy rope around her neck which trailed to the floor.

Among the tall wooden gallows at the hill's peak, three executioners waited in wide-brimmed hats and bucket top boots; a Priest ambled to and fro waving a thurible of burning incense as he read from an open Bible. The Judge stood dutifully to one side of the gallows with two of his Clerks. The man took no pleasure in this spectacle, feeling a natural discomfort in the forced death of a healthy life. But a Witch, of course, cannot be endured and the law was such that to invoke evil spirits was—justifiably—punishable by death.

As she was helped delicately upon the ladder and the rope painstakingly secured to the horizontal beam, the crowd had lost its boisterousness to be replaced with a quiet respectfulness. The leaden sky threatened rain and the mood of the death party was one of hurried efficiency, not merely to avoid a soaking but more so to be swiftly done with this unpleasant affair.

She was now ready.

As the Judge overlooked the preparations, with palpitating heart, he cast his eyes over the soaring church spires and rooftops of the town far behind; he was grateful for this momentary escape. The Priest closed his bible with a clap and inverted his head solemnly. The Chief Executioner, ready with his men at the base of the ladder, looked attentively towards the Judge, awaiting his call. As the Judge looked at the woman, a fleeting moment before he commanded the end of her existence, he was astonished to see that she was staring straight at him. There was no panic or frenzy as he had grown to expect in such situations, but a fixed calmness, even the suggestion of a smile. Something she said carried on the wind, perhaps.

A whisper: "*Beware your Fear.*"

Shaken, but also aware of all eyes upon him, the Judge gave a decisive nod and the ladder was pulled violently away from beneath the woman. Without a cry, her body fell, coming to a horrible jerk as the rope reached its full length. Her neck did not break. Legs kicked, torso twisted and a guttural choking polluted the air. Urine streamed from the woman's feet as her eye balls bulged, threatening to leave their sockets. Mercifully, the frenzy became gradually weaker until finally the corpse swung gently on its creaking rope, dead tongue lolling and neck extended at a freakish angle.

Heavily under the weight of duty, the Judge and his clerks turned and walked with bowed heads, back to their horses.

Humbled into silence, the crowd slowly dissipated to continue about their business and their lives.

Mike Forrister's wife was still at work, both of his daughters were away at university. He settled into his favourite armchair with the chill of evening firmly shut outside and so began to read his newspaper. A welcome few days away from work gave him a warm, contented feeling. He had been overworked lately and knew it. All the anguish he had to deal with on a daily basis as part of his job was highly stressful. He must relax over the next few days and just take it easy....

An *almighty* thud in the bedroom above.

Forrister was up onto his feet in the centre of the lounge.

Silence.

The central heating hummed.

What the hell was that?!

Like chains being dragged over bare floorboards....

The Witching Hour

Joseph Rubas

lexandru Anton watched nervously out the window as the car navigated the winding road to the village of Zela, high in the steep forests of Transylvania. Since leaving Bucharest early that morning, Alexandru had been reading the dossier provided by the Securitate, and with each page his disquiet grew. Now, the lush green hills and hunkered country cottages seemed sinister, a façade masking menace and magic. The weather didn't help. In the city, it was warm and sunny, but the farther into the wild they got, the darker the sky became, so that now, at one in the afternoon, it verged on twilight.

"How much farther?" Alexandru asked.

The driver, a large, broad-shouldered peasant in black, grunted. "Ten kilometers."

Ten kilometers. They were close. Alexandru swallowed.

Despite the reassurances of his handlers, Alexandru had the distinct feeling that they would know him when he arrived, that the witches would watch him through drawn curtains as he pulled up, aware of who he was and for whom he worked. That was ludicrous, of course, for witches possessed no actual powers, but even though, he couldn't convince himself otherwise.

"Proceed with extreme caution," the dossier said. "Consider them dangerous."

From what he'd read, he agreed wholeheartedly; reports of missing persons, harassment, and murder. Was it all true?

Could it possibly be?

It all began five months before, when a loyal member of the Party wrote a letter to the regional Committee complaining of "Witchcraft and Devil worship."

"They meet in the woods at night," he charged, "and practice black magic. My own daughter was approached to join them but wisely declined. Now we fear for our lives."

The Committee replied, asking for more details, and his next letter was full of them. "I don't know who precisely is involved, but the night before last, I left my house about midnight and went into the woods south of the town. Shortly, I came to a clearing where a fire roared. In the shadows, I saw roughly a dozen people dancing about. They were chanting. I couldn't discern the language, though I thought it was Latin. The next day, I found a dead dog lying on my doorstep. Its throat had been cut and its eyes were removed. I took it to be a warning."

Later in the day, he returned to the clearing and found bones from multiple animals, along with "Other signs of witchery." Not too long thereafter, another Party member wrote to the Committee, claiming that an old woman by the name of Dalca had placed a spell on him, and now his son was sick and his car no longer started. "She's a terrible old woman with no teeth and a puckered face, a prime candidate for Lucifer worship."

Several days later, authorities were informed that both men had mysteriously died and been buried in the local cemetery. No other explanation was given.

"Religion is the enemy," the director of the Securitate said, and that was the Communist Party line through and through. "It distracts man from his social obligations and diverts his loyalty from the State. Witchcraft is especially heinous."

Now, here he was, on his way to see for himself whether witches really met at midnight. And if they did, he was to report back to headquarters. After that…

"We are close," the driver said.

The road rounded a harrowing hairpin curve and there, in

the distance, Zela rose on its hill, a tight cluster of ancient European buildings along a narrow cobblestone street. In the flat lands leading up to it, lone cottages rotted in the twilight. An old wooden bridge carried the road across a lazily stagnant river; from there, the road began to rise. On the right, an old woman in a headscarf forked hay into a wooden carriage. She stopped to watch as they passed.

His official story was that he was a college student from Targoviste touring the countryside. If pressed further, he was to profess a love for the novel *Dracula*, which was partially set in Transylvania. That would, the Securitate hoped, allay suspicions, as Dracula was banned by the Communist Party. If his favorite novel is one that is banned, they reasoned, people will trust him not to be a government agent.

But people, even peasants, aren't so easily fooled. Not always. What was one small lie from a government that told many, big lies? And would they accept him as a college student? Though he was young and fresh by agency standards, he was still close to thirty. It was true that he had a boyish face, but could he pass as twenty-two?

Presently, the car entered the shadow of Zela. On either side, brick and wood structures loomed, blocking out the remaining light of day. A few people moved sluggishly along the sidewalks, bags of groceries in their arms. Their clothes were old and threadbare, their faces hard and weather-beaten. A few Romanian flags hung over open doorways, the red, yellow, and blue bars just as faded as the people who flew them. At least one of them lacked the coat of arms of the Romanian People's Republic. A sign of disloyalty.

The car came to a stop in front of the town inn, a quaint two floor building with a pitched roof, its crisp white face crisscrossed with wooden beams, reminding him of buildings he'd seen on a trip to East Germany. A wooden sign hung above the door: INN.

"Two days," Alexandru said as he got out.

The driver nodded. "Two days."

He would return in two days. If, by then, he'd found nothing, the government would send another man.

Alexandru was afraid that if he didn't find anything he'd be demoted.

Outside, the day was damp and chilly. Alexandru took his bags from the back, and the car pulled quickly away.

He was alone.

Sighing, Alexandru went into the inn. Its lobby was dim and warm. An archway to the left led into a type of sitting room. A fire burned in the stone hearth. Chairs sat empty around it.

Ahead, a desk flanked the foot of the stairs, which turned before disappearing. Alexandru sat his bags down, rang the bell on the tabletop, and waited several minutes before a short, plump man in a white shirt came in through a doorway leading who knew where.

"Good afternoon," he said with a smile. His face was red and warm. Alexandru thought he resembled Nikita Khrushchev, late leader of the Soviet Union, except Khrushchev had never been particularly plump.

"Good afternoon," Alexandru said with a nod, "I'd like a room, please."

The man smiled. "Of course. For the night?"

"Two nights, actually."

The man beamed. "Wonderful. Are you alone?"

"Yes," Alexandru said.

The man pulled out a big logbook and wrote down the details. "Would you like dinner? We eat at six."

"Are there any cafés around?"

The man nodded. "Yes. Directly across the street is one. The food there is good."

"I'll probably eat there."

The man noted that in his book. "Let me show you the way."

The man (who introduced himself as Adam) led Alexandru up the stairs. There were six rooms along the hall, and two of them were already taken. Alexandru's was small and Spartan, boasting only a bed, a nightstand, a desk, and a single forlorn chair.

"It's perfect," Alexandru said.

The café was busy when Alexandru ordered his dinner; though he sat in a far-off corner, he could feel himself being watched. The waitress—a pretty woman—brought him his food with a smile and left him alone. He thought he saw something in her eyes, suspicion maybe, but she was gone before he could study it.

People in the countryside were naturally suspicious of outsiders, he knew that, but he couldn't help feel that the suspicion here was different, more profound. Several times as he ate, he looked over to find people openly staring at him.

Shortly before he finished, a man slid into the chair across from him, startling him.

"Good evening, Sir."

The man was in his sixties, thin with a thick gray mustache. His eyes were sparkling blue and his lipless smile revealed rows of yellow, rotted teeth.

"Good evening," Alexandru replied. Though he could feel the eyes of everyone on him, he resisted the urge to look.

"My name is Florin."

"I am Alexandru."

"It is nice to meet you, Alexandru."

They shook hands.

"Are you on vacation?"

"Yes. I am touring the countryside."

Florin nodded. "I was a traveler as a young man. When the Soviets liberated us from the Nazis, I traveled with them to Berlin."

"I've never been," Alexandru lied.

"It's a beautiful city. How are you liking our town?"

Alexandru swallowed. "To be honest, I feel like a zoo animal."

Florin laughed. "Do not take offence to it. We rarely see anyone from the outside. We have no television, no radio. The world is a stranger to us."

"What is a stranger but a friend you haven't met?"

Florin laughed again. "That is true. What do you do for work?"

"I am a student," Alexandru said.

"So, you are a Party member?"

"Yes."

Florin nodded. "Good. It is good to know you are a friend. I apologize for interrupting your meal. Have a good night."

"You, too."

Later on, back in his room, Alexandru went over the encounter in his mind. Had he handled it correctly? Florin would most certainly spread the information he had given him, thus the entire town (or most of it) would know that he was a student and a member of the Communist Party. Would that tip them off that he was a government agent? Many people were members of the Party, including many people who didn't particularly like the Party; being a member was the only way to advance in life.

Presently, it was close to eight o'clock. At eleven, he would leave the inn and set out for the clearing. The dossier indicated that it was on the other side of the bridge into town, nearly a kilometer into the wilds.

Now, the wait.

At eleven sharp, Alexandru left the inn and began walking toward the edge of town. The streets were empty save for a few men staggering home from the tavern. They didn't seem to take any special notice of him as they passed.

Past the lights of Zela, darkness crashed down around him like black sea water. The sky was still overcast, so neither moon nor stars lit the way.

At the bridge, Alexandru paused for a moment to get his bearings. The clearing was to the east, which, after a quick calculation, was to his left. The papers said it was rather large, and so shouldn't be too difficult to find.

The brief stop lasted roughly ten minutes, and by the time he was ready to get back underway, the sound of voices in the night stopped him cold. Someone was behind him, walking the same route he had. For a beat, he was paralyzed. How would he explain being here, at this hour?

Just as quickly as it set in, the paralysis broke, and training kicked him; moving quickly yet quietly, he ducked off of the road and into a cluster of reeds at the water's edge, startling a frog into flight.

The voices drew nearer. Footfalls came on the bridge. *Clunk-clunk-clunk.*

"…night."

"I know. I know. I hate it too. But we must in order to keep His blessings."

Women.

Alexandru listened closer.

"How is she taking it?"

The second woman sighed. "As well as can be expected. It is *her* child being killed tomorrow. She knew this day might come, and she's willing, but she isn't happy."

Child? Killed?

"I wish there was some other way."

"So do I, but He demands a sacrifice. It's for the good of the village."

God in heaven! They were going to sacrifice somebody!

The women were on the road now. They steered left, and shortly disappeared into the woods.

For a long moment, Alexandru remained where he was, digesting what he had just heard. A child was going to be killed tomorrow tonight. A sacrifice to the delusion of Satan! Righteous anger flooded him. Leave it to religion. It didn't matter who was in charge or who was worshipped, they were all the same, kneel at the altar of fantasy and render unto the killer-god your children or theirs. Wasn't that the central tenet of all faiths? Death? God smites this group, Allah smites that. God commands blood. The vampire in the sky needs nurture.

These beasts…their sacrifice was literal. No crusades or fat-was here, just simple, pagan murder.

More voices approached.

Resisting the urge to strangle whoever else was coming along, Alexandru huddled down and waited.

He recognized Florin's voice.

"…of him. You can't trust Communists. They have a lot of funny ideas."

"No," a man said, "you can't."

Florin sighed. "If Martin was one of ours, I'd have him killed tonight."

"Do it anyway," the other man said. "How can he stop you?"

Florin was quiet for a moment. "We're not to harm him. He doesn't want it."

It was the other man's turn to be silent. "If he is a spy, we have His protection. What's the worst that could happen?"

Florin grunted. "I wonder."

They crossed the bridge (*clunk-clunk-clunk*) and disappeared into the woods.

So, the innkeeper wasn't in on it. That was good. When he got back later, he'd have to talk to him.

Alexandru remained in the reeds for a while longer; several more people crossed over the bridge. When his watch read midnight, he decided it was safe to move on; they would all be at the Black Mass.

The woods were alive with the croaking of frogs and the chirruping of crickets. He found a well-worn pathway, and followed it through the thicket; around him, trees and snarls of undergrowth loomed and sought like undead hands.

After several hundred yards, Alexandru began to notice a flickering light through the branches ahead. Closer, the sound of low, monotonous chanting rose into the night; it had the quality of a thousand bees buzzing in a hive.

When he reached the edge of the clearing, Alexandru crouched down, making himself as small as possible. A massive fire burned in what he took to be the center of the clearing, its light dancing across the shaggy ground; even as far back as he was, Alexandru could still feel the heat against his face.

The figures amassed around the blaze weren't dancing; rather, they were standing, their hands—or so it seemed—linked to form a Satanic circular chain. The chanting continued apace. It did sound curiously like Latin. The buzz was maddening. His eardrums thrummed with it, and his brain ached. A wave of nausea crashed over him, and he fought back the urge to puke.

As he watched, the chain broke, and the worshippers all took several steps back in unison. In time with each other, they raised their arms, and the flames themselves appeared to mimic the gesture. When their arms dropped, the fire dropped, devolving into a mere bed of embers. When they rose their arms yet again, the fire roared back to life, only this time it wasn't red or orange or yellow, it was purple, trimmed with green.

Alexandru's breath caught. The revelers began dancing at this point, and the fire kept time. The buzzing intensified, like tape wound too quickly through a spool, and an icepick of pain cleaved Alexandru's brain. Clapping his hands over his ears, he fled, staggering back down the path. When he was out of earshot, the agony in his head disappeared, and his eardrums no longer vibrated, though his ear canals itched.

Free from that damned oppressive buzz, he became aware of a strange, body-wide pins-and-needles sensation. It was slight, but pronounced.

He had to get back to the inn.

He met no one on the way back.

Inside, the shut the door and locked it behind him. He pulled the curtain away from the window flanking it and peered out; nothing moved. He wasn't followed.

At the door to Martin's private quarters, Alexandru knocked loudly and waited, glancing occasionally over his shoulder, each time half-expecting Florin to be there.

Finally, the door creaked open and Martin appeared, dressed in a bathrobe and a pair of slippers. His eyes were puffy with sleep and his voice was thick. "Mr. Anton? Is everything alright?"

"I need to talk to you," Alexandru said.

Martin looked puzzled. "I'd be happy to talk to you, but can't it wait?"

"No."

"Alright," the innkeeper sighed, stepping out of the way. "Come on."

"I know what's going on in this town," Alexandru said, concluding his tale. "Or some of it."

Across the kitchen table, Martin Seczk was pale. He hadn't touched his coffee, and when he moved his hand, he nearly knocked it over.

"I heard Florin say you're not one of them. I can trust you."

Martin nodded woodenly. "I suppose. I don't know much. I'm an outsider here."

"Tell me what you do know."

The old innkeeper shifted uncomfortably in his chair. "It started when the Communists took over. There were…shortages of everything. People didn't have enough to eat. They were dying. When Gheorghiu-Dej sent his men to collectivize everything, they were…*so* brutal. People reached their limits. They said "If God won't protect us, maybe the Devil will.""

"Florin started it. Didn't he?"

Martin nodded. "He was the mayor long ago. People looked up to him, they respected him. When he said that the Devil would do for us what God wouldn't, people listened."

"So he was doing it long before anyone else."

Martin nodded. "Behind closed doors. When he saw his chance, he spread it. You have to understand *why* they're doing this. When the Germans invaded us, they took everything. Our food. Our clothes. When the Russians beat them back, they came right through Zela. Our buildings were burned, our friends and neighbors were dead. The years right after were hard for us, but when the Communists took over, it got worse, and they were desperate. They were tired of seeing their children sick and hungry. They lost their faith in God. They started...doing what they do now, and things got better. The Dark Prince watches over his own."

"You think the Devil is actually rewarding them?"

"Yes," Martin said, "I do."

Alexandru sighed.

"They can still be saved, though. If I can just get them...

"That's why you haven't said anything? You think you can save them?"

Martin only nodded.

"Well, you aren't doing a very good job of it. A child's going to be killed tomorrow. If you won't stop it, the State will."

Alexandru stood, and Martin did likewise. "Do what you must," Martin said, and Alexandru detected a hint of weariness. "God's Will shall prevail."

In his room, Alexandru locked the door and wedged a chair against it. Still dressed, he sat down on the bed and thought about what he'd seen...the strange purple fire and the buzzing, the damned buzzing.

When he slept, his dreams were dark and devilish. Florin, clad in a black robe, chased him through the empty streets of Zela, a spear fashioned out of bone held high above his head. When he reached the clearing, dead bodies began coming out of the ground, their faces rotted and their clothes hanging in tatters.

Alexandru woke with a start long past dawn. Pale morning light fell through the window.

Downstairs, he knocked on the door, and Martin appeared, as if he had been expecting him.

"Do you have a telephone?"

"Yes."

In the parlor, Alexandru dialed his driver's number. He answered on the third ring.

"Come get me. I've seen enough."

"I'll be there in half an hour."

Back in his room, Alexandru gathered up his things, and then carried them down the stairs. He was surprised to find the car waiting for him; the driver must have driven like a madman.

Back downstairs, he paid Martin for both days, and then carried his bags out. The driver helped him put them into the trunk.

"Are you okay?" he asked as they pulled away. Several people in the street watched them depart, their mouths and eyes wide as though they'd never seen a car before.

"I'm fine."

Thirty kilometers away, they stopped at a police station in the town of Kalza. When Alexandru flashed his Securitate ID card, the desk sergeant went from gruff and suspicious to warm and servile.

Alexandru's fingers trembled as he dialed the number. When his commanding officer answered the phone, Alexandru said, "We have a problem."

"What problem?"

Alexandru quickly ran through what he had seen and heard.

"Damn it. Okay. I'll contact the base of Medvala. Proceed there. I want this town razed."

The village of Zela huddled darkly against the sky. Alexandru Anton turned to the man behind the wheel of the armored transport and said, "The orders are to kill everyone."

The driver nodded.

Behind them, several other armored vehicles plodded along, each one featuring a wicked machine gun turret on top. If they couldn't gather everyone up nicely, they had orders to open fire with the machine guns. "Satan will recognize his own."

The bridge was coming up. Beyond it, Zela.

"I want this..." Alexandru started, but stopped. All of a sudden, the buzzing was in his head, stronger than it had been the previous night. The driver heard it, too, for his face contorted in something like discomfort.

"What the hell is that?"

"It's…" The driver burst into flames.

"Jesus Christ!"

The fire seemed to come from within, starting at his center and spreading forth,

creeping along the ridges and contours of his body. Within moments, he was fully engulfed.

Alexandru felt no heat.

Wailing, the driver jerked the wheel. The transport left the road and splashed into the river. Cold water gushed into the footwell. Screaming, Alexandru forced open the door and half-fell into the water. Behind him, the other vehicles were also in distress. He saw flames in the cabs of each.

Slack-jawed and wide-eyed, Alexandru watched as the last truck in the convoy exploded. The one directly in front of *it* slammed into the one in front of it, and the flaming driver smashed through the windshield. Screams of agony rose into the day. Troops began piling out of the transport directly behind Alexandru's, and each one in turn erupted in flames. Smoke. Screams. The odor of burning flesh. Heat.

Alexandru turned, toward the town, and there, on the bank, was Florin.

He was holding a pistol.

Alexandru screamed and threw his hands up.

The first bullet ripped through his outstretched palm and tore through his right eye, exiting out the back of his head.

The second struck him in the nose.

But he was already dead.

"We have to leave," Florin said.

The townspeople were gathered in front of the inn. Below, smoke and fire billowed into the sky.

"But we're protected," someone said.

"How far?" Florin asked. "How far will He go for us? How much of a burden will He allow?"

No one spoke.

"They'll send more. And more. And He will not expend His powers etern…"

Florin burst into flames.

Shadows & Dolls

DAVE DORMER

eeklong hunger drove her from the dust and grime of the mining tunnels and she crouched beneath balsam boughs on the encampment's fringe, studying its occupants. Sunlight vanished and campfires ignited throughout the trees. Long, ghostly shadows began to stir, making the villagers appear as sickly giants. From her perch within the foliage, and in a final evening frenzy, black flies and mosquitoes fed on her salty skin and blurred her view of the three partridge breasts sizzling atop the blackened grate of a nearby fire pit. Her mouth watered and stomach growled as she watched the owner of the succulent dinner disappear beneath the ragged flapped entrance of the canvas tent that she had to assume, served as his home. She was in the company of the living again. She couldn't help but feel like a square peg trying to squeeze into a round hole.

An uncommon smile spread across her dirt-smudged cheeks. Her eyes closed and her breathing slowed. The sound of the crackling fire awakened memories of camping trips with her family when she was young. She remembered long walks on hiking trails beneath the canopy of trees and trailing behind her two older brothers. Out of earshot from their parents, her brothers mocked her about her dolls and how everywhere she went, one of the ugly things were tucked in the crook of her arm. Her dolls weren't store-bought, but handmade using unconventional materials and she knew the truth, those dolls terrified her brothers. That made her smile. To see their fear was worth their taunts.

Her thoughts drifted to the beginning of all this, when two years earlier, her parents and brothers writhed and choked on the ground outside their home while it simply altered her. Moraya's eyes opened to the campfire's piercing light. She focused on the flickering flame and imagined the warmth it shed.

Her physiology was still changing, she was sure. She was still learning, and the side effects of her change would come at a price. She didn't choose to live within the darkened tunnels of the mine, trespass in shadow's realm, or exist alongside the dead. She knew no one would ever accept her or her newfound skills. It didn't take her long to discover that her feelings helped manipulate darkness. She understood that her affliction from exposure to the biological attack two years prior was the primary reason for her survival. She missed her family. She wondered if she'd always be alone.

Translucence enveloped her and her form flickered into greying mist. Moraya drifted from concealment within the foliage and escaped the insects and as she approached, the unattended fire, the encampment, the trees stood twisted and diseased. Everything was warped and any movement caused a thin, ink-black tendril to trail in its wake that eddied then dissolved. The soil beneath her feet became nauseatingly spongy. After several visits to the mirroring world, she could hold down the contents of her stomach and began mastering control of her motion so as not to appear as a stumbling drunk. The nagging hunger ended the moment she joined with shadow, but she knew it would be there waiting when she returned. She couldn't escape the need for nourishment yet—she simply succumbed to it less. She snatched the partridge breast from the grill without as much as a blister. The campfire's blaze now only a dull glow among the hundred other muted lights that marked fire pits within the village of survivors. Clear juices from the meaty breast ran down her arm at the clench of her fingertips. She instantly extended her unique ability to include the new chunk of flesh that lay in her blurred hand.

She returned to the cloaking forest and sat down, placing her supper on a fallen leaf beside her before it could affect her skin when she returned to the material world. As if she had fallen, her head lolled forward and her shoulders slumped at the sudden return of her physical weight. Her back arched and her head rolled slowly side to side in a stretch before she removed the black blade from its sheath at her hip. She began slicing her dinner, then froze at the sound of a crisp slap against skin that she was sure escaped the canvas tent a short distance away. Her knuckles whitened on the knife's pommel at the sound of muffled cries from a young woman. As the burly hunter lifted the canvas flap of his tent, she became certain of the sound's origin. He returned to his fire and refastened the belt on his stained wool pants while the furrow of his brow deepened. He stood scanning the radius of the fire's light for the thief that stole his supper.

Moraya watched and waited in a crouch with her blade ready, when a young woman, barely twenty, with a tangled mess of greasy hair, exited the tent. The young woman pulled her jacket closed tightly around her while her eyes never left the ground.

"Try to be early tomorrow, Rae. You know it's not polite to keep a man waiting. Now, go on home. I'm sure there are more chores for you to do."

The young woman vanished into the darkened foliage without a sound while Moraya watched. The hunter grabbed a partridge breast from the grill, and ignoring any pain, tore a bite out of it as if it were an apple. Moraya's stomach heaved. She was used to working alongside men in the construction trade and it hardened her, but since the attack, men grew more revolting. Moraya studied his camp through teary eyes convinced the world had been cast violently back into the Stone Age. Her jaw tightened. A trickle of blood stemmed from her lower lip.

Roots, stones and firewood would impede a quick and quiet escape, she reasoned, and then she spied the leather shoulder strap sheathing twin daggers that hung from the brawny man's shoulders. As a hunter, he'd chosen this ideal site at the outer reaches of the park when they first organized. Its existing trails laid out in an efficient grid that separated electrical and nonelectrical sites, and despite disrepair, the park's services remained intact and functioning.

On Moraya's right, lantern light bobbed and dipped down the trail that separated Moraya from the hunter. Mumbling male voices accompanied that light and she inched farther back into the underbrush. In moments, two men strode into view, one carrying a kerosene lantern, and swinging a strange club at his side, while the other man wore a sword at his hip. Her heart pounded in her ears and eyes blurred from tears, but she knew three against one odds would be suicidal. It would take some time before she could rejoin with shadow again. Under held breath, she watched the two sentries pass by unaware of her.

She couldn't deny her envy of their curious weapons. She marvelled at the club that looked like something she read about in history books. It was two feet long, slightly curved, and ended with a four-inch diameter ball fitted with a small spike. The sword appeared intricate—medieval, and although its blade hid in its sheath, it had to be about four feet long and had an unusual curve. She knew both weapons were replicas, but she wanted them. She needed them.

She would wait.

Only the wealthy or village council members lived in tent trailers or campers—everyone else, like the young woman's family, suffered in tents or sheltering tarps that cluttered the park. Anyone who noticed the young woman's passing on her well-worn trail and aided by firelight simply lowered their heads. They all knew she, like many others, were luxuries extended to the village's hunters.

Rae walked the litter-strewn trail passing site 97 E again.

She couldn't help but spy on the pregnant woman and her haggard-looking husband. The woman was cleaning up supper dishes wearing the same clothes as she had on the day before, while he struggled to split firewood atop a massive stump for the following day. Rae wondered if the baby was his or the offspring of one of the village elite. She wondered if the baby would be *special*. Would it inherit any defects from the attack?

Rae often laid awake at night thinking about that baby—it wouldn't know anything about the world before this. It wouldn't know what it was like to drive a car, attend a school dance, or eat fast food. Finally, it struck her, almost as cruelly as the hunter's slap against her cheek—what if the hunter got her pregnant?

How could she ever raise a child in this?

Having a boy stood a better chance at normalcy, she decided. He could grow up to be a hunter or a guard for the village. He may even move up in rank to become a member of the Council, but to give birth to a girl held fewer alternatives. She would inevitably serve as a slave to men. Rae's mind spun with assumptions. The finality of her existence here was claustrophobic. Tears filled her eyes as she approached her family's site. Her mother, heavyset but beautiful, moved slowly toward her and embraced her in a hug. Her mother's hands moved to Rae's flushed cheeks and wiped tears away with her thumbs, "You know I would take your place if I could, but it's not me they want."

Rae's head lowered, "I know, for Jeremy." Rae broke away from her mother's arms and quietly slipped into her tent. Wrapped only in her damp sleeping blanket, she awaited the familiar wolf's howl, an ominous reminder to those who might consider breaking the rules.

Rae's younger brother, Jeremy, who sat poking the campfire with a stick next to his father, watched Rae disappear into her tent, "Where does she go every night, Dad?"

"She's just...hanging out with friends," the boy's father replied, a lump building in his throat.

"Tomorrow, I want you to take two guards with you and scout Elliot's camp." Scott sifted through topographic fishing maps of the region and removed a tattered map he rescued from the park office.

The stench of wood smoke and sweat-soaked feet infected Scott's twenty-eight-foot camper. Dishes, empty cans, and dirty clothes littered the once immaculate travel trailer and Rick moved to sit beside Scott at the cluttered table to study the map his boss held in his hand, "Jeez-us, Rick. How many times do I have to say this—I don't want to look at your face. Sit over there." Scott handed Rick the map and pointed to the empty bench on the other side of the table.

"Get over it, Rick." Scott said seeing Rick's hand subconsciously move to cover his pockmarked and scarred right cheek. "It was your own stupidity—they gave you specific precautions when handling the shit. They told us the VX and botulism combo was unstable—all you had to do was deliver the stuff."

"Why the sudden interest in Elliot's camp?" Rick asked, trying to escape further ridicule.

"The mine owners promised me unlimited resources and a small share in gold if we command all survivors in the region—that's why." Scott replied. "*You*, my friend, will assume leadership of their camp when we take over. I'll even give you one of our *friends* in the amphitheater to help you maintain discipline."

"What do you need me to do?"

"We need to know how many remain in the village, their defenses and their weapons." Scott inched his way out of his seat, his bulging stomach almost upsetting the table, and opened the door to let Rick know this meeting was over. "And if you fuck this up, I'll feed you to our *friends* myself."

Rick folded the map Scott gave him and tucked it into his back pocket before grabbing the bag of garbage outside Scott's camper door. If this was what he had to do for a chance at being a boss of another village, and away from Scott, so be it. He hoisted the leaking bag over his shoulder and made his way down trail C toward the amphitheater for feeding time.

"Evening, Rick," came the greeting from more than one campsite as he walked by. He was immortal. No one would dare challenge or disobey him—he was the boss's right hand. Soon he would be 'Scott' in another village, and maybe he would become even more feared. The stench of the amphitheater broke him from his reverie and the man standing guard began to climb the stairs leading to the roof of the twin cages he protected. Rick followed the guard to the rooftop while the grunting and snorting sounds erupting below told him he was late again with their evening snack. The guard unlocked the trapdoors fashioned into the den's roofs while Rick took a deep breath, held it, and emptied the bag into even portions below with a sickening splat. He watched darkened masses move directly beneath him like hunting sharks and couldn't help but pity rule breakers past and future. He thought about what Scott said earlier about having one of their *friends* join him when they took over Elliot's camp. He knew if he had a choice in the matter, which of the two creatures he would choose.

Moraya's eyes never strayed from the trail as she bathed in the cold river. Gooseflesh plagued her skin as she tried to rid herself of the funk from traveling underground. She felt more at home in the mining tunnels anyway—she could always keep a wall at her back.

She lowered herself in the water of the riverbank among the reeds. Only her head remained above the surface when voices broke the still, autumn morning.

"Okay, guys. Fill your canteens. This is going to take us all day." The apparent leader of the trio of men spoke.

Moraya was like a boulder, not stirring a ripple of water around her as she listened to the riverbank's intruders, "Where are we heading, anyhow?" One guard asked, as he squatted by the edge of the water.

"We're doing a recon of Elliot's. Scott has his sights set on his village and he's intent on taking it." Rick replied trying to disguise a grin.

Moraya watched the men, two of whom she saw the night before on patrol, fill canteens then climb the bank and cross the wooden bridge that spanned the river. She waited until they disappeared into the bright yellow and orange foliage of the tree line before escaping the chilly water. With wet skin, she struggled to dress then grabbed her gear to follow them. The wooden bridge, only a hundred feet away and built for the park's past trail enthusiasts, now lay ignored by the village's current inhabitants. As far as she could tell from her week of scouting the village, it seemed more a border and rarely patrolled.

At the northeast end of the village in the park office, Scott's office, he barked orders to the squad of waiting guards. They stood spread out chaotically in front of him, "People are getting too comfortable around here. We need to shake things up!"

Scott waited to let the threat of his words hang. His men tensed at his pause then shuffled to form an orderly line. If he intended to take Elliot's camp, he needed everyone on high alert and disciplined.

"I think it's time for an assembly."

He called out six guards by name and continued, "You guys go in pairs. Grab the gators and a bullhorn and *invite* the people to an assembly. Everyone will attend. One hour, no exceptions." He turned to look at the remaining three guards and whispered, "You three, come with me."

Rae and her family sat at their flaking, burgundy-painted picnic table eating breakfast alongside a smoldering fire when the roar of ATVs shattered the calm. Her mother wrapped an arm around her son and pulled him closer as tears began to stream down his cheeks. They all knew what this meant. Rae could see the color escape her parent's faces and knew worry would all but paralyze them.

"Assembly in one hour, NO EXCEPTIONS." The repeated cry from a bullhorn echoed throughout the village as the green, six wheeled ATVs paraded by.

"They won't come for us," Rae said, looking squarely at her brother.

She had done everything expected of her to ensure her brother's safety. That was Scott's threat when he assigned her to service his hunters. She had done her chore diligently for months without squabble or complaint, and she knew now no other man would touch her because of it. She would never marry because no one could love her. Rae and her family waited in silence, hoping no guard would enter their camp and take one of them away. Forty minutes went by before they left their camp and joined the solemn parade toward the amphitheater.

Row after row of benches filled with people around the amphitheater originally designed for children's educational performances when the camp was a camp. Now the adapted stage resembled two natural caves or dens built side by side complete with iron bars and gates at their mouths and hatches in their ceilings.

Rae scanned the benches that formed a semicircle and descended toward the mouths of the caves looking to see who was missing. It was selfish, she knew but she was glad they arrived early to get a seat as far away from the caves as possible. She watched Scott amble up the stairs to the roofs of the caves and her mouth began to water as if she would be sick. Even from this distance, she could see the condescending grin on his stubble-chinned face as he glared at the gathering crowd below him. After everybody filed in, was accounted for and seated, he motioned with a wave of his hand for the proceedings to begin.

Down the center aisle, two people were escorted with hands bound behind them, legs restricted for minimal movement by rope, and Ty-wraps. The guards ushered the gagged man and woman who screamed through fabric that bit into their cheeks toward the mouth of the caves. Rae stifled her sobs when she recognized the couple from 97 E.

Rae watched the guards parade the couple in front of the iron bars for what seemed like eternity. The crowd remained silent and the remaining guards on duty milled about the stands, weapons ready. Rae was certain a puddle of liquid formed at the couple's feet as they watched the creature's pace across the iron bars growling and snarling.

Scott waved his hand again and the couple were dragged up the stairs.

Rae couldn't take her eyes off Scott and his eyes never stopped glaring at the crowd. Behind him, one guard unlocked the padlocks to the roof hatches and flipped them open with a crash, while the other guards persuaded the bound couple to the edges of the dual openings. Rae looked to her mother, who now covered Jeremy's eyes. Then she looked around the crowd, most of whom had eyes squeezed shut, but she was sure, all had the same thought running through their minds—I'm glad it's not me.

Rae's attention snapped toward the caves after hearing two nauseating thuds. The wolf—mangy, mottled, and grey—pounced on the unmoving form of the man, who lay twisted and broken from his fall. Its face; hide peeled back revealing bone, muscle and sinew, buried into the soft midsection of the man who wasn't screaming any longer. In the adjoining den, jagged bone protruded from the brow of the mammoth bear and it buried its muzzle into the pregnant woman's shoulder. Spared the gruesome sight to come, the onlookers watched the hulking form drag her body to the darkest recess of its cave.

The timeless magic of dolls and Moraya's affection toward them since childhood kept her traipsing thin borders between the physical world and shadow. Each doll was unique: she fashioned them with care and emotion, and this unwittingly brought her an early understanding of the spirit world's two laws: contagion and similarity. The pack she carried on her back included materials to continue creating the only things she loved. As soon as the three men she followed stopped for a rest, she decided she'd begin fashioning a likeness of each one of them. She stalked the trio like a killer through the winding trails. Foliage engulfed the forest's trespassers instantly and Moraya was mindful to keep distance between them, but remained close enough to hear them talk when shadow's draw called on her again. Her skin itched and her hands trembled. It became an addiction. Each time she walked its realm became more difficult to escape its comforting blanket of energy.

The biological attack to the province's water treatment plants years earlier triggered her neurosis. It bridged a gap in her network of nerves allowing her to make the leap into shadow's veil at will. The attack affected beings in unusual ways and some creatures went unscathed from residual effects.

To walk among the living and bodiless spirits of the dead here still confused her. Luckily, any emotion she felt went numbed. In time, she learned to notice the difference; the living cast reflections of their current selves with energy diluted by physical being and soul, and the dead emitted an energy that was unbroken. She discovered early on, bodiless spirits gave off the strongest emotion—despair being most common and shadow consumed this energy, and amplified negative emotion. This, she found, was key, as long as she remained conflicted spiritually her access to this world would solidify. She could engage gloomy spirits wandering hearts of thick forests, building ruins, and underground tunnels and caves. She exploited the working tunnels of the region's mine responsible for the attack to travel between villages, gather supplies and avoid the inevitable condemning glares when the province's survivors decided she was a witch.

Moraya's eyes strayed from her quarry when a shudder pulsed through the gloom and staggered her to her knees. Behind her and somewhere in the center of the village a momentary ripple formed between the planes. Only when an act of true evil occurred in the physical world would this happen. The overlapping planes were thin in many places, they said. She uncovered many secrets speaking with the dead. She hesitated and then continued tracking the trio of men, not able to see the two new inhabitants entering shadow, the energies of a husband and his pregnant wife.

She could follow them much closer now, taunt the men, and listen. She needed to learn their names. One by one, her breath chilled the back of their necks as she plucked free a strand of hair from them and drawing confused looks. She walked alongside them, holding back branches, only to let them snap back into the face of the man behind. She grasped and raised dead branches that littered the trail and sent the men cascading forward into one another.

"How is it that they managed to keep anyone from nosing around for so long?" One guard asked Rick while stoking the fire.

"Holy shit, you're an idiot. Don't you remember? They publicized it as an environmental tragedy—one that could take years to clean up." Rick replied. "The clean-up crew *is* the mining corporation and the clean-up will take as long as it takes to empty the tunnels of gold. The area will remain quarantined until then."

Enveloped in thick foliage with her gear spread out in front of her, Moraya watched and listened to the three men while they rested and ate by the fire. She emptied a few drops of oil onto her hands from a long-since exhausted perfume vial and furiously went to work kneading and sculpting the wax she removed from her pack. Certain the group would be on the move again soon, she worked quickly, sculpting a doll to resemble each man and embedding it with their own strand of hair. With the tip of her knife, she etched the men's names into their effigies nine times while muttering curses. She escaped the foliage and approached the group, "Sorry guys, but I need *those* weapons."

Before they could respond and bolt towards her, she had already tossed her three curious creations into their fire. They scrambled for their weapons and charged the lone intruder while flames began to dance and lick their skin. Each man erupted like a walking torch and flailed in futility while she raced to rescue the sword and club from the guards' quickly liquefying grasps. Her stomach heaved at the stench of charring hair and flesh, but excitement surged between her thighs at their gurgling screams that eventually dwindled as she began retracing her steps back to the village. A grin spread across her face as she admired her newest acquisitions that she couldn't wait to test.

Sounds of grunting and thrusting outside the hunter's canvas tent told Moraya that she wasn't late for the young woman's visit. Again, muffled cries escaped the tent's flap. Moraya eased the sword from its sheath and slipped into the darkened tent. Without her unique ability she would have fumbled hopelessly, but the darkness now was little obstacle. The hunter's wide back faced Moraya when she entered and it shrouded the slight, young woman beneath him. She ran the sword's curved blade along the back of his thick, hairy legs, just below his buttocks. He lurched forward, howling, as tendons separated and no longer supported his hulking mass. The young woman struggled to free herself as she kicked and squirmed against sweaty skin. Moraya watched him struggle and scream, trying to right himself while she slid her sword back into its sheath. As he rolled onto his back, she grasped her club and her knuckles whitened. The young woman looked to Moraya with tears streaming down her cheeks, a darkened silhouette standing calm. Then she looked at the hunter, who scrambled frantically to gain a handhold. His hands clawed, reaching to squeeze the life from someone. The young woman rolled away, out of reach from his massive hands and then, with a sickening crunch, she felt warm liquid spatter across her naked skin.

Moraya placed a booted foot onto the hunter's unmoving chest and pulled her club free from his devastated skull. She knew she would see him soon in shadow and be able to continue his torment. Moraya smiled at the young woman, removed the bowie knife and its sheath from her belt, and tossed it to her feet before escaping the hunter's foul tent. There was one thing left to do, she decided, before lingering forever in the spirit realm. Battering locks from their cages with her club; she opened the heavy barred doors and released the two beasts from the amphitheater.

She could still hear the screams.

A Quiver Full of Dirt

DARA MARQUARDT

Ma and Theresa always said we don't choose our animal but it chooses us. That doesn't explain why I killed those pigs. Or what happened to them after. I was seven at the time and I could think I didn't really understand what it was I was dealing with. I could claim the mystery of who we are and what we did was all swirled with incense smoke and Aunt Theresa's tarot cards lining the kitchen table like spider-veined money that banks wouldn't trade.

But that would be a lie.

Because I did know how dangerous it was, how furious it could be, what it felt like to draw from the roots of plants and herbs and flowers their quiet, whispering chatter. I knew how it felt to hold that language in the base of my dry palm and that's what I did out back of the trailer with the pigs all around making valleys in the mud with their hooved, sharp feet.

I was out back because Aunt Theresa was inside with her crystal ball (she got it through a mail order type company that also sold little river rocks with last names carved on their sides that some of the up-to-do-folk in Pitkin, Louisiana put out on their front steps in the summer months) and a client. She always called them that, "clients." As if by assigning them a business class label it dignified their venture into a doublewide leaning on cairns of cinderblock; somehow quieted the cheap sound wooden bead curtains made as the strands swayed together, dignified the thirty-minute sessions purchased for the $43.97 Aunt Theresa charged. I don't know if her clients found it more dignified or not but I do know she was sorely attached to that silly crystal ball, even though it was nothing but smoky-looking glass with little bubbles of air trapped inside.

So maybe I knew how serious it really was but thought Aunt Theresa and her jaded crystal ball made it cheap, like stage makeup. Kind of like the movies made blood and guts look like butcher's meat and chocolate syrup.

I stood in the little barn out back, quivers of hay drifting in the heat of high July, wishing for all I could that Jetta's mom hadn't taken Jetta and Kimbo to N'arlins (it was New Orleans but that's how Jetta's mom said, it: "N'arlins") to visit her uncle who was a jazz player in a tambourine street band.

I was wondering what a tambourine street band sounded like and if I could dance my feet to it. Sometimes me and Jetta, with her crazy tufts of unkempt hair, danced to her momma's records in her bedroom. One time we tried on her lipstick and she whupped both our hides for that.

My momma was away, plugging at the Laundromat until five and then Dob's Bowling Alley until close. Bell to bell she pulled those days. Aunt Theresa, a cigarette jumping from the big pout of her bottom lip at every syllable she spoke, clucked her tongue at that and told my mother to quit it with the washing and stacking pins. Said she was made for more than washing other people's skid marks and filling their drinks. Said she'd been gifted more than a decent grasp of arithmetic, surely had more brains than a simple table-waiting job at Dob's Bowl-O-Rama required. Said she'd be better off at home, sending in $69.99 for her own crystal ball. Even offered to lend out her tarot cards so she could read the fortunes.

But my mother, proud and stiff-lipped, worked her shifts with a kind of quiet defiance.

Only now do I understand what all those red calluses on her palms were for. The sting of laundry soap coming off her skin and the smell of other peoples' cigarettes in her hair. She was running from something. Something she knew was fierce and dangerous. Something she knew ran as thick in her blood as it did in mine. I wonder if she thought she could keep it away with enough scrubbing, enough ice cubes clinking in drink cups, enough cracking pins put to right again. There ain't nothing that can keep away what's inside a person, I know that now.

I was in the barn and thinking about Jetta and wondering if I wished real hard could her uncle maybe get sick or something, nothing serious like the pox but a cold or something, so Jetta and Kimbo would have to cut their visit short, maybe see the tambourine street band another day. I was wishing and hoping and the pigs were in their pen, just three of them, three fat hogs with pink white fur netted on their backs. I was praying and thinking and all the smells, the thick, heavy scent of dung, the sweeter scent of fresh hay, even the warm, baked smell of sunlight, came on strong. So strong my nose burned with it and I found the darks of my eyelids and realized my eyes were closed. My hands were warm rocks bundled in the pockets of my dress and I'd taken off my shoes. They were stuck in mud.

My feet were bare on dirt and for a quiet moment I could hear the sighs of the cotton fields circling the little land we rented from McGlover and his shrew of a wife. I could hear all the fields, thirty acres strung together by fronds of white cotton, breathe in at once. My lungs filled with it. And then all of a sudden I was on my knees, trying to breathe out, the seeds of the crop lodged in my throat, my air coming out like I was the choked fan motor on Momma's Dodge. I was coughing and shrieking, trying to, and the hogs were screaming and the day was bright as X-rays.

I came to a few moments later. Aunt Theresa hadn't heard a thing. I could hear her, softly, a mute voice from sixteen yards away, the trailer window open as she said,

"There will be a dark figure." I could see her, although at the time I thought it was just in my mind's eye, caressing the polished orb of mail order glass twinkling between her and her "client". "They will come quickly and slip quietly into your life. Be wary of them because in their quiver they carry arrows, a goodly amount."

In their quiver they carry arrows

A goodly amount

I got to my feet, thinking Momma would be mad as a plucked hen at my shoes stuck in the mud like that, not remembering exactly when I had slipped them off. *Why* I had slipped them off? I know now it was to feel the ground beneath the soles of my feet. I know now it was to feel the cotton breathe in the field. I went to them and bent, plucking them from the mud, frowning at the little dark worms of muck that had found their way to the arches, and that's when I saw the pig.

All the pigs. They lay on their sides, their bellies still, their ribs all expanded. They were holding their breath and their eyes were open, their snouts parted. I could see the mid-sized one, the one me and Jetta called Stinky Sue, had a cavity on her back tooth.

I should take the tooth, I thought. I should take it to show Jetta. I was horrified at the pigs, they were dead and we needed them to sell to McGlover's wife who would pay twenty cents a pound, and my mother would be mad. Aunt Theresa might even whup me for it.

I went to Stinky Sue, my knees all mud-covered now and the hem of my dress dirty as the bottoms of my toes, and touched her ear. She was warm like fresh-dried velvet. I touched the tooth, finding the abscess, and recoiled at the texture. It was warm mush. I pulled my hand back and began to cry.

Aunt Theresa's client left and she found me in the barn, leaning over Stinky Sue, crying rivers onto the white quills of her hide.

"How'd this happen?" she asked, a hand on her hip but the cold edge of her eyes softened at the tips.

I cried harder.

"We have to bury them now. Quick. If we don't they'll spoil the dirt."

So, wiping my nose with the knob of my wrist, I hauled the

pigs out, one by one. We used the shower curtain—we didn't own a tarp—and dragged the pigs out of the barn. Immediately I felt better, stronger somehow now that they were out of that place that smelled of sour dung and sweet hay. That place where I'd been wishing and thinking of a tambourine band and jazz music and how fast my feet could dance, wishing on all I had Jetta and her brother Kimbo, annoying as he was, would come running up the lane with trinket dolls or a bag of candy from N'arlins.

We dug the earth with two small spades. We had to borrow one from McGlover but we did it secret-like. Secret-like meant I shimmied through the plastic-covered window in their backyard shed, got the spade off its wall hook—all tidy-lined up with the rest of McGlover's garden tools, and shimmied back out just as slick.

We dug their graves on the west side of the little barn so...

"So they'll know that each day they must lay to rest. Sometimes they will prowl, sometimes when the sun hides behind the moon's shadow, you'll hear em out here bawlin', maybe wanna come look. Don't."

"Why not, Auntie?"

"They'll see you before you see them, little Lilly Tucket. Every day the sun sets they'll lay back down in their bed of dirt. You bury 'em on the east side and they'll think they can roam forever. Least this way they's limited to twelve hours or so, less in the winter time."

I didn't question her anymore. I simply dug the holes.

I put a flower on each of their pill-shaped graves, saying a little word of niceness to Stinky Sue, saying how I was sorry about how the day went.

It was that night, shortly after my mother came home, when she was sitting in front of the television, watching about some kind of flood that washed out Earhart and Carrollton streets down in N'arlins, that I heard it. I was lying in my bed and wishing I could make peace with how the pigs looked, lying on their sides like that. I even rolled onto my side so I faced west just like Stinky Sue and her friends. I was wondering if Jetta was asleep in her uncle's spare room or if her uncle even had a spare room. A jazz-playing man in a tambourine street band couldn't have *that* big a place, could he? Maybe Jetta and Kimbo and their momma were all cramped up in their little car, sleeping with ass and elbows and knees all running into each other, waking often with car-cricks and neck cramps, just like I used to when it was just me and Momma because we hadn't come to Aunt Theresa's yet.

I was thinking about these things when I heard their cries, their slow, long, *yeee-upps*. These long, crazy, sad cries and I knew we'd done it wrong. The pigs were confused and thought night meant for waking, not being still, and pigs crying in the day weren't so bad but pigs going *yeee-upp yeee-upp yeee-upp* in the night was something else. Something miserable. So I waited until the whole trailer was filled with steam and the scent of juniper shampoo and I could hear the sponge slide over my mother's callused hands while she showered and I tossed back my cover quilt.

My mother started singing, "In their quivers they carry arrows…a goodly amount."

It was horrible to think of the shower curtain so near my momma, the same curtain we'd used and dragged across the dirt, hissing plastic, the corpses of the pigs on top of it.

"In their quivers they carry a-rrooooows…a goodly amount."

I ran outside in my bare feet. I ran until I saw them, three of them, loafing around the barn.

Their eyes were gone. The flowers had wilted and were smashed among the mud. White petals from simple daisies had turned dark, wet with dirt. I shushed them, trying to pick which one was Stinky Sue, unable to tell because they'd expanded with death, filled with gas now, their skin whitish blue, the pink all drained.

Aunt Theresa's warning, *they'll see you before you see them, little Lilly Tucket,* sounded in my ears and I shut my eyes tight as gator jaws, as if I could keep their hollowed sockets blind that way.

I could hear the bowling pins falling and the big green

clothes washers spinning and that same breath the cotton took earlier breathed again now and I wasn't missing my shoes—they were drying in the dish rack by the sink—and I inhaled. I breathed in every star trembling from their clefts of heaven and I inhaled all the nighttime bugs, the crickets and the longtails and the big fat green frogs croaking from the shores of Mud Lake down the way. I breathed in the sound of cypress leaves rubbing on one another. I inhaled all of the air bubbles trapped in Aunt Theresa's mail order crystal ball.

And when I exhaled all the pigs fell down, trembling, their cloven feet shaking like pieces of scrap quilt fluttering from wooden pegs on the laundry line. Dirt and cottonseed clung to my lip and fell like a caul over the bloated forms of the pigs.

A star fell, and another, and one more, and when my heart beat again Stinky Sue huffed, a great cloud of dust streaming from her nostrils, and she got to her four feet. Her cavity tooth glittered in the dirt. Then the other, smaller hog. Then the third. Then they were all standing, stunned, eyes solid and glazed, breathing in the dooryard while the moon hung like a witchin' charm in the night of a July sky.

In their quivers people carry arrows. A goodly amount. But I had killed the hogs, and the quiver I carry is filled with dirt.

Judex Est Venturus

Jennifer Loring

eather cracked over naked white flesh. He gritted his teeth and closed his eyes as a slow burn built beneath his skin. Blood crawled down his back like insects. He tossed back his black hair, moaning softly in an entreaty to God to expunge the evil from his soul. Over the left shoulder, over the right, thongs chanted their own iron-tipped atonement to Him on the drum of his body. *Kyrie Eleison, Kyrie Eleison, libera me Domine...*

Father Radcliff gazed up at the crucifix on an otherwise bare wall. His Savior, bloodied as he was, dying in agony for a wretch like him. The austerity of his room could not cleanse his mind of impure thoughts. He picked up the cat o'nine tails again, and the rawhide tongues once more licked a back already aflame with agonizing offerings to a Lord he despised.

He saw Rebecca for the last time that morning, bound to a wooden post on a dais in the town square, wrists tied together and folded against her chest in a forced mockery of prayer. Whole villages turned out for such events, and that day was no different except that the accused today should not be the typical old woman, malformed recluse, or midwife—but a lovely young girl, an angel in the shapeless white shift that clothed her.

The priest stood before her. She watched him with large, dark eyes innocent of the transgressions for which they had convicted her. Thus, she refused to confess, no matter the tortures put to her.

"Witch!" the crowd shouted. What passed in silence between the priest and the girl was their eternal secret, theirs and God's alone.

"*Confiteor Deo Omnipotenti,*" he intoned, "*quia peccavi nimis cogitatione, verbo et opere.*"

Her lips remained sealed, but the confession of sin was as much for his contrition as for hers.

"Confess," he hissed, "and save your soul!"

"*Tibi, Pater,*" she whispered. "Only to you." She lifted her gaze heavenward, hands clasped now in true supplication. "*Gere curam mei finis. Dona nobis pacem. Sit sempiterna gloria.*"

For a few moments, he could only stare at her, his heart twisting in the throes of hypocrisy. Flames might burn away her flesh, but her spirit would not suffer the agony of eternal damnation, not like his. With trembling hands, he held out the elaborate silver cross he'd been clutching to his chest. She kissed the ruby in its center.

He closed his eyes, counting his breaths. One, two, three...

"If the girl will not confess to the accusations set forth against her," cried the Archdeacon, "then she cares not for the state of her soul! She has chosen damnation rather than the grace of God! Let her burn!"

"Burn the witch!" the crowd responded as if it were a participatory sermon and not a human life hanging in the balance.

"She has made her choice, Father." The Archdeacon laid his sausage-fingered hand on his shoulder. "We must give her over to God's punishment, now."

The young priest gazed at her one last time, pleading silently with her to confess. Yet betrayal of any kind, whether of herself or of him, was a concept completely foreign to her. Rebecca peered back at him, and the corners of her mouth turned up into a small, sweet smile.

My savior, dying for my sin.

"Come, Father."

The priests stepped down from the dais. A hooded executioner, blazing torch in hand, lit the pyre below her. Sweat trickled down Rebecca's face. She thrashed against the post, flames lapping at her unprotected feet. Acrid black smoke swirled up and outward, and the nearest spectators coughed.

"Deo!" she screamed when the fire began to devour her legs. *"Sit sempiterna gloria!"*

Smoke stung Father Radcliff's eyes, a believable excuse for the tears he shed. Perspiration from his brow and upper lip rolled down his neck. A shimmer of heat rose from the pyre and her head rolled back, face glistening, her gown and her body blackened. Her skin bubbled and peeled.

His knees buckled, and he pitched to the ground in a tacit appeal for forgiveness. She was falling all over him like snow, and no matter how he tried to brush her away she remained, ever more of her.

What has she done that I can feel the flames raging through my body?

When the wind shifted, the last remnants of an earthbound seraph swirled upward toward the Heaven that called her home. He wondered if she journeyed there alone.

Last night marked her third day in the cold cell, a frigid subterranean room beneath the courthouse, while snow blanketed the village above. Rebecca lay naked on a dirt floor with no fire to warm her. Almost ironic, given the death she was to face in the morning. And she would die whether she confessed or not, innocent or guilty. Most of the priests, being amongst the few educated men, recognized that condemnation was a double-edged sword, only a question of dying as the liar the tribunals needed in order to appease peasant hysteria.

Father Radcliff visited her twice a day in the hope of coaxing a confession from her, if only to end the torture. Her hair had begun to grow back during the weeks of her incarceration. She curled up in a corner with nothing to hide the shame of her nudity, so out of respect, he set his lantern on the far end of the chamber, where its light could not touch her.

"I won't speak," she said softly. "If they mean to kill me, so be it. You know what will happen if I do. They will find out! Do you want that?"

"I can leave. I can start over in a new town—"

She shook her head, ever the wiser of them. "Word will catch up with you soon enough. My doom has already been written. Why destroy both of us?"

"But it's because of me that you…" He knelt down. "I betrayed you to protect myself," he murmured. *"Mea culpa."*

He breathed a white puff of air onto his chilled hands to warm them. She reached the few of her fingers not mangled by thumbscrews through the bars, and he linked his own with them. "I am not free of guilt, if guilt is what God commands us to feel," she said softly. "I will do penance for all of us."

"I am a coward. God will not have me, and yet I pretend to be His servant."

He squeezed her frozen hand in the hope of transmitting some of his warmth to her. Instead, a tingle of heat generated by her slender fingers passed into his body. She was some sort of magical creature after all, but no witch. In his mind, the Inquisitor recited words from the *Malleus Maleficarum: Women are by nature instruments of Satan—they are by nature carnal, a structural defect rooted in the original creation.*

"You need only ask His forgiveness," Rebecca whispered. "You are frightened. You have much more at risk than I."

"You know that isn't true. Not now."

"They would excommunicate you. Better to die than that." She sighed a little. "Such a wondrous thing we have done. How is it sinful, Father? It does not feel like sin."

He kissed her knuckles. He had no answer for her or for himself, and God did not respond to his queries, no matter how many lashes he endured.

After the evening visit, when the village had long since retired to bed, Father Radcliff made his way back down the damp, dark stone stairs to the cold cell. His black robes rustled along the floor, sending rats skittering back to their hideaways in the crevices along the wall. Each night, he feared disturbing her, but she did not awaken. With the lamp placed just to his left, allowing a dull golden haze to illuminate the cell, he pressed his face against the bars, curled his fingers around them, and stared at her.

She was a pale goddess curled up in the shape of a child, shivering uncontrollably with cold and bad dreams. Every curve of her sleek body captivated him, and as she trembled, he longed to gather her into his arms, warm her velvet flesh with his hands. He drank in the swell of her breasts, their small nipples erect with kisses from the winter air. His gaze drifted over silken thighs, lingered upon the shadow between them and the beautiful mystery they sheltered.

"Forgive me, Father," he whispered, crossing himself as tears blurred his sight. He sinned merely by looking at her. The instrument by which he must free her from his veins awaited him in his room, bloodstained leather for a back scarred with each thought of her.

Forgive me, Father, that I love her more than You.

"Arrest her!" he had cried weeks earlier, when the witch-hunts swept through villages like the Pestilence two centuries before. Rebecca's neighbor accompanied the men.

"It is she who has been making me ill!" Goodwife Oldham shrieked. "She who has destroyed our cattle!"

The men who burst into Rebecca's home at the young priest's behest latched their arms around hers, lifting all but the tips of her toes from the wooden floor. She did not resist, only cast a knowing glance at him before they carried her outside to the witches' cart. Her humble possessions would be gathered and sold to pay for the costs of her arrest and imprisonment, and ultimately, her execution.

No evidence here, none that anyone could see, for the burden he carried in his soul was his alone.

Father Radcliff followed them to the courthouse. Villagers threw rocks and rotten fruit at the cart in which she crouched, and she allowed their abuse with an interminable sadness in her eyes. She pitied them, he knew, those same neighbors whom only a week before had sought her services in healing their ailments. She pitied their ignorance, which the Church fostered in their susceptible and easily-molded minds. His elders planted the fear, the suspicion. Any one of them, tortured enough, would confess to the same crimes of which she was accused.

He did not believe in pacts with the Devil any more than he believed she could curdle the milk of her neighbor's cow.

They jailed her overnight. At dawn, he waited on the dais in the center of town, watching the horse-drawn witches' cart rumble over cobblestones. The Inquisitor and tribunal, along with hundreds of spectators, awaited her arrival as well.

The men dragged Rebecca from the cart. Her stiff legs could barely support her. They grasped the collar of her simple dress and yanked downward, shredding it to the waist. A blush that began on her chest crept up her neck, into her cheeks, and she covered her breasts with her arms.

"Please…"

One of the men backhanded her. The priest looked away, but only for a moment. They removed the rest of her dress and her underclothes, leaving just the sunlight and her glorious waist-length hair to clothe her. She was the color of fresh cream and perfectly smooth. He memorized every curve, every angle, as if studying an ancient sculpture.

The other man hacked away at her hair, and if she had been nothing short of impassive before, now she broke down into heart-wrenching tears. The priest lowered his head. They took razors to what remained, shaving her to stubble lest she weave their fates into her hair.

The first man knelt before her and, forcing her legs apart, scraped away at that hair as well. Her dark curls joined the thick mass already fallen to the stones. Tears rolled down Rebecca's cheeks, as did thin streams of blood down her inner thighs. He exposed the soft pink folds and even parted her lower lips to complete the job. Father Radcliff grasped a post on the dais, for his knees quavered at the sight of the man's fingers inside the poor girl. He did not need to look at the crowd to know the men offered more than a few lustful leers for that rosy flesh.

"Enough!" he shouted at last. "Let her be questioned!"

Her breast heaved with a sigh of relief, and before the men turned her away from the platform, he caught a glimmer of gratitude in her eyes.

"Approach the dais," said the Inquisitor. The Church had appointed him, an educated man from the city who traveled from village to village in the service of the witch hunters. Employment abounded in these times for lawyers and judges, for jailers, executioners and the men who sat on the tribunals. Even for humble village priests, who heard the confessions of perhaps scores of women apiece.

Rebecca walked backward, so as not to give the Inquisitor the evil eye. With each sonorous tolling of the church bell, she took another awkward step. She stumbled often and crossed one arm over her breasts while cupping her other hand between her quivering legs. Her entire body turned crimson with shame.

"You have been seen mixing potions in the woods," said the Inquisitor.

"No—"

"Has she not, Father? Did her accuser not state for the tribunal that she has attempted to peddle such potions to the good townsfolk?"

"This woman…she came to me in the woods one day— likely after her visit with the Devil—and claimed she could heal my illness." His tongue felt made of stone, his lips as dry as the eyes of the Inquisitor who stared without compassion at the frightened girl. "I pray and pray to God in order to remain strong, for I shall never turn from Him no matter what devils the witch sends for me."

"What have you to say to this accusation?"

"I say that…he does not speak the truth."

"You dare call a man of God a liar?"

Her shoulders tensed. She was so radiant in the aureate light of morning, so flawless despite the red welts and blackish contusions disfiguring her back, that it seemed she would sprout wings and fly back to Heaven. He envisioned her shoulder blades breaking the skin to reveal feathers of white and gold, the incomprehensible beauty of an angel taking flight. The priest smiled but caught himself before anyone else noticed.

"Yes, he is a liar," she said, and she was still but a human girl.

"To the courthouse with her! We must put her to the question at once."

Her tears had dried, her face calm and composed once more as they thrust her back into the cart. The crowd jeered and shouted curses at her.

He accompanied the Inquisitor to the courthouse in the latter's carriage. "I was watching you," the man said. "You mustn't let one's youth or beauty soften your heart, for the Devil uses it to charm the strongest of men."

"I have no tenderness for evil," Father Radcliff replied, looking straight ahead. "She was a faithful parishioner. I merely regret that she strayed."

"Best to dispense with regret. We must have no sympathy for the Devil."

"For he has no sympathy for us," murmured the priest.

She survived the first torture. Most did without confession. The Inquisitor allowed her twenty-four hours in which to recover and speak to the priest.

"You could end the torture now," he pleaded. "Only tell them what they want to hear!"

"And then I would truly be damned as a liar. They will burn me anyway, for things they say I should not feel."

He hung his head.

"My heart breaks," he whispered. "God Himself has sent you to test me, and I have failed. I have failed us both. I do not deserve your mercy, or His."

"You mustn't let them see you like this. Be of good cheer, Father, for we will meet in Heaven again one day."

He looked up at her dirt-smudged face, bruised but more beautiful than any of God's wondrous creations. "May that day arrive sooner than later."

She smiled and kissed his brow through the bars.

Most women confessed after the second torture, but she repudiated the Inquisitor yet again. He invited Father Radcliff into the chamber for the third and final torture, knowing the man would carefully gauge his every reaction. The priest was certain he could not brave for long the sight of her disrobed and bound to the rack.

"In the name of God, confess!"

"No."

A thumbscrew pinched her finger. She whimpered, bit down on her lower lip until it bled, but remained ever obstinate.

"Did you not poison your neighbor, Goodwife Oldham? Did you not try to poison this holy man while he walked in the woods?"

Her eyes glimmered with tears. "No."

A fingernail and the tiny bones beneath it crunched and shattered, ripping from her a shriek so horrifying that forever onward, even in waking hours, it often echoed in his mind.

"Rebecca, confess!" he cried, hands over his ears. "Please confess to me!"

"No!" she screamed.

Father Radcliff ran up the staircase. He did not care what the Inquisitor or the Archdeacon thought of him. More than one person broke beneath the weight of Rebecca's torment, and he could attend it no longer.

"He is very young," one of the torturers said as he fled for the church.

Then they released the thumbscrews and imprisoned her with her ruined digits for her final slumber before death.

Father Radcliff had often walked the woods in the early spring evenings after fulfilling his many church duties. He had much to learn, as his elders were grooming him to be an Inquisitor. One night, he happened upon a small fire and a group of young women gathered around it, sharing news of births and deaths and all the things women were wont to speak of when together. But at his approach, they scattered in the natural fear that, should he identify them, the next stake erected in the town square would be theirs.

Only Rebecca stayed. She never missed a church service, and the community recognized her as an expert in the healing arts. Lately there was talk she had studied with a midwife, allegations whispered about town but not yet brought to the Archdeacon's attention. An only child, she'd been orphaned some years ago and inherited her father's land, enough to make a literate and well-spoken woman the envy of her less fortunate peers. That and her extraordinary beauty, though she scarcely seemed aware of it. However, the young priest, who often made any excuse to spend a few moments in her company, had noticed. Too many moments, perhaps, stolen from others in need of his services.

"Hello, Father." She tucked behind her ear a lock of dark hair that had escaped her pins and white linen caul.

"I've frightened your friends away."

Her face blanched in the firelight. "It was a harmless gathering."

"I am not questioning that. May I sit with you?"

"Of course, Father." She shifted a little to her left, and he sat beside her on the grass. The air smelled of wildflowers, new leaves, and wood smoke. "Father...it has happened."

"What has?"

Rebecca placed her hands over her belly. He needed no further explanation.

"It is a sin in the eyes of God."

"But is it a sin in yours?"

He looked away from her to the blades of grass he grasped in his fist.

"I know they are turning against me, Father. I give them medicines and birth their children, and yet the Archdeacon demands they name me. I see how Goody Oldham watches me from her window. I see her staring at me in church. She will accuse me and spare herself."

"It has happened in every village to women like you."

"Father...are you happy with the life you chose?"

He gazed into the flames as though they would give him the answer, if only he looked hard enough. He had been the man of his household since his father's death six years ago. The priesthood seemed his only escape from the rigorous life of a peasant.

"My family is poor. What other life is there for me but this?"

"The one we might have had together. With our child."

Father Radcliff tossed the grass into the fire. Not a day passed that he didn't imagine such a life with Rebecca, raising a family and learning some trade with which to provide for them. A true father, not a fool who merely pretended to offer guidance and direction for those who depended upon him. How God must abhor him to dangle his dreams within his grasp, to give him a child he must deny.

"No," he said, hoping to set his heart against her. Or to make her hate him, inspire her to purge the child with her secret herbs so that nothing of him remained in her. "Not with a witch."

She patted his hand but did not speak another word as she rose to leave. With tears in his eyes, he watched her walk away into the gathering darkness.

Offerings

STEPHANIE BURGIS

That Wednesday, the witch found five silver paper-clips laid across her doorstep, next to an apple and a sharpened No. 2 pencil. She regarded them gravely as the breeze from the lake swept up through the pine trees and ruffled her upswept black hair. Then she turned to see if she could spot any signs of who had left them.

The dirt road was empty behind her; a single squirrel raced back and forth across her front lawn, chittering manically as he hunted for food.

The witch shrugged. "'Back to school,' I suppose." She scooped up the offerings and carried them with her into the small wooden house.

As usual—as the rules required—she set the day's offerings on the altar in her living room before she even shrugged off her jacket, and she said a blessing spell across them for who-ever had left them to her. If she'd been more certain of their meaning, she could have made the spell more focused; as it was, she wished the giver luck in new ventures and an open mind for knowledge, and she hoped she hadn't missed the point entirely.

Once she'd finished the spell, though, she couldn't dismiss the offerings as neatly as usual from her mind. Sitting on her back porch, drinking coffee with her high-heeled work shoes kicked off and her hair released from its clips, she gazed into the rippling waves of the lake that bumped up against her sloping back yard and found herself thinking back to her own school days.

Apples, paperclips, multiple-choice tests…simplicity. Order. Her lips curved, ruefully.

Alexander had always said she had a mind as rigidly shut to opposing theories as any Victorian school textbook.

The witch's smile snapped off as quickly as a light bulb going out. She flipped her loose, long, black hair over her shoulder and stalked back into the house, clenching her fingers around her coffee mug.

A long, low wave swept the lake behind her, in her wake. Ducks fluttered up out of the water to avoid it, squawking.

The witch's door was already closed.

The next day, she had to stay late at work, dealing with a crisis. She was still muttering to herself, her shoulders tense, as she walked across the neatly-trimmed grass of her front lawn, side-stepping the squirrel in his usual hyperactive race. She almost tripped over the tiny pile of offerings that had been left that day on her doorstep: a long, narrow candle that looked like it had already been lit at least once before, and seven candy hearts, pink, yellow and orange, neatly arranged into a tiny "U". She stopped herself just in time, before the tip of her shoe could crush the bottom heart—that would have broken all the rules—and she looked down at them, baffled.

"'Love,' I suppose," she murmured. Her eyebrows drew together. "But why the 'U'?"

There was no one to answer her except the squirrel, chittering as he scurried up the trunk of the closest pine tree.

She picked up the offerings carefully, keeping the hearts in their proper order, and carried them into the house. At the altar, she dutifully offered a blessing spell to the giver, wishing him or her luck in love. But she felt oddly itchy as she did it, and she found herself glancing out the big front windows to make sure that no one was watching her. Only the squirrel's beady black eyes looked back at her from the prickly branches of the pine.

Yesterday's offerings had already been transmuted into a

part of the altar, cool and finished. They offered her no help.

She sat down in the kitchen instead of going to the back porch. The sky outside was beginning to darken. The candy hearts lay in their "U" formation on the altar in the living room, where she'd left them. She nudged off her high heels but left her hair firmly clipped up as she gazed into the depths of her coffee cup.

It had been a long time since she'd wished for love for herself. That had been the point of accepting the old witch's offer of this house and all the responsibilities that came with it. That was the reason behind the house's rules.

Upstairs, in the attic, there was a box that held photograph albums from her college years. She hadn't looked at them since a week after graduation, almost three years ago.

She would not look at them now.

The squirrel's chittering sounded through the kitchen window. With a flash of irritation, the witch pointed her finger at the radio on top of her refrigerator. It burst into sound, covering up his noises and her too-uncomfortable thoughts.

But it couldn't cover up her growing conviction, which she would have preferred to drown out: the same person had left both days' offerings. That meant her first blessing spell hadn't worked—or it hadn't been enough. That meant, somehow, she had missed the underlying message.

The witch didn't like making mistakes.

For the first time in years, she found herself reluctant to come home to her safe, quiet house, the next night after work. She'd left the office early, to make up for her long hours the day before. Instead of coming home, though, she wandered through the downtown area, gazing idly at expensive jewelry and useless crafts she didn't want. Her reflection in the display windows was cool and professional, blending in neatly with the early evening crowd. No one would know, from looking at her, what she truly was. Only Alexander, of all the men she'd ever met, had known her for a witch. But that, of course, was only because he himself came from a long line of wizards.

Stupid, hard-headed wizards. She ground her teeth together, grinding old hurt into anger.

She wasn't the one with a closed mind. She wasn't the one who'd given ultimatums. She wasn't the one who'd left town the week after graduation and never come back.

The shop assistant gave her an odd look through the window, and the witch realized she had been glowering. She lifted her chin and stepped away. It was time to go home.

The evening air was cool as she walked across her front lawn. The tangy scent of pine mingled with the fresh, sweet smell of the lake. As always, the dirt road was empty. Her closest neighbor lived half a mile away, and even supplicants so desperate that they would drive hours to the witch's house never dared linger to see her accept their offerings. Were they really afraid of her, she wondered? Perhaps they were more afraid to admit what they believed. Only the squirrel was there when she arrived, running back and forth across her lawn, searching desperately for...something. She dismissed him from her mind as she saw her front doorstep.

A bright orange life jacket, limp and deflated, lay propped against her door. Frowning, she scooped it up.

"'Help?'" she asked.

No one answered her.

She walked into the house, closing the front door firmly behind her. As she set the life jacket down on the altar, her fingers brushed against a set of tiny holes in the fabric.

Teeth marks. Very, very small teeth marks.

The witch kept her mind utterly blank as she spoke the blessing spell for safety and aid in great endeavors. She kept her mind blank as she changed out of her professional clothing into a bathing suit. She chose her most modest and all-covering suit, despite the fact that she had no neighbors to see her. She walked out the back door, across her carefully-tended back lawn, and dived into the lake.

The water was cold and piercing, like knives, or knowledge. She swam deep under, trailing her fingers through the thick, slimy weeds. When she surfaced, gasping for breath, her hair lay cold and clinging against her shoulders. The squirrel was running up and down the steps of her back porch, looking frantic.

A strong, cold wave swept through the water, sending birds and insects fluttering away from it in alarm. The witch didn't move as it swept over her, stinging against her open eyes.

It was time to face the truth.

The next morning, she called in sick to work. She put on her most expensive black blazer and skirt, pinned her long hair neatly atop her head, and drove out of sight of the house. Then she cloaked herself in silence and stillness, and walked back to sit, invisible, on her front lawn.

She didn't have to wait very long.

It took a great deal of effort for the squirrel to drag all the different sticks he'd gathered across the yard. Even more effort, chittering and anxious, to arrange them into letters, nibbling at the ends of the sticks to shape them properly. The witch watched, her anger rising and falling from moment to moment. She waited until he had stepped back, preparing to jump into the safety of the trees.

Then she undid her cloaking spell.

"So you've given up on symbolism?" she said.

The squirrel froze. His beady black eyes stared at her. His big, bushy tail twitched.

The witch stepped up beside him to read the awkward number and letters formed by sticks.

4give.

"The rules say I have to take these to the altar," she told him. "The rules say I have to say a blessing spell over them, whether I want to or not."

He stared up at her, his black eyes shining.

The witch said, "I only agreed to the rules because of you. To keep anyone else from hurting me the way that you did."

He looked up at her, shivering. She couldn't tell if it was from the breeze or from nerves.

She ignored the sticks. Instead, she scooped up the squirrel. He froze in her hand for a moment, then raced up her arm to stand on her shoulder. She set her mouth in a grim line and walked into the house, to the altar. He hopped onto it, looking nervous.

On the altar, all his offerings were frozen into place around him, fixed for all time.

The witch took a deep breath and remembered cold water, sharp and bracing against her skin. She did not let herself remember the albums upstairs. She closed her eyes and said the spell.

She heard the altar shatter before she opened them.

Alexander was thinner than he had been three years ago, and he stood naked before her. His human eyes were dark and focused with intensity, and she had to look away from them to keep hold of her breath and righteous anger.

"You couldn't just phone me?" she snapped. "If you finally changed your mind about your stupid ultimatums—"

"I changed my mind less than a week after I left," Alexander said. "Do you know how long it takes a squirrel to cross the country?"

"If you hadn't been careless enough to turn yourself into a squirrel—"

"I wasn't the one who did it," he said.

"Well, I certainly didn't—" She stopped. "Wait. Is this some family curse? All those wizards in your family..."

Alexander shrugged, flushing. "I turned my back on love, so my ancestors jumped in to teach me a lesson. I agree with the message, but I wouldn't have chosen their methods."

"Well," the witch said. Her lips twitched. "Well."

She looked down at the offerings, fresh again and unfrozen, scattered across the floor with the remnants of the altar.

Paperclips, pencil, apple. *I want to learn.*

Candle, candy-hearts in a U. *I love you.*

Life jacket. *Help.*

And, outside: *4give.*

She felt a shiver in the air around her, signaling changes underfoot. The rules had been broken. Anything could happen.

The witch said to the wizard, "You'd better come into the kitchen with me. It's warmer there. We'll have coffee."

Finis

Biographies

STEPHEN BLAKE lives in a small seaside Cornish town in the UK with his wife Sarah. He copes with eight cats, whilst Frodo the Border collie tries to maintain some sort of order. He's been previously published in a number of anthologies such as *Airship Shape & Bristol Fashion* and *Toys in the Attic: A Collection Evil Playthings*.

TANYA BRYAN is a Canadian writer and poet currently based in Toronto, Ontario. Her work has appeared in *Feathertale Review*, *Latchkey Tales*, and *Drunk Monkeys* as well as in the anthologies *Dear Robot* and *My Cruel Invention*. She loves to travel, writing and drawing her experiences, which are often surreal and wonderful. She is currently working on her first novel.

STEPHANIE BURGIS grew up in East Lansing, Michigan, but now lives in Wales with her husband and two sons, surrounded by mountains, castles and coffee shops. She has published over thirty short stories in various magazines and anthologies, and her trilogy of Regency fantasy novels was published in the US as the *Kat, Incorrigible* trilogy. The first book in the trilogy won the Waverton Good Read Award for Best Début Children's Novel by a British writer, and the whole trilogy was recently re-released in the US as *A Most Improper Boxed Set*. Her first historical fantasy novel for adults, *Masks and Shadows*, will be published by Pyr Books in 2016.

DIANA CORBITT is a retired elementary school teacher who has lived her entire life in northern California. She and her husband, Michael, have two sons who, although grown up and out of the house, still live close by.

Ever since she was a kid Diana loved to be scared, either by movies or books. She started writing her first scary story in sixth grade. That one never got past six pages, but now that she's retired she can't stop writing. Besides short stories,Diana has written one adult novel and one middle grade novel which she is currently shopping around. When she's not trying to scare herself silly, Diana enjoys working with stained glass making lampshades and mosaic sculptures. She also likes to travel, and eating popcorn at the movies. Those don't have to be scary. Just not chick flicks.

JONATHAN CROMACK is a writer of historical ghost and horror stories. He has stories pending release in December 2015: "Blood Red Dahlias" appearing in *Short Sharp Shocks II*; *Spawn of the Ripper* by April Moon Publishing; "Where All Light Fades" appearing in *Winter Shivers* by Inkstained Succubus Productions and "The Shadow of Ippikin's Rock" due for release in early 2016 in *The Secret Life of Ghosts* by Martinus Publishing.

LAWRENCE DAGSTINE is a 42-year-old writer born and raised in the Big Apple. He studied journalism and creative writing in the 90s, and is workshop-certified in proofreading. His work is available on Amazon, Nook, Smashwords, Apple, Kobo, and in a variety of other formats. He is best known for his small press stories—publication in a plethora of science fiction, fantasy, and horror magazines during the 2000s era (what he affectionately labels the Millennial Pulps, before digital became mainstream). He mostly writes video game news and comics these days, and offers affordable proofreading services. He is the author of a half dozen ebook novelettes and novellas (including *Family Reunion & A Child Weeps in Moscow*), has been published with companies such as Damnation Books and Steampunk Tales, and is the author of two popular but out-of-print collections: *Death of the Common Writer* (out of print), *Fresh Blood* (out of print). He enjoys *Walking Dead, Doctor Who*, collecting *Star Wars* memorabilia, console gaming, and comic books. Reach him on Facebook, Twitter, or other popular apps and social media.

DAVE DORMER lives and writes in North-Western Ontario alongside his wonderful (and patient) wife and four children. His love of horror began at an early age and he spent many classes devoting his divided attention from the regular curriculum to write gruesome tales. He distinctly remembers and is thankful for his seventh-grade teacher who displayed an uncommon tolerance for his interest in writing by reading Dave's stories aloud to his class.

DEB "SPINSTER" ESKIE is a resident of Massachusetts and has an M.Ed in creative arts education. With a background in women's studies, her focus as a writer is to expose the woman's experience through unsettling tales that highlight the dilemma of sexual repression and oppression. By combining the genres of feminist and horror/science-fiction she aims to not only disturb readers, but deliver a message that is informative and thought provoking.

In 2005 Eskie's play, *Tell Me About Love*, was featured in the Provincetown Playwright Festival. She has been featured in various online magazines such as *Deadman's Tome*, *Bad Moon Rising*, and *69 Flavors of Paranoia*. Eskie has a number of short stories published by Pill Hill Press, Post-Mortem Press, Scary Tales Publications, and Cruentus Libri Press, among others.

KEVIN M. FOLLIARD is a Chicagoland fiction writer with a degree in English and creative writing from the University of Illinois in Urbana-Champaign. His published fiction includes scary stories collections *Christmas Terror Tales* and *Valentine Terror Tales*, and adventure novels for 12 and up such as *Jake Carter & the Nightmare Gallery*, *Violet Black & the Curse of Camp Coldwater*, and *Jimmy Chimaera & the Temple of Champions*. Folliard's work has appeared in *Sanitarium Magazine*, and he has also developed films and web series for the Champaign-based studio Neon Harbor, including the acclaimed video game parody *Press Start* series.

FLYNN GRAY writes fantasy and horror fiction, consumes unhealthy amounts of coffee, and blogs about writing, books and horror at www.flynngray.wordpress.com. When not writing, curled up with a great book, or binge watching horror films and TV series, Flynn can usually be found procrastinating on social media.

SILAS GREEN is a lover of stories. He grew up on a paradise island in the middle of the Pacific Ocean, where he went to school and graduated from the University of Hawaii. Encouraged by his parents, his childhood was spent daydreaming and visiting fictional worlds, and he never quite got over it. These days much of his free time is spent either reading or writing, and most of the stuff he reads and writes is fantasy, trying to meet a very grown-up need for magic.

S.K. GREGORY lives in Northern Ireland, where she works at a local TV station. She is a blogger, author and journalist who writes in the horror/fantasy genre. A huge fan of Stephen King and Kelley Armstrong, she loves reading. In her spare time she offers reviews to writers through her blog at www.storyteller-skgregory.weebly.com.

COY HALL is married to a wonderful woman, lives somewhere in Appalachia, and, aside from writing horror stories, makes a living as a history professor.

K.A. HARDWAY was born and raised in North Carolina, where she lives with her husband, son, and many pets.

She has loved writing since she was old enough to do it. She writes mostly horror/supernatural stuff, often laced with elements of heart-tugging nostalgia and bright spots of cheeky, irreverent humor.

She just started getting her feet (or maybe just a pinky toe) wet in the getting-published-pool in 2014.

Stephen King, Ray Bradbury, William Faulkner, and Joyce Carol Oates are her tip-top favorite authors.

She spends most of her time finding her own voice, honing her skills, reading, and trying not to let all her ideas make her forget where she's going while she's driving.

LIAM HOGAN is a London based writer and host of the award winning monthly literary event, Liars' League. He was a finalist in Sci-Fest LA's Roswell Award 2015, and has had work published in Leap Books' *Beware the Little White Rabbit #Alice150* YA anthology, and also in *Sci-Phi Journal*.

HEDDY JOHANNESEN has been published in *Eternal Haunted Summer Ezine*, *Essential Herbal* magazine, *Circle Magazine*, *Naming the Goddess* anthology, *Paganism 101*, *Horror Novel Reviews: One Hellacious Halloween* Ebook and *Chicago Literati*.

J.T. LAWRENCE is an author, playwright and bookdealer based in Parkhurst, Johannesburg. She is the mother of two small boys and lives in a house with a red front door.

She has written various plays for SAFM including *The Shelter*, *Unspilling the Milk*, *Every Breath You Take*, and serials, the most recent being the crime drama *Jigsaw*. Her short story collection, *Sticky Fingers*, will be broadcast in the last quarter of 2015.

Her first novel, *The Memory of Water* (2011), is about a writer who would do anything for a story. Her 2015 offering, *Why You Were Taken*, is a sci-fi thriller starring a synaesthete, and takes place is a futuristic Jo'burg burdened by infertility and a water crisis. It was optioned by the national broadcaster, SABC, for a radio adaption.

She is currently working on her new novel, *Grey Magic*, slated for 2017, about an eccentric modern-day witch, accused of murder, who must explore her past lives in order to keep her freedom—and find her way back to magic.

JENNIFER LORING lives in Philadelphia, PA with her husband, their turtle, and two basset hounds. Her short fiction has appeared in numerous magazines, webzines, and anthologies. In 2013, she won Crystal Lake Publishing's inaugural Tales from the Lake writing competition; in 2014, DarkFuse published her novella *Conduits*, and in May 2015, Omnium Gatherum released her debut novel, *Those of My Kind*. She recently signed a deal for a contemporary romance trilogy with Limitless Publishing; the first book, *Firebird*, is due out on October 20, 2015. Jennifer She is currently at work on the second book in *The Firebird Trilogy* as well as a paranormal romance.

DARA MARQUARDT is a writer living in the High Rockies of Colorado. A complete list of her published work can be found at heartsintheattic.wordpress.com.

VIRGINIA M. MOHLERE was born on one solstice, and her sister was born on the other. Her chronic writing disorder stems from early childhood. She lives in the swamps of Houston and writes with a fountain pen that is extinct in the wild. Her work has been seen in *Cabinet des Fées*, *Jabberwocky*, *Lakeside Circus*, *Goblin Fruit*, *Strange Horizons*, and *Mythic Delirium*.

TIFFANY MORRIS is an emerging writer and practicing witch from Nova Scotia. Her poetry, horror fiction, and creative nonfiction have appeared in anthologies and online, including *Siren's Call* eZine and Hocus Pocus & Co.'s *Halloween Night* anthology. A sucker for folklore, Gothic romanticism and all things 90s, her current projects include *Athame*, a YA novel about punk rock, witchcraft, and ghosts in rural Canada.

D.T. NEAL is a fiction writer and editor, a lifelong Midwesterner, and resident of Chicago since 1993. He won second place in the Aeon Award in 2008 for his short story, "Aegis," and has had his short fiction published in *Albedo 1*, Ireland's premier magazine of science fiction, horror, and fantasy. He is the author of the werewolf novel, *Saamaanthaa* (2011) and its sequel *The Happening* (2015), the horror-thriller, *Chosen* (2012), the novellas, *Relict* (2013) and *Summerville* (2013), the vampire novel, *Suckage* (2013), the science fiction anthology *Singularities* (2015) and is currently working on several new works of fantasy, horror, and science fiction.

He recently contributed a short story, "The Wolf and the Crow," to the *Thunder on the Battlefield: Swords* anthology (2013).

He's very fond of history, art, music, masks, Westerns, and ancient ruins. He enjoys cooking, photography, and making things grow. He is currently working on several new works of horror, fantasy, and science fiction.

MEGAN NEUMANN is a speculative fiction writer living in Little Rock, Arkansas. Her stories have appeared in such publications as *Crossed Genres*, *Daily Science Fiction*, and *Luna Station Quarterly*. She is a member of the Central Arkansas Speculative Fiction Writers' Group and is particularly appreciative of their loving support and scathing critiques.

COOPER O'CONNOR is an imagination seeker, and when he isn't writing stories, he's exploring for lake monsters in his kayak.

JEFF PARSONS is a professional engineer enjoying life in sunny California, USA. He has a long history of technical writing, which oddly enough, often reads like pure fiction. He was inspired to write by two wonderful teachers: William Forstchen and Gary Braver.

Jeff got his first break with *SNM Horror Magazine*. SNM published his book of short stories titled *Algorithm of Nightmares* and also featured his stories in the SNM *Bonded by Blood IV* and *V* anthologies.

He is also published in *The Horror Zine* and *Dark Gothic Resurrected Magazine*, and the *Chilling Ghost Short Stories*, *The Moving Finger Writes* and *Golden Prose & Poetry* anthologies.

MIKE PENN has been an Associate Editor for *Space and Time Magazine* as well as the Editor of the horror/suspense anthology, *Tales From a Darker State*.

His story, "The Cost of Doing Business," originally appeared in *Thuglit*, Issue 24 won the Derringer Award for best mystery.

One of his stories, "The Converts" was recently filmed as a short movie. Another story "The Landlord" was recently translated into a play.

Fiction of his can be found in over 90 magazines and anthologies from 6 different countries such as *Alfred Hitchcock Mystery Magazine* in the USA, *Here and Now* in England, *Crime Factory* in Australia. Comic book publishers include IDW and JKOR Graphics.

Organizational Affiliations include The Mystery Writers of America and the International Thriller Writers.

LORI G. PETROFF was born in Scarborough Ontario, lived in a smattering of places all over Ontario and a bit of Nova Scotia, before finding herself immersed and comfy in cottage country. Lori Grace lives in a cottage house in farm country on Georgian Bay. She daydreams part time at a Thrift Store, on occasion does Reflexology and Quantum Reiki, and works part time as a spiritual counselor together with her tarot cards and all the voices in her head. And sometimes, she writes it all down.

JOSEPH RUBAS has been featured in a number of 'zines and hardcopy publications, including: *[Nameless]* (professional paying 'zine), *The Horror Zine, Thuglit, All Due Respect, The Storyteller, Eschatology Journal, Infective Ink, Strange, Weird, and Wonderful*, and *Horror Bound Online*. His short stories are also collected in *Pocketful of Fear* (2012) and *After Midnight* (2014).

CYNTHIA WARD has published stories in *Asimov's Science Fiction Magazine* and *Witches: Wicked, Wild & Wonderful* (Prime Books), among other anthologies and magazines, and articles in *Weird Tales Magazine* and *Locus Online*, among other webzines and magazines. Her stories "Norms" and "#rising" made the Tangent Online Recommended Reading List for 2011 and 2014. Cynthia is the editor of the anthologies *Lost Trails: Forgotten Tales of the Weird West Volumes One* and *Two* (WolfSinger Publications). With Nisi Shawl, she coauthored the diversity fiction-writing handbook *Writing the Other: A Practical Approach* (Aqueduct Press). She lives in Los Angeles, where she is not working on a screenplay.

JO WU is a proud Cal Bear born and raised in the San Francisco Bay Area, where she can be found scribbling in notebooks or typing away in her Google Docs, accompanied by a giant Jack Skellington mug that's constantly refilled with green tea and hot water. When she isn't writing, she's hiding away from the sun and drawing in her sketchbook, sewing her newest cosplay, cuddling with her dogs, or modeling under the alias Carmilla Jo.

She has been published in a few anthologies, and her short story, "Devoured by Envy," was praised by Publishers Weekly as "the most Gothic of the successful stories" from the gothic romance anthology *Darker Edge of Desire.*

Copyrights

✳